VEX NOT HER GHOST

Gill Calvin Thomas

First published in 2024 by Blossom Spring Publishing
Vex Not Her Ghost Copyright © 2024 Gill Calvin Thomas
ISBN 978-1-7385023-6-3
E: admin@blossomspringpublishing.com
W: www.blossomspringpublishing.com

"What all school children learn
Those to whom evil is done
Do evil in return."

(W. H. Auden, 1939)

"I shall gather myself into myself again,
I shall take my scattered selves and make them one,
Fusing them into a polished crystal ball
Where I can see the moon and the sun."

(Sara Teasdale, The Crystal Gazer, 1926)

POOLE, DORSET

SEPTEMBER 2003

My name is Charlie Bond. I'm an ex-police officer, working as a private investigator. I met Caitlin just over a year ago. As I reflect, I understand how I failed to recognise the careful planning; the manoeuvring that led to tragedy. The gift of hindsight has allowed me to see how I was drawn into her story; how I became part of it, my life intertwined with hers.

Caitlin was obsessed with unravelling the mystery of her mother's death. She couldn't see she was playing with fire. No, that's not fair, I didn't see she was playing with fire, until it was too late. Was it natural justice? I simply don't know.

PART ONE

CHAPTER ONE

ROCK HOUSE, SATURDAY 6TH JULY 2002

CAITLIN

I had developed a routine, each morning I walked down to the seafront, rain or shine, then I would go for coffee. Today was no exception. The owners of the café greeted me by name. It was a good feeling; I was beginning to feel part of the community. Lately however, my new-found happiness was draining away. I put off going home as long as I could. I didn't want to leave the warm atmosphere of the place.

Outside, I found myself dragging my feet as I trudged up the hill. Each step beating out a mantra: "It shouldn't be like this." I stopped to catch my breath and turned to stare at the sea below me. I felt hot, sweaty, longing for respite from the midday sun. Eventually, I left the road and walked through the entrance to my drive shaded by tall beech trees on either side. Then the house came into view. Rock House, my haven, my safe space. Only it was going wrong.

I opened the heavy front door and walked into the hallway. Shutting the door behind me, I closed my eyes momentarily as I experienced an intense sense of melancholy. When I turned round, I saw an ethereal figure standing at the window. Tall and thin, wearing a long floral dress, her dark wavy hair tied back with a blue ribbon. I had seen her before. I whispered, "Please tell me who you are." She looked straight at me, her blue eyes brimming with tears.

Overcome with dizziness, I put my hand on the desk beside me knocking the phone to the floor. I heard it clattering on the tiles. To my horror my hand seemed to slide through the wood, then everything went silent. When I came to, I heard Dennis's voice. He was standing beside me. I asked him if he had seen her but he shook his head. "Oh, for God's sake Caitlin, it's all in your mind. Sit down before you fall down."

I wasn't going to argue with him. I sat down, closed my eyes and I was back in a room I remembered as a child. I reached for a memory but couldn't grasp it. Dennis reappeared with a mug of tea. He'd put sugar in it. I hate sugar.

I had vivid dreams that night. When I woke I wasn't sure where I was, but mercifully I was alone. The sun shone through the window. I could see dust motes dancing in the air. Then he came in. As ever, I tried to lighten the mood. "What shall we do today? We could go out somewhere." Dennis grimaced. "I've got stuff to prepare for tomorrow."

"Well, I'm going to get up and go for a walk. You can do whatever you like." Showered and dressed, I prepared a packed lunch, picked up my rucksack and shouted goodbye. Dennis, still in his pyjamas, stood at the top of the stairs staring down at me. "I'll expect you when I see you."

The early morning was misty with the promise of sun breaking through. Although Rock House was on a hill, getting up to the cliff path meant yet another steep climb. I needed to watch my step, the stony paths could be slippery. I saw the town and bay below and the dark silhouette of the Isle of Wight just visible on the skyline.

I carried on walking until I reached one of my favourite spots. I took off my rucksack and pulled out a plastic sheet; laying it on the grass, I sat down. I had grown to appreciate the rugged beauty of the landscape. The grassy mound I sat on was created by old quarry workings. I looked closely at it and could see a clutch of pyramid orchids amongst clover and vetch. I tried to lose myself by drinking in the beauty of the natural world around me. I should have been content but I couldn't rid myself of a sense of impending menace.

I had trained as a social worker. I was self-sufficient. I would never be rich in my chosen career but I was happy enough, that is until thirteen months ago, when a letter from Barrett and Jones Solicitors turned my world upside down. It could have been a dream come true, but I should know by now, life isn't like that. The letter informed me that my father had died and as the only child, I had inherited my mother's estate. I couldn't grieve for him. I barely remembered him.

I'm normally self-reliant. I had had occasional casual relationships but none that I wanted to take further. I met Dennis, shortly after I had moved into Rock House. He worked for a local estate agent. He was confident, handsome with blonde hair, grey eyes and a tall rugby player's build. I was flattered by his attentions. It felt good to be with him, to be part of something. He began stopping over, moving his gear in bit by bit. By the time I noticed what was happening it was too late. He had his feet under the table. He was living in my house.

At first, he had been tender and considerate. He couldn't keep it up. He became moody. I asked him not to smoke in the house, but he did. I found myself trying to second guess what he wanted, trying to please him, a habit I had picked up as a child. A couple of days ago I had spotted him sitting in a café reading a newspaper. I went in and called his name thinking we might have lunch together. He looked round, his face lighting up. Then he saw it was me. His face fell. Whoever he was expecting, it wasn't me.

I wasn't going to waste any more of my time thinking about him. I jumped up, grabbed my plastic sheet and headed onto the top of the cliffs. The walk through wildflower meadows, followed by the cries of skylarks, was delightful. I came upon my favourite bench on the headland overlooking, what seemed to me, to be an infinite expanse of sea. The bench had been erected in memory of a young woman. I read the inscription and wondered who the woman had been. Her death had clearly come too soon, as had my mother's. However, my mother had no such memorial, at least not one I had been able to find. She had given birth to me at age thirty four, the age I am now. Four years later she was dead. Living in her house had made me recognise the unresolved grief I carried inside me.

Of one thing I was certain, Dennis was an unwelcome distraction; a distraction I would have to deal with soon. The search for my mother, Cecilia Rose, was my goal. I had no idea who she had been. There was no physical trace of her. I didn't know what she looked like, what she had done in her life, or how I came to be. I didn't even know how she had died. When I took possession of the house it was a shell. It was only later I discovered the attic. For some reason, whoever had cleared the house had forgotten the attic.

I sat down on the bench, staring out over the sea. For the last couple of months I had been obsessed with the thought that misfortune was waiting to strike. Then I had begun to see the ghost and had become convinced she was my mother. Whoever or whatever she was, she was warning me.

I ate my lunch then walked home. I would find a way to rid myself of Dennis. I couldn't tolerate him in my life anymore. I needed to find my mother. For the rest of the day, Dennis and I were polite to each other. We spent a boring evening watching the television.

The following morning I watched his car disappear down the drive then went out to the garage to find a stepladder. It was awkward to carry but I managed to move it into the house and up the stairs, placing it underneath the loft door. I manoeuvred myself around boxes and made for the far corner where my old trunk was hidden from view. I was an expert at hiding secrets. Inside a shoe box I found the bundle of envelopes I was looking for. My father's letters marking birthdays and Christmas. They were all unopened apart from the one I was given after his death. It contained a single sheet of paper. I settled myself down to study his last confusing message.

Memories flooded back. I was nearly eight when my father told me he was taking me for a farm holiday in Pembrokeshire. What I didn't know was that he had decided literally to farm me out. I never returned and I never saw him again.

CHAPTER TWO

CAITLIN

I clambered back down and was storing the step ladder away when I heard a voice.

"Morning Caitlin, have you got time for a quick chat?" I turned round to see Bob grinning at me. Middle aged and of medium height, he was thin and wiry and very brown from working outside. His dark eyes were edged with laughter lines. He had been working in my neighbour's garden. Now he came to work for me a couple of times a week. A man of few words, he was knowledgeable and a hard worker. As the months passed I had grown to trust his judgement and to feel comfortable in his company. "No builders today?"

I shook my head. "They've finished the kitchen. I want a few weeks respite from mess." We stood beside each other looking towards the house, our backs to the avenue of mature Beech trees that give the impression of driving up to a grand house. It isn't. Rock House is weathered and solid looking, built with locally quarried Purbeck stone.

"You're doing a fine job. Come round the back with me, let me show you what I've been doing." I gasped when I saw a secluded area. I was sure it had been covered in brambles a few days ago. "Oh Bob, it's a secret garden." I was captivated by the statue standing in the middle of the ground. The sun, just coming out from behind a cloud, lent it a radiant milky glow. "I gave her a good scrub, she was covered in moss. She's a beauty, isn't she? And look over there, a lovely old fashioned rose, a rose for Caitlin Rose." I walked over and inhaled its scent, then stumbled back feeling dizzy and disorientated for a moment. "Are you OK?" I felt Bob holding onto my arm. "I feel as though someone just walked over my grave. What a weird feeling. I'm OK, probably in need of caffeine. Come and have a coffee with me." I led the way back into the house. "What do you think of the new kitchen?"

"I like it." He ran his hand over one of the kitchen cupboards. "The wood's good. You've managed to keep the character of the old place." He sat down at the table whilst I grappled with my new coffee machine, not quite sure yet which switch did what. I managed to make two passable cups of coffee. We sat sipping, both of us comfortable with silence, but I must have started to look serious as Bob interrupted my thoughts. "You're looking solemn today. Is there something bothering you?"

As soon as the words were out of his mouth, I could see he wished he could take them back. He was thinking about Dennis. I was thinking about my mother. I could see by the look on his face that my next statement surprised him. "Rock House has stirred up all sorts of memories. Dennis thinks I'm mad but I'm sure I see my mother standing looking out of the front window. Do you believe in ghosts?"

"Not really, love. Do you think it could be a memory? Now you're settled, why not do some research. Your mother was a local lass, wasn't she? There'll be people in the town who remember her. How old would she be now?" I told him she would be in her sixties. "My mother or aunt might recall her. I can mention her and see if they do. Remind me of her name."

"Cecilia Rose. Her birth name was Roberts. I'd love to talk to someone who remembers her. To feel she really existed. I know nothing about her or my past, and it's time I did. I have another appointment to see the Executor of my father's will this afternoon. See what he can tell me."

He looked at me, a serious expression on his face. "You may find things you don't expect." I shrugged, "What have I got to lose."

CHAPTER THREE

The office of Barrett and Jones Solicitors was in the High Street. Caitlin was asked to take a seat in the waiting area. When Mr Jones came out he saw a young woman dressed simply in jeans and white tee shirt, long legs stretched out in front of her. Her short dark hair framed a strong face, rather than a beautiful one. She sat very still. When he spoke her name she looked up at him with a pair of remarkable blue eyes.

They shook hands, Caitlin withdrawing hers hastily from his moist grip. "How very nice to see you again, Miss Rose. Do come in." Caitlin assumed he was middle aged. Shorter than her, she could see his sandy hair was receding, but he had combed over longer strands. He wore old fashioned horn rimmed glasses, magnifying his hazel eyes. Despite the warm day he was wearing a three piece suit. The waistcoat buttons looked as though they might pop. His face was shiny with perspiration. The office smelled unpleasant, perspiration mixed with Old Spice aftershave. A vase of chrysanthemums added to the overpowering smell in the room. Caitlin, trying not to show her distaste, asked him to open the window. Whilst he did, she sat on the chair in front of his perfectly organised desk. When he rejoined her, he withdrew a file from his drawer and glanced at the top page. "It's been quite some time since all your affairs were settled. What can I do for you today?"

"I'd like to ask you about my mother's will and the Trust Fund. When you first told me about my inheritance, I was too shocked to ask much. I simply took the cheque to the financial adviser as you advised. Then I was busy making Rock House habitable. Now I'm more settled

I've been thinking. The Trust Fund held a great deal of money. I never saw a penny of it until my father died. I was fostered by an elderly couple. They had a monthly allowance to look after me, but it didn't amount to much and they told me it stopped when I reached sixteen. So what happened to all the money? What was my father up to and why did my mother, a young woman with a husband and small child, write a will instructing a trust fund be set up for her child? Was she expecting to die?"

"The old files will have been archived. The best person to talk to might be my father. He's retired now but I believe he acted for the family. I can talk to him when he's back from his holiday. But I seem to remember your father left a letter for you. Didn't it contain an explanation?"

Caitlin stopped smiling, her composure shaken. Could she trust this man with her father's last message. "After what he did I burned it unopened."

Mr Jones looked down at the file, "I see. Well, there is your cousin Arabella Rose of course. Have you spoken to her?" Caitlin stared at him. "What cousin? I didn't know I had a cousin. Who is she? Where does she live?" Mr Jones rifled through the file in front of her. "I can't give out any personal information, but what I can do is phone her and let you know her response." Caitlin clasped her hands, her eyes looked luminous. "I'd like to talk to your father, and I can't believe I have a cousin. I thought I was little orphan Annie, all alone in the world." She grinned at him and he smiled. Caitlin expected solicitors to be rather distant and business like. Someone you neither liked nor disliked but trusted to give sound advice. At that moment, with a smile on his face, he looked vulnerable; almost boyish. When he realised she was observing him he averted his eyes, then he looked up and smiled. His eyes seemed to glint behind his glasses. "So, tell me how you are? How are you getting on in the house?"

"Slow but sure, but I've been distracted. I thought I'd found a helpful partner. I'm afraid it's turned out badly. He's about as much use as a chocolate kettle." She chuckled, then immediately became serious. "I'm going to have to ask him to leave. I suppose I should have had more sense. This is a small town. People must have known the Roberts family were wealthy. I suspect he's a parasite."

"Oh my dear, I am sorry to hear that. Are you going to be alright on your own? Will you have someone else in the house when you ask him to leave?" His question made her stop and think. She felt a frisson of anxiety. "Yes, I think so." Full of nervous energy she stood up. Mr Jones pushed himself from his chair with some effort and walked round the desk. They shook hands. "I'll do as we discussed and contact you as soon as I can."

She left the room with a sense of relief. Why on earth did men wear overpowering aftershave. It had been a very whiffy half an hour. A cousin should be able to help her with her search. She had believed she was the last of the family line, yet suddenly Mr Jones had found her a cousin. How very odd.

Caitlin was eager to be out in the fresh air, so, instead of turning up the High Street to head for home, she walked half way along the sea front and sat down on a bench. Apart from her delight on discovering she had a cousin, Mr Jones's question had left her feeling vulnerable – should she be alone asking Dennis to leave.

Her head was telling her to make a clean break from him. She dreaded the thought of confrontation. She ambled home but was no closer to a plan when she reached the house. She recognised how anxious she was becoming. She decided to swallow her pride and ring her best friend.

Caitlin and Sally had met in Pembrokeshire College, both young aspiring chefs. They had unusual childhoods which seemed to draw them together. Sally had spent her formative years with her elderly grandparents. They were members of the Methodist Church and held strong beliefs. College brought both girls freedom and Caitlin tried hard not to lead Sally astray. They were good for each other. Sally, in return, helped Caitlin believe her life was worth living and worth living well. They had remained close friends and when Caitlin moved to Dorset Sally came too, finding a live-in job in a hotel nearby. Caitlin's plan had been, once the house was habitable, to ask Sally to come and live with her. Unfortunately, Dennis had intervened.

Caitlin rang her hoping she would pick up. "Hello stranger, I thought you'd forgotten me now you're all loved up." Caitlin immediately felt guilty. "Hi Sal, I'm sorry it's been so long and I'm not 'loved up!' Could you come over here one evening? Even better, would you come and stay?" Caitlin explained what she had in mind and to Sally's credit, she didn't reply "I told you so." She would take some leave and stay with Caitlin the following week. She made Caitlin agree that she would leave things as they were until then.

Dennis and Caitlin tiptoed around one another that evening. Unusually, he came home with a bottle of wine and some flowers. Caitlin feigned a headache and had an early night, suggesting he sleep in the spare room. He looked irritated and she was left wondering whether she should put off asking him to leave until Sally arrived. The following morning he brought her tea in bed. Crossing her fingers she broke her promise. "We need to talk tonight." He gave her a suspicious look, screwing up his eyes as he contemplated her. When he walked away she heard him say, "Anything for you my darling. Have a good day, see you later."

ARABELLA

When the phone rang she had felt annoyed. It was disturbing her peace. Tetchily she picked the phone up. After the call she stood looking out of the window. She was going to have to be very careful not to give anything away. She had agreed to the caller's request. She had a short time to prepare herself. She stood in thought for a few moments, then picked the phone up again.

CHAPTER FOUR

TUESDAY 9TH JULY

CAITLIN

It was a beautiful day and it didn't take me long to decide against sorting the attic in favour of gardening. Last winter Bob had cleared some of the flower beds at the front and we had replanted them. There was weeding and dead heading to do. I worked steadily through the morning then went in for lunch. Mr Jones's secretary rang to give me my cousin's phone number, so at least I could get on with that. I called her that afternoon. She seemed delighted to hear from me. We arranged to meet at her cottage in North Cornwall on Saturday afternoon.

I prepared supper and changed into clean clothes. I was beginning to get butterflies. I laid the table and opened the bottle of wine Dennis had bought the previous day. When he saw the effort I'd made, he kissed the top of my head; asked how long supper would be. When I told him, he wandered outside for a smoke. I thought, typical - it wouldn't occur to him to offer any help. Eventually I went into the garden to find him. He was standing staring at the statue Bob had cleaned, his hand resting on her head as though he owned her. He was smoking one of his ghastly little cigars. When he saw me, he took another puff, then dropped it close to the base of the statue, grinding it out with his heel. Something snapped in me. I glared at him, shaking my head in disbelief. "I want you to leave. Get out, you don't belong here."

"Why! What have I done?" He looked stunned. "You

take it for granted that I'll clean all your mess. Look at where you've just thrown that cigar. How dare you! Go back to where you came from and leave me alone." He stared at me, his eyes narrowing. "You're chucking me out, just like that?" I noticed how stained his teeth were. I could smell his foul cigar breath. I stepped away from him with distaste. He came closer. I stood my ground, quietly responding, "It's simple. This is my house, my garden. I don't want you here any longer. Take your things and go." He seemed bewildered. His eyes shiny now with unshed tears. He began to plead. "I fell in love with you the first time we met. I've been trying to find the right moment to ask you to marry me. I said I wanted us to grow old together. Don't say it's over. It can't be over. I won't let it be over." I tried to remain calm. "It's the house and money you love."

"How can you say that? I've never asked you for a penny. You'll regret it if you make me walk out now. I'm the only one who can help you." I glared at him. "No more bullshit. Just go." He came closer, looming over me. I was startled, but he only put his hand out to touch my hair. He was trembling. We stood staring at one another. Then he broke the gaze and strode back into the house. I followed him into the hall and saw him disappear up the stairs. I could hear him pulling open drawers and slamming doors. Ten minutes later he struggled down with two bags and stood gazing at me as though willing me to change my mind. I remained silent. "I'll be back for the rest of my gear. I meant what I said, I won't give you up. Think about it. I know we can be happy together, you just haven't given us enough time."

"I'll put all your stuff in the garage. It won't be locked." He gave me a last desperate look then slouched out slamming the front door behind him. I was shaking and felt sick. What did he mean, he was the only one who could help me? What was he playing at?

I've always been claustrophobic and I needed fresh air, but I could only pace round the house, shut all the downstairs windows and lock all the doors. I tried to ring Sally. She didn't pick up. The only other person I could think of was Bob. Taking a deep breath, I rang his number. "It's Caitlin – are you doing anything? I have a lasagne in the oven and no-one to share it with, and I need to talk to someone. I've told Dennis to leave. He warned me he wouldn't give me up. He's packed his bags and gone for now, but I'm sure he'll be back."

There was a silence for a moment. "I've just got in from work. Let me clean myself up and I'll be with you." Then he put the phone down and I wondered what I had done.

Bob lived in a small stone cottage on the High Street, approximately a hundred yards from the house he had grown up in. As a young man he wanted to travel and ended up working in Australia. He met a woman on a paddle steamer, cruising down the Murray River on the legendary Emmy Lou. They settled down together on the outskirts of Melbourne. It was beautiful, but he felt out of place. The beginnings of homesickness, although he didn't recognise it as such. When the break up came it was amicable. He saved enough to book his flight and flew into Heathrow on a cold, wet November day. When he walked out of the terminus he held his face up to the rain. He was home, freezing cold but very happy to be back amongst his own.

His parents loaned him money to buy his cottage. He

set himself up in business. The town attracted retirees as well as holiday makers, so there was always plenty of work. Now he understood where he belonged. He was a contented man.

His friendship with Caitlin added spice to his life. She was one of those people who seemed to court disaster. He couldn't quite make her out but he was becoming fond of her, and she needed help. Someone dependable rather than a knight in shining armour. He was glad she trusted him enough to ask for help. Dennis struck him as a total git. He couldn't figure out what she saw in him. Half an hour later he pulled in at the front of Rock House and knocked on the door. She opened it immediately. "Am I glad to see you, Bob. After Dennis left I realised I hadn't asked him to give the house keys back and I panicked."

"No need to panic. Locks can be changed." He could see tears beginning to well up in her eyes. He didn't want to spook her but she needed a brotherly hug, so that's what he did, and it did the trick. She had a bit of a weep, then broke away and blew her nose. "Better?"

"I think so. I can't believe what an idiot I've been. Sal's coming to stay on Sunday, I should have waited but when it came to it I couldn't bear him here for another minute." He grinned. "How could I refuse to come to your rescue or resist the supper you promised me? Oh, and to be on the safe side, I'll stay here tonight. My cousin, Justin, and I can change the locks tomorrow, then you'll be secure."

Her lasagne was delicious. She offered wine, but he turned it down in favour of a glass of water. He wanted to keep a level head. They had been involved in the garden together, and they had chatted in the pub, but this was a different Caitlin. She was open. She told him how it had been between her and Dennis. Kept on repeating what a fool she had been. Bob wasn't going to agree. He gave her the sort of advice a friend would give. Get over it. He's not worth it. Move on. They talked about the town, her plans for Rock House and about her friend. He told her a little about himself. It was comfortable and they both relaxed, enjoying each other's company.

After supper Bob rang his cousin. He would get some new locks and help fit them. Bob wasn't going to leave Rock House until he knew it was secure. Although he was offered a spare bedroom, he chose the sofa. He was alert to every noise. The old house produced a myriad of creaks and groans. He could hear Caitlin pacing around upstairs. She was having a bad night too. He did drop off eventually, waking around first light. Eventually he heard floorboards creaking then Caitlin appeared, her hair damp. She handed him a bath towel.

"I've finished in the bathroom, it's all yours. I'll see what I can rustle up for breakfast. Are you a tea or coffee man?"

He had a strange feeling as he climbed the staircase to search for the bathroom. He noticed the plaster was cracking and the paintwork faded. He was nearly at the top when he was startled to see his side reflection in an ornate full length mirror. It hung close to the top step. He stood there and looked down at the front hall, the long window and the old red and gold Victorian floor tiles and shivered. Perhaps Caitlin was right, there was something not quite right here.

His cousin Justin arrived with the new locks. They spent the next hour fitting them, attaching chains to the front and back door. Justin suggested erecting gates and some security cameras at the top of the drive. Caitlin looked uncomfortable. It seemed she had a horror of being enclosed. She sighed, "What a mess I've got myself in." Bob agreed, "You have and he'll not give up easily. Sorry Caitlin, we've got to go. We've both got jobs to get to." He stopped her when she suggested she pay both of them. "Pay Justin for the locks and his time, not me. You and I are friends, aren't we? Gardening's different, that's my day job." She reached out and clasped his hand. "That's a relief, I can't lose my gardener." She smiled at them both. "Friends."

As Bob left she reminded him about her trip to Cornwall. She would see her cousin on Saturday, returning on Sunday evening when her friend Sally was due to arrive. "I guarantee you'll like Sally. She's my ginger ninja chum. If Dennis gives her any nonsense she'll use a karate kick on him. Until then I'll stay securely at home thanks to you and Justin."

Bob drove away thinking how naïve Caitlin was. Dennis had targeted her. Moving in to Rock House and having money to employ builders to renovate it - she was clearly not short of a bob or two. The question was, who was he and how did he find out about her? Who had been talking? She wasn't the sort of person who indulged in chit chat. She struck him as a reserved, private person. Slow to trust and form friendships, but steadfast when she did.

CHAPTER FIVE
CAITLIN

Saturday arrived and I set off for North Cornwall with high hopes. I found Arabella's cottage tucked away on a small side road. Painted blue with a neatly trimmed lavender hedge, it was a picture postcard of a place. I sat in my car for a few minutes. My excitement was rising. A long lost cousin popping up out of the blue doesn't happen every day. I grabbed the flowers I'd bought at a petrol station, stepped out, opened the gate and rang the bell. Arabella opened the door instantly. I was surprised to see such a tiny woman. At five foot eight I towered over her. She was petite, her mid length blonde hair held back from her face with a yellow Alice band. Dressed neatly in cream shorts and a pink and blue check shirt, she looked fit, tanned and healthy; pretty in a painted doll sort of way. If I had hoped seeing her would prompt a memory, there was nothing. I wouldn't have known her from Adam or indeed, Eve. "Caitlin, how wonderful to see you. I can't believe it, after all these years. I thought you had disappeared for good. Do come on in."

The front door was low, I had to stoop my head. She led me through to her sitting room. It was small and cosy. I was beginning to feel like a giant. She smiled, "The difference is you've grown into a tall, elegant woman, and I'm only five foot nothing in my stockinged feet. You're lucky to take after your mother. Shall we go and get some tea – or would you rather something a bit stronger? I have white wine chilling." I followed her into a neat kitchen. The cupboards were painted light blue; there was a small painted dresser with blue and white china displayed on it. I sat down at a pine table and watched whilst she placed the flowers I had given her in the sink. She leaned over to open a door underneath a marble effect worktop to reveal the fridge, and produced a bottle. The offer of tea forgotten. She turned and smiled at me. "You've still got your beautiful dark hair. I remember when you were little. It was long then. I used to brush the tangles out for you." "My father had it cut off, he couldn't be bothered to braid it for school. Perhaps it did me a favour. With me, what you see is what you get." Ignoring my comment, Arabella poured wine into two flute glasses and handed me one, "Do you remember, your father brought you over to visit us before he took you to Wales? You were such a cute child. Thinking about him, I must tell you, his funeral was a sad affair, hardly anyone there to mourn him. I'd hoped you would be there." I tasted the wine before replying. Good thing it was well chilled. Oaked Chardonnay, my least favourite. "I didn't know anything about it. I hadn't seen him since I was eight. The solicitors told me weeks afterwards. They had to find me first. I hope you're not expecting me to feel guilty. Had I known I wouldn't have gone, not after what he did." Arabella reached across and touched my arm. "I'm so sorry. We all lost touch. I worked away for years. I only came back when Mother became ill, she died four years ago. I would have contacted you, but I didn't know where you were."

"I'm sorry for your loss, Arabella. What a strange family. I'm afraid I don't remember you, but we're first cousins, right? Mr Jones, the solicitor, the one who rang you, said my father and your mother were siblings. Have you any brothers or sisters, any more cousins I don't know about?" She sipped her wine. "Oh, please call me

Bella, no-one calls me Arabella now. The last person was my mother - usually when she had something to complain about. George and my mother had one child each, that's us two, and as far as I know, they were the last of their family. I'm afraid we are all that's left of the Roses. I can hardly believe we're together again. It's lovely to have you here. Are you able to stay?"

"I'm afraid I have to go back tomorrow. I've booked into a hotel for the night, but we've got a bit of time to catch up, and we can arrange to meet again. Right now, I'd love to stretch my legs after the journey. Do you fancy a walk by the sea?"

We strolled from the cottage down to the beach. The tide was out, the distant sea reflecting the blue of the sky. The beach looked as though it went on for miles. We wandered down across the soft sand and I searched for some flat pebbles to skim in the water. Bella joined in the game for a few moments then said, "It's such a lovely afternoon, shall we walk for a while?"

"Yes, it seems I've lost my stone skimming skills – not easy to say that! Let's walk and you can tell me what I was like as a child." Bella stopped for a moment, a sad expression on her face. "I don't know if I have the strength to do what I think you want." That took me by surprise. What a strange thing to say. "I don't want to talk about anything distressing, Bella. I've got a story to tell but I wasn't going to talk about it now. I'm just so excited to see you. I thought I was alone in the world. What I was hoping was that you'd remember my mother. I was so young when she disappeared from my life. I haven't even got a photo of her. I've found old boxes in the attic at home. There may be photos in them, but I haven't got round to sorting them properly yet."

Her friendly expression changed. Her eyes narrowed momentarily. She looked puzzled. Then she smiled again. "Of course I remember her. We often had family parties on the beach. She was tall and had dark, wavy hair. She loved being in the sea. I'll see if I can find anything in my mother's old photo albums."

Something wasn't right with Bella. I wondered if my mother's death had upset her. "I'm glad you remember her. It's weird, but since I've been back at Rock House I think I've seen her ghost. She wears a floral dress, her dark hair tied back with a ribbon. In a strange way, I've found it comforting. I suppose it might just be a memory."

Bella stood still for a moment, looking out to sea. "Yes, that's got to be a memory. Ghosts don't exist, Caitlin. People want them to and conjure up all sorts of fancies." Ouch. No sympathy there. We carried on walking, stopping occasionally to look at shells washed up on the shoreline. We watched sanderlings floating on the waves. There were several walkers throwing balls for their dogs. One fit, young black Labrador was continually running and swimming out to fetch his ball. He ran up to us, shaking his wet coat, splashing us. I laughed, "I wish I had your energy, boy!" The dog dropped his ball at my feet looking up at me expectantly. I threw it for him then turned and waved to his owner. We were almost at the end of the bay by now so we found a couple of large rocks to sit on.

"Caitlin, can I give you a piece of advice? I may be able to find some photos of your mother if that's what you want, but it would be best not to rake up the past. I mean, why do you need to know? Uncle George left you all the money and the family house." Her attitude had changed. Was that resentment in her voice? The veneer of friendliness had gone. Although I wanted to say that I had a duty to use the Roberts money wisely as my ancestors had done, I didn't. It was none of her business. I snapped back at her. "It was my mother's money and her house. Nothing to do with your uncle. My mother's family had invested their money over the years, so it was held in trust for me, and let me tell you, I **am** going to find out what happened all those years ago, and why I got sent away." I softened my tone then, "But honestly, that's not why I'm here. I just wanted to meet you again and get to know you."

Bella's eyes were cold, my words had hit home. She shrugged her shoulders. "I'm a couple of years older than you, but I was never told why you left home. Children were seen, not heard, and my mother certainly never talked about it. I'm worried that you'll find out things you'd rather not know, that's all. There must be a dark past. My mother became a bitter, twisted, lonely old woman and Uncle George died of cirrhosis – he drank himself to death."

"Are you blaming me for that?" Bella flinched, "Of course not. I'm trying to think what's best for you. You're a wealthy woman. You can do what you like. You don't have to cause yourself pain." Bella was irritating me now. "I see. So, you can't help." She shook her head. "I didn't say that." I found myself sighing although I wanted to shout at her. "I think you just did."

I was struck by how stilted our conversation was. Although maybe it had been like that from the beginning. I just hadn't noticed. There was no warmth, no empathy. No excitement on finding a long lost cousin. In fact, OK, she was pretty, but she looked unfriendly right now. Her eyes were unkind and she had a mean little mouth. She turned away from me looking out to sea. When she turned back her expression had changed. "Forgive me. I honestly would like to know more about my long lost cousin. I've been alone so long, it takes a bit of getting used to that's all." She looked as though butter wouldn't melt in her mouth. She leaned over and pecked me on the cheek. I felt too confused to respond. What on earth was I doing here. We had absolutely nothing in common. Eventually I said, "I'm sorry too, Bella. I'm tired. Let's walk back. I'd like to check into my hotel. Then I think I'll have a meal and an early night."

"We're not getting off to a very good start are we, Caitlin? The tide's coming in, we ought to make tracks. By the way, where are you staying, I don't think you said." I don't know why but I didn't want to tell her. "I can't remember the name of the place. It's the other side of town to you." I walked away, Bella, on her short legs, had a job to keep up with me. I wasn't quite sure why I was reacting the way I was. I felt so irritated. We were both relieved to get back to the cottage. "I'll give you a ring in the morning Bella, but I'm planning to go home in the afternoon. I have a friend coming to stay."

She smiled at me. "I can book us in for a lunch at the pub we just walked by if you like. They do a really good Sunday lunch; I promise I'll have a look for photos. See you tomorrow lunchtime. I'll be there by midday." With that she turned, walked up the path, opened her door and closed it firmly behind her.

I backed the car out of the lane, found my hotel and checked in. It was too early to eat and I was feeling restless so decided to go and find the local canal walk. The main street was bustling. It was good to see small independent shops doing a good trade. I browsed for a gift for Sally, then I took a short cut down some steep steps finding myself near the road to the beach. Not quite sure which way to go I stepped into a doorway so I could look at my street map. I could hear someone running down the steps. I don't know what made me move deeper into the doorway but I was glad I did. The man looked remarkably like Dennis. If it wasn't him, he had a double.

Keeping my distance, feeling slightly ridiculous, I followed him, and eventually saw him stride into Bella's road. I ran as quickly and quietly as I could and hid behind Bella's front hedge. I heard the door open. "What on earth are you doing here? You knew she was coming today. Are you trying to ruin everything?" I heard her say. "I had to see you. It's a mess, it's all going wrong." She clearly wasn't amused. "For goodness sake, come in." I heard the door slam and crouched there for a few moments trying to figure out what I had just witnessed. One thing was certain, I had allowed myself to be played for a fool.

I did my Miss Marple impersonation back down the lane, concealing myself as much as I could before quickening my pace. I walked back to the hotel. What on earth should I do next. I was meeting the scheming little snake tomorrow.

CHAPTER SIX

I sat on the bed endeavouring to make sense of the afternoon. Whichever way you cut it, it was contemptible. Arabella, if that really was her name, chatted to me as if she had prepared a script; she was wooden, there was no warmth, no empathy. Despite her painting a picture of family beach parties, I had no memory of them, or of her, and I didn't like her mean little mouth one little bit. I could think of numerous motives, all of them fantastic. If I hadn't been traced I presume Arabella, as next of kin, would have inherited. She and Dennis had been manipulating me. He said he wanted us to marry. Then what did he intend to do with me? I was afraid now and made up my mind to give nothing away.

Despite the turmoil I was in, I was hungry, so ate in the hotel restaurant. Taking a book, I tried to read, but my heart wasn't in it. Should I ring Arabella (I no longer thought of her as Bella) to cancel the lunch? Should I go home? No, she mustn't think there's anything wrong. I would just have to be patient and put on a good performance.

After dinner I walked along the front to get rid of some energy. Dusk was stealing the day and I shivered from cold or possibly fear and hurried back wanting reassurance. Should I ring Bob or Sally. In the end I rang Bob. I suppose I wanted to save the juicy bits for Sally tomorrow night. I've always been a bit of a show off. "Have you got time to talk, Bob? I've got a lot to tell you."

"Yeah, Justin and I are in the pub. Are you OK down there. Hang on a minute, it's so noisy, we're going out.

...That's better, now, are you OK, what's been happening?" He sounded concerned.

"I'm alright but things are not what they seem here. I met Arabella, it didn't go that well. Later on I was strolling around the town when I saw Dennis. I followed him at a distance. He went straight to Arabella's cottage."

There was a sharp intake of breath. "Whoa, what did you say, you saw them together? What the hell is he doing there? Stalking you? Look, do not attempt to play the detective. You could be putting yourself in danger."

"I know, but I had to find out. They didn't see me." I knew I didn't sound very convincing. "I'm meeting her for lunch tomorrow. I'll check out of the hotel and drive to the pub. I'll just be nice and friendly, not give anything away, eat my lunch and go. If I leave at two I should be home by five thirty."

"The sensible thing would be for you to get in your car right now and come home, but you're not going to do that, are you? Look, ring me just before you get to the pub so I know you're OK. I'll ring you after, say an hour and a half, and give you an excuse to leave."

"Thanks Bob, that would be good. I'll keep the conversation going. Arabella has promised to look for photos of my mother, I wonder what she'll come up with. I'll park in the main car park in plain sight. Don't worry, I'll be alright, and I'll see you tomorrow."

"Cat, be careful, I mean it, no heroics, this isn't a game. You don't know what you're dealing with. I'll see you tomorrow. I haven't just found a friend to lose one."

Bob was right. I had been treating it as a game. I was frightening myself now. What if Dennis was still in town, saw my car, disabled it and I broke down half way home. I'd be at his mercy. "Stop it, stop it, stop it. Don't be ridiculous. How would he even lift the bonnet? He could have taken my spare car key." My brain was in overdrive. To calm myself I went down to the bar and bought a large glass of wine and chatted to some residents. I left when I felt my eyes drooping. My last thoughts before dropping off were, I am not going to allow that pair to get the better of me. Strangely enough, I slept really well. Could have been the red wine.

I arrived at the pub as we had arranged and found myself a window seat. It was an old building, with a flagstone floor, black wooden beams, a large fireplace and little nooks and crannies housing small oak tables and chairs. The bar was filling with people who all seemed to know one another. I bought myself an orange juice and settled down with my book. Arabella was late. When she eventually arrived she looked flustered. "Oh good, you're still here Caitlin. A friend stopped by and I lost track of time. Shall we order?" She handed me a menu. "Thanks." I scanned it. The usual choice for a Sunday. "I'll have the beef with all the trimmings."

"Excellent choice, I'll have the same." She looked at me for a moment. "OK, I'll go and order. Would you like another drink?" I refused and she went off to the bar. I didn't offer to pay. She came back with a glass of white wine for herself. "How did you sleep? I always find it difficult to sleep in a hotel room."

"I slept well, didn't wake up until gone nine, so I skipped breakfast ready for an early lunch." She looked at me with a very innocent expression on her face, and asked whether I had gone out last night. With an equally innocent expression I said I had felt too tired after the drive. She barely hid her relief. "What did you do with yourself?"

"They have a lovely terrace overlooking the sea so I relaxed with a book. Here it is, *Cold Comfort Farm*. I like to read it once every year or so, it never fails to make me laugh. What do you do to relax?"

"When I have time I play tennis at the club. Most evenings I end up watching TV. I'm a bit of a sports fanatic. I planned to go to the Commonwealth games this year but couldn't get away. It's hard when you're on your own, but you must know that." Our lunches arrived so conversation thankfully ceased. When we'd finished I asked about the photos. Her hand flew to her mouth in a wonderfully theatrical way, "Oh, my goodness, I'm so sorry, I forgot." I bet she did!

"That's a shame, I was hoping you'd find some old family snaps. I just wish I could see what we all looked like then, it might help me remember. If you do find any, could you keep them for me? I'll try and get back down to see you before too long."

"Yes of course but I've a horrible feeling I've dumped them. You know what it's like when you have to clear a house after someone dies. Oh, silly me, no you don't really do you? You've not had to deal with the mess, the endless trips to charity shops." I didn't rise to the bait but smiled at her, trying to look as though I was hanging on her every word. I was relieved when my mobile rang. It was Bob. I explained I had to go as my friend was on her way to me. "Is Sally coming to you for a holiday?" How did she know my friend was called Sally. A bit of a giveaway there. I kept a straight face, "No, she's coming to live with me. She's going to help with the renovations. You must remember Rock House. I'm sure it was beautiful when my mother was alive. It's very dilapidated now and in need of major works. It's too big a job for one. I rattle around the place not quite knowing what to do next. I need someone to share it, help me with the design. Sally will spur me on."

Arabella looked thoughtful. Yes, I thought, you planted Dennis as my little helpmate didn't you? Well, that didn't go so well. He didn't lift a finger. I surmised that she and Dennis had been hatching something up to get him back in my good books. Now she knew Sally was coming they would have to change their plans. Her face gave nothing away, "That's nice, well I guess I mustn't keep you, you've got a long drive. You may hit weekend traffic going back. It's been so great seeing you. We must do it again." She couldn't wait to get rid of me to contact Dennis, to warn him I daresay. She walked with me to my car, standing on tiptoe to kiss my cheek. "Don't be a stranger." And with that she left. I watched her until she was out of sight. I had a horrible feeling I was being watched.

She was right about the traffic. The drive back was slow and I stopped to pick up shopping on the way. I was relieved to be going home to friends who would support me. I also felt dread. I was being targeted by two unscrupulous people.

CHAPTER SEVEN

ROCK HOUSE, SUNDAY 14TH JULY

SALLY

Caitlin gets herself into such scrapes with men. She portrays herself as an independent woman, but inside she's still a scared, little girl. Men sense it and try to take advantage. They soon find out that the little girl when pushed is spirited and determined.

Dennis was charming and attentive when they were first together, but there was something fake about him. At the time, I figured I was jealous because Cat was spending all her time with him. She didn't seem to notice. When we did have the occasional evening out, he'd turn up and try to join us. It was obvious he was trying to control her and he didn't like us being together. Lately she's looked anxious and jumpy, so when she rang and told me she was going to ask him to leave I was relieved. He's a big strong bloke. I'd be wary of him becoming violent. I often felt he was capable of it.

I love her like a sister. When we first met in college, we were chalk and cheese. There's me, not able to say boo to a goose, overweight, spotty; with ginger hair, the butt of jokes. Cat stood up for me. She recognised a fellow wounded soldier. We told each other our stories and have since formed a lasting friendship. Hers was hard to believe. Her mother dead, her father abandoning her to strangers, but despite that there's something joyful about her.

Unlike Cat, I'm Welsh, a real Celt with my red hair, white skin and freckles. I'm an orphan, with kind grandparents. God and the Methodist chapel formed their world. I was a hindrance, particularly as I grew into such an awkward child. It was Caitlin who gave me faith in myself. She told me I was beautiful, and encouraged me to be myself. Here I am now, tall, Rubenesque with long Titian hair, the sort that Pre-Raphaelite painters would have died for. You notice how I've changed the word "overweight" to Rubenesque and "ginger" to Titian.

Right now I'm parked round the back of Rock House, waiting for her. She rang me forty minutes ago to say she would be home in an hour. I've been strolling round the garden. From the top you can just see the sea. It's a beautiful place. Her plan is for me to live here with her. I'm very tempted. Her words were, "Why work for a pittance, I have enough dosh for both of us, and I'd rather live with you than anybody else. Come on, even if it's only for a while. Let's have some fun. There's plenty of room. You can have your own flat on the third floor if you want."

"Yeah" I replied, "I can be the mad relation locked away in the attic!" But she knows that I can't sponge off her, my pride won't let me. So the next part of the conversation went, "I'll put up the money for a café in town. We can both cook, but you can run it. We can have home-made cake and people can sit and read the paper." I like the idea of a café. I've been working in a large tourist hotel. We have a revolving two week menu and I'm bored stiff with it. I've always dreamt of running a French style bistro, with a daily "Plat de jour" and a salad bar, oh, and the cakes, with Caitlin there's got to be cake. Well, it's a dream. Who knows, dreams can come true, look at Caitlin.

As I wandered back round to the front of the house, I

briefly saw the back of a person hurrying up the drive, then the sound of a car starting up. Rock House isn't very secure, and it's tucked right out of the way. Not a good idea to have every Tom, Dick and Harry wondering in. I continued my exploration of the garden then sat in the car. Caitlin had left me a message to say the locks had been changed, so my key wouldn't work. I don't know why she didn't think to leave me one hidden somewhere. Anyway, she should be back any minute. I wonder who that person was.

Here she is bang on time. That's the Virgo in her and she's still driving her BMW. I would have thought she'd have upgraded by now. Typical of Caitlin. I could immediately see the strain on her face and put my arms around her. She held onto me for a long time, her body shaking. "Whatever's the matter?"

She pulled away from me. "Let's go in and I'll tell you everything." She unlocked the boot picking up her overnight bag. I carried her shopping to the front door. She turned round pressing the key fob to lock her car, something she didn't normally do. Inside she dropped her bag, shut the door and put on the safety chain. I picked up the post and we walked through into the sitting room and sat down on the sofa together. By this time I was truly concerned, "Tell me what's been going on. You look scared."

"I think I've frightened myself. I'll be alright now you're here Sal. I've had a stressful few days. I don't quite know where to start."

"Start at the beginning. Have things got worse with Dennis? You haven't told him already, have you?"

"I'm sorry, I just snapped and told him to go. He was angry then I thought he was going to cry. He flounced out and then I realised I hadn't asked him for the door keys. So I rang Bob." That surprised me. "Who's Bob?" "He's the gardener, I don't think you've met him. He rescued me, got the locks changed." I sighed. "Oh lord, Cat, don't jump from the frying pan into the fire." She shook her head. "It's nothing like that. We've become friends and I trust him." Then she proceeded to tell me what had occurred over the weekend. No wonder she's scared. I always knew there was something not quite right about Dennis. "The question is, what can be done about it. Do you want to go to the police? Are they committing a crime?"

"I don't know. There are so many questions, for example, is Arabella really my cousin? We don't look alike, and try as I might, I can't remember her. The solicitor gave me her phone number. If she's not my cousin he could be in this too. It's like something out of a book. It's too fantastic. I've driven myself nuts going over and over it. Come on, let's do something normal. Let's cook some supper, it's getting late and I promised I'd ring Bob when I got back. We could invite him to supper too – you can vet him, make sure he's genuine!" It was good to see the sparkle back in her eyes and I laughed.

It's great working in the kitchen with Cat. She's an intuitive cook. I'm the sort of chef that has a recipe, weighs ingredients and follows instructions. Cat enjoys experimenting, throws things together and hey presto, they work. The kitchen is spacious enough for us not to get in one another's way. I wonder whether she had thought of the café idea before designing it. The cupboards are solid wood with practical marble work surfaces. A large scrubbed pine table stands in the middle of the room, big enough to seat a crowd. I could imagine an old rosy cheeked cook kneading the daily bread for the household on it. Anyway, this evening, we are going to make a simple linguine with mussels and prawns and focaccia bread to mop up the juices.

We decided to lay the table in the dining room, which is just across the hallway from the kitchen. Cat has furnished the room with an old Welsh dresser and a beautiful dining table she found in an antique shop. She has polished them to a glossy sheen. With French windows opening onto a terrace leading into the back garden, it's full of natural light. Feeling warm I opened the doors, then Caitlin, making a funny face at me, shut them again. I should have thought.

Bob turned up bang on time. I presumed he hasn't got other commitments to be able to just drop things. I watched them hug each other affectionately. "Bob, meet my best friend Sally." He turned to me, a big grin on his face. I could immediately see why Cat likes him. He's a comfortable looking man, neither too short nor too tall. He's got a mop of darkish hair and his eyes twinkle. He greeted me with a soft Dorset accent. I thought, yes, this one's OK. In fact, he's not bad. "It's great to meet you Sally. She called you her 'ginger ninja chum,' it hardly does you justice."

I felt myself blushing as Cat burst into laughter. "Just don't mess with her. Years ago we took self-defence lessons; then Sally went on to do Karate. She doesn't take any nonsense. She can chop things in half with her bare hands."

"Nonsense, stop teasing Cat." She laughed and walked towards the door. "Let's go in the sitting room. Gin and tonics all round. I've told Sally the Dennis and Arabella saga. The telling of it has made me more confused than ever. I'm so glad you're both here. Between us, perhaps we can figure it out."

Bob settled himself in a comfortable chair. "I've been asking around town about Dennis. He's illusive. Keeps himself to himself. No one knows where he came from. His flat's rented and there's talk of a woman living there. Now you know there's a connection between him and your cousin we'd better dig a bit deeper. The question is, is she really your cousin?"

I saw Cat tense up. "I'd just like to forget it, turn the clock back, pretend it never happened." I took her hand and squeezed it. "I'm going to be a shadow at your side. If there's a conspiracy, we'll get to the bottom of it, and they will get what's coming to them. At the moment you have the upper hand. We could play them at their own game."

"You're right Sal. We can look on it as a mystery to be solved. Maybe there's a link somewhere with my mother's life. She has been on my mind so much lately." Bob snapped his fingers, "I'm glad you reminded me, I've chatted with my aunt. It turns out, she was in primary school with her. She remembers her as Cessie. She didn't want to tell me much, said she'd speak to you." Caitlin's face lit up, "Oh, that's fantastic news. What did she say about her?"

"Sunny, that's what she said. She had a sunny disposition and was always laughing. Sounds like you, when you're not worrying about conspiracies." Cat grinned. At that moment, I thought Bob's sensitive and he cares about Cat. We had all finished our drinks and rather than suggest another, I thought it was time to move things on.

"Right you two, let's have a nice evening together, and tomorrow, it may seem quite different. I had a thought, when we were cooking Cat, you said you can't face the attic? I'm going up there and I'm going to fetch down three of the boxes. When we've sorted those, I'll bring down three more. That way, it'll get done and you won't feel trapped up there. We might even find hidden treasure." Cat stood up, "Thanks Sal. Marvellous what a bit of lateral thinking does. Now, let's go and eat."

CHAPTER EIGHT

CAITLIN

I drew back the curtains the next morning, the sun was shining; the sea sparkling in the distance. I began to take stock of the last few days. Alright, there may be vile things to contend with but I'm so happy Sal is here with me, and Bob is the most honest, relaxed man I've ever met. I hope he's gay or falls madly in love with Sally! What strange thoughts pop into my head. I padded downstairs and made two of mugs of tea and went back up with Sally's. "Morning my lovely, rise and shine!"

"Thanks Cat, you're a treasure." Sally sat up in bed and took the mug from me. "When you're ready to get up, the water's hot, and there are plenty of towels in the airing cupboard. I'll leave you to it." I went back downstairs and picked up the post. Then I remembered Sal had picked some up when we came in last night. I settled down to sort it all out. Two of the envelopes had been hand delivered. I recognised the writing and my heart skipped a beat. Ripping the first of them open, I scanned through three paragraphs of unadulterated sentimentality. Dennis saying how much he loved me, how he couldn't believe I had asked him to leave with what we had going for us. With a PS saying he had collected his gear from the garage. Then another PS asking me to ring him.

The second letter had a different tone. "I'm sorry if I'm moody sometimes, it's when I get a migraine. We need to meet, I have something urgent to tell you." He asked me to come on my own. "Please, please come, we can't let our relationship die after all we have been through together." I sat there feeling slightly nauseous – what a complete bastard. Why did he want to be with me? If I was honest with myself, he hadn't liked me much, let alone loved. And what was this about migraines? He complained of headaches sometimes, that's all. Meet him alone, I think not, I never want to be alone with him again. What did he mean, after all we'd been through together, for goodness sake. The rest of my life, how long did he intend that to be?

The first letter must have been posted before he'd found out that Sally was coming to live here. What had the ghastly pair cooked up afterwards? The only way to find out would be to meet. Right now, I was seeing him through a different lens. Instead of the solid, confident character I had taken him for, was he really weak and easily led? He might be, but he was still physically strong. I mustn't let my guard down.

When Sally came in, she examined the letters. "Before you got back yesterday afternoon I'd been looking round the garden and saw someone disappearing up the driveway. It must have been Dennis. I thought at the time a gate with a post box would be kinder for the postie, save a walk, but an automatic gate would give you more security particularly with the high hedges." I tried to be ironic. "We could be like film stars. What fun."

"No Cat, it's not fun. This is serious. You need to find out what he's up to, but in a setting of your choice, with back up. Let's have some breakfast then we can figure out the best way to deal with this. And, I haven't forgotten, I'm going up in the attic and I'm fetching three boxes down."

"OK, we'll do the three B's: breakfast, boxes and then I'll ring Bob. We can have a pow wow later." I found myself laughing, couldn't help it. I read a lot of Enid Blyton as a child. I loved the mysteries the children solved and was always looking for secret tunnels. Now we have our very own mystery to solve and despite everything I was beginning to feel like my old self again.

SALLY

"Corr heck, it's hot up here! Are you ready for the first box, Cat?" When I looked around the attic, I understood why Cat's heart sank at the thought of it. So many boxes, and so many cobwebs, but at least I could stand comfortably and the strip lighting illuminated the space well. I shivered, fearing I might see big black spiders lurking around. I grabbed the nearest boxes lining three up next to the opening. "Careful Cat don't hurt your back. You can balance the box on the top of the stepladder and then just ease it down."

We dragged the boxes into a spare bedroom which looked as though it had once been a nursery. The wallpaper was peeling but you could see it had been pretty. "Does this room bring back any memories?" Caitlin looked around her. "Not this room, but out there, at the top of the stairs, I have a hazy memory of my mother wearing a long grey dressing gown looking down at me. Oh, there used to be a gong up there. I think I was allowed to go up and hit the gong when meals were ready." She sat back for a moment. "That's just come back. How weird! I hadn't remembered the gong. I wonder what happened to it. See, with your help, memories are slowly returning. It's a bit scary. You remember I told you about seeing a ghost looking out of the hall window. The last time she was weeping then she faded away, or at least I faded away. I'm sure she was my mother and I knew then that I was sad and would weep too."

I put my arm around her shoulder, she looked at me with raised eyebrows. "I might start remembering all sorts of things. I'll be conjuring up ghosties and ghoulies!"

I didn't like the sound of that. "No you won't, just stop it. You dealt with Dennis and between us we'll find out what's been going on. If the woman at the window is your mother then you've helped her rest. You haven't seen her since have you?"

"No, I think she knew I was in danger but I'd like to see her again looking at me with a smile."

"Nice thought, now get on with doing the boxes woman, or it'll be time for coffee and cake before we even start!" The first box contained a porcelain tea set wrapped in old 1962 newsprint. Everything was wrapped as carefully in the next two boxes. We found silver cutlery, pewter jugs and glass vases, and one little cup and saucer. It was beautifully painted in green and gold with markings underneath we couldn't decipher. Cat examined it with a quizzical expression on her face. "This is so pretty. Let's take it downstairs and put it on the dresser. If only it could speak and tell its story." We stacked the boxes in the corner of the room and went back downstairs, our sorting job done for the day.

I think Cat's fallen in love with the coffee machine. She messes about with it. It makes me smile to see her so relaxed. The ceremony of tea or coffee making is important for her, and she always has homemade cake. It's charming and I love her for it, although the scales will tell me otherwise. I don't know how she manages to stay so blooming slim.

CHAPTER NINE

BOB

Caitlin rang as promised. She offered to feed me again, but I didn't want her to think I was taking advantage, so I went in my working clothes, and we sat round the table in the kitchen. Sally is so good, she had done exactly what she said she'd do. She had started them off on the great attic clearance. They were like a pair of excited children showing me what they had found.

I'd been able to fix up a meeting with my Aunt Ann. Caitlin looked solemn and must be worried. Unfortunately she has every reason to be. I'd like her to tell me a little about her childhood, Ann needs something to gauge how much to divulge when they see each other tomorrow. In the meantime both girls agree arrangements should be made to meet Dennis. The idea is for him to believe Caitlin wants to remain friends. Keep him guessing whilst we try to figure out what to do next. I suggested a lunch in one of the hotels in town, but to leave it until the weekend.

"I'd like you to be on the next table Bob, but Dennis knows you. Do you think Justin would agree to come? I want someone there I can trust."

"I'm sure he would and we could rope in Aunt Ann. It would look quite normal, mother and son out for lunch. You'll both have to reserve tables and get there early to make sure it goes according to plan." She grinned. "I can feel my 'Miss Marple' coming on again. I'm almost enjoying it."

"No," Sally interjected, "this is deadly serious, you shouldn't be joking about it. The meeting is to find out what their next move might be." Caitlin frowned. "Point taken, I'm just getting a bit carried away."

I wanted to introduce childhood memories to help Aunt Ann but I'm not good at subtle. After all, I'm a gardener not a shrink. "Caitlin, can I ask you about your childhood? You said you'd been farmed out. What did you mean?"

"Well, it's quite a long story. I'm happy to talk about being on the farm. Do you really want to hear about it?" I nodded. "OK, well, you know I said I'd left here when I was nearly eight, my so-called father told me we were going to spend the long summer holiday with Aunty Sylvia and Uncle Barry on their farm in Pembrokeshire. I don't know how he knew them, I assume now that he advertised. We went, and he left me with them. I probably shed a few tears but they were lovely and I just accepted them as my aunt and uncle. I thought at the time they were very old. Actually, they were in their late sixties, taking on a young child.

Sylvia was wonderful. She read me stories every night and we made cakes together. Barry was a bit gruff at first but he taught me all sorts of stuff about the animals on the farm. The farm was quite isolated. During the first week, they walked me right round the farm and then allowed me to go out on my own. The best thing of all was that they had a pony waiting for me. Betsy, a sturdy little mountain pony. She was a bit frisky and I was nervous. The first time I tried to mount her, I had my foot in the stirrup and she turned round and bit me! But that didn't put me off. I learned how to look after her, saddle her up and soon felt secure riding round the fields. It was the best holiday ever.

Then just before my eighth birthday, they sat me down

and asked if I would like to stay with them forever. I could go to school nearby and I'd be able to keep Betsy and if I wanted I could have a dog of my own to look after. I suppose I should feel guilty about it, but I was as happy as a lark. Sylvia was a substitute mother. Instead of having to get used, or not, to a string of 'aunties', I had security. I accepted things as they were. Although quite frankly, palming a young child off on an elderly couple shouldn't have been allowed. Anything could have happened.

I grew to love the farm. I helped with the milking. It was my job to go with Barry to fetch the cows in. I'd put scoops of cattle cake into the troughs to feed the cows whilst they were being milked. I drank milk straight from the cooler. Barry said it would make me big and strong. It did!

Christmas came. I didn't remember what a traditional Christmas was. We made decorations and we had a Christmas tree. I was given presents, but the best present of all was a Corgi puppy. I called him Rusty. Barry explained that we would train him to be a cow dog and that's what we did.

My first spring was magical. Primroses and snowdrops bloomed in the hedgerows. Later on I found a whole field full of cowslips. Barry teased me. He asked me to pick all the cowslip heads so he could make cowslip wine. I was an obedient little girl. I remember crying, when he told me he was joking. He didn't really understand children.

I started school. It was in the countryside near a Second World War aerodrome. I remember long underground buildings with grass roofs. I can't remember much about the teachers or lessons. I do remember having to say times tables, forwards and backwards. I can still do it at a push. I made some school friends, but I was generally quite a solitary child."

"You sound as though you enjoyed being on the farm, but weren't you curious about your father?"

"I didn't forget him. My aunt and uncle told me they received money to look after me, and he sent me money for birthdays and Christmas, but he never came to see me. Not surprisingly, I was torn between the security and love I'd found, and anger at being abandoned. I thought he'd chosen a girlfriend over me. Anyway, I began to hate him. I made up stories of why he couldn't see me. I stopped opening the birthday and Christmas cards, hiding them in a cupboard. I still have them in a box in the attic, all unopened."

"Full of £10 notes I daresay!"

"Well yes, but I think that's why I don't have much regard for money. I wasn't going to let him buy me. It's ironic that I've inherited a fortune and all I've ever wanted is independence and enough to pay my way. Anyway, life was good on the farm but when I was fifteen Sylvia had her first stroke. She was in hospital for a while, then home, and now it was my turn to look after her. I left school as soon as I could at sixteen and stayed at home. I remember Barry saying something about my allowance stopping then. A year later dear Sylvia had a second stroke and never recovered consciousness. Barry and I were devastated. After the funeral he sat me down and said I must think about myself. I needed to have a profession. I'd always liked cooking so I plumped for going to the local college to do a catering course. That's where Sally and I met."

They smiled at one another. Sally sat patiently

listening to a story she had probably heard many times before. I was fascinated hearing about Caitlin as a child, coping with all the shit she'd been dealt.

"Barry had been a smoker all his life, he'd been off colour, and it turned out he had lung cancer. I looked after him as well as I could, until he died. Then I was homeless. The farm was rented so everything was sold and I had to find somewhere to live. There was some money from the sale, so I could pay my way, but I was a wreck. Sally rescued me from a lonely life in a bedsit. I went to live with her and her grandparents. I'll never forget what my aunt and uncle did for me. They were wonderful people, and you Sally, I may not have survived without you."

Catlin's expression was difficult to read, but I wanted her to finish her story. "What happened next?"

"After Sally had put me back on the straight and narrow, I learned to look after myself. I was a working girl. It was through cooking in an old person's home that I decided I wanted to become a social worker. So I did an OU course to gain enough points to apply to university. It took me four years. I carried on working so I could pay my way. The area of Pembrokeshire I lived in was known as 'Little England beyond Wales'. I never learned much Welsh. Working in Wales without Welsh wasn't really an option, so I crossed the border into England. Sally and I remained friends, we've always followed one another. Now she's almost as English as me!"

"So when George Rose died, how did the solicitor trace you?"

"Well, I'd kept my name although I'd thought of changing it when I lived on the farm. My aunt and uncle talked me out of it. One day, an envelope popped through the door, and the rest is history. It seemed stupid to carry on working when I have so much to do here, and Sally and I have tentative plans to go into business together. I'd like to put the Roberts money to good use. So another chapter of life begins."

After hearing her story I'm sure fate has drawn me here. I didn't know George Rose, but had seen him around the town. He was well known in the pubs. Difficult to believe he was Caitlin's father, she's nothing like him. Being taken in by foster carers may have saved her. Why did George Rose send her away? I reckon this must all hinge around money. Well one thing is certain, I am going to do everything I can to keep Caitlin Rose and Sally Thomas safe. Whatever Dennis and Arabella have planned, they are not going to get away with it. Caitlin's going to need our support when she learns what happened to her mother. She's been through so much in her life already. Quite frankly, there's no justice in this world.

CHAPTER TEN

CAITLIN

Tuesday brought a sea fret over the bay. The hills were shrouded in mist but by lunchtime it looked as though the sun would break through. Sally and I had spent the morning sorting through another three boxes (she's a hard task master). We've started putting things we want to keep to one side. We'll give the rest to charity. There are still no signs of photographs or pictures.

I set off to find Aunt Ann's house. As I sauntered along, I remembered Arabella's warning, why put yourself through pain? Well, if there was pain, so be it. The retelling of my story last night helped me put my life in perspective. Before he abandoned me, my father neglected me. Goodness knows how I survived. I was one of the few children who liked school meals. Sylvia and Barry were subsistence farmers. They may have given me a home for the pay they received, but that didn't matter. What mattered was the love they gave to a shattered little girl. Looking back on it now, it can't have been easy having a damaged little person living with them. I was plagued by nightmares and it took me time to settle into life on the farm. When I tell my story, I only ever talk about the good times. I never disclose any of the unhappiness. I was fiercely loyal to Sylvia and Barry, which might be the reason why, until recently, I hadn't consciously been thinking about my mother. I just knew there was something missing in me.

Work became my saviour. I loved working with older people. Some people work to live but during that period I lived to work. That wasn't a bad thing for me. George

Rose dying freed me from the deep knot of hatred I had held inside me. If only I hadn't met Dennis, I'd be further along the journey, but I'm not going to beat myself up over that. I believe the whole scenario with Dennis was engineered to trap me. In addition, I think my mother has been trying to warn me.

At this point in my thought processes I realised I was walking along Ann's road. I found her house at the end of a long terrace. A wild flower patch at the side of it. I think she's going to be my sort of person. I rang the bell and heard a cacophony of barking. "Coco be quiet, stay there." I heard the sound of a door closing and then the front door opening. "You must be Caitlin, come on in. I'm sorry, Coco gets so excited. She won't stop until she's made a fuss of you." I was greeted by a ball of dark brown fur hurling herself at me, then running around in pure joy. "What sort of dog is she?"

"A miniature Schnauzer. She'll calm down in a minute." I leaned down to stroke her.

"It's OK, I love dogs. Come on Coco, let's make friends." It wasn't hard, she was delighted with the attention. Ann gave me a treat for her. She sat immediately, tongue hanging out. "No more barking now." I put the treat on the palm of my hand; she took it gently and trotted over to her bed. What a little sweetie.

"Let me look at you." Ann put her hands on my shoulders and examined me closely. "Oh my goodness, you look so like your mother. Your hair's different, hers was dark like yours, but long and wavy. Maybe it's because yours is short." I shook my head. "No, it doesn't make any difference. It grows dead straight." She smiled at me, "I can hardly believe I'm looking at Cessie's daughter. Do you remember me at all? I used to come to

Rock House, but there was no welcome for me there. George Rose had no time for any of Cessie's friends." I thought how attractive she was. Her face was beginning to show her age, but her hair was still light brown. Her dark eyes had looked sad but now she smiled. "Follow me my love, I'll make you a cup of tea or whatever you'd like and we can sit in the conservatory."

I walked through with her, noticing how comfortable and lived in her lounge/diner looked. There were two large squashy sofas scattered with cushions and a small dining table and chairs. Light poured in from a large front window with clean white nets obscuring the room from passers-by. A patio door at the other end of the room looked out over the garden. Lots of family photographs, including one of Bob and Justin grinning into the camera. I settled myself down in the conservatory whilst the kettle was boiling. I could see the hills emerging out of the mist. I hadn't realised quite how high Ann's road was. Coco padded in and plonked herself by me on the sofa. She nuzzled up to me so I would stroke her.

"I see you've made friends with Coco. She's always a good judge of character. Where shall we begin? What can I tell you?"

"Bob said you'd been to primary school with my mother. Can you tell me what she was like?" She nodded. "We were in the same class at the convent school. In those days we had nuns teaching us. Cessie was named after Saint Cecilia, but there was nothing saintly about your mum. She used to get into terrible scrapes. She was never nasty or spiteful, just mischievous. I've unearthed an old school photograph. Have a look, see if you can pick me out, then look second along on the right." She handed me a black and white school photo. Two long rows of children wearing school uniform. I imagined the photographer telling them to say "cheese." I studied their little faces, but I couldn't differentiate the girls from one another. "I give up, can you show me?" She pointed to a little girl sitting at the front. "And there, look, that's Cessie with her cheeky little face."

"Oh wow, yes I can see her. You both look so bright and smiley." I felt excited. Here was a real little girl with a future ahead of her. My mother, looking playful and full of life. "Can you tell me anything you know about her. I don't remember her much or remember the early part of my life. I may have blanked it. Trauma can play strange tricks. I don't know whether Bob has told you, but I've had these experiences lately. I see a young woman standing looking out of the hall window. The last time she turned and looked straight at me, her eyes brimming with tears." Ann looked very serious. "Oh my dear, I do wonder whether she is at peace. Describe what you see."

"She's tall and quite thin. She has her hair tied back in a ponytail. She has blue eyes, a small nose and square jaw. She's wearing a sort of floaty dress. I don't see her for long, it's more like a dream. Bob thinks I'm projecting a memory and I think he's probably right. I have a vivid memory of her standing at the top of the stairs in Rock House, so somewhere inside me, her image exists."

I could see Ann was taking me seriously. "Do you have these visions anywhere else?"

"Rock House is the catalyst. I did have a funny turn in the garden. Bob had uncovered a statue but I didn't see her then, I just had this really strange feeling."

"What's it like afterwards?" I struggled to find the right words. "It's difficult to explain. I almost grasp hold of a memory or an image, then it slips away from me. Momentarily I feel dread then it all fades away. It's something about my mother. Now I'm back here I feel as though we are two halves that need to be made whole again. I'm desperate to understand how we would have fitted together."

I looked at Ann and could see she was crying. That started me off too. She got up and came back with a box of tissues. "Oh dear, oh dear, oh dear, what a pair! Come on, let's drink our tea, and today I'm going to tell you about the first part, the happy part, of Cessie's life. I have two brothers and a sister but Cessie was an only child. I think she may have been adopted. The Roberts' adored her. They gave her everything. When we were little she just wanted to make dens and climb trees. She was a right tomboy. The nuns didn't make much impression on her; she wasn't going to be turned into a young lady, I can tell you. Anyway, instead of coming to the local grammar with us, she got sent to a posh boarding school over the other side of the county. Maybe they were trying to turn her into a young lady. I don't think it was a good move for her, although I suppose they wanted the best education for her. She was a weekly boarder so was home most weekends joining in with us gang of girls. It was a long time ago, but I suppose we did what the youngsters do now, hanging around together, playing music, dressing up and trying to attract the boys. She was always full of fun.

Strangely enough we both went into nursing. I trained locally, but Cessie went up to London. She trained in Barts. I stopped round here, got married and had a family, Cessie had the wanderlust. She wanted to travel, worked all over Europe. She'd come home quite regularly; her parents were getting on by then. She was in her late twenties when she came home to work. I think she may have been in a relationship, but I don't know for sure, she didn't confide in me. I always expected her to fall for a dashing young doctor but suddenly I had an invitation to her wedding to George Rose."

"Did you know him then?" She shook her head. "He was older than me. I didn't know him but I knew of him. He'd been evacuated from London as a boy. We had quite a few evacuees here during the war. Some, like George were orphaned and stayed. I wouldn't have said he was her type at all. He was shorter than her, dark hair pomaded back, he had a stupid little moustache. We all thought it was very strange."

"When I was little he seemed tall, but I remember the moustache. I hated him kissing me. It's difficult to believe you're describing my father." I shivered a bit at the thought. I don't like men with moustaches even now.

"That's the thing darling, I don't think I am. My theory, for what it's worth, was that she'd been having an affair and fell pregnant. Maybe the man was already married. Cessie's elderly parents were pillars of the community and devout Catholics. They would have been mortified to be told their daughter had got herself into trouble. She wouldn't have wanted to put them through that. Marrying George Rose wasn't an act of love, it was an act of convenience.

He was a hard drinker, I know that. I might just have some pictures of him. He was at our local carnival a few years back and joined a group of us at the bar. If I could find those pictures we could look for similarities but I have to say I can see no trace of him in you."

"The plot thickens and if this is true I can't tell you

how pleased I am! It doesn't matter that much though, it's my mother I'm interested in. If I find a father somewhere, that'd be a bonus." I felt quite excited by the thought.

"You're a brave young woman, Caitlin. Mind you, I wouldn't have expected anything else of Cessie's daughter. I'm feeling very guilty. We should have rescued you. Bob's told me about your foster parents, and I'm so relieved you found some stability with them. But you know, as a community, we did nothing to save you."

"Please don't feel bad. Our culture makes it difficult. People don't feel comfortable interfering, and when they do, it doesn't always end well." I could see the memories Ann was reliving upset her.

"Thank you love. You know your mother was loved and seeing you now, I can see you're a person who will always be loved. Can we carry on with Cessie's story another day?"

I too felt as though I needed a break. It was a lot to take in. Ann offered me another cup of tea, but I wanted to have some time on my own. Coco got excited when I stood up and started running round and round again. "Coco, stop it!" Ann spoke in a firm voice. "One day, she's going to trip somebody up and hurt them. Just ignore her love. I'll get her lead and walk up the road with you." As I went to leave her at the corner, she turned and said, "See you on Saturday."

"Oh, good lord, I'd almost forgotten the lunch. What must you think of me. I'd forgotten you're Justin's mum." I could feel myself biting my lip. "Don't look so worried, it's OK. With everything you're going through, I'm not surprised you didn't guess. Justin came along as a bit of an afterthought, I assumed I'd finished with babies. But, he's a proper handsome young man isn't he? My pride and joy!"

"Golly, yes, he is handsome. Thanks for being so understanding. I'll be in tears again in a minute. I'd better go. We can catch up on Saturday evening if you and Justin are free. The least Sally and I can do is cook for you all. It could be a proper family affair for you with Bob as well." With that I left her and Coco and went back down the hill towards the sea, then sat on a bench to think things over. The sun had kept its promise and broken through. I thought about the children breaking up from school in a few weeks, the excitement of the summer holidays ahead of them. Then the season getting into full swing and the town buzzing with life. So many happy families. I felt myself letting out a big sigh. Tomorrow I'm going to renew the attic search, there's got to be documents and photographs up there somewhere. I want to see my mother and me before it all went so horribly wrong. I looked at my watch. It was just past five, time to get home and ring Dennis. I should have done it yesterday.

CHAPTER ELEVEN

SALLY

When Cat dropped her bombshell about inheriting her mother's home, I remember how gobsmacked I was. Then I saw Rock House for the first time and I was caught up in the excitement of it all. When I came over she was always my focus, so I never had the chance to be on my own. Today, with Cat visiting Bob's aunt, I had time for a bit of a mooch around the town. It was an easy walk down the hill apart from the uneven paving. A trip hazard in waiting. I walked down some little alleyways then out into the main shopping area. I spotted a shop selling curios and hats. Thinking that I could do with a hat (I have the kind of skin that burns and freckles) I wandered in. I found just the one. Straw with a nice wide brim, and a spray of daisies tucked into a green ribbon. I was going to pay, then noticed there were clothes at the back of the shop. Walking round I pounced on the 50% off sale rail. My build, being of generous proportions, means that I'm usually lucky. Larger sizes are harder to sell. Today was no exception. I thought I'd died and gone to heaven. How could I possibly resist the long cotton dresses that floated around my body. Tight, belted dresses that show waistlines and pert little bums just don't suit me. I came out of there with a large bag full of goodies and my new hat placed jauntily on my head. I sighed. Better go back. I've got a long walk up a very steep hill. My bum is bound to get sassier if I keep this up.

I could hear Cat on the phone, having a heated exchange. I tiptoed in. She glanced up and put her finger to her lips. "Look, this is it, take it or leave it. I've booked us a table at the Imperial for twelve thirty on Saturday. No, I'm not being bossy but if it makes you feel better, you can pay." She was silent for a minute, "I'm not always going on about money, and I'm not controlling you, it was the other way round, you were always trying to control me. Why are you being so bloody awkward. I've agreed to meet you, the table's booked and I like that hotel. If you don't want to come, I'll go with Sally."

She was biting the skin at the base of her thumb nail. She always does that when she's anxious. "Of course I read your letters. Look, let's just meet on Saturday. There's no point in going over and over this. I'm putting the phone down now." She looked at me, her eyebrows raised. "How was that. Did I give a good performance or what?"

I had to laugh, "Are you alright?" She burst out laughing and there we were both laughing, even though we both knew it wasn't funny. "Do you remember the time at college when a bloke asked you out, and you tried to put him off by telling him you would only go out with him if he wore trendier clothes?"

"Oh God, Sal, and he turned up all smart, and I didn't know what to do and we both fell on the floor laughing. That was so cruel. Taught me a lesson though, didn't it? I learned how to say no. Pity I forgot when it came to Dennis." She shrugged her shoulders, looking far away for a moment, "Despite complaining, I reckon he'll turn up on Saturday. I've booked the two tables, one in Ann's name and one in mine. I've got collywobbles at the thought of seeing him again but it'll be OK with the others nearby. You know how good I am at playacting.

I'll think myself into the part, because I was playing a part when Dennis and I were together; I'm glad I'm able to be myself again." She sighed, "I think I need a drink, the sun must be over the yardarm by now." I looked at my watch, it was six thirty already and I'd said I was organising supper for us.

"I hadn't realised it was so late, why don't I pop down town in my car and get us a takeaway? I'm dying to hear about this afternoon." So, that's what I did and we had an interesting evening, eating Indian food and chatting. Cat had clearly liked Ann. Watching her face I began to understand how the stories Ann told her had brought her mother back to life, made her real in Cat's mind. I could imagine how that felt. As we retired for the night, Cat asked me if I could bring more boxes down after breakfast.

I had a disturbed night, curry has that effect. I was up early and crept downstairs for a glass of water. With the patio doors open I could hear the birds singing their dawn chorus. It was magic. I sat looking out over the garden, thinking about the last few days. I had once read that the secret of happiness is not doing what you like but liking what you do. Cat and I had long ago learned how to compromise and we enjoy even the most ordinary things together. I've had a few relationships with men in my time but I've never managed live in harmony as I do with Cat.

I put the kettle on and made Cat some tea. Rock House had been built at a time when people had servants. There is a narrow staircase near the kitchen that I could have used to go straight up to the bedrooms. However, the main stairs are wide and easier to negotiate. As I ascended, holding a tray in my left hand, whilst holding onto the banister with my right, I imagined Cessie, the tomboy, sitting on the banister and sliding down the smooth wood all the way to the bottom. I would love to see a photo of her as a child.

As I walked along the corridor towards Cat's bedroom, I thought I heard something, but the house is bound to creak with the passing of so much time. Cat sat up in bed as I came in. "Tea, how lovely, I need something to wake me up this morning. I was listening to the radio until the early hours, my tummy was in revolt."

"Snap! It's what you get when you eat chicken madras and drink beer in the evening." I went over and pulled the curtains open. "It's warm but I don't think it's going to be a great day. I can go and disturb the spiders in the attic after breakfast if you like."

A couple of hours later, I was treading carefully around a jumble of boxes nearer the back of the attic. They looked different, older and haphazardly stacked. One of them was heavy. I looked inside and could see a jumble of documents and old toys, so that's the one I hauled over and helped Cat manoeuvre down. Then I went back up for two lighter boxes and managed to get them down on my own.

She was sitting on the floor pulling papers out. "Look, these are my mother's old school reports. Here's some of her art work." We spent time looking through all the material. It was interesting, but not what we were looking for. I thought the second one was going to be the same until I pulled out an old rucksack. "I reckon you could get this repaired and use it, it's beautiful leather." Cat took it from me and looked inside. "There's an old biscuit tin in here. Walkers shortbread!" She shook the tin,

"There's something in it. Have we found treasure or have we found some ancient biscuits." Inside we found some folded newsprint, a bundle of letters and loose photographs. "Bingo! It looks like we've found treasure." Cat looked at me, an anxious expression on her face. "I thought I'd be excited but I'm terrified. Let's take it downstairs, then we can sit and look through it in a bit more comfort."

The newsprint had been cut out, as though destined for a scrapbook. Underneath there were several pages from a magazine. We unfastened a rusty bulldog clip holding the papers together and laid them out on the dining table. The newsprint was yellow and fragile. Cat smoothed the pages out very gently. The first page was a short report of an avalanche in Davos that struck on 26th January 1968. The second page listed the casualties. A circle had been drawn around the names of one family, Dr Claude Gabin, his wife and two teenage sons buried in the avalanche. The third page reported their deaths. Dr Gabin, his wife, Monique and their eldest son Marcel were found dead, their younger son Jacques died in hospital.

A long magazine article reviewed Dr Gabin's life as a dedicated orthopaedic surgeon and keen mountaineer who had climbed many of the world's most dangerous mountains. "Oh, my goodness Cat, this might be your father. Why else would these papers be saved and hidden. Look, there's a photo of him. I reckon you have his nose."

"You noodle Sal, don't jump to conclusions." She stared at some of the other photos, he was a fine looking man and he did have a patrician nose rather like hers.

Caitlin felt her heart beginning to beat faster and told

herself to calm down. She collected the cuttings and photos and carefully clipped them together again. Picking up the bundle of letters she could see a loose sheet attached to the front. Sally got up and offered to make coffee. Caitlin settled down to read. The loose sheet was folded over, held together with a paperclip. It was handwritten and difficult to decipher, as though it had been written in a hurry. Caitlin started to read, saw her name and shivered.

My darling Caitlin,

Something is very wrong here. I don't know who to trust or what to do. I'm hiding all these letters to you in the hope you find them one day. My will is with the solicitor. Everything is for you, the house and the contents, the money. They can't alter that. He's frightening me now. I need to get us both away from them. I wanted you to know I have and will always love you.

"Cat, are you alright? You look as though you've seen a ghost." Sally put the coffee down and hurried over. Caitlin was very pale and visibly shivering. She kept repeating, "Oh my God."

"Come on darling, you're frightening me. What's happened?" She thrust the note into Sally's hand. "I don't know if I can bear the letters. Please, will you read them to me. I won't be able to see for tears." So, that is what Sally did. Starting at the beginning.

63

CHAPTER TWELVE

SALLY

The first letter was dated 22nd November 1968.

My beloved daughter. You're three months old already and it's time I told you how we both came to be. I don't want our history to be forgotten.

I was born on St Cecilia's feast day and given away on that day in 1934. My mother was called Kathleen, I believe she was Irish. We both have her blue eyes and dark hair. It haunts me now as I look at you. I imagine poor Kathleen having her baby ripped away from her arms. I couldn't have survived that happening to us.

Your grandparents, my Ma and Pa, are the kindest of people. But the story I want to begin to tell you is how you came to the world. I want you to know everything. I've made some mistakes, but you, my darling, were never a mistake, you were meant to be.

I was working on an orthopaedic ward when I met Claude. He was the registrar. I'd always wanted to go to the Himalayas. Claude was going and I persuaded him to take me along with his party as far as the base camp. On the expedition, we got close. I knew it was wrong and it had to end there on that mountain. That's how you came to be, Claude and I, a long way from home.

By January I knew I was pregnant. I'm not sure I would have told him, but that was never put to the test. On January 26th 1968 Claude and his whole family were skiing and were buried by an avalanche. I don't know how you and I survived the trauma but you are all the more precious to me because of the senseless loss.

Your grandparents, my Ma and Pa, are devout Catholics, I feared they would insist I have you adopted too, like my poor mother, so I came up with a plan. I would find someone to marry, it didn't matter who, as I had no intention of remaining with them. Ma and Pa were in their late eighties, neither of them very well. When they passed, I would divorce.

You are the most dear thing in the world to me. Your grandparents adore you. They have twigged that my marriage to George is rather unusual, but no matter. We are friends and we are coping. I am going to keep writing to you. I wish Kathleen had been able to write to me. I'll try to trace her when Ma and Pa have gone.

All my love
Mum

Cat stared out of the window, a faraway look on her face. "It's all fate, all of it. I wasn't abandoned, she loved me. I had a father, who never even knew I existed. Oh God Sal, I feel so peculiar. I can hardly believe it. Will you read the other letters to me. It helps listening to your voice."

I read the other letters out. I don't know how I managed to keep going. They were so tender. Cessie had recorded all Cat's milestones in detail. It was an outpouring of delight and love. The last letter was written on 26th August 1972 just after Cat's fourth birthday. There had been a party. Cessie had baked a cake and packed up presents for all the children.

Cat was looking out of the window. Tears running down her cheeks. "Thank you. I need to be on my own for a bit." She stumbled out of the room; uncertain footsteps climbed the stairs. I didn't know what to do. How was she going to come to terms with all this? It was a game before. Unravelling a mystery, but not really believing there would be one. I folded the letters carefully and put them away in the tin, then sat reading the article about Dr Gabin, studying his picture. He had the same dark hair as Cat but, unlike Cat's, his eyes were a liquid brown. A tall, handsome man, what a tragedy it all was.

Then I looked at the note again. Cessie had been frightened. It sounded as though she feared for her life. My mind was in overdrive. Ann knows how Cessie died and if she does then Bob does. No wonder he looked so worried. I grappled with my conscience. I didn't want to go behind Cat's back but he and Ann could help in a way I never could. I went out into the hall and found Cat's address book in the desk drawer.

I phoned Ann. "Ann, you don't know me, I'm Caitlin's friend, Sally. Could I speak to you for a minute? We found a note and some letters her mother wrote for Caitlin. She's very upset, and I don't know what to do. All I can think is that she must know the rest of her mother's story."

"Where is she now?" Ann asked.

"She's upstairs, and she's heartbroken." There was silence for a moment.

"Would you like me to come over? Yes? I'll come now."

I went outside, wandering into Cat's secret garden. I felt devastated for her. We have a solid friendship and love one another for who we are, but she could be like a chameleon. She saw herself as an outsider; capable of reinventing herself depending on who she was with. I prided myself that I was the only one who really knew her. I had watched from the outside with her for long enough. Unlike Cat, I had known who my parents were. I knew my lineage – I came from a long line of Welsh Methodists. I was grateful Cat had rescued me from the tentacles of Welsh chapel, their preachers like black crows, warning of fire and brimstone.

I walked over to the statue Bob had uncovered. She looked at me serenely, radiating tranquillity. For a moment I imagined she was expecting me. I laid my hand on her head and said a little prayer to any god that might be listening.

ANN

How on earth am I going to tell that dear girl what I've always suspected. I don't want to make things worse for her. Is honesty really the best policy? I'll walk up to Rock House, give me time to think.

How many years is it since Cessie was killed – thirty years? At the time people were horrified; the whole town buzzed with gossip. Then it all died down. We went on to something else. Why didn't we ask more questions. The easy answer is, we wanted to trust the police.

I wasn't surprised when I heard Caitlin was seeing her mother in the house. She never had any justice. Maybe after all these years we can find a way to bring her peace.

CHAPTER THIRTEEN

SALLY

I opened the door to Ann, she looked exactly as Cat had described her, but Cat might not have seen the deep frown lines on her face. She put her hands on my shoulders and leaning over, kissed me on both cheeks. "What a good thing you're here, Sally. How is she?"

"It was a game before, but now it's real, and deadly serious. She's devastated.

Shall we go up and see her." We went upstairs and knocked on Cat's door. It was worryingly quiet, so I opened the door to see her lying on her bed. She must have cried herself into a state of calm. I sat down beside her and stroked her head. Eventually, she opened her eyes, they looked sore and bloodshot. A smile flickered on her face then switched to an expression of infinite sadness.

"Darling, I didn't know what to do. I rang Ann, explained what we discovered. She's come to tell you what she knows about your mother's death." Cat let out a big sigh. "You're so kind to come all the way up here. I've cried all the tears I'm going to cry. I'm ready to hear what happened."

Ann came over and sat down on the other side of Cat. "I've been dreading telling you, ever since Bob first asked me to talk to you. I'm sorry if it causes you more distress. It happened one evening in late August. According to George Rose, he and Cessie went down the town to meet friends. They were in the pub until closing time. His story was they all had a lot to drink and went for a swim near the pier. Cessie was a strong swimmer and George said he saw her swimming across the bay. He went back home as he was worried about the babysitter. In the morning he realised that Cessie hadn't come home and called the police.

The currents took Cessie's body over to the north of the bay. She was found later that day. The local press picked up on it. Our little town was famous for a day or two. I had the impression even then that the police had already decided it was an accident. I don't think they took it seriously. I attended the inquest. The post mortem indicated a head injury and bruising, and the conclusion was that she had been swept onto rocks. Analysis of her blood indicated intoxication. So the verdict was death by misadventure."

Cat nodded her head, "George Rose killed her, didn't he?"

"He may have done, but there was no proof." We sat there in silence, Ann on one side of Cat and me on the other. She put her head on my shoulder and Ann and I reached our arms around her, holding her close. Then she looked up with a sad smile on her face. "Do you think my mother would be proud of me?" Ann reached for her hand, "Very proud."

I don't think I have ever felt so close to two other people in my life before. Women together are unbelievably strong. Cat looked at us both, "I can't believe my mother went out to get drunk, not with a young child at home. Something must have happened. I can imagine George Rose holding her head down in the sea until she stopped struggling, then letting her body drift away as the currents took her."

The three of us sat there, deep in our own thoughts. Then Cat squeezed our hands and stood up. "Come on, let's go downstairs and into the garden. When I first saw Cessie's statue I knew there was something or someone there. Let's go and talk to her and help her rest in peace." So that's what we did. It was almost like praying, drawing us together in close harmony.

Afterwards we sat outside in the warm afternoon sun, Cat telling Ann what she had learned from the letters. How she had found and lost a father. Found and lost her mother. A mother who had loved her. Later, Ann said she had unearthed some old photos of George Rose, "If you feel you can, come and see me tomorrow."

CAITLIN

That evening, Sal and I walked down the town together strolling round to the coastguard station, then back past the pier and over to the furthest end of the bay where Cessie's body had washed up. A south westerly breeze livened the sea causing waves to break onto the shore. I kept thinking of my mother being buffeted in cold, dark water. Had there been a moon that night? Surely the story that they had seen her swimming across the bay couldn't be true. I was convinced it wasn't true.

We sat on a rise of pebbles at the very end of the beach. We must have walked two miles from the coastguard station to get to this point. Our legs spread out in front of us, we threw small pebbles into the sea watching ripples form. The sea was calmer here, sheltered by the cliff. Still early evening, the air warm with just a light breeze ruffling our hair.

"You know Sal, I can't help thinking what a miracle my birth and survival have been. I was only ever told my mother had gone to heaven. If I cried for her, George would put me to bed. I learned to be quiet. Poor desolate little girl. Learning that my mother's life ended here, maybe on this very spot, tells its own story. Maybe it was a dogwalker who found her, or children playing on the shore. Imagine the shock of finding her poor dead body."

Sal put her arm round my shoulder and pulled me close. I turned towards her so I could look into her eyes. "You've been wonderful Sal, and I've not even asked how you are. You read Cessie's letters so well. It was as though she was there. I shouldn't have put you through that."

"I wouldn't have had it any other way."

We sat there quietly watching the waves, thinking about the day. The day everything changed. It struck me that now I know who I am, I don't have to try to be anything other than me. Yet I'm the same person I always was. My best friend is the same person. Sal, steadfast and true. If I was on my own now, would I have crumbled? Dissolved. Maybe taken to the bottle. I struggled to my feet and grabbed Sal's hand to pull her up. "Shall we go to the pub and have a meal? I don't think I've the strength to walk all the way home from here."

Sal smiled at me. Her dark eyes full of compassion. She wasn't going to let me get away with making light of anything. "This part of the beach is so different from the town beach. When we walk here in future, we'll always think of your mother. We should build her a pebble monument, close to the cliff, where the sea would leave it be." She shook her head, "All I can think of to say is hold on. Hold on to the love you and I share for one another, and the new life and friendships we're making."

We stood there, listening to the sound of the sea and the cry of the gulls. Sal's eyes were bright and full of tears. Then she smiled, her eyes creasing so tears flowed down her face. Pulling out some tissues from my bag, we both blew our noses and set off for the town, back to a new normality.

CHAPTER FOURTEEN

THURSDAY 19TH JULY

Caitlin and Sally walked down to Ann's the following morning. Greeted by excited barking; Coco running round and round with joy. She sat down obediently when Ann spoke firmly, but as soon as Sally sat she leapt up on the sofa beside her, placing her head in her lap.

Unusually for her, Sally had put her hair up on top of her head. Tendrils escaped softening the outline of her face. She had dressed in a loose, light green linen dress and brown leather sandals with thongs tied around her ankles. A picture entered Caitlin's mind of a Celtic warrior queen. She imagined Sally standing in a chariot, holding a spear, about to face Roman soldiers.

Ann came in with a tray of coffee interrupting Caitlin's daydream. Then sat beside Caitlin and handed her a photo. "See that man there, that's George Rose. It was taken at the Carnival about four years ago. There he is with one of his girlfriends. He was always smartly turned out, but he wasn't nice-looking. There was something furtive about him. Beats me why he attracted women."

Caitlin peered at the photo. "I might be looking at my mother's murderer." She looked more closely. "Have you got a magnifying glass, Ann?" Ann rummaged through a drawer and then handed Caitlin a small magnifier. "Ann, do you remember that woman?"

Ann peered at the photo. "Yes, I think she used to work at the local Spar shop. She's a dainty little thing. Goodness knows what she was doing with that George."

Caitlin gasped. "I'm almost certain I recognise her.

Are you sure they were together?"

"Yes, definitely. Look, here they are again and they're holding hands." She handed Caitlin another photo. "They're clearer in this one."

Caitlin peered at it. "The plot thickens. That, unless I'm very much mistaken, is the woman who calls herself Arabella. I had no idea I had a cousin until the moment Mr Jones, the solicitor, said he would put me in contact with her."

Sally walked over and looked at the photos. "When you think of it, it's a ridiculous notion. You don't just forget a relative. Remember we used to call ourselves 'the Orphan Annies' at pub quizzes?"

"Yes but, if a solicitor states you have a cousin, you're bound to believe him, why wouldn't you?"

Ann stood up. "OK, before we jump to conclusions, give me a few minutes, I'll walk over to the Spar and see if any of the staff remember her. They may have a name. Come on Coco, walkies!"

CAITLIN

Sal and I looked at all the photos Ann had unearthed. Happy people standing at a bar smiling into the camera. George, not part of the group, was leaning on the side of the bar waiting to be served. Yesterday had been difficult and I wanted some peace today. But despite myself I felt a quiver of excitement. We had stumbled on something important.

"When I was little I was terrified of George. He never hurt me, but I learned to keep out of his way. I knew he didn't want me there. He was a sleazy weasel. His image in the photo gives me the creeps. He's holding hands with a woman half his age. Yuck. She has the same stature as Arabella, it could be her. Her hair's different." Sal raised her eyebrows at me, she's good at that. "It's intriguing. I'll give you that."

Ann came back with a big grin on her face. "As luck would have it, the manager remembers her. Her name is Alice Brown. She worked in the shop until a couple of years ago. She's been seen in the town since, although they think she moved away."

My brain was in overdrive, all manner of scenarios flooding it. We needed clear evidence. An old grainy photo wasn't good enough. If only I'd taken my camera with me when I visited "Arabella", we could compare them. "OK, here's what I propose. We have to be sure of our facts, so I ring Arabella/Alice and say we're passing her way, maybe next week, and would love to drop in. We'll just be relatives visiting, all perfectly natural, and what could be more natural than you wanting to take a photo of us both Sal, two cousins together. What do you think?" Ann had a stern expression on her face. "Slow down you two, let's think this through. I can't help thinking this is history repeating itself. We can't let anything bad happen to you, not after what happened to Cessie. Be sensible Caitlin."

"I'm sorry Ann, you're right. A few days ago I was gardening and thinking about how to rid myself of Dennis. Since then we've found my mother, discovered who my father was, uncovered a murder, and exposed a conspiracy. It's incredible. The problem, as I see it, is we have very little proof. If we went to the police, they would probably dismiss us as hysterics."

Sal was sitting with Coco in her lap, stroking her head, tickling her behind the ears. Coco was looking at her adoringly. I couldn't help smiling. What a tonic a dog is. "You're both right. What about trying to find a private detective? They must exist in real life, I've read enough books about them!" Caitlin shook her head. "I think we might be up against the same problem. We have very little evidence. I still think a visit to Arabella would help us make sure the person in Ann's picture is the same person as Arabella."

Ann sighed, "I'm out of my depth girls. I honestly don't know what to say, and I'm losing track of time, it's Thursday isn't it. On Saturday you have your meeting with Dennis. Doesn't give you a lot of time to think about what you want to achieve when you meet him."

"When Sal, Bob and I talked about it, we'd simply thought of playing for time; keeping him on side so we could figure out what he and Arabella were up to. It occurs to me now, we might set a bit of a trap." Sally stopped stroking Coco and sat bolt upright, "Don't you dare! That's exactly what you shouldn't do. First we find someone to help and get proof. Then we think again."

Ann was looking at us both curiously. "How things can change in the space of a few hours. Caitlin, I met you a couple days ago and Sally yesterday; now I feel as though I've known you all my life. Do you want an old woman like me tagging along? I'm old enough to be your mother."

"You're exactly what we want Ann. We both need a wise woman who will bring us down to earth. So, if you agree to be our mum, less of the Caitlin and Sally and more Cat and Sal. What do you think?" Ann got up and bowed, and then all three of us held hands and did a little circular 'Ring a Ring 'o Roses' dance round the room. Coco ran round and round us barking delightedly.

CHAPTER FIFTEEN

The wind had picked up during the night, clouds were scudding across the sky. Caitlin and Sally were sitting in the kitchen eating toast. "I don't feel strong enough this morning to tackle any more boxes, Sal. Let's leave the clearing until next week sometime. The weather forecast isn't brilliant, but we could go for a walk this morning. How about it?"

Sally agreed, "It's windy enough to blow the cobwebs away that's for sure. How about driving over to the heath? My car could do with a run." Two hours later, they were sitting on top of a rise admiring the castle ruins in the far distance. "Have you thought about what you are going to say to Dennis tomorrow?" Caitlin grimaced, "I've been trying not to."

"What intrigues me is what you ever saw in him. I could see you were always nervous around him. Did he ever make you happy?"

"Yes, in the beginning I was. It was something about his body and his hands." She bit her lip and made a funny face. "I know that sounds peculiar. It was when he held me, he was big and comfortable. You know, sort of muscular and manly. Oh dear, how to explain? It was the holding. The only way I can describe it is you know when mothers swaddle their babies to help them feel secure, it was like that."

Sally looked puzzled, "No, I haven't a clue what you are on about, except maybe you wanted to be smothered in some way. What was the sex like?" Caitlin frowned. "That's the strange thing, non-existent really. He was remote. I'd go to bed thinking he would follow, but he didn't. In hindsight, I think he either wasn't interested in sex, or he didn't find me attractive."

"Oh Cat, that must have been awful." She smiled. "I didn't mind so much about the sex. I used to tell myself, our relationship shouldn't be like it was, not at the start. I'd walk for miles on my own trying to figure things out. He didn't have to do an awful lot to keep my interest did he, but he couldn't bring himself to. He would criticise little things I did, right down to me listening to Radio Four, so I stopped. I stopped a lot of things I liked doing. I was frightened he would get in a bad mood with me. The scales came off my eyes one day and I realised his behaviour was controlling me. It wasn't as though I needed him. I knew I had to break the ties. He was trying to make me dependent, and the more dependent I became, the more he took my obedience for granted."

"Are you still attracted to him?" Caitlin looked down for a moment. "I don't know to be honest. There's a bit of me that still wants him to want me. Pride I suppose. I used to ask myself why he wasn't more affectionate. Now I know he was playacting. He couldn't even carry that off. When I asked him to leave he was shocked. I suppose he had taken me for granted and hadn't expected me to turn on him."

"Stop that Cat. Remember what Bob said. There was another woman in his flat. He was doing a job. You were the job and you ended up sacking him because he wasn't very good at it." Caitlin blinked. "I hadn't thought of it like that. So, when we meet up tomorrow I'll be very reasonable and nice and make him despise me even more."

"Remember, he's got something to tell you, something he and his woman have cooked up. You're just going to have to play it by ear and keep him guessing. You'll have Ann and Justin close by and I'm going to come in by the time you have finished your meal. On no account are you going to be alone with him."

"Point taken. Come on, we'd better head back, I don't like the look of those clouds. It feels more like October today than July."

Later on they were in the kitchen finishing the preparation for a casserole for their evening meal when the doorbell rang. Caitlin heard an excited bark and went out to see Coco running round and round the hall. "It's Ann, how lovely, come on in. We're in the kitchen, follow me."

"Sorry if I'm disturbing you. I had this urge to come and see you after the trauma of the last couple of days. I wanted to have a chat about tomorrow as well. I lay in bed last night worrying about you. Do you really have to meet him? You won't do anything silly, will you?"

Caitlin sprang up from her chair; walked over and kissed Ann on both cheeks. "Please don't worry too much. I'm going to listen to what Dennis says; keep him guessing. I can be a good actor when I put my mind to it. I'll be careful not to give anything away, I promise." They went into the sitting room with a cup of tea each and settled comfortably. Coco immediately jumped up on Sally's lap. "Are we taking you over, Ann? Will you see us through this patch, or is it too much to ask?"

"Of course I will Cat. You don't think now I've got a chance to help Cessie's daughter I would turn you away. We're going to be great friends, I know it. Bob thinks you two are the bees knees." She smiled widely, "I agree with him."

"That's kind, and I'm relieved. I lay in bed worrying last night too. You must be fed up with us wanting to know about my past. Then I thought about you. I remembered you saying you had Justin late in life, when you thought you were finished with all that."

Sally felt uncomfortable for Ann. "Forgive my friend here, she's very nosy. It's the social worker in her."

"I don't mind telling you at all. It's quite funny really. My husband, Will, came in late after his darts team won the County competition. I was in bed fast asleep when the silly old fool became amorous and nine months later there I was, a woman of forty eight with a new born baby boy. A twenty five year gap between our daughter Margaret and baby Justin. I didn't think it funny at the time, mind. It took me a long time to forgive.

Justin and Will loved making things in wood. Will and the boss of one of the local carpentry firms were old mates, and before you knew it, Justin was sorted with an apprenticeship. You'll get to know this town when you've lived here a bit longer. It operates on family connections.

So here I am, at sixty eight, the mother of a twenty year old carpenter. He's doing very well for himself and I'm as proud as punch. I just wish Will had lived to see him now. One minute he was the tall, strong husband I had always been able to rely on, then eighteen months ago, he was felled by a massive heart attack. Our little family didn't get a chance to say goodbye. That was extra hard for Justin but he has always been mature beyond his years, and he was, and still is, a tower of strength for me.

He's brave too. I realised early on he wasn't interested in girls. When he told me he was gay, I couldn't help but feel shocked. This is a small town, people gossip." Ann looked ashamed for a moment, "I'm embarrassed because

I listened to bigots when I was young. Thank God Justin trusted me and didn't try to hide how he felt from me."

Caitlin, compassionate by nature, found just the right words. "Justin is a fine young man and he's lucky to have you as his mum. Will sounds nice, it must have been very hard losing him so suddenly."

"It was a mercy for him, he wouldn't have liked to have been disabled. We had ups and downs in our marriage. It wasn't plain sailing, but you're right, he was a nice man, and a good friend. I'm very lucky to still have my family close by."

Yesterday, Caitlin's life seemed to be spinning out of control and Sally wasn't sure how she would be able to cope. When Sally looked at her today, she saw a resilient young woman who was handling having her life turned upside down.

Caitlin offered to show Ann round the house, but Ann looked at her watch and got up with a sigh. "Can we do it next time, I should be going. Time to feed Coco. I have to keep her to a routine otherwise she takes advantage. I'll see you at the hotel tomorrow. It's not often my son buys me a meal, I'm going to make the most of it."

CHAPTER SIXTEEN

Sally lay in bed the following morning thinking what lay in front of her friend. Meeting the man who had targeted her would be a challenge. Glancing at the clock, she realised how late it was getting; she dressed quickly and went down to the kitchen. Caitlin was nowhere to be seen. The patio door was open, so she grabbed a coffee and went to find her friend in the garden. She was sitting on a bench deep in thought. "Morning Cat, I thought I'd find you out here. Did you sleep well?"

Caitlin got up with a big smile and kissed her friend on the cheek. She was in a contemplative mood. "You know I always thought I was English. The clue, of course, was my name. Now I know I'm probably a mixture of Irish and French. So you can't tease me any more, my Welsh buddy. Anyway, with your hair, you've probably got a touch of Irish." Sally's eyes twinkled. "We're certainly both Celts."

"I've been thinking I'd like to change my name. It's not hard to do by deed poll, you just have to make sure all your documents are altered." Sally chuckled, "Have an exotic name. Be a mysterious, dark lady."

"I wasn't thinking like that. My mother was a Roberts. I was going to use her name. Anything but Rose." Caitlin gazed out over the garden, a dreamy expression on her face. "I wish I'd known at the beginning that George Rose wasn't my father. I could never understand what I'd done to be sent away. I thought it must be something terrible. That was cruel of him. I expect he did well out of the Trust Fund money so wouldn't have wanted the facts broadcast. I wish he was here now, I'd confront him and get the truth out of the bastard."

"Can a dead man be convicted of murder?"

"It would be great to get justice for my mother, but I guess it's unlikely, and anyway, I don't think I want revenge. That might eat me up, change me again, and I don't want to be that sort of person." She got up from the bench. "Have you had breakfast Sal? I can't face food this morning, my body's in revolt at the idea of eating lunch with Dennis. I'm going to have to try to act normally; I don't suppose he'll be surprised if I'm nervous. He'll think I'm worried about upsetting him."

"Knock him dead. Dress up a bit. Why don't you wear your sunflower dress, I love you in that." Caitlin smiled at the thought. Dennis had always criticised the way she dressed. "Which one? The bright yellow fitted one. Well, I suppose I could if I don't eat too much and keep holding my tummy in. I'll go up and try it on."

Sally watched her friend walking back to the house. She imagined herself in Caitlin's shoes. Walking slowly, trying to put the moment off. Unfortunately, she still seemed to have a soft spot for Dennis even though he might mean her harm. Sally felt a fierce surge of love for her. She would defend Caitlin with her own life if necessary. Making a face as she sipped the last dregs of cold coffee. She drifted back into the kitchen, made herself another cup and put some bread into the toaster.

Half an hour later Caitlin reappeared. "Wow, you look stunning. I have just what you need to complete the outfit. Hang on, I'll be down in a tick." Sally came back with a small box and handed her friend a pair of drop earrings made of a clear resin with tiny flowers embedded in them. When Caitlin put them on, they reflected the colour of her dress as though they were made for it.

"Thanks Sal, they're lovely. I remember you buying these. They'll be my lucky charm for the day." She groaned, "It's eleven forty already. If I walk there, I'll be ten minutes late, keep the swine waiting. Will you drive over and pick me up around two. Come into the restaurant and rescue me. I'll tell Dennis we are off somewhere."

"Of course. I'll stick to you like glue. He's not getting you on your own again." Caitlin frowned at her. "I know Ann and Justin will be there, but they won't be part of the conversation, and don't forget, he's a nasty piece of work. Just try to keep him at arm's length. He's likely to try to wheedle himself back into your good books." Caitlin grimaced, "That's not going to happen."

CHAPTER SEVENTEEN

The Imperial had been built in the Victorian era, when the town had become popular as a seaside resort. Updated but with many of the original features preserved, it was luxurious although not ostentatiously so. Wooden floors, William Morris wallpaper and quiet music greeted Dennis when he swaggered in at twelve twenty.

At six foot three he was an imposing figure. Broad shouldered, he was wearing a soft cream and brown check shirt and a pair of brown corduroy trousers that revealed the beginnings of a paunch. His dark blonde hair cut short at the back was longer at the front, giving him every opportunity to smooth his hair back nonchalantly with his hand, a habit he had developed as a teen, hoping it made him look cool. He was keen on looking cool. His skin was baby soft. No stubble to be seen. A man keen to show himself at his best. He stood tall, spine erect, shoulders back. A little too stiff, too studied, holding himself together. His grey eyes told the story. Bulging slightly they looked over bright. He was not totally in control of himself.

He looked around. It was early so there were only a few diners, mostly older people. One table was occupied by a woman and a young man who looked like a relative. It was all very discreet and genteel. He was ushered to a table overlooking the sea, ordered a double gin and tonic and settled down in anticipation.

He had been adored as a child. His mother's golden haired boy. Everything he wanted lavished on him; consequently he had developed absolute self-confidence, enabling him to sail through life with little thought for anyone but himself. As many self-obsessed people do, he was unable to think empathically and failed to understand why Caitlin had rejected him. It didn't make any sense. He had been specifically chosen for this job. He knew he could do it. He'd lay on the charm again. Should be easy enough to win her back.

She had been totally malleable when they first met. She couldn't get enough of him. Simpering over him, buying him little gifts, doing everything to please him. Then came the ghost. Stupid cow, they only existed in storybooks. Suddenly she was no longer the sweet woman he had groomed. She had turned into a nutter. It was the only explanation. She had looked to him for help. What on earth had she wanted him to do, exorcise it? The others had advised him to humour her. Well, he'd done his best, but the ghost had won. That was it, the ghost had won. It wasn't his fault at all.

He sighed, the thought of having to go back to live in that dreary house with Caitlin left a bad taste in his mouth. The way she went on about her mother got on his nerves. From what he heard about the woman she had been po-faced, a real killjoy. Caitlin obviously took after her. She might be a meal ticket, but she was unbelievably dull. They would have to organise an accident sooner rather than later, otherwise he would die of boredom.

He looked at his watch and was irritated to see twelve thirty had passed. The place was beginning to fill up. One of the many things he detested about Caitlin was her compulsive timekeeping. "I can't help it. I'm a Virgo." What a load of bollocks. She never kept him waiting. Well, quite frankly, she never made much effort. Throwing the same old clothes on. He felt ashamed of being seen with her. It wasn't as though she didn't have the money to buy herself some decent clothes and wear some makeup. She was mean beyond belief; she didn't care about him spending his good money on hotel prices when they could have gone to the pub.

More and more exasperated, he looked round for the waiter who was nowhere to be seen. Struggling to keep his temper, he went to the bar for another drink. His hand shook as he poured a small amount of tonic into the gin. That was another thing, the looks she gave him when he came in from work and had a drink. He walked back to his seat. Glaring at the old woman and boy at the table next to him. What were they staring at? He plonked himself back into his chair. He knew he was winding himself up but was unable to control his thoughts or feelings. He was beginning to wish he hadn't stopped off at the club on the way. He'd only meant to have one pint... He sat looking out at the sea, tapping his foot. Gulping the gin then remembering he should make it last.

At twelve fifty Caitlin walked through the door. He hardly recognised her. She was wearing a dress and actually looked attractive. He let out a sigh of relief. "She's trying to please me. She wants me back. She's kept me waiting deliberately. This is going to be a doddle." He got up from his seat and waved to her, an elated smile on his face. "I've not seen you wearing that dress before. It looks great, and you look wonderful. I've missed you so much." She looked embarrassed. "I'm sorry I'm a bit late, I got held up. Have you ordered?"

"No, not yet." He gestured at the waiter who continued to ignore him. "What is it with bloody waiters. I don't know why you chose this place. It's a bit over the top isn't it? I thought a pub was more your style."

"Oh come on Dennis, I like dressing up and being

waited on sometimes. Anyway we have a great view of the sea, and the seafood is supposed to be excellent."

"Fair enough, but really Caitlin, you should know by now I'm allergic to fish. I hope they do a decent steak. You see if you can get that waiter's attention, I could do with a drink. Flutter your eyelashes or whatever it is you women do."

"Don't patronise, Dennis. You just have to be polite and smile a bit." She leaned past him and waved to the waiter, a slim young man, dressed smartly in black, his dark hair combed back from his forehead. He looked barely out of school. He nodded at her and came over. Dennis was tapping two fingers loudly on the table. He scowled at the waiter, who continued to ignore him. Caitlin, a tense expression on her face, glanced at the waiter's name badge, "Could we have a couple of menus, Jack? Dennis, what do you want to drink?" He looked down at his empty glass, "Haven't you brought the wine list? What sort of place is this?" The waiter frowned, "I'll bring one immediately, Sir."

Caitlin was embarrassed, "There's no need to be rude. He's young and probably new, just give him a bit of slack." The waiter appeared promptly and winked at her. For a moment she seemed surprised, then looked over at Ann and Justin who she could see were watching the interchange.

Dennis studied the wine list and ordered a bottle of Burgundy. Caitlin raised her eyebrows at him and turned to the waiter, "I'll have a small glass of Muscadet please." He passed her a menu, "Oh thanks, I'm looking forward to your fresh fish. Can you just give us a moment or two."

The waiter came back over with the wine. He handed

Caitlin her glass of Muscadet, then uncorked the bottle for Dennis. "Would Sir like to try it?" Dennis glared at him. "Just pour the bloody stuff." His mood improved when he sipped his wine. "Decent wine. I'll have steak, medium rare, with all the trimmings. What do you want Caitlin?"

"I'll have the sea bream, thanks, oh and a large bottle of sparkling water." So, they settled down to wait for their food as Dennis poured himself another large glass. "What's the good news?"

Dennis looked confused for a moment. "Oh, my grandfather died." Caitlin stared at him, trying to look disconcerted. She wanted to laugh. Is that the best they could come up with? "That's your good news? I'm so sorry, were you close? I don't remember you talking about him."

"I wouldn't, he was an irascible old bugger. He didn't like me much." Caitlin raised her eyebrows. "Anyway, blood's thicker than water so they say, and he's left me some cash. I want to book us a holiday, all inclusive, somewhere like the Dominican Republic. We can start again, relax in the sun and enjoy ourselves. I always felt that money came between us. You're a wealthy woman. Now I can splash out on you, spoil us both."

"Oh, Dennis, that's not true. Money didn't come between us. I never said I was wealthy either." He looked irritated, "Well, I thought money was a problem so I'm offering you an all-in paid holiday. Just say thank you."

"Um, thank you for the thought, but I can't think of anything I would like less than an all-in holiday. Don't waste your money on me, I much prefer travelling around if I'm going overseas. I wouldn't be very good company on a beach holiday." He responded in a high voice, trying to mimic her. "Oh, travelling, not package holidays then, like us hoi polloi." He was beginning to slur his words. "Would you like a glass of water?" He laughed, "You know what fish do in it, no thanks, I'll stick to this. Where's that food, they're taking their time."

"It's cooked fresh. It won't be long now. Don't be so grumpy and please don't feel you have to take me on holiday. I'd much rather be at home or do short trips. Sally and I are going down to Cornwall for a few days soon. You know I told you about my cousin Bella, well, she lives in Cornwall. We thought we'd drop in on her. That's a thought, why don't you come with us sometime and meet her too. I'm sure you'd like her." Caitlin smiled, endeavouring to appear friendly.

"You really are the most annoying woman. You're turning down a luxury holiday with me for a sleezy weekend with your girlfriend. It beggars belief." She smiled. "So you don't want to come down with me to visit Bella?" He didn't reply, rescued by the waiter bringing their meals. "Can I get you anything else?" Dennis grunted. "No, we're just pleased to get our food at last. Hang on, haven't you forgotten something? You haven't brought me a steak knife."

"You won't need a steak knife, Sir. We pride ourselves on our steak. We source it locally. You'll see, it cuts like butter." He looked at Caitlin's empty glass, "Would you care for another glass of wine, Miss?" She shook her head. "No thanks." He leaned over and filled her water glass. She beamed at him, "This all looks delicious." Dennis poured out the last of his wine, looked pointedly at the waiter and gestured for another bottle. "Is that wise Dennis? I don't want any. Why not just have another glass with your meal?" He glared at her. "Don't tell me what to do." Elbow on the table, she put her hand on her forehead and groaned, "For God's sake."

"Okay, you win." He turned back to the waiter, "I'll have a large glass of your house red." Caitlin settled down to eat her meal with relief. She glanced over at Ann and Justin sitting opposite them and frowned. Relieved that Dennis was eating with gusto, if rather noisily whilst knocking back more wine, she allowed herself to relax slightly. "Sally's coming in about two, we're off to do some shopping. There are some good sales on at the moment."

He was undeniably slurring now. "Why don't you go up to London or somewhere. Act like a real woman. Buy yourself something expensive for once. Always penny pinching!" Caitlin glared at him. "I've told you often enough, I like shopping locally. It's better to put money into the local economy." He shook his head. "You haven't got a clue what I mean have you? Get some bloody happiness in your life, loosen up." Seeing her reaction, he reached across the table, and tried to take her hand in his. She snatched it away. "Look Dennis, I'm a sensible and practical woman, that's what I am. If you love someone, you don't try to change them. You love them for who they are. Ever since we met, you've tried to change me. I'm not going to change. I am who I am. This is getting us nowhere. Drinking buckets of alcohol doesn't help either does it?" She could smell his breath. A sour smell. Alcohol mixed with cigarettes. It made her feel sick.

He narrowed his eyes. She thought for a moment that he was going to yell at her. Then he suddenly crumpled. "Maybe I needed Dutch courage. I love you Caitlin. You are the only one for me. I won't give you up." Caitlin tried to appear acquiescent. "Maybe we could try to be friends. There's no point in us sniping at each other. I'm sorry. Perhaps meeting here was a bad idea of mine."

The waiter came over to clear their plates and asked about desserts. "Not for me thanks. How about you Dennis?" He shook his head. "We'll have the bill please."

"What are you doing with yourself now? Still communing with your ghost?" Caitlin didn't appreciate his sarcasm. He had never believed her. "She still appears to me in the same floral dress, with her hair tied back. She's spurred me on to try and find out more. We're clearing the attic. I've been looking for old papers and photos." He looked up. "What have you found?"

"Lots of my grandparents' old china and ornaments. But there must be something of my mother's up there, otherwise what did my father do with everything. It's as though she never existed. We're sorting things out in the spare bedroom at the end of the corridor." Realising that she was giving a lot of information, she frowned and stopped. She was losing control. Turning round she was relieved to see Sally standing at the entrance to the restaurant. "Oh, look there's Sally."

Caitlin waved at her. Sally was wearing one of her new dresses, her bright red hair framing her face and curling down her back. She called over, "Hello darling, will you join us for coffee. How about some coffee, Dennis?" Dennis couldn't hide his irritation at Sally's untimely arrival. He was curious. She was about to tell him she'd found something important. He glared at them both.

"If you can get that waiter back it'll be a miracle, and he's supposed to be getting the bill. Idle sod." He scowled at Sally. "She's your guest Caitlin, not mine. I'm going. I'll pay our bill at the bar." He got up unsteadily. "I'll ring you next week." He began to weave his way across the room. Sally looked worried and followed him. "You're not driving are you Dennis? Wait a few moments and we can give you a lift. I've got the car out the front."

"With you? No thank you. I'll get a taxi. By the way, it's so nice to see you scrounging off Caitlin again. Don't make yourself too comfortable. I'll be back soon, and you'll be out on your ear."

"Don't be so stupid Dennis. Haven't you got the message yet?" She bit her lip. Cat was stringing him along. She wasn't supposed to be telling him to sod off.

He grinned at her and held two fingers up. "We'll see. Make the most of it while you can." Giving him one last disgusted look, she turned and strode back to Caitlin's table. They could hear Dennis complaining loudly at the bar and watched him in silence.

The waiter came over, "Are you alright Miss? I'm Justin's friend. Don't get up, he's just outside the door, watching. I can give Ann and Justin a message for you if you want to go."

"Maybe he's not as drunk as he seems Sal. Let's just have coffee." She smiled, "Two coffees and then we'll be off. Thanks Jack." Caitlin looked over at her friend; frowned and shook her head. "Whatever made you follow him? He was drunk. He could have turned on you."

"He did, he more or less told me to drop dead. Swore he would get me out of the house. I only went after him to try to be friendly. I don't know what I've done to him, but he really hates me." She looked upset.

"It's because you're getting in their way. Do you

remember I said yesterday I had this urge for him to still want me. It's gone. I hope I never have to see him again."

CHAPTER EIGHTEEN

Ann and Bob stood looking out at Cat's secret garden. The dining room doors were open wide. The warm evening air sweet with the fragrance of roses. Bob had planted a small cherry tree to shade the statue, and the pond was ready to fill. He and Cat planned to have running water to make the space a peaceful and contemplative part of the garden. It was a labour of love for both of them. Cat felt a strong association with her mother there, and so, had ordered a bench from a local stone mason as a memorial for Cessie.

Ann felt excitement flow through her. For the first time she sensed Cessie's presence. She almost expected to see her standing in the garden. She imagined her friend, tall and slim, her long wavy hair pinned up at the side. She had had such poise, innocent of her beauty and the impact she had on those around her. Cat's features were stronger, she was handsome rather than beautiful, but she had the same poise and amazing blue eyes.

Ann remembered the last time she had visited Rock House after Cessie's death. It was mid-morning. George answered the door looking as though he had just got out of bed. The house was already looking unkempt. When she had asked after Caitlin he had told her to mind her own business. Was she out playing, where was she? He accepted her homemade cake with bad grace, then ushered her out. To her shame, she hadn't gone back. The whole community had let him get on with it. That poor little girl.

Bob put his arm around his aunt's shoulder, "Penny for your thoughts."

"I was remembering how it was for Caitlin when her

mother died. I should have tried harder to help." He pulled her towards him. "It is what it is Ann. We can't change the past, although the past is here. I'm not prone to superstition but there's something not quite right. Have I been to the house before, maybe as a youngster? Cat and I are about the same age. The night I stayed after Dennis had left, I had a strong sense of déjà vu."

"I don't know love. It's possible. We know from Cessie's last letter that there was a birthday party. You may have gone to that. I agree about the strange feeling. Maybe Cessie has been trying to tell Cat something. If we can help the girls unpick what happened between George Rose and Alice, we might get somewhere." She looked round, "Where have Justin and Jack got to? They've been gone a long time."

"They're exploring the garden. Shall we go and find them? Hopefully Cat and Sal will be serving up soon, delicious smells coming from the kitchen. I'm getting hungry."

Caitlin and Sally were indeed in the kitchen. It delighted them to be able to give their new friends good food. They had made a variety of individual savoury flans to serve with potato salad, coleslaw and a large green salad. Instead of a dessert they laid a selection of cheeses and crackers onto a large wooden platter. The centrepiece was a huge china bowl full of fruit.

Justin and Jack walked in from exploring the garden just as Ann groaned, "That looks fabulous. What are you two trying to do to me. I had a big meal at lunchtime!"

"It's OK for you, I didn't get invited, and I'm starving." Bob winked at Cat. "Come on, let's all sit down, I want to hear about this afternoon. How did Dennis react? What did you think Ann?"

"He wasn't a pretty sight, and as time went on he became very agitated. Cat walked in looking gorgeous and his expression changed to a self-satisfied smirk. What did you think Jack?"

"He was drunk. He smelt of booze when he arrived, then swigged down two double gins in quick succession. By the time Caitlin came in, he looked ready for a drinking session. Ann's right, he had a puzzled expression on his face, then relief when you walked in Caitlin."

"You winked at me Jack. I loved that." She grinned, "Please call me Cat. I feel as though I've done something wrong when friends call me Caitlin. I'm seeing Dennis in a different light. He can't cope without adoration. He thought he'd have me eating out of his hand; told a stupid story about his grandfather dying and leaving him money. I hope I played pliant woman well enough. I kept looking at him and wondering what on earth I saw in him."

Justin smiled at Jack and back to Cat. "Well that's a good thing because one thing's for certain, he doesn't care much for you. His eyes are emotionless, his body language closed. Does he always drink so much?"

"He usually had a bottle of wine on the go. One of the few things he did buy. I never saw him drunk though, he controlled it. What worried me today was how aggressive he became and in the end, how openly hostile he was to Sal. That was new. He'd get maudlin, not nasty. I hope he hasn't guessed anything. What do you think Ann?"

"I don't think he's got a clue. The man's a bully. A straw man. Whoever chose him to win you over didn't know him very well. He's good looking, that's about it. Picking on someone who wasn't able to answer back like Jack was cowardly. All in all, he's shown himself up for

97

the nasty piece of work he is."

Bob looked anxious, "Listening to what you're all saying, I'm more certain than ever that you two are putting yourselves in danger. He's targeted you for a reason Cat. It's time to get help."

Cat looked round the group, observing their concern, "I agree." She turned to Ann and Sally, "We talked about a private detective, but I'm still thinking we haven't enough evidence to go on. That grainy photo of Alice Brown who might be Arabella isn't good enough. Let's try and get a photo of her." Bob interrupted, "No Cat, if you hire someone, you can ask them to do it. All they'll need is a copy of the photo and Arabella's address."

"I understand what you're saying Bob, although I must see Jones senior, the solicitor. I'll find out what he knows then I'll look for a suitable person to investigate the Alice/Dennis conspiracy. How does that sound?" Bob cut in, "Please think about how vulnerable you both are out here. We can fit gates and a security system, you just need to say yes."

"I'm saying it, YES, please do the work. But you must let me pay you both for your time as well as everything else. Deal?" Justin looked up, "I'll sort it out. But listen, I've been sitting here thinking about your mother's death Cat. Have you tried to investigate who George Rose's drinking buddies were? Who was with him that night? Jack's right about Dennis. He was ready for a drinking session today. It may be far-fetched, but is there a link between him and George? Both of them drinkers – is that coincidence? I like talking to the old chaps in the pub, listening to their yarns. Someone in the town will have known George and may remember the night your mother died." They all looked at one another, serious expressions on their faces. Ann seemed particularly uncomfortable with her son's proposal. Bob slapped his forehead, "Why didn't I think of that? It's OK Ann, I promise to look after your boy." Justin leaned across and poked his tongue out at his cousin, "Yes, you should know by now, I'm a genius and by the way, I'm not a child anymore. Is it OK with you Cat? We're more likely to get a result than a stranger poking around." She nodded, "Yes, please ask, but be careful. It won't take long for rumours to get round the town. Now, have something to eat, we don't want lots of leftovers. Come on, tuck in. Let's try and forget all this for a while. Enjoy!"

CHAPTER NINETEEN

SUNDAY 21ST JULY

Set adrift in a unique set of circumstances at such an early age, Caitlin had learned to control her emotions. Her more settled life with foster carers had taught her to be self-sufficient and resilient. It would take time for her to find closure, yet already she was beginning to come to terms with what she had learned about her mother's life and death. The initial shock had turned to a dull pain and a steely determination to find out the circumstances of her death and George Rose's part in it. Despite what might lie ahead of them, Caitlin felt a sense of belonging at Rock House. A sense that she could take root, make a good life for herself and Sally.

They had both been restless in the night, and had risen early, taking their tea outside. A pleasant, cool breeze played on their bare arms. When Caitlin had moved into the house, the area that was now lawn had been waist high in grass. Bob had tamed it, fed it, mowed it and now it sparkled with dew in the clear, early morning light. On its border, mature shrubs rescued from bindweed shaded the bedding plants Caitlin had planted for colour. Beyond that, out of sight, stood a dense, neatly trimmed beech hedge, surrounding the front of the property.

"Two Sundays ago, I walked up on the cliffs and decided I was sleepwalking through a rotten relationship that I had to finish. Now look what's happened. Forgive me for involving you in this mess Sal."

"Don't be so daft. Remember when we met? You were very unhappy and so was I. We found strength in friendship. It's carried us through all these years. We'll manage the Dennis thing. What happened to your mother goes deeper, but I'll help you all I can."

"You are a brick Sal, I don't know what I'd do without you. As long as we're both agreed, shall we try and find out what happened to Cessie that night? Justin and Bob will surely find someone who remembers."

"OK, but we are not going to try to unravel Arabella and Dennis's part in this, we are only going to manage it. We'll leave that up to a professional, right? The two things may link, and it could turn out to be dangerous." Sal looked at her empty cup, "Have you finished your tea? Let's go and walk round the perimeter of the garden. There's no point in putting in a high gate if it's easy to get in anyway."

They found gaps in the hedge that could be blocked. The property on the other side of Rock House had a well maintained high fence. At the back, beyond the secret garden, the path led up an incline, with a distant view of the sea. There was a wire fence and a low spindly hedge marking their boundary; separating them from the meadow beyond. They could just see the outline of a path running along the side of the farmer's hedge with a stile in the very far corner. Caitlin looked in dismay. "I don't want to live in a fortress. I like this being open, but if anyone wanted to get into the garden here, they could. What am I saying? This is sleepy Dorset. Let's go back in, have a think over breakfast."

Later that morning Sally and Caitlin looked through their local Yellow Pages for a private detective, making a list of agencies within a thirty mile radius. It would be Caitlin's first job on Monday.

It was a fine day and they decided to see how difficult it was to clamber out of the garden and walk through the meadow to the town. It was easy at first, then it became steep and rocky in places. Just about walkable in dry weather. Arriving at the bottom, feeling hot and bothered, they dropped in to one of the local pubs. Delighted to find a band was playing, they settled down for a relaxing afternoon.

CHAPTER TWENTY

First thing on Monday morning, Cat rang several of the agencies on their list. She was fed up with listening to answering machines. She was almost at the end of the list, when the phone was picked up. A female voice answered brightly, "Good morning, Charlie Bond's office, how may I help?"

"Could you put me through to Mr Bond please."

"Certainly, hold the line." Caitlin held, then what sounded like the same voice said "Charlie Bond, Private Investigator at your service." Caitlin snorted, "You're the same person. I'm sorry, I assumed you'd be a man." She heard a chuckle, "You'd be surprised how many people model their ideas on Philip Marlowe."

"Who's Philip Marlowe?"

"Oh, you know, the Raymond Chandler books, Humphrey Bogart and all that. I can do a passable American accent."

"No, please don't." Caitlin was laughing now, "What sort of private investigator are you?"

"A very good one. I'll tell you why. I'm average. I'm five foot five with brown hair and I wear plain clothes. My face is symmetrical. I'm nothing out of the ordinary, so no one notices me. But if I need to look stylish, I can wear a suit and high heels and look stunning or simply fade into the background."

"Well, that sounds like private investigator perfection. May I come to see you and explain what I want. I'd prefer not to talk about it on the phone. Could you fit me and my friend in as soon as possible? We don't live far from your office."

"How would tomorrow suit you? You had better give

me your details."

With the appointment made, Caitlin sat back in her chair pondering what she had set in motion. Charlie Bond sounded quite a character. She hadn't banked on a woman, but neither would Dennis or Arabella, and if she came face to face with them, they would hardly pay any attention to a small, ordinary-looking woman.

She picked the phone up again and dialled the solicitor's number. Put through to Mr Jones, she didn't know whether to be excited or scared that Jones senior was at home and willing to speak to her. Taking the bull by the horns, she arranged to go out to see him later that afternoon.

Sally drove Caitlin to a modern estate in the town. It was bungalow heaven or maybe hell. Compact modern buildings set behind immaculate front gardens. Sally found the right address and parked a little way beyond it. "This estate is giving me the creeps, Cat. It's all too perfect. I wish you'd let me come with you. I'm not happy about you going in there alone."

"I'll be fine, and I'll make sure I've got an escape route." Sally sighed. "Well, I don't like it. Just be on your guard. I'll be here waiting." Caitlin got out of the car, walked briskly down the drive stopping to admire a green Mazda sports car. Noticing a tennis racquet bag on the front seat, she felt a spasm of fear. Was there more than one person in the house? She rang the bell. Within moments the door was flung open by a tall, athletic-looking, older man. If she'd been expecting to meet a replica of Jones junior, she couldn't have been more mistaken. Jones senior was dressed for tennis in a white polo shirt and navy shorts. He almost gleamed. His white hair was slicked back from his face, his eyes obscured behind a pair of wire framed spectacles. He had a neatly trimmed, white beard and his smile revealed several gold teeth.

"Oh" she burst out, "You look very different to your son, and you've been playing tennis?" He smirked, looking down at his trainers, "How did you guess!" She grinned, "I saw your racquet bag in the car."

"Ah, that's it! Please come on in. I'm David by the way." She followed him down a pink carpeted corridor to an untidy-looking sitting room. He apologised for the mess, moving newspapers off a chair for her. "Since Trevor's mother died, I'm afraid I've let things go but I rather like the muddle. Babs always kept the place like a new pin. Never a thing out of place."

"Trevor's your son, the Mr Jones who's acting for me? Forgive me, it's just you're nothing like him. I suppose I was expecting a doddery old man in a three piece suit wearing too much aftershave." Caitlin covered her mouth with her hand, "Oh, my goodness, that just slipped out. I'm so sorry, I didn't mean to be rude." He sat down opposite her. She couldn't help her eyes being drawn to his muscular brown legs, splayed out in front of him. It was all rather disquieting. He chuckled, "He's not exactly a 'chip off the old block' is he? He's like his mother, and just as straight laced. Now, I believe you've come to see me about your own mother."

Caitlin found herself telling him all about her search. He listened in silence. "So, you see, I want to know why a young wife and mother would have taken the trouble, at that point in her life, to make a will and leave everything to her daughter in a trust fund. It doesn't make sense."

"Caitlin, may I call you that?" She nodded, "I

remember your mother very well, a serious young woman. You're very much like her. I was new to the firm at the time, so it was my partner, John Barrett, who drew up the will for her. I recall there was inherited wealth from her father's side. So when both her parents died, as their only child, she inherited the whole estate. Naturally, she wanted to put her own affairs in order. It was as simple as that. But I remember the last few times she came to the office, she'd lost a lot of weight and looked very unwell. John told me she had cancer. There was no reason for us to disbelieve her, though it wasn't mentioned at the inquest. Be that as it may, there was something very wrong with her and it led to tragedy. After her death, John handed the case to me, he was about to retire. I carried out her wishes, setting up the Trust Fund as she had instructed."

"It's difficult to make any sense of this David. I knew nothing about the Trust Fund until my father died. As regards my mother, she had hidden letters for me. She wanted me to know about my father, because she hadn't known about her own birth parents. There was nothing in the letters to say she feared she was ill. Her last note implied that she was frightened. If the police had seen those letters at the time, maybe there would have been a different outcome." He looked surprised, "You found letters in the house, after all these years? Where were they hidden?"

"They were concealed in the attic. She'd obviously meant to hide them well."

He licked his lips. "Have you taken them to the police?" She shook her head. "Not yet, but I think I should, don't you?"

"If it makes you feel better, my dear Caitlin, you

should. But think very carefully before you rush into anything. It's been thirty years since your mother's death; it's highly unlikely that any action would be taken. You said she had implied some concern, but that could mean anything. It could well have been about her health. I don't want you to end up feeling worse than you already do. Now forgive me, I hadn't expected you quite so early, do you mind if I go and get changed then I can rustle up some drinks. Give you a chance to think things through."

Once he had left the room, Caitlin sat bolt upright. Could she trust what this man was saying? She'd meant to ask him how the Trust Fund had been administered, but she didn't want him to think she was suspicious. No, she couldn't trust him and he was worried, otherwise why would he ask if she'd shown the letters to the police. Whatever else she did, she must convince him that she was happy with his explanation.

Feeling restless she got up to look around. She walked over to a modern oak bookcase containing a strange array of books ranging from thrillers to historical romance and a whole shelf full of travel books and maps. The fireplace was obscured by an embroidered screen, a brass carriage clock ticked softly on the mantelpiece. Looking closely, she saw it had an inscription. A retirement gift for Barbara Jones. His wife presumably. What had happened to her? She sat back down and picked up the Daily Mail from the floor flicking through it, her mind elsewhere. She badly wanted to run away.

David came back in carrying a jug of orange juice. Thankfully he had a pair of trousers on. She sipped her drink, hoping that she was giving the impression of quiet composure despite the adrenalin coursing through her veins. "Thank you so much for seeing me David, it makes more sense now, and you're quite right, it would be best to let sleeping dogs lie. After what you've told me, my poor mother must have been suffering with some form of illness." She hesitated for a moment, then continued. "Despite how young I was at the time, I still have a hazy memory of her. Sometimes, I think I see her. She stands at the window in a floral dress, her long hair tied back with a blue ribbon. I suppose it is no more than a hazy memory; my mind playing tricks."

"Grief can take you many ways. It will pass my dear. It's natural for you to want to see her. We all need our mothers and you lost yours so early. But you had a good life away from here didn't you. Where did George take you?"

"He abandoned me in Wales, actually. It was no thanks to him that I had a good life." David seemed surprised. "Oh, come on. George was a funny old stick, but he would never have wanted you to come to harm."

Caitlin wanted to shut down the conversation. It wouldn't do at all. She had to stop; get out. She felt as though she was suffocating. Although it felt too soon she stood up. "Thank you so much for your time. You've put my mind at rest. Excuse me for rushing off. A friend's outside waiting for me. Thank you for being so kind and understanding." She gave him what she hoped was a playful look, "I might see you on the tennis court one day."

His smile was ingratiating, "What a shame you have to go so soon. I don't often have such beautiful company. I suppose you must be busy. I'm sorry if George let Rock House go to rack and ruin. The will stipulated he could remain living there, but as far as I remember, no provision was ever made for the maintenance of the place. I'd love to see what you've done to make it your home."

Caitlin's eyes widened as she thought to herself, "You wish!" but she said, "Of course, I'd be happy to show you around when it's finished." As she stepped towards the front door, he stood in front of her. He leaned over her and placed his hands on her shoulders, kissing her on both cheeks, "Goodbye my dear. If I can help you with anything, you know where I am."

As Caitlin walked back down the driveway, she shivered. What a creepy man. There was something about him that disgusted her. She found a tissue in her pocket and rubbed her cheeks roughly where he had kissed her. She had let down her guard and stupidly disclosed details she had meant to conceal. Reaching the car she threw herself into the passenger seat, "Let's get going Sal, get me out of here."

David Jones stood at the door and watched Caitlin being driven away. "Naïve young thing, and still so pretty and innocent too." He ambled back down to the sitting room, mulling over their conversation. If there was evidence, what difference would it make now. She didn't seem to have any misgivings about the Trust Fund. If doubt was thrown on Cecilia Rose's death, questions would be asked. Trevor, that fool son of his, might take it upon himself to delve into the accounts. Somehow he must make sure that Caitlin meant what she said. He had mentioned her foster carers and she hadn't responded. In fact, had she suddenly closed down? She capitulated very suddenly. Maybe not as innocent as he first thought. He would dearly like to see those letters. He snapped his fingers, "Damn it, what was I thinking." He knew what he must do.

Sally was relieved to have Caitlin back in the car with her, but she looked shaken. She gripped her bag so tightly that her knuckles had gone white. Sally pulled up outside Rock House, leaned across and touched her shoulder. "Are you going to tell me about it?"

"I'm sorry, Sal, yes of course I am. Let's go in and get a cup of tea and I'll tell you everything."

Whilst Caitlin excused herself in the bathroom, Sally went into the kitchen and put the kettle on. She reached in a cupboard for the tea pot, mugs, milk jug and biscuit tin. When the kettle boiled she warmed the pot, added Lady Grey teabags and poured boiling water on top. Then she sat down munching on a biscuit waiting for Caitlin to appear. It took some time.

"Sorry I was so long," Caitlin poured herself some tea, "I've been trying to work out what happened. He wasn't what I expected at all. He had white hair but he's probably not much more than mid-sixties. He sat on a chair opposite me wearing shorts that didn't leave much to the imagination. He was friendly and casual and now I'm sure it was all a ploy. The man's a slimy snake."

"Why do you think that?"

"He suggested that my mother was simply sorting her affairs out after she inherited her parents' estate. I found myself telling him that I didn't buy that because of the letters. I'm afraid when I told him about my search I also may have hinted to him that George Rose wasn't my father. He was interested in the letters and asked me if I'd been to the police.

He left me for a while to get changed out of his tennis things. Then when he came back I told him that I would let sleeping dogs lie and not try to investigate further.

I'm not sure if he believed me. He was really creepy Sal. I'm sorry now that we didn't both go in together, I might be reading him wrong, I just don't know."

"You're a good judge of character. We should get those letters into a secure place, just to be on the safe side."

"Oh golly – what have I done?" Caitlin put her head in her hands then looked up, a determined expression on her face. "He's not going to get away with it. I'm as sure as I can be, he's crooked. We'll take the letters to the private investigator tomorrow and ask her advice. We can ask her to investigate Jones Senior as well as Arabella and Dennis. She's going to be a busy woman."

CHAPTER TWENTY ONE

The following morning, after a pleasant trip on the ferry, Sally and Caitlin found themselves driving round and round looking for Charlie Bond's office. They had been up and down side streets in the old part of town. Caitlin, who hated being late, was jittery. Sally was puzzled. "This doesn't make sense, it's here on the street map, so it must be close. Why don't we park and walk?"

They found a multi-storey car park, took a ticket then drove up several ramps, finally finding a gap and manoeuvring Caitlin's BMW into a small space by a pillar. They just about managed to shuffle themselves out. Sally looked for the exit. Hurrying down a fusty-smelling stairwell, they came out at ground level and marched to the end of the street checking the map. They walked until they found the right street name. Now to locate Charlie's office. "You should be good at this Cat, or how did you manage as a social worker."

"I was always getting lost. Drove round and round just like this morning." She laughed, "Here we are, this is the right number, and we're not all that late." They opened the door following a sign directing them up the stairs, then walked down a dingy corridor peering at doors before spotting the investigator's name plate. They knocked and entered a well-lit room. There was a mullioned bow window directly opposite the door. In front of that, behind a cluttered desk, sat Charlie. One wall was taken up with a book case displaying a neat array of box files, a metal filing cabinet beside it. The other wall housed a cupboard with a kettle and a variety of cups on a tray, and next to that, a photocopier. The only additional furniture was two chairs placed in front of

Charlie's desk. She stood up and walked over to them holding out her hand.

"Which one of you is Caitlin?" Caitlin stepped forward and shook her hand. "You must be Sally then." She turned and grasped Sally's hand. "So pleased you managed to find me. Do come and sit down." Charlie was just as she had described herself, except she hadn't said she had a wicked grin, twinkling hazel eyes and perfect white teeth. She walked back behind her desk and sat down. Contemplating them both she said, "Now, I want you to tell me all. Just as it comes. I'm not going to interrupt you, and I'll be taking notes. If at the end of this consultation you decide not to employ me, then I will give you the notes. We talked about expenses and fees on the phone; I can go over them again if you wish."

"Thanks Charlie, I'm happy with the money side and we'll do our best to tell you what's been happening. Shall I begin?" Charlie and Sally nodded. "I'll try to tell you briefly. It all began a very long time ago, and if you don't know about my childhood it won't make sense, so bear with me." It did indeed take Caitlin some time to recount. When Caitlin finished Charlie put her notes down and resting her hand on her chin, she looked at both women. "Thank you for sharing your story, Caitlin. Have you anything to add, Sally?"

Sally looked at Caitlin, "I think the only thing you've missed out is your ghost. It all started with her didn't it. Your unhappiness and falling out with Dennis." Charlie raised her eyebrows, "A ghost?"

"I suppose I didn't say anything about her because it sounds fantastic and I didn't want you to dismiss me as a nutcase. But, there is a presence in the house and in part of the garden. I think it's my mother, that's the honest truth."

"We can never explain everything rationally so why not look on her as a catalyst who was able to alert you to danger. I'm glad you've come to me, and I am taking you seriously.

What I'd like to do now is read back my chronology. See if I've missed anything, or maybe prompt anything that you have left out. Would you like a drink before we start. I've got tea and coffee, milk's fresh and I've even got a few biscuits."

She got up, put the kettle on, made their drinks and settled back down looking at her notes. "Well, here goes. Your mother marries George Rose in 1968 and you were born in August of that year. In late August 1972 your mother dies, leaving you, a four year old child with your father. In 1976 when you are eight years old, your father places you in private foster care with an elderly couple living in Pembrokeshire. You have no idea why he did this, or how he arranged it. You have a happy childhood with them. You never see your father again, although, as a small child, he sends you birthday and Christmas cards.

When your foster parents have both died, having struck up a friendship with Sally, you move in with her. You put yourself through university and become a social worker.

In June 2001 you are located by a private investigator working for Barrett and Jones Solicitors. Your father has died and you find out that you are the sole beneficiary of your mother's estate. You said at this point, you were too shaken to ask many questions and had no idea how the Trust Fund had been set up. The legacy is substantial and includes a house. When you see it you realise it's your old home.

In September 2001 you move into Rock House. It needs substantial renovations and you set to work. In November Dennis Gough enters your life. He seems very taken with you and over the next few months you go out together and eventually he moves in. At first it goes well, but you begin to realise he's controlling you and you decide you want him to leave. During this period you have been thinking about your mother. I'm guessing that's when you began to see your ghost." Caitlin nodded. "You met with Jones, the solicitor, and he advised you that his father would be able to tell you more about your mother than him. He also tells you that you have a cousin, Arabella, and he offers to contact her on your behalf.

So now we are up more or less to the present. You have a falling out with Dennis and ask him to leave. He does so with veiled threats. You call on your gardener to rescue you as you'd already struck up a friendship with him." She looked up at Caitlin, a twinkle in her eye.

"You contact Sally. You then contact Jones the solicitor and find out where Arabella lives, and arrange to go and see her. Arabella is apparently your father George Rose's niece. It's an awkward meeting, you feel she is working to a script. Later that evening you are surprised when you recognise Dennis in the town and follow him to Arabella's house. You hide behind the hedge and listen to their conversation. They know one another and your suspicions are raised.

Back at home Sally arrives and she meets the gardener, your friend Bob. It turns out his Aunt Ann had been to primary school with your mother. You meet with Aunt Ann and she tells you about her. You strike up a friendship. You find hand-delivered letters at home from

Dennis. He wants to meet you. You decide to string him along and arrange to meet him at a local hotel. You ask Ann and her son Justin to be on hand.

You find letters hidden in the attic from your mother to you. You learn about your biological father and your mother's life with George Rose leading up to her death. Ann tells you about the night she died. You fear she was murdered. Ann has photos of George Rose. Although the photo isn't very clear, you think you spot Arabella. She's holding hands with George Rose. Ann recognises her as having worked in a local shop and the manager confirms that her name is Alice Brown. You suspect the solicitor is involved in a conspiracy.

You meet with Dennis. He spins a cock and bull story about his grandfather dying and wanting to take you on holiday to rekindle your love. He appears drunk and becomes aggressive when Sally turns up. Discussing it with your friends, you decide that you should seek help. You contact me but in the meantime you also make contact with Jones Senior. He catches you off guard and you feel you have given him too much information. He mentions your mother's inquest and he seems very interested in her letters."

Caitlin interjected, "I have the letters here if you would like to see them. I wondered if you could store them for me." She handed over the folder containing the letters. They watched whilst Charlie looked through them. "If you wish, I'll copy these and store the originals for you." Caitlin nodded.

Charlie leaned back in her chair pushing her hair off her face with both hands, then rubbing her eyes she contemplated the two women in front of her. "Perhaps you could tell me what you want to achieve and how you think I can be of help?" Caitlin leaned forward on the desk, her left elbow balanced on the edge, two fingers squeezing her lower lip. "I wanted my mother's life to mean something, but now, I'm frightened. I could understand if it's just Dennis wanting a rich wife, I could deal with him. But who is Arabella? What part does she play in this? I need to know. I've brought the photo with me." She reached into her bag and pulled out an envelope, passing it over to Charlie. "That's George Rose on the right of the bar, holding a woman's hand. She's the one who the shop worker remembered as Alice Brown. I think she's Arabella. We need a clear photo of her to show the shop worker, and that's where we'd like you to start."

"OK, I can do that. If I may, I'd also like to make an observation. Jones senior took up the case when his partner retired, yet he remembers your mother's inquest. That strikes me as odd. I'm not an expert on trust funds, but they're usually time limited until the beneficiary reaches a particular age. You didn't hear about it until your stepfather died. Fishy, don't you think?" She narrowed her eyes, "Your Jones senior warrants further investigation."

Both women nodded. "He was creepy. I expected to meet a fusty old man; he certainly wasn't that." Caitlin leaned back in her chair, folding her arms. "It's about justice. Being able to put some closure to this story. I believe George Rose killed my mother and used the Trust Fund to finance himself. The money stopped coming to my foster parents when I was sixteen."

Charlie got up and stood looking out of the window. "I'll start with a trip to Cornwall. I'll take photographs of Arabella and try to find out more about her." She turned round, "Then, if you instruct me to, I'll make some enquiries about Mr Jones senior. How does that sound?"

Caitlin and Sally got up. Sally breathed a sigh of relief, "Thank you Charlie. You have no idea how relieved I am. Cat's brave but we can't do this on our own. With your help, we should get to the bottom of it. Bob and Justin are enquiring around the town to see if they can find someone who remembers the night of Cessie's death. That might lead us somewhere." Charlie looked puzzled, "Remind me who Bob and Justin are. Oh, is Bob the gardener?"

"Yes and Justin's his cousin, the one who changed the locks and watched over Cat when she met with Dennis."

Charlie nodded, walked over and shook both their hands. "I'll get to work and hopefully resolve this for you. In the meantime, I would suggest you stay away from Dennis. Maybe get away for a few days. Let me do my work and then we'll meet up." She followed them to the door, "Be careful, please leave this to me."

"Thanks Charlie." Caitlin chuckled, "I rather fancied being a Miss Marple, but I don't think I'm really cut out for it. By the way, I'm glad you turned out to be a woman." Sally took Caitlin's arm, "Come on Cat, let's get back home. Lot's to do in the house. More boxes in the attic!"

"OK, I'll do as I'm told. We'll lie low. Thanks for listening Charlie." They waved as they walked down the stairs out into the bright sunlight.

Charlie watched the two women disappear down the road. Then she stepped round her desk, stood in the middle of the room, and suddenly whooped loudly and broke into a strange warlike dance. Cavorting around, lifting one knee and raising the opposite arm, then leaning over, kicking one leg back and raising the other arm. Round and round, bobbing up and down, laughing and whooping, then flopping down into one of the chairs.

"At last, fabuloso!" This was why she had spent six unhappy years in the police force trying to ignore the sexual banter and misogyny of male officers, but in the end it wore her down. She researched investigation services in her area, all male orientated. A year ago, almost to the day, she had set herself up as Charlie Bond Investigations and had worked steadily ever since. Almost all enquirers expected a male. Almost all were more than happy to employ a female. Most of the cases had involved infidelity, looking for missing persons and the occasional missing pet. This case would require skill and resourcefulness. She was ready.

She got up and paced around. She needed to come up with an idea to be able to approach Arabella. She went back to her desk, opened her laptop and started to type, smiling with satisfaction. When she had finished she checked her diary, a follow up was necessary with one client. She would do that this afternoon, then prepare for the investigation.

CHAPTER TWENTY TWO

WEDNESDAY 24TH JULY 2002

CHARLIE

I packed a small overnight case and a backpack. What I planned had required working in the evening. So, a leisurely drive down with lunch on the way. Caitlin hadn't queried my fees. So for once I might be able to claim proper expenses, what a luxury.

Driving into the town that afternoon I realised I had miscalculated. The town was bustling. School holidays in full swing. Accommodation was going to be difficult to find, and probably expensive. I drove slowly through residential streets until I saw a vacancy sign in a B&B. An old terraced house with three floors. Nets at the windows looked clean. The small front area was tidy. Luckily, I found a parking space, got out of the car and rang the bell. Eventually the door was opened by a large woman, her grey hair tightly permed, glasses perched on the end of a bulbous nose. She was wearing a stained apron and holding floury hands out in front of her. She looked irritated.

"I'm so sorry to disturb you. I've had to travel down unexpectedly. I saw the vacancy sign in your window. Could you put me up for a night or two?" The woman sighed. "I don't take people for one night, it's not worth the bother. I have a double room at the back of the house. There's a sink in the room, the bathroom's down the corridor." She eyed me up and down. I must have passed inspection, "You can have that if you want."

I thought, "Awkward old cuss." and gave what I

hoped was one of my sweetest smiles, "I'm so grateful, but I don't want to disturb you whilst you're baking. Shall I park up, and come back, in say, twenty minutes?"

"Yes, I'd better have your name. Oh, and cash please, in advance, two nights with breakfast will be £120."

"OK, and I'm Charlotte Taylor. I'll be back in twenty minutes or so."

I went back to the car; a grey Rover that had belonged to my father. It had sleek lines and was still smart although it was beginning to sound clunky. I promised myself a new, nippy bright red sports car one day but I couldn't part with the Rover just yet, it reminded me of my dad. I imagined it still smelled faintly of his tobacco. Two years dead now and I still missed him terribly. I often sensed his presence at home and would tell him about my day. I understood very well how Caitlin felt about her "ghost".

Consulting the street map, I drove towards Arabella's road and her cottage. Perfect layout, a mixture of housing: some terraced, some semi-detached. Arabella's cottage was detached. There was the lavender hedge Caitlin had hidden behind. I wasn't going to hide, I planned to knock on doors all the way up Arabella's road posing as a prospective independent councillor. The forms I designed were to test opinions about local services. It shouldn't take too long, my guess was that many of the properties would be holiday lets. I hoped Arabella would be in and that I'd be able to wheedle my way into her confidence. I could pretend to feel faint, it had worked before.

After visiting a cashpoint, I went back to the B&B and this time the door was opened promptly. The landlady had removed her apron revealing an ample bosom enhanced by a flowery summer dress. Without glasses obscuring her face, she looked rosy cheeked and homely. Her full lips parted as she rewarded me with a warm smile and welcomed me in. Not such an awkward old cuss after all.

"Sorry, you caught me at a bad moment before. I'm Sandra by the way. I'll show you the room, see if it suits you." She led the way up the stairs and down a corridor. I counted four rooms, mine would be number five. The landlady took out a key and opened the door to reveal a large airy room, comfortably furnished with the same deep pile blue carpet that I admired as I entered the house. It had the usual television on the dresser and tea making equipment laid out on a cupboard.

"Thanks Sandra, this is lovely." I walked to the window and saw a small walled back yard with pot plants, a table and four chairs. I could just see the top of a head and someone's arms holding a newspaper.

"Would you like a cream tea. You can sit outside if you wish. The scones are fresh from the oven."

"Ah, that's what you were doing when I disturbed you. Yes please, but could you show me the bathroom first."

So, I took up my short residence at Number Three, Maple Gardens. I unpacked and went downstairs, wandering out into the backyard. A man looked up and smiled. "Hello, you just arrived?" He looked smart in light coloured trousers and a blue short-sleeved shirt, a navy tie loosened at the collar. His brown shoes were polished to a bright shine. His face was thin, and lined, possibly from too much exposure to the sun. His dark hair was peppered with grey. Not bad looking, and not a holiday maker.

"Hi, I'm Charlotte, just down for a few days. How about you?"

"John's the name, and snap. I'm staying for a few days. I have some business down here." He didn't expand on what business, and I suddenly had a horrible thought that he might be a police officer. I know the type. Just then Sandra came out with a tray of tea and scones. "Hope you enjoy my homemade raspberry jam, and our proper Cornish clotted cream. I've made a pot of tea for two, hope you don't mind sharing."

I wasn't sure why, but the thought of sharing a teapot with John unsettled me. The scones were delicious. I ate mine, drank my tea, then excused myself. I wasn't in the mood to sit there chatting, particularly if John was going to ask me questions. In my experience the least said the better. Lies have a way of finding you out. That's why I use my real name. I went upstairs and lay down on the bed thinking about the job in hand.

At six p.m. I made sure I had enough forms and pens in my backpack and left for my evening's investigation. It was a warm evening, so I walked from Maple Gardens to Arabella's Road. Beginning at the bottom, I started knocking on doors, clipboard and forms at the ready. The first three pretty terraced cottages were holiday lets. Key lock pads were the clue. I struck gold at the end cottage. It hadn't been prettified. The windows and front door looked original and were in need of a lick of paint. Whoever owned the other cottages were probably hoping to acquire this fourth one. I surmised there might be an old person within and knocked and waited. I could hear footsteps, and stood back from the door. I was right. She was tiny, neatly dressed in a tweed skirt and blouse, thick brown tights and sensible shoes. She still had the Marcel waved 1930's hairstyle I remembered from old films. White hair carefully curled at the sides. Maybe kept back with pins and a hairnet at night. She looked at me, standing there with my clipboard, bright little brown eyes full of curiosity.

"Hello, I'm sorry to disturb you. My name's Charlotte and I'm hoping to stand for the Council next time as an independent. I'm trying to find out what services people need. I have a short questionnaire. Would you be very kind and help me?"

"You'll need to speak up my dear, I'm a bit deaf. Why don't you come in, I'll be able to hear better."

Just what I was hoping for. I've met so many lonely people, particularly older people, who simply want company. Often their friends have died, houses sold, done up and let. So instead of familiar neighbours, people come and go. Another community broken. Progress I suppose. She showed me into her front parlour and I stepped back in time. Echoes of my father, who had retained the familiar utility furniture he and my mother had acquired after the War. I blinked, here it was again. The same sofa and two chairs but these were covered in pretty chintz material, arms and back protected by exquisitely worked lace antimacassars. Photographs in silver frames adorned a highly polished utility sideboard. I went over and peered at one. A happy bride and groom stared back at me.

"That's me and Harry. We married when he came back on leave from the Navy in 1942. We had forty nine years together, didn't quite make our Golden Anniversary." So many photographs, so many silver frames. "Are these your children and grandchildren?" I asked.

"I've been blessed, but they've moved away, no work here." She looked gloomy, "I suppose that's what happens. The old folk are left behind with their memories. My son rings me on a Sunday. My daughter comes over every month. Goes through my cupboards, gives me lectures on sell by dates. A load of nonsense. But you wanted to talk to me, was it the council you said?"

I explained again, and she asked me whether I would like some tea. I've had some awful experiences in my time, but this lady was neat and tidy, I accepted. Hopefully I wouldn't have to pour the tea away in a pot plant. She brought in a tray loaded with tea things and poured me a cup. We got down to business. I explained the questionnaire was anonymous and confidential, but she wanted to give me her name. So I wrote her name down at the top of the form and thought no more of it. We went through the questions. "Has no-one ever asked what you want or feel about services?"

"No, they come round knocking on doors at election time with their shiny leaflets asking for my vote. I haven't got time for any of them. Nothing changes."

"I've noticed there are lots of holiday lets on your road. Do many people actually live here? Do you speak to one another?"

"There are no jobs, that's what you need to change. The wages youngsters get hardly cover the cost of rent, let alone buying somewhere to make into a home. It's all topsy turvy. I've got a relative up the road. Alice was such a sweet girl. She loved nature, always looking for plants to make old fashioned remedies. Then she went away and came back all hoity toity. Suppose she must have made her fortune. I don't know what she does, but she's not here all the time."

"I'm glad you have someone close by."

"Oh, she doesn't take an interest in me. She knows my children will inherit everything. She came to see me a few times, poked around, but I have nothing of value for her. I fell out with her mother years ago, but that's another story." I looked at the name at the top of my paper, Ethel Brown. Was she talking about *the* Alice? If so, I'd struck lucky.

"Well," I said, "You can't choose your family."

She smiled at me, then got up from her chair. "It's been lovely meeting you, but I expect you want to get on. There's a few other houses up this road where you might find someone in. If Alice answers her door, say I sent you, or she'll give you short shrift. Hers is the cottage at the end."

"Thank you for your time Mrs Brown, You've been really helpful, and I hope, if things go according to plan, I might be able to make a difference." I walked away. Sometimes I feel like a rat. The positive was that I'd spent time with her and she was interested. Maybe when the election came round she could make a difference by asking questions rather than listening to empty promises. You never know. Anyway, a few more doors to knock, then into the lion's den.

I found one other person at home and had a lively chat on their doorstep. Then I opened the gate in the lavender hedge, walked down the path and rang the bell. No answer, I rang it again and waited. I saw a face glancing briefly out of the front window, and then the door was flung open. There was a resemblance to my Mrs Brown. This woman was tiny too, but there the likeness ended. She looked as though she had seen a bit of life. Maybe in her mid-thirties. Her blonde hair tied back; revealed sharp features, a thin mouth and suspicious brown eyes. Nothing welcoming or curious about this one. "If you are trying to sell me something, don't bother. I never buy from the doorstep."

"I'm not selling anything. My name's Charlotte. I've just come from your aunt. She suggested I come and talk to you." I went into my spiel again. She wasn't impressed.

"I suppose I can spare you ten minutes." She wasn't going to let down her guard. We stood on her doorstep and went through the questions. Her answers were abrupt and disinterested. After I'd asked the last question I tried praise. Sometimes that works. I looked around me, hoping that I showed admiration. "I love the way you've planted your garden, and your hedge is gorgeous. Have you been here long?" Bingo, she softened, relaxing a little. I smiled and she actually smiled back, even giving me some eye contact.

"I was born round here. Now, if you don't mind I really am busy. Good luck with your campaign." With that, she turned round and shut the door.

Storing the clipboard away in my backpack, I walked back down the road. It had gone better than I had hoped. From Caitlin's description she was the woman who had called herself Arabella. Now, I needed some photos of her. I'd take care of that tomorrow. Caitlin had mentioned a pub nearby. Time for something to eat and maybe some gossip.

The pub was easy to spot in the middle of a long terrace of old stone houses. Colourful hanging baskets, wooden benches and a menu board lent it a welcoming appearance. I walked through the front entrance straight into the bar. It was surprisingly spacious inside going back a long way. People were sitting on tall stools at the bar and at small tables. There was a large fire place with logs stacked in an alcove beside it. I could imagine how cosy it would be in the winter. This evening it was pleasantly cool and shaded within.

Sometimes when I walk into a pub I feel uncomfortable. Here, instead of stares, there were smiles from the men at the bar, as they made some room for me to order a drink. I could see they warmed to me when I ordered a pint of Doom Bar. I wanted to chat, ease myself in, then see if anyone knew Alice Brown. I genuinely enjoy meeting strangers and listening to stories. Giving someone an opportunity to talk often pays dividends in my job. Tonight was no exception, I soon had the group of men at the bar engaged in lively conversation.

I tried to think up a good reason to ask about Alice. In the end I said she was a friend of a friend but I only received blank looks. They were older men, so maybe their age range was wrong. Refusing the offers of another drink, I ordered some food and when it arrived sat at one of the small tables. I was just finishing my scampi and chips when I heard a familiar voice.

"You were asking after a friend." I looked round. John from the B&B was standing near the fireplace smiling at me. I explained that a friend had asked me to look her up. "Do you mind if I join you?" I could hardly refuse and I didn't refuse his offer of a drink either. He turned out to be amusing company as he very cleverly tried to pump me for information. Needless to say, I got about as much information from him as he got from me. There was a point where we both gave up and talked about the state of the world instead. I liked him and he was good looking in a world-weary sort of way. He saw me glancing at the gold band on his ring finger and raised his eyebrows. I grinned and told him that I didn't want to be messing with a married man. When he told me he was divorced, I wanted to believe him.

We walked back to Maple Gardens together and I found myself agreeing to have dinner with him tomorrow. Back in my room, I sat and thought about our encounter. Of all the pubs in the town, why was he in that one? There were closer ones to the B&B. Why was he interested in Alice? I could sniff something, but couldn't figure out what yet. I would stake out Alice early morning and get the photographs I needed. I might just meet a neighbour who knew her, but I didn't want to arouse suspicion. Then it was dinner with John and return to report the following day.

CHAPTER TWENTY THREE

Caitlin relaxed on the sofa, closing her eyes for a few minutes. Seeing how tired she looked, Sally had cooked dinner and insisted she would clear the dishes. Caitlin dozed off to the clatter of pots and pans, a smile on her face. They had caught a bus to Lulworth that morning and hiked all the way back along the coast paths, stopping off at a pub for a pasty and a pint along the way. Caitlin came to with a start when the phone rang. She could hear Sally answer it out in the hall. "Bob, how are you?"

She tried to open her eyes but dozed off again to the hum of voices. When she woke, she saw Sally sitting opposite her. "You looked so peaceful I didn't want to wake you. That was Bob on the phone with news. They've found someone who might be able to help. It sounds promising." Caitlin sat up. "Oh gosh, spill the beans Sal, tell me all."

"Justin and Bob did a trawl round the pubs in town last night. They were looking for locals in the sixty to seventy age range. No luck. Too many tourists. So they went to the British Legion. There were a few older men at the bar. Some of them remembered Cessie's death, but no-one recalled being out that night. Then they struck gold. A woman called Edna is married to a man who, she says, was there. His name's Bert Savage. She said he's not a well man and it might do him good to get things off his chest. The thing is, his best friend Harry, who had been with them that night, was dead four months later. He committed suicide that Christmas by throwing himself in front of a train. According to Edna, Bert never got over it, and listen to this, he blames George Rose."

Caitlin sprang up and stood looking out of the window, unconsciously mimicking the stance of her ghost. She turned to Sally, her brow furrowed. "That's given me goosebumps. How did Bob and Justin leave it?"

"We can go and see Edna and Bert tomorrow morning. They live quite close by. Bob said to go gently with Bert. He knows him from the darts team. He has bad lungs now. Asbestosis from working on building sites."

"Poor man, but we're getting there Sal. Terrifying isn't it? Are we about to uncover a murder?"

They found Silverthorne Cottage tucked away just off the main road into the town. It looked as though it had once been a barn. A long, single storey building with small windows and a low front door. The front garden was a profusion of colour. There was a trellis overrun with fragrant sweet peas on one stone wall and against the other tall hollyhocks swayed majestically in the breeze amongst an abundance of California poppies and snapdragons.

Caitlin and Sally walked up to the front door and knocked. It was answered by a small, nervous-looking woman in a blue overall. Her hair was very dark in contrast to her face which was lined and anxious. She had shadows underneath her brown eyes. She smiled at them both.

"I'm glad you've come." She turned and gazed at Caitlin, "I think I remember your mother. I moved here when Bert and I married in '67, so I only have dim memories of her. It's your height and blue eyes that makes me think you must be Caitlin. Am I right?" Caitlin nodded. "So," she continued, "you must be Sally, and I'm Edna. I did warn Bob that Bert's unwell. He may not be able to talk much, he had a bad night last night. He still wants to see you though. Fate must have sent me to your friends. I don't go out much in the evening with Bert being so sick, but I was up the Legion last night for a birthday. You could have knocked me down with a feather when I overheard Bob talking about Cecilia Rose. I've heard her name so many times over the years. I had to say something. I hope they didn't think I was tittle-tattling." She clucked to herself, "Sorry, I talk too much, please come in."

Crossing her fingers behind her back, Caitlin followed Edna into the front hall and through a door into a large sitting room. Sally hung back at the entrance. Her eyes took a moment to adjust. Bert Savage sat in an easy chair in one corner. He was breathing through a mask attached to an oxygen cylinder. His breath sounded laboured and shallow. He looked up from his mask staring at Caitlin with an unnerving intensity. You could sense he had once been a handsome man but now his face was gaunt, his skin paper thin and his dark eyes over-large and red rimmed. His hands looked swollen.

When he spoke his voice was hardly more than a whisper. "I wondered if this day would come. I was never asked." He breathed into his mask for a few moments. "You're like your mother." Caitlin knelt down in front of him and touched his arm. "Thank you for seeing me. I'm so grateful to meet someone who remembers my mother." Her eyes filled with tears, tears for her mother and for Bert. They held each other's gaze for a moment.

"I see no evil in you. He was evil." Caitlin frowned, "Who are you talking about?"

"Your father. He did away with your mother, and he

killed my best friend." He gasped, and reached for his mask.

Caitlin sank back and let him catch his breath before she spoke. "George Rose was my stepfather, and I think you're talking about your friend, Harry? Can you tell me what happened. Were you there with them?" With an effort he pulled himself more upright, turned and looked at his wife. She gave him a sad smile, "Tell her Bert. Tell her what happened. She has a right to know. If you don't say now, it'll be too late." Edna spoke softly to Caitlin. "He has mesothelioma, it's spreading. There's nothing more the doctors can do."

Caitlin turned back to Bert. "Nothing is going to happen. I don't want revenge, I just want to know the truth. Please help me." She knelt down on the floor beside him.

Bert started to talk slowly, stopping when he needed to hold the oxygen mask to his face. "It started as a lark. They said she was too po-faced and they were going to loosen her up. They started buying her doubles. Honest, I didn't like it. But me and Harry, we didn't stop them. I'd been drinking whiskey chasers. When they said they were going to swim, I was too drunk. I stayed. They went out laughing, and I never saw her again." His head drooped as he fumbled with the mask. Edna came round, knelt down in front of him and held both his arms. "Have a rest love. I can tell Caitlin what Harry said. You've told me often enough."

He nodded his head and she continued, "Harry went out with them to Monkey beach, but he held back, sat on the wall. He wasn't a good swimmer, and it was dark. He saw the three of them stripping off. He said he thought he heard splashing and a cry, but he did nothing, thought it was horseplay. They came back without her. Said she was swimming across the bay. The men dressed and they all went back into the pub. Everyone knew Cecilia was a good swimmer, and they just carried on as though nothing had happened. Poor Harry blamed himself. He tried to tell the police it was deliberate but they did nothing. He became more and more depressed, and well, the rest is history."

"Thank you for telling me. I'm so sorry about your friend Harry." He looked up, tears filling his eyes. Removing his mask for the last time he whispered, "Forgive us." Caitlin got up from the floor. "I have nothing to forgive you for, Bert. It wasn't your fault. The tragedy is that my mother ever met George Rose. He's the one who's to blame for all of this, and you're right, he was evil. I'm so sorry remembering has upset you. You should rest now." She leaned over and kissed him on the cheek. He held onto her hand. She smiled at him and nodded. His breathing was very laboured, but he squeezed her hand and said in a barely discernible whisper, "Find the locker man."

Caitlin and Sally followed Edna out into her kitchen. "Sit down my loves. I'll make us all a cup of tea. Poor Bert, he hasn't got long to live. It's good he's unburdened himself but he's left it with you, you poor girl. What a terrible thing. I'm so sorry."

"I believe George Rose manipulated my mother into a situation she couldn't control. I don't think we could prove it was murder, but maybe we could get somewhere by following the money." Edna perked up, "What do you mean?" Sally interrupted, "Oh, it's nothing Edna. I think you ought to leave it Cat." Caitlin took the hint. "How are you managing to look after Bert? Do you get help?"

Edna was keen to talk, they listened sympathetically. Afterwards they walked back down the road together in silence until Caitlin said, "She's a chatterbox isn't she? It'll be all round the town before long. Well, there's nothing to be done now. We need to talk to Bob and Charlie tonight."

Instead of walking down the main street, they struck off on a farm track, following bridleway signs that took them up to a maze of steep tracks. Sally's hair was being blown across her face by a stiff breeze. She kept pushing it back; getting annoyed and vowing to either have it cut off or find a way to secure it on top of her head and out of the way.

They kept walking until they recognised a landmark and stopped at a vantage point with a clear view of the town below. The sea looked choppy. Small sailing crafts scudding across the bay, their white sails spread out to catch the wind. They flopped down on the grass for a few minutes to catch their breath. Sally combed her fingers through her tangled hair and sighed. "Edna isn't the sort to keep anything to herself. We have to be prepared for gossip. Your Jones senior will probably get wind that you're not letting it go as you told him."

"I'm going to try and think the best of Edna. She genuinely wanted Bert to get what he knew off his chest. I had to stop myself going into full social worker mode. I hope they have someone to help them." Caitlin looked into the distance. "I think the poor man is close to death. I've seen that faraway look too many times. He said something odd at the end which I didn't quite catch. I wish I'd asked him to repeat it."

"I didn't hear anything I'm afraid. I was moving out of the room by then. What did it sound like?"

Caitlin made a face, "Locks, he said something about locks or a locker. Doesn't make any sense to me. Come on, let's go, it's lunchtime." She sprang up and held out her hand to help Sally up. "I'll race you home."

CHAPTER TWENTY FOUR

CHARLIE

I rang Caitlin and Sally before I left Cornwall satisfied that I had a good idea of Alice Brown's character and some clear photographs of her. I arranged to go over to see them that evening. Instead of putting the radio on, I diverted myself by recalling the evening I spent with John. I glanced in the mirror. Yes, a definite rosy glow. He said he'd ring me. Well, if nothing came of it, we'd had a great time, coming in late and creeping into the B&B together like a pair of teenagers. He intrigued me and for the first time in ages, I felt a tingling of desire.

I went back to the office and checked phone messages and emails. I'd been sneezing on the way home, the change of air in Cornwall seemed to have set my hay fever off. I fumbled in a drawer and managed to find some antihistamine tablets. A sneezing detective isn't a lot of use. I managed to get some work done, then headed out on my journey.

Travelling across on the ferry, I felt as though I was going on holiday. There was a sense of anticipation in the air. People in bright summer clothes stepping out of their cars enjoying the sea air; taking photographs of each other. But after landing and going through the toll booth it became a different story. A story of endings. On the opposite side of the road a queue of cars containing hot-looking adults and children were waiting for the ferry. Glancing at my watch I saw it was five fifteen. After a day on the beach, parents were trudging up the road, carrying chairs and bags. They looked tired. Fractious children walked beside them. Dogs on leads, except one, an overexcited chocolate coloured Labrador had got free and was darting in and out of the traffic, the owners nowhere in sight.

The traffic thinned out as I left the village behind. I followed the signs, checking the directions Sally had given me. The country roads were narrow, so I drove slowly watching out for cyclists and walkers. A couple of miles further on I drove down a steep, winding hill and entered the town. The road meandered around until a long, sandy beach came into view. The tide was coming in, nevertheless I could see holiday makers sitting on the beach, the sea almost lapping at their feet. Scantily dressed people were walking along the promenade above. I badly wanted to stop for an ice cream or a cold drink. Despite having the windows wide open I felt hot and bothered. The drawback of driving an old car without aircon.

I left the bay, changing gear as I started driving up what seemed like a never ending hill. I found the road I was looking for near the top and drove slowly along looking for the house. Eventually I spotted a gap in the hedge and a partly obscured sign. I had to get out and peer at it. *Rock House* faded but just about decipherable. Reversing the car I turned down the drive. There were tall trees on either side giving some welcome shade. Then I caught my first glimpse of Rock House. It reminded me of old stone houses I had seen in Brittany. Long front facing windows virtually at ground level and on the third floor, at roof level, small dormer windows looking out over the garden. I had been brought up on a council estate, secure in the knowledge that my parents, friends and neighbours were never far away. After her mother had died, Caitlin must have felt isolated and lost despite, or maybe because of, these beautiful surroundings.

I walked up three stone steps to the front door. It looked old and solid, but it had a shiny new mortise lock as well as an old lock that would need a large key. I couldn't see a bell, so used the door knocker, it sounded very loud. I heard footsteps. The door opened a fraction, held back by a chain. I was glad to see that Caitlin and Sally were taking security seriously. "It's me, Charlie."

Sally opened the door wide and stepped out. I thought she was going to shake my hand but she gave me a quick hug then stood back and grinned at me. "We've been swimming. I bagged the shower first, but Caitlin won't be long. Do come in, but watch that step, it's easy to trip." A timely warning, as indeed, I nearly did.

"Thanks Sally, you saved me." I stepped onto an original Victorian tiled floor, then my eyes were drawn to the broad staircase. "I can imagine an elegant woman posing there, then sweeping gracefully down to greet her guests."

Caitlin appeared at the top of the stairs. "I think you're right Charlie. They could admire their appearance in the mirror before descending." She pointed at a long mirror opposite the first stair, "Not a very safe place to stand and look at yourself. I'm going to move it when we get the decorators in." She came running down the stairs, her hair still wet and smelling of shampoo. Her skin looked tanned. Her face less drained than when we first met. The dark shadows under her eyes had disappeared. "It's good to see you again. Come on in. Would you like a cold drink? It's been such a hot day."

I followed them into the kitchen. Sally opened a big American style refrigerator and took out a jug of juice.

"Here's one I prepared earlier." She grinned, "Elderflower. Is that OK?"

I accepted the drink gratefully and sat at the long pine table whilst Caitlin fetched glasses. "Phew, that's better. I'd misjudged how long it would take to get over here in the holiday season. I remember my parents bringing me over with my bucket and spade; the taste of sandy sandwiches on the beach with mum and dad. Happy memories. How are you both? I hope you've been lying low." They looked at each other then back at me. "Is that a slightly guilty look I see?"

Caitlin was quick to reassure me, telling me briefly about their visit to Bert and Edna, eager to hear about my investigation. Sipping my drink slowly, I told them how I had set about tracking Alice Brown, then reaching into my document case, I pulled out the photos. We compared them to the photos Ann had of her and George Rose. There was no doubt about it, Alice and Arabella are the same person, and the Alice in the photo was clearly an item with George, their body language said it all. Caitlin sat back in her chair. "We're on the right track. Ann's expecting us to call. I'll organise a time with her for us to go and talk to the manager of the corner shop. You know, I thought I'd be elated or angry, but I just feel flat. Maybe I was hoping that Dennis was a good guy after all. How can people be so wicked?" Sally looked fondly at her friend. "You see the best in everyone Cat. He's not a good guy."

I finished my drink and sat waiting for Caitlin or Sally to break the silence, but they both seemed deep in their own thoughts. I broke the silence instead. "I'd like to write up my notes. Can you tell me what happened when you visited Bert and his wife please."

Caitlin recounted how ill Bert Savage was. She said Bert thought George Rose was evil and had "done away" with her mother. The story unfolded of a surfeit of alcohol and the swim, with his pal Harry as an unreliable witness. Caitlin was of the opinion that Harry's suicide had led Bert to believe that George Rose was responsible.

"You may be right Caitlin, there's nothing much to go on. We have to keep digging. By the way, when I say we, I mean me, not you. Was there anything else that worried you when you talked to Bert. Anything you can recall."

"He said something as I left. He had his oxygen mask over his mouth, I could hardly hear him. It sounded like 'lock' or 'a locker'. And there may be an issue with his wife. She liked to talk and heard everything Bert and I said. Sally and I both thought it would be round the town by now. Well, let's face it, nothing much happens here. It's bound to be hot gossip."

"Okay, we'll have to deal with that. But what he said interests me. Is it possible you could go back and see him?" Caitlin looked uncomfortable. "I'd rather not Charlie. The poor man is close to death. Do you really think it's important?"

"It could be, and something's niggling at me. Tell me again what Edna said about Harry going outside. Try and recall it word for word. Take your time."

Caitlin deep in thought, her eyes closed, started to speak, "She said Harry went out with them to Monkey beach. He held back, sat on the wall. He wasn't a good swimmer, and it was dark. He saw the three of them stripping off. He said he heard a cry, but thought it was horseplay. They came back without her. The men dressed and they all went back into the pub." She sat bolt upright.

"Why didn't I see that before. She said he saw three of them stripping off. Who was the third person?"

"Well remembered. Now, think again. What did he whisper at the very end. Something about a lock or a locker. Just that, or anything else?" Caitlin put her elbow on the table, her hand on her forehead. "There was something else. If only I could remember." She paused, "Of course, he said 'find the locker'. He wants me to watch out for someone."

"Yes, and now something really is niggling at me. Just let me go back through my notes." Sally got up and poured me another glass of juice while I sat checking. I always keep copious notes when I'm on a case. Impressions and any evidence, no matter how unimportant it might seem at the time, is all noted. "Ah, here it is. You refer to Jones senior, but he introduced himself as David. I wonder if he was Davey as a young man. You've heard of Davey Jones's Locker?" Sally and Caitlin both looked puzzled. "It's nautical folk lore. Davey Jones's Locker is a euphemism for the deep dark sea. Your mother drowned in the deep dark sea."

Caitlin leaned over towards me, her hand covering her mouth. Her eyes looked huge. Then she slumped and turned her face away. Sally reached across and touched her arm. "I'm sorry Caitlin, I shouldn't have said it like that."

"Don't apologise. I'm beginning to see how it was. It was that phrase. It conjures up the most horrible picture." She sighed, straightened her posture to look at me. Her face said it all, an infinite sadness for a loved one lost. She took a deep breath.

"According to Bert there were four men there that night. George Rose, Bert, Harry and someone who may be called Davey. Harry sat back on the wall whilst George, my mother and Davey stripped off to swim." She shut her eyes for a moment. "I remember now. Bert said 'the locker man, watch out for the locker man'. Oh God, no wonder Jones had so much information. He was there. He's complicit in all this. When we were talking he called George Rose, 'old George'. He didn't just take on the work after my mother died, he and George Rose were friends." Sally got up and went over to the window, her back towards us. "Courage Sal. We're doing a better job than the police did thirty years ago, and we're doing it for Cessie." Sally came back and sat down. Two gutsy young women together. I had confidence in their resolve, but I didn't have so much confidence in them being able to keep safe.

"Now we've something to go on. I'd been puzzling how to get information from the solicitors office, but now I'll start with David Jones. You told me he'd been playing tennis and that he talked about a club. What I want you two to do is find out when the club days are. When he's safely on the tennis court, I'll get into his house."

"You mean," Sally interrupted, "you're going to break in."

I chuckled. "Not exactly. You'd be surprised how many people hide a key outside. If I can find one it'll be easy, otherwise I'll have to use other methods."

"You'll need a look out." Sally grinned at me. "It can't be Caitlin, he knows her. I can watch him on the tennis court and alert you when he finishes. He doesn't know me from Adam, so it wouldn't even matter if he did spot me."

"Okay, but remember Sally, this isn't a game. Find

out when he might be playing tennis and I'll come back over."

"Justin and Jack are both fit young men. I wonder if they play." Sally looked at Caitlin and me with a big smile on her face. "I feel better now. I knew I could be useful. I think this calls for a little glass of wine, don't you? Let's go out in the garden." We sat in a shady spot, sipping white wine, until I started to sneeze uncontrollably. Hay fever is a curse. Time for me to leave.

Sally rang Ann that evening to arrange a meeting at Ann's local shop the following day. Next had been a long phone call to Bob, in which Caitlin recounted her conversation with Bert and Edna, and the subsequent revelation.

Sally was keen to talk to Justin about the tennis club. She was about to ring Ann's number again when the phone rang. She picked it up, listened for several minutes without speaking, then said, "She's not here" and put the phone down. This was true. Caitlin was in the bathroom. When she came down, Sally, looking shamefaced, told her what she had done.

"So, you didn't say anything, whilst Dennis spoke of his undying love, then told him I wasn't here. Oh dear."

"Sorry Cat. Maybe you'd better ring him back. He'll be angry with me not you."

She shook her head. "Let him wait. Justin first. See if he can help us with the tennis club. Let's get things sorted, then we can relax." Ann picked up, Justin was out. They left a message for him to ring. Caitlin sighed. "I'll ring the dreadful Dennis. He's going to want me to meet him. I'll make an excuse." It would be Caitlin's birthday in August. There followed a conversation about getting away for a few days. They were both fans of music festivals and the Cambridge Festival was on soon. It would be a good excuse to put Dennis off. With that agreed Caitlin got up and went out to phone him.

Sally could hear her speaking in a soft voice at first. When her voice rose, Sally went out into the hall. "How many times do I have to say, you're not welcome in this house. No, it's nothing to do with Sally." She listened for a few seconds, "I've changed the locks Dennis. You won't be able to get in. If you come, you can knock all you like. I'll simply phone the police." She put the phone down, looking exasperated. "He'd been drinking. Started making all sorts of wild threats."

"I'm sorry. I provoked him. It's my fault, and now he's threatening you. Could you take out a court order against him or something?"

Caitlin scratched her head. "Don't blame yourself, he's ridiculous and he's getting worse; losing control. Not sure about a court order. They're not that effective. I'll ring him again tomorrow, there's no point in trying to talk to him when he's drunk. Like we said, we'll go away for a few days. Let Charlie do her investigations, then we'll contact the police. By tomorrow we'll know if Arabella really is Alice Brown. Come on Sal, smile. If she is, then, as Sherlock would have said, the game's afoot Watson!"

CHAPTER TWENTY FIVE

SATURDAY 27TH JULY

The local convenience shop was at the top of the High Street. Caitlin and Sally met Ann outside. With Coco safely tied up, they went in and looked for the Manager. They were to be disappointed. It was her day off. Ann wanted some shopping so Sally and Caitlin looked around. Walking up one of the aisles they could see the back of a dark haired woman wearing a blue overall. She was filling shelves. As she moved over to let them by, Sally exclaimed "Edna, it is you, isn't it?" Her face broke into a smile. "Sally and Caitlin, how nice. I do a couple of hours here in the morning, just to get out of the house. Are you shopping?"

"We're here with our friend Ann." Caitlin said, "We're trying to find someone who may have worked here." Sally frowned, "Don't take any notice Edna." She turned to Caitlin, "We'd best wait to talk to the manager."

"Oh, come on Sal. Edna works here, she may know my cousin. We could at least show her the photo." With that Caitlin pulled the photo out of her bag to show Edna. She took it to the light and peered at it.

"Yes, I remember her, she worked on the tills for a few months. Now, what was her name. No, it's gone. My memory's terrible. Hold on, I'll go and ask Janine." She took the photo and disappeared from view.

Sally looked anxious, "What have you done Cat? You should have waited." Caitlin shook her head and put her finger to her lips as Edna came back.

"Janine remembers her. She's called Alice, and she thinks her surname was Brown, but she couldn't be sure.

So, she's your cousin?"

"Yes, I think so."

Edna looked very pleased with herself. "Is she a long lost cousin or something?"

"We don't know. We're simply trying to find her. Thanks Edna – you've been a great help. How's Bert, I hope he's no worse. If there's anything you need be sure to contact me. I'd be pleased to help you, especially after all you've done for me. Well, we'd better go, Ann will think we're lost." They were not going to shake Edna off easily. She followed them. Sally could see Ann waiting outside with Coco and went to join her. Edna took Caitlin's hand, "Good luck with your quest. It helped Bert being able to tell his story."

Outside, Caitlin looked at Sally and Ann, her eyes twinkling. "Shall we walk down town. Go and get a coffee." At a safe distance from the shop Sally exploded. "What on earth did you do that for? Edna will tell everyone, and before you know it...."

"Exactly," Caitlin interrupted, "It's time we stirred the pot. We'll let them simmer for a while then see what pops up." Sally strode off, then turned round angrily. "That's not funny. You are putting yourself in harm's way." Ann stood watching, surprised at Sally's outburst, "Maybe you two would like to tell me what's going on."

"She only showed Edna the photo and told her she was looking for her cousin."

"Well," Ann said calmly, "It's done. Probably not wise. Let's go, Coco's getting impatient. Caitlin's going to treat us to coffee and cake - isn't that right?"

They chose a café where they could tuck themselves away. Caitlin ordered, then sat down looking shamefaced. "Sorry Sal, I had a sudden urge for mischief." She turned to Ann, "Arabella was positively identified as Alice Brown. So we're a step forward. We've established Alice is posing as my cousin. Such a lot has happened, I'm not sure you're up to speed. I told you about visiting Jones the solicitor, didn't I?" Ann nodded. "Have we told you about our discovery – we think we know the name of a third man who was with George Rose that night."

"Who?"

"Bert whispered something to me as we left, it sounded like 'Watch out for the locker man'. It was Charlie who came up with Davey Jones's locker, and we put two and two together. We think it was David Jones, the retired solicitor. From what he said when I met him, he knew George Rose well and he was administering the Trust Fund. It must have been him who planted Alice Brown as cousin Arabella, creating a next of kin. All the evidence we have leads straight to him. So the plan is for Charlie to get into his house and search for clues."

Ann raised her eyebrows, "Break in. Is that wise? How will she do it?"

"This is why Sally was hoping to talk to Justin. We know David Jones plays tennis, and he talked about being a member of the tennis club. So we figured, two athletic young men like Justin and Jack might play." Ann laughed, "Oh yes, and not just athletic young men, old birds like me play. You should have asked, I'm a member."

"Oh wow, that's brilliant, so tell us, when are the club days?"

Sally clapped her hands, "Do you know a David?"

"Club days are Monday and Wednesday between nine thirty and eleven thirty. I do know a David. What does he look like? There are a few men called David." Caitlin answered, "I'd say, he's late-sixties. He's quite tall, maybe six foot. Sports a white beard. When he smiles he shows a lot of gold teeth. Wears metal framed spectacles. When I met him, he was flaunting himself, wearing short shorts, and he's creepy." Ann nearly choked on her cappuccino, "Of course, I'm being stupid! He's that David. I usually play with a group of women so I haven't mixed with him. We call him 'Jones the grope'. Apparently, he's got no idea of personal space. He's tall; looms over you and leers. You survived a meeting with him on your own Caitlin. Well done." Caitlin grimaced, "It wasn't pleasant. You're right about the loom and leer. He did that to me. Kissed my cheeks. Yuck. Anyway, one thing's for certain, by the time we've finished with him, he'll get his just desserts."

Ann raised her eyebrows. "You're playing with fire Caitlin. I hope Charlie knows what she's doing. Surely by now you should bring the police in. Not play at being detectives."

Caitlin shook her head. "Too soon. We need some solid evidence and I've got every confidence in Charlie. We could try for Monday. Can you arrange to play tennis on Monday? If Jones is there, give Sally the nod. She's going to watch from the top of the gardens. Then as soon as Jones finishes, she'll ring Charlie."

"OK, I'll do my bit. Usually we put our names down on the board by Sunday evening, so I'll check and let you know tomorrow."

Caitlin looked thoughtful, "How long have you known him? Is he a good player?"

"I've played at the club for more years than I care to remember. He used to be a very handy player, slowed down a lot now."

"Do you think there are any photographs of him as a younger player? Maybe if he won a cup or something."

Sally was still feeling irritable. "What are you doing now? Are you trying to broadcast your story to the whole community?" She scowled at her friend. "Don't be cross with me, Sal. I'm interested. I just want to go and look at some photos."

"I'm sorry Cat. If you think it will help, go and look." She sighed, pointing at her plate, "Look at this piece of apple cake. It's huge. Who wants to help me finish it?"

CHAPTER TWENTY SIX

MONDAY 29ᵀᴴ JULY

At nine o'clock sharp Charlie was sitting in her car with a good view of David Jones's bungalow. At nine fifteen he appeared, carrying a racquet bag. He was dressed in white shorts and tee shirt, a navy jumper over his back, the arms of the jumper loosely tied at the front.

"Very well turned out." Charlie muttered as she reached for her camera. He fished in his pocket for the key to the green Mazda parked in the drive. She quickly took a couple of photographs for her file. He started the car, reversed slowly out of the drive, picking up speed rapidly as he progressed down the avenue. She waited in the car for the call from Sally to tell her he had reached the tennis courts.

Earlier that morning, Sally considered what to wear. She wanted to blend in with her surroundings, but only had a limited amount of clothes with her. The majority of her clothes were still in the hotel. She would have to decide what to do about her job soon. She had brought some 'slopping about' hareem trousers with her. She chose an old, soft, cotton shirt to go with them and completed the outfit by wrapping a dark green scarf round her head. She surveyed herself in the mirror as she stood at the top of the stairs. "Not bad."

Caitlin was in the kitchen. "Morning early bird. I'm about to make us scrambled egg on toast." Sally nodded, "Lovely. Is my outfit OK? I want to blend in. It might look a bit strange me sitting up there if the tennis carries on for a whole two hours."

"You look great. I like your turban. Take a book.

You don't need to keep your eye on the game all the time."

"Good thinking. Well breakfast, then I'll get going. Charlie has asked me to ring her as soon as David Jones arrives. What's the time now?" She looked at her watch, "I've got forty minutes, then I need to leave."

Sally was driving away from Rock House by nine ten, a flask of coffee and a copy of *The Life of Pi* she had borrowed from Caitlin in her bag. She parked on the road, a short walk from the gardens. Seeing a gate in the hedge, she walked through and found a bench underneath trees. Perfect, she'd be shaded. She sat and waited. It was now nine twenty five. She could see tennis players on the court and surmised they were sorting out who was playing with whom. She spotted Ann. She saw a tall bearded man sauntering onto the far court. He fitted Caitlin's description of David. On cue, Ann looked up at her and waved. Time to ring Charlie.

CHARLIE

At nine thirty I got the call from Sally. I walked up the drive to the front door and knocked. Then walked round the back. I hadn't seen anyone, but you never know who is watching behind net curtains.

The back garden was quite different to the manicured front lawn. There was a path leading round to a washing line. Everywhere else had been gravelled. The gravel was covered in weeds. There were two flower borders containing perennial flowers almost swallowed up by bindweed. A path led round to a ramshackle looking garden shed. The door was open. I could see a lawn mower, and garden tools set against the wall. Dilapidated garden furniture and old plant pots were almost spilling out of the door.

I needed to look for a key. I started by checking under the doormat. It's amazing how many times I've found a key that way. No luck. Then I ran my fingers over the top of the door lintel. Next, I tried the pots outside the door. Hidden in an overgrown shrub in the last pot, I saw a grey stone. I had seen one of these before. I picked it up, and yes, it was made of plastic. Underneath there was a plastic slider. I managed to pull it across. It had not been used for a very long time and was encrusted with dried mud. The inside of the fake stone was hollow leaving just enough room to hide a key, and there it was, protected by a small plastic bag. I crossed my fingers and hoped it was the back door key.

Getting up off my knees, I went over to the door. I was in luck. He had not left a key on the inside of the door. The key turned and I entered a small, untidy utility room that in turn led through to the kitchen. What looked like several days of crockery was piled in and around the sink. There were half empty mugs and an overflowing ashtray on the table. I wrinkled my nose in distaste. It smelled rancid. So, David Jones was all show. He cultivated a playboy persona with his sports car. In reality he was a dirty old man.

It was a sizeable bungalow. Large double glazed windows would have let in light, but curtains were half drawn. The windows were all closed. It was stuffy. I began to sneeze, found some tissues in my bag, and blew my nose. My eyes were beginning to stream. Trying to ignore how uncomfortable I felt I carried on looking in all the rooms. The thick pink carpet muffled any sound I made. His bedroom was unkempt. The bed unmade and grubby. Dirty glasses had been left on the bedside table. The living room was untidy. Lots of books and papers lying around, but cleaner. Somewhere for him to entertain.

I carried on opening doors. I discovered a dirty bathroom and toilet. The toilet by the front door was clean. For any guests I presumed. The dining room looked out onto the back garden. At last I located a small office. It held a desk on which a large computer screen stood. No filing cabinet, but there were two cupboards mounted on the wall that might once have been kitchen cabinets. I opened one. It held a jumble of files and papers. The other was full of old law books. I sighed. If there was something here, it would most likely be hidden, or it could be hidden in full view. I started to open some of the folders. Mostly a jumble of utility bills, old guarantees and bank statements. There was a bulging folder marked 'Holidays' in which the papers were tidily filed. He was evidently keen on expensive holidays.

Glancing at my watch, I saw it was already ten fifteen. I scratched my head and blew my nose again, shoving the tissue up my sleeve. OK, there has to be a locked drawer somewhere. I walked round the desk. There was a space for the computer and a set of three drawers. I opened the first drawer. It contained the usual mixture of pens, post it notes, paper clips. I felt round the top and right to the back. Nothing. The second contained paper. I checked the back and felt round the top. There was something taped up there. I drew it out. It was a white envelope, yellowing with age. I carefully unsealed it. Inside was a sheet of paper dated 15th September 1972. I took a photo then quickly read it through. I whistled. That's how they did it.

The bottom drawer was locked. I fished out my set of lock picks, got down on my knees and manipulated it. Click, and bingo. The drawer held a black ring binder. Sitting down at the desk I began to look through Caitlin's Trust Fund accounts. It looked as though the capital of the fund had been left intact. An income had been drawn on the interest. I spotted one capital outlay for a house purchase. I took photographs of the transaction. I carried on searching until I came to a wodge of email correspondence between David Jones and George Rose. I reached for my camera again. The phone rang. Sally. Panicking. He had just driven off. She was sorry, she hadn't been able to get a signal.

There was only one thing for it. I unclipped some of the email correspondence and put it in my bag. I locked the drawer again, and hurried out, glancing around to ensure I hadn't left doors open. I could hear a car. I ran out to the back door, locked it and replaced the key in the plastic stone fumbling with the slider. I heard the front door slam, so keeping low, I ran and hid behind the shed. Please don't let me start sneezing again. I reached for the tissue in my sleeve, just in case. Not there. What had I done with it? Probably in my bag. I got another tissue out and mopped my eyes and nose.

I remained hidden. Five minutes went by. He opened the back door, I smelled cigarette smoke. Then I heard him bang the door shut. Ten minutes later he drove off. I stayed where I was for another ten minutes then very carefully extricated myself and walked out, looking as though I had every right to be there. There was no sign of the green Mazda or David Jones. I walked briskly to my car and drove away.

Sally flung open the door. "Oh Charlie, I'm so sorry.

This is all my fault. You've been a long time. Did he catch you?" I tried to look stern, but couldn't keep it up. She looked so distraught.

"Come on. It's OK. I got out of the bungalow. Then I hid in the garden until I was sure he had gone out again." I told her about the shed. How he had come out to smoke a cigarette. Not wanting to cause more distress, I didn't voice my thoughts. It was evident from the ashtray in the kitchen that he normally smoked inside.

"What am I thinking. Come in. Caitlin's in the garden. Let's go and join her, tell us all about it." The stone bench and table Caitlin had ordered as a memorial for her mother were now in situ in the secret garden. Italianate in design, they reflected the style of the statue. A large cream umbrella erected beside them offered shade. Caitlin was sitting reading a newspaper. She was wearing a halter necked top and shorts, her long legs stretched out in front of her. She leapt up when she saw us coming. "How did it go? Sal was worried about you. I had to stop her going down there to rescue you."

Sally looked shamefaced, "Well, I wanted to help and instead, I nearly messed it up."

"Please Sally, don't worry. As soon as you rang, I put everything away, locked up and as far as I know, he wasn't aware I'd been there."

Caitlin looked straight at me. Her eyes said it all. She was no fool. "What did you find out?"

"I found what I was looking for. There was a hidden envelope that set out how the Trust Fund would be manipulated dated September 1972. I've also got photographs of part of the accounts. Then I found an interesting email exchange between George Rose and David Jones. I was reaching for my camera when Sally phoned."

"You see," cried Sally, "I did mess it all up."

I extricated some of the correspondence from the file. "Au contraire." I fished in my bag and drew the papers out with a flourish.

CHAPTER TWENTY SEVEN

The three of them sat on the stone bench. Charlie explained, "I'm no expert, but it looks to me as though they used the interest from the Trust Fund as an income. I've taken a photo of a hidden document. The text was too legal for me to make sense of it. Your name appeared, but as we know, the only money that was used for you was during the eight year period when you were at the Warrens', and you said that came via George Rose. It stopped when you left school at sixteen. The interest must have been substantial. Whether it was divided up between George Rose and David Jones wasn't evident. I've taken photos of as much of the accounts as I could. We'll have to wait for the film to be developed. What interested me was one capital outlay on 28th September 2000 for £275,000. I suspect that was to buy property. We'll come back to that."

Caitlin, elbow on table chewing at her thumbnail, shook her head. "Crooked bastards. Money was the motive all along. Why on earth wasn't the Trust Fund audited. I'll answer my own question – David Jones would have got one of his chums to do it." Her eyes narrowed. "Did you spot when the payments stopped? I never received a penny until a month after my meeting with the solicitor. Had they managed to cover their tracks so well that Trevor Jones didn't see that anything was wrong; is he incompetent or did he know all along?"

"I don't know Caitlin, but once the film has been developed you will have evidence to take to the police. They'll do a forensic examination. Now let's have a look at those emails."

The three of them sat there in silence. Charlie read the

first page, then passed it over to Caitlin and Sally, before going onto the next one, and the next one, until they finished. They looked at one another. "Was this all, Charlie?"

"No, I just grabbed a few pages, but I think we've got the gist of it, don't you? We have enough to go to the police." Caitlin looked thoughtful. "How soon can you get the photos developed?" Charlie had to confess, "I'm sorry, stupidly, I didn't use a digital camera. I used my old Leica and a black and white film for clarity. I'll take the film in this afternoon. They're pretty quick, usually within days."

Caitlin took it well, too well. Charlie realised she wanted to delay for some reason. She looked quite cheerful. "We're due to go off to Cambridge on Wednesday. We could go for a couple of days Sal, come back on Saturday." Caitlin looked over at Charlie, "I guess the photos should be back by then."

"Are you sure you want to go?" Sally looked surprised, "I know it's all booked, but it would be easy to cancel." Caitlin smiled. "No, I promised you we'd go to the music festival. Besides, Dennis knows we're going. I want to keep him cooking for a bit longer. I'm sorry. It's difficult to explain, I just want to get away for a few days." Charlie's eyes narrowed as she watched Caitlin. She was acting strangely. Maybe it was shock but surely she should be jumping up and down with excitement. Charlie broke the tension, "I could do with a coffee. Then I think we should examine the emails further. I'm beginning to see how they did it. Tell me Caitlin, when you moved in, did you find a computer? George Rose must have had one to be sending emails."

"No, the place had been cleared. It was just an empty

shell."

"Take pity on me girls. I've had a busy morning. Give me a coffee. I need to think. I'd like to make some notes with your help." They left Charlie sitting in the garden. She went back through the emails. Why would David Jones have kept all of them? Was it an insurance against the threats George Rose had made? Was it pure carelessness? He had got away with things for so long he had become blasé.

Caitlin and Sally came back with three mugs of coffee and the biscuit tin. Charlie helped herself. "Right, let's go through page by page." Charlie fished her notepad out of her bag and found a pen. "These emails start at the millennium. Remember, it was a huge milestone. Maybe they felt it was for them too. Threats of computers going haywire; aeroplanes dropping out of the sky."

Caitlin picked up the first page. "It's dated 5th of January 2000. An email from David Jones asking George Rose for a meeting. Then two days later he sends another email setting out what they agreed." She read aloud from the page: "I am retiring as senior partner at Easter. I will attempt to continue as the administrator for the Trust Fund although it is likely my son will take over. We agreed I will begin a search for Caitlin, however we decided there should be a contingency plan. We agreed we should 'find' another potential beneficiary. You suggested Alice Brown."

"Well," Sally said, "That explains Arabella, although why on earth did they bother to change her name?" Caitlin interrupted, "They were living in cloud cuckoo land, for goodness sake."

"He's retiring for some reason Cat. I guess they needed a plan to keep milking the fund."

"It doesn't sound very plausible. But look, they do progress with it. By the end of February David Jones says, he has the documentation in place, and the files are up to date. My guess is that Alice moved away about this time. When I was in Cornwall her aunt told me she had recently moved back. I think David Jones misappropriated the funds. He diverted trust money to make an investment in the house in Cornwall. We may even find the deeds are in his name."

Charlie continued reading, "That thread of emails stops. Then we have this interesting one. On 4th March there is a note stating Caitlin has been located. In the next email George Rose is threatening David Jones. He's going to tell his wife, Babs, about Alice. I think David Jones had been seeing Alice behind his friend's back, don't you? Then the really interesting bit - he says, 'If you hurt one hair on Caitlin's head I will make you pay this time.'"

Caitlin shook her head, "Thieves falling out. But I don't understand. George Rose seems to be worried about me." She got up from the table. "This is awful. I don't know what to do. I need some time to think." She got up from the bench. "I'll go and have a wander round the garden. I'll be back."

Sally and Charlie continued scouring the emails. The last page showed how sour their relationship had become. George Rose threatened to blow it all apart. Charlie exhaled, "I'm becoming convinced that David Jones is a very dangerous man. George Rose was dead by the end of March 2001. According to Alice Brown, he died of cirrhosis of the liver, in other words, liver failure."

When she reappeared, Caitlin asked Charlie to photograph the emails and leave her the originals. She wanted to examine them further. The revelation that George Rose may have been a pawn in the conspiracy cooked up by David Jones had clearly unsettled her. She promised to keep the papers safe. By the time Charlie left them that evening, they had a plan in place. They agreed to wait for photographs of the accounts to be printed then approach the police with the evidence.

As Charlie sat waiting for the ferry, she couldn't shake the uncomfortable feeling she had about Caitlin. Why was she so keen to leave just as the case against David Jones and his co-conspirators was becoming clear? This was no longer a game for her. Maybe it never had been. She was shaken by George Rose's reaction. Charlie had a sneaking suspicion that she had found something out that she wasn't prepared to share. She had no option but to trust her and her ability to keep Sally and herself safe. The sooner the police were notified the better.

CHAPTER TWENTY EIGHT

SALLY

Cat was quiet after Charlie left. I let her be that evening. She had a lot to think about. When morning arrived I itched to ask her how she felt about George Rose. She had hated him for so long. First for abandoning her and then suspecting he had murdered her mother. Now she knew he had been concerned for her welfare. Had he hidden her in Pembrokeshire for all those years to keep her safe? It didn't exonerate him even if he was easily led. From what Charlie had told us yesterday, David Jones was the instigator. A clever, crooked solicitor. Jones the Grope. It all fitted. I would wait for Cat to start a conversation. I didn't know how I would be able to support her. For the first time I felt out of my depth and fearful for the future.

We are off to Cambridge tomorrow. I must pack a few things. Luckily it will be a short trip as the clothes I have brought with me are limited. Today might be a good day to talk to her. I have resolved to leave my job. I like her idea of setting up a business; I could work and pay my way. It might take her mind off what she will be facing when we return. By lunchtime I had made my mind up. After we had eaten, we went into the garden with our coffee. When I told her my decision, she beamed with sheer delight.

"That's the best news Sal. I'm so happy. Why don't you write your resignation letter now? I don't want you to change your mind!" I could almost see the wheels turning in her brain. She has a way of ordering her thoughts rapidly that I could never master. She doesn't jump straight into things. However, once she gets going she's like an arrow winging towards a target. By the time we'd finished our coffee, I could see she had an idea. "I'm going to phone the junior Jones solicitor and say I want to consult him over a property." I looked sternly at her, "Well, I do, don't I? I'll make an appointment for next week."

"I know what you're doing Cat. If he is part of his father's schemes your phone call will put the wind up him. Is that wise?" She grinned, "Yes. Let them suffer. We're off tomorrow. There's nothing they can do to us. We'll have them bang to rights before you know it." I wanted to smile with her but I couldn't. Who was in control? I certainly wasn't. I let it go. She was determined.

I did indeed write my resignation letter that afternoon. Later on I heard Cat on the phone and presumed she was ringing the solicitor. The conversation went on for a long time. I couldn't help myself. I went to the door and listened. She was talking to someone. A friendly conversation. No raised voices. She said we were off tomorrow. It sounded as though the person wanted to meet her for coffee. She turned them down telling them we were leaving by ten. Then she said, "When we're back I'll show you. You'll be amazed."

My heart skipped a beat, what was she up to? I went back and sat down. When she came in she was her normal self. I didn't feel able to quiz her about her mysterious conversation. We spent the rest of the day quietly. I went out and posted my letter. On the way back I missed my footing on an uneven paving flag and turned my ankle. It wasn't swollen, so I figured it would be OK after a night's rest. I was packed, and looking forward to a few days of normality. I wasn't going to let anything spoil our few days away together.

CHAPTER TWENTY NINE

It was a warm but cloudy day with a light, south-westerly breeze. Sally and Caitlin had their breakfast and looked at the map to plan their route to Cambridge. Caitlin wanted to pick up some supplies for the festival before leaving. She confessed that she hadn't packed. They agreed they would stop in Salisbury for a late lunch in a restaurant they both liked and would leave at twelve thirty.

Sally had time to kill. Caitlin suggested she could drop her off at the castle; she could do her favourite easy walk back via the cliffs and the fields. They both went upstairs to get ready. Sally came down in a tracksuit. Her hair pinned on top of her head in a bun. Before they left the house, she pulled a cap firmly down on her head to keep the sun from her eyes. They drove out of the gates at nine fifty.

At ten forty, a green Mazda sports car turned into the drive. The car traversed slowly round to the side of the house and stopped. David Jones levered himself out. He was dressed in dark trousers and a black polo shirt. He stood looking around, listening for any sounds as he slipped on a pair of thin latex gloves. Satisfied he was alone, he fished a key out of his pocket and tried the back door. The key didn't fit. He had been told the locks had been changed, but he thought it was worth a try. He looked around the outside. Tried the key under the mat trick, top of the lintel trick. Nothing. There were several plant pots. He felt round each pot. Nothing. He lifted each one, peering underneath. He scowled. If he couldn't find a key he would have to smash a window. He walked round the house. He struck lucky. The French windows to the dining room appeared locked but on pulling the handle down firmly, it opened.

He went in. He knew the house well. He idly went from room to room staring in. A curious expression on his face. Then smiling to himself, he crept up the stairs. He had been told the information he needed should be in the old nursery at the back of the house. He was taking a risk all because that stupid boy had refused. Spineless. When you need something doing properly, do it yourself.

He walked silently down the corridor in his new trainers. He had seen them leave, but it didn't harm to be careful. He found the room he was looking for. He pushed the door open and saw a figure in a grey cap squatting over a box. Without thinking he picked up a heavy brass lampstand. The person sensing his presence turned round. Her eyes were wide and terrified. She tried to protect herself as he brought the lamp down on top of her head; whimpered, fell onto her side and lay still.

David Jones stared at her for a moment. He had seen them both drive away, the one in the cap had been in the passenger seat. What the hell was she doing here? He was angry. She had made him hit her. He dropped the lampstand on the floor beside her, his eyes narrowing with rage. She had had a good look at him. Well, she was collateral damage. He bent down and tried to find a pulse. No matter. He must hurry and find that folder. He looked over, saw a chest of drawers and pulled the top drawer open. Got it. He picked the folder up and glanced inside. He smiled to himself. He had found what he was looking for.

Staring at the unconscious woman lying on the floor, he shrugged and left the room walking down the corridor towards the stairs. He thought he heard a creak, turned round, nothing there. He continued to the stairs. This time he was sure he heard footsteps. Looking to his right, he caught a reflection in the mirror. What the hell. He turned and saw a woman in a floral dress. Her long dark hair flowing down to her shoulders. She looked straight at him and pointed. Those huge blue eyes, staring at him.

He cried out in horror. His foot caught on a carpet grip. Holding onto the folder with his left hand he flung his right arm out to regain his balance. His right hand caught the top of the mirror; he saw it dislodge and clatter down the stairs. It shattered on the tiles below. For a brief moment, time stood still. He couldn't stop himself falling. Letting go of the folder, he tried to catch hold of the banister but it was out of his reach. The impetus of the fall sent him tumbling down the stairs. The papers from the folder floated down around him. The last image he had was that of Cecilia Rose. The woman he remembered from so long ago. Then his head met the red and gold tiled floor on the hall with a sickening thud.

CHAPTER THIRTY

Caitlin, her head down carrying a bag full of bottles of water, energy bars and baby wipes for the festival, almost collided with Bob outside the local shop. "I'm off to spend a few hours, clearing, pruning and mowing your neighbour's lawn."

"You're so good Bob. Is that at Marjorie's?"

"Yeah, one of my favourite customers." He winked at her. "Aren't you and Sally supposed to be off to Cambridge this morning? What time are you going?"

"I'm on my way back now with all this lot." She put down her bag and looked at her watch. "Gosh, it's gone eleven." Bob looked surprised, "Already, I'm going to be late."

"So am I, I've got to pack up the car yet and we're off at midday. We'll see you when we get back. I'll try and get you some interesting CDs." She leaned over and kissed his cheek. He thought how lovely she was looking in a flowery summer dress and cream pumps. She often wore shorts in the garden - he thought about her bare brown legs then quickly looked away in case she read the expression in his eyes. As he walked back up the road, he called, "Stay safe and enjoy the music. See you when you get back."

Caitlin hurried in the opposite direction, unlocked her car and drove back to Rock House. She parked the car under the trees at the side of the house, close to the garage. She opened the boot and picked up the bag of supplies. Standing with it in her hand, she looked around her. No sign of Sally yet. There was no point in taking the bag inside, just to put it back in the car again. Instead, she opened the passenger door and deposited the bag there, thinking with satisfaction that it would leave plenty of space for their cases, coats, blankets and camping chairs. She just had to locate everything in double quick time now.

She walked back round to the front, rummaged in her shoulder bag for the door keys and opened the door. Looking down at her feet she spotted something shiny. Bending over, she saw it was a sliver of glass. She picked it up with great care, frowning as she did so and laid it down on the ground outside. She stepped through the door looking around to see if there was any more glass on the tiles. She stood still. There was glass scattered all over the floor. It must be glass from the mirror.

She glanced up to look for the gap where it had once hung; instead she couldn't help her eyes focusing on what looked like a bundle of clothes at the bottom of the stairs. She stepped in to investigate. Her foot went down hard on a piece of glass, she slipped and fell on her hands and knees. Crying out in pain and shock, she tried to get to her feet, pushing up with her hands but encountering more glass. She sat down, wincing as she pulled out a large piece of glass from her knee. Hardly noticing the blood coursing down her leg she quickly pushed what glass she could see away from her, smearing blood on the floor as she did so. She managed to get to her feet, wiping her bloodied hands on her dress. Photographs and papers were scattered all over the floor.

What had looked like a bundle of clothes was in fact a figure dressed in black. Lying on its front, one leg bent back at a strange angle; the white trainer at the bottom of the trouser leg oddly clean. She limped over and stared down at it. The head was turned to the right, the cheek resting on the manilla folder she had left upstairs.

Peering down she could see a large piece of the mirror had lodged in the neck. There was a trickle of blood resting on the front of the folder. Not much. She knelt down, ignoring the pain in her left knee. Gold framed glasses twisted on its nose. Eyes wide open. The dead eyes of David Jones staring at her. She clutched the bottom of the banister to haul herself up, then stood over his body a slight smile on her face. "He's dead Cessie." She murmured, "The bastard's dead."

She backed away then turned and limped to the other side of the hall; picked up the phone and dialled 999. "Police and ambulance quickly. There's been an accident. I think he's dead. Please hurry." A calm voice asked her for details. "We'll be there as soon as possible."

The front door was still open. She looked at her watch. It was eleven thirty. Should she go outside and wait, but she desperately wanted to pee. Meaning to go to the bathroom, she walked back to the bottom of the stairs cocking her head to one side. Had she heard a faint sound? "Cessie, are you up there?" She considered the body then stepped over it and began to climb the stairs. She heard the sound again. It must be her mother. There couldn't be anybody else here. Reaching the top, she looked down at David Jones and shuddered, then walked down the corridor willing her mother's ghost to materialise. She felt like her four year old self, needing to be comforted and reassured. The nursery door was open. She stood on the threshold. There was someone lying on the floor. She saw the grey cap and cried out, "Oh Sally, no, no, no. What are you doing here?"

Sally groaned, her eyes flickered for a moment. She sighed and went quiet again.

Caitlin fell to her knees, ignoring the pain. "Sal, look

at me. This shouldn't have happened. Come on, please wake up." A heavy brass lampstand lay on the floor beside Sally. On reflex, she reached over and touched it, then snatched her hand away. "You bastard Jones, I hope you rot in hell."

She heard a shout. "Hello, is anybody here?" She eased herself up from the floor, wincing she ran down the corridor to the top of the stairs where she saw a young male police officer looking up at her. "What are you doing up there Miss? What's happened here? Are you the homeowner?" Caitlin moved closer, as though she was going to come down. "No, stay where you are for now Miss."

"My friend's injured up here. Where's the ambulance? She needs help." They both stood still listening as sirens began to sound in the distance.

The police officer, trying to appear calm, called up to Caitlin. "How badly hurt is your friend? I'm going to call in for more help." He reached for his police radio. He stared down at the dead body. "Is this man known to you?"

Caitlin shook her head in disbelief at his repeated questions and turned round, limping back in to Sally. Sitting at her side, she held her hand in her own bloodied one. "It's going to be alright, help's coming." She thought she saw Sally blink and held her hand more tightly. She kept talking. "I can hear them downstairs. There's a police officer down there, he'll send them up. You're going to be alright Sally."

Two paramedics stood at the front door. The police officer, breathing a sigh of relief, called to them. "Over here. Careful, there's glass all over the floor." They walked over and the female paramedic squatted down to look at the body. She felt for a pulse and looked up at both men. "He's gone." She peered closely, "There's glass lodged in the neck, but I doubt if that killed him." The police officer looked very pale. "Are you alright constable? Don't faint on us."

"I'm OK. There's someone else upstairs injured." He looked nervous, "Oh lord, we're going to have to disturb the crime scene." The paramedics stepped over the body and without hesitation ran up the stairs. Caitlin heard their footsteps and shouted, "We're in here." She saw two paramedics dressed in green. They saw a dark haired woman sitting beside a body. She seemed unaware that her leg was bleeding and that she had cuts to her arms and hands. She pushed her hair off her face, leaving a trace of blood on her forehead. "My friend Sally's been hurt. Help her please."

One of the paramedics immediately strode over, bent down and felt Sally's pulse. "She's breathing." He looked at the lampstand beside her. "It looks as though she's had a blow to the head." He turned to Caitlin, "What's your friends name?"

Caitlin looked dazed. "Oh, thank god she's alright."

"No, I didn't say she was alright. We need to get her into hospital. What are your names?"

"I'm Caitlin Rose, and this is Sally, Sally Thomas."

"OK Caitlin, when my colleague comes back we are going to lift Sally onto a stretcher and take her out to the ambulance. We will treat her there before we take her into hospital. You are coming too. Let me see that leg and your hands." Caitlin looked up at him. "I'm alright. I fell, that's all."

"You're not alright Caitlin." He looked with concern at her leg. "Looks as though you still have some glass lodged in there. We'll patch you up as soon as we can. Just hang on in there and keep talking to Sally. We won't be a moment. My name's Gary and my colleague's called Joan. We're going to be looking after you. As soon as Joan's back we'll get going."

Joan strode into the room, carrying the stretcher and a bag. The police officer followed. He gazed down at Sally. Caitlin thought he looked so young. Poor man, he doesn't know what to do. He's pretending to be brave. "What's happened to her? How did she get hurt?" Turning back to Caitlin the police officer demanded, "Where were you when all this was going on?"

Gary, the paramedic looked up in disbelief. "That can wait Constable, we need to get both these young ladies to hospital." Addressing Joan he said, "This is Sally Thomas, she may have a brain injury. Caitlin has been injured and is clearly in shock and your questions Constable, can wait."

Caitlin sank further to the ground, her head in her hands. The female paramedic put a blanket round her. "Come on love. We'll get Sally comfortable on the stretcher, then we'll take you both down to the ambulance." Caitlin tried to lever herself over onto her side to get up, wincing as pain shot through her leg. "Careful, I can see a piece of glass in your leg. Let me help you." Joan opened her bag and took out some dressings. Squatting down, she examined Caitlin's knee, gently covered the cut with gauze, bandaging it in place. Then she plucked a piece of glass out of Caitlin's leg with a pair of tweezers, causing blood to spurt out. Giving Caitlin a dressing, she asked her to hold it firmly onto the area. Applying pressure, she taped the dressing in place staunching the flow of blood which had been running freely down Caitlin's leg. "Just sit there for a moment, while we lift Sally. Then I'll help you up. Do you think you can walk down the stairs?" Caitlin nodded. By now tears were streaming down her face. "What a mess." She whispered, "It was Cessie. Did you see her when you came up?"

The police officer frowned, "Is there someone else here? Where are they?" Caitlin shook her head. "No-one else."

The paramedics had lifted Sally and were ready to take her down to the ambulance. Joan looked over at the police officer. "Caitlin's clearly in shock. We need to get them both into hospital. Can you help her down the stairs please. There's nothing we can do for the man down there now. That will be up to your forensic team."

The paramedics led the way, followed by the police officer holding Caitlin by her right arm. They manoeuvred the stretcher down the stairs, stepping over the body. Caitlin held onto the banister with her left hand. The police officer went to stop her. She looked him square in the face. "Haven't you noticed, the dead man's wearing rubber gloves? There won't be fingerprints." She bit her lip. "This is awful. I can't bear it." Looking shamefaced, he steered her round the body. "Careful now, don't slip on the glass again." Very close to tears, her voice shaking with emotion, she whispered, "He's only got what he deserved." The police officer looked startled. "You know him, Miss. Why didn't you say?" She shook her head, and walked away.

The paramedics had lifted Sally into the ambulance. Joan stepped back out to help Caitlin inside. They heard a vehicle rattling down the drive. Caitlin turned round and saw it was Bob's van. She wanted to get out and speak to him, Joan shook her head. "No, love, we need to go. The sooner we get Sally in and comfortable the better. I'm sure our young Constable here can deal with it."

"Please, I just want to ask him to do something." Bob got out of his van. He called over. "What's happened?" He saw Caitlin standing at the door of the ambulance, "Oh god Cat, you're injured." Her voice shook as she called out. "I'm alright, it's Sally who's really injured. She's been attacked. Can you ring Charlie for me?"

"Yes, but what's happened to you?"

"Sir," Joan interrupted, "We need to go. The Constable can fill you in." She shut the ambulance door and strode round to open the driver's door. With sirens blaring, the ambulance passed a police car approaching them down the drive. Reinforcements had arrived.

Bob stood watching as the ambulance sped away. Puzzled and apprehensive he saw two plain clothed police officers climbing out of their car and walking over to talk to the uniformed officer standing on the front door step.

CHAPTER THIRTY ONE

BOB

I left Caitlin in a reflective mood. I had been told about the outcome of her talk with Bert and the discovery of incriminating material in David Jones's bungalow. Despite the pace of the revelations she seemed strangely upbeat and relaxed. The magnitude of the recent breakthrough may not have sunk in. Well, good luck to them going away for a few days. Caitlin was going to need all the encouragement we could give her when the police started investigating her mother's death, the fraud and the failed entrapment.

I heard the first siren but I was so absorbed in pruning back overgrown bushes in the back garden that I thought no more of it. Sometime later I heard another siren in the distance. The sound increased as the vehicle turned into our road. I walked to the front gate to see where it was going but it had already disappeared. My customer came out to ask me if I knew where the ambulance had gone. She had seen it coming up the road from her upstairs window and was worried something had happened to one of her elderly neighbours. Despite me trying to reassure her, she asked me to find out. I hesitated, not being one to pry into other's affairs, but I acquiesced and wandered up the road. I couldn't see where the ambulance had gone. I felt my heart lurch, if indeed a heart can lurch. Rock House has a long driveway, if the ambulance had gone there, I wouldn't be able to see it from the road. I quickened my pace. As I hurried round the last bend I saw a police car and an ambulance. Caitlin, a blanket wrapped round her shoulders, was being helped into the back of the ambulance. I ran towards her as she called out to me. She let the blanket slip; I could see blood on her arms. Her left leg had been bandaged. My heart really did lurch now. She called out to me to contact Charlie before the doors were closed and the ambulance pulled away.

I stood still for some minutes trying to digest what I had just witnessed. She had said she was OK but Sally had been injured. My thoughts turned to Dennis. He had been threatening both of them. What had he done? I turned and looked towards the house. A second police car had pulled up outside the front door. Two plain clothed police officers, their backs towards me, were conversing with a uniformed officer. I walked towards them. As I drew closer I recognised the tall figure of Sam Huxley wearing a uniform fitting loosely over his gangly frame. He had been in the same year as Justin at school. Teased about his big feet, the other children called him Mr Plod, and now here he was a real Mr Plod, kind and helpful Sam, his innocent young face screwed up with anxiety.

He was so engrossed, he didn't notice me, but I heard what he was saying. "I think there is someone else in there. I couldn't leave the injured women to search. Shall I search the house now?" One of the officers snapped, "Check the perimeters, but first repeat what the woman said." I couldn't help smiling as I watched Sam. His demeanour was of a naughty boy being ticked off by a school teacher; trying to think up an excuse.

"She said, 'did you see her? Cessie must have done it.'" I moved in closer.

"Excuse me butting in but I might be able to help you." Both plain clothed officers turned round. The older of the two frowned and asked me who I was and what I was doing there, so I asked them who they were. They both pulled out their ID; that's how I first encountered Detective Inspector Paul Benson and Detective Sergeant Harry James.

Sam blurted out, "It's Bob Saunders. What are you doing here Bob?" I explained that I was a friend of the family and worked for Caitlin; that I had heard the sirens and had come to investigate. "I overheard what you thought Caitlin said to you. If she said 'Cessie' then you won't find anyone else in the house. Caitlin thinks she sees her mother's ghost. It's a long story - Cecilia was killed when Caitlin was a child. Can you tell me what's happened here. A man has been threatening them recently. Did he attack them?"

Ignoring the glares from the other officers, Sam said, "A man fell to his death down the stairs. Do you know the identity of the man who was threatening the ladies?" He turned to the others, his eyes wide. "Bob might be able to identify him." DI Benson nodded his head. Both officers pulled on blue latex gloves and I followed the three of them to the front door. What met our eyes will haunt me. The floor was covered with glass; despite the colour of the floor tiles I could see smears of blood. A figure in black lay at the bottom of the stairs, his body at a strange angle. I could hear the sound of glass crunching under my feet as I walked over and stared at eyes that would normally have been disguised behind wire-rimmed glasses. I knew I was looking at pure evil.

The DI bent over the body. "Is this the man who was threatening them?" I shook my head. "No, but I know who it is. He's a retired solicitor by the name of David Jones."

David Jones was wearing similar gloves to the detectives which struck me as strangely incongruous. His head resting on a manilla folder. I could see papers strewn around the floor. Looking round me, I couldn't help commenting. "It looks as though he found what he was searching for. He must have been surprised by something, bringing the mirror down as he tumbled down the stairs. Caitlin has been saying that mirror needed moving. She was waiting for the decorators."

The DS raised his eyebrows. "You know a great deal Sir, but we mustn't jump to conclusions, must we? Did he fall or was he pushed? I've heard some excuses in my time but a ghost takes the biscuit."

I stood there thinking, you sarcastic bastard. I wasn't going to let it go. "If you're jumping to the conclusion that Caitlin Rose has anything to do with this you couldn't be more mistaken. I was with Caitlin until gone eleven when I went to work at number six. You should concentrate on finding out what this man has been up to. Look at his gloves for God's sake." I could feel my voice rising with indignation.

"Well, me thinks you protest too much Sir." DS James said in a sardonic tone. "Having a fling with the young lady are you?" DI Benson intervened. "That's enough Sergeant. Constable Huxley, take Mr Saunders' details and ask him to come to the station later to make a statement, and escort him out. Thank you." They both turned their backs on me. "Total bastards." I muttered under my breath as I stamped out heedless of the glass. Sam followed me outside. "Not a good idea to get on the wrong side of that pair, Bob. You're not involved with the young lady are you?" The attitude of some police officers infuriates me, but not Sam's. I softened, "No

Sam, I'm not. I garden for Caitlin; we're friends, that's all. Just let them try and stitch her up." Sam looked crestfallen. "Sorry Sam, it's not your fault. I'm working at Marjorie Wheeler's. I'll square it with her and then come down to the station to make a statement, OK?" He nodded. "Caitlin said Sally had been injured. Can you tell me what happened?"

"It looks as though she was hit over the head. The paramedics stretchered her out. She seemed to be coming in and out of consciousness. The other lady slipped on the glass and hurt herself. They've taken them both to the county hospital."

"Thanks Sam. You'd better go back in and supervise." He grinned at me and went back into the house. I walked slowly back up the driveway. I remembered Caitlin had found Charlie Bond's name in the Yellow Pages. I needed to contact her asap.

CHAPTER THIRTY TWO

Constable Sam Huxley went back inside. This was the first violent death he had attended; he was unsure what to do with himself. DI Benson was watching his sergeant go through the dead man's pockets, and Sam was watching the DI. He didn't like him much. He had a reputation for getting the job done but despite that he had the look of a man disappointed with life. His hair had receded to a stage where he asked for a number one at the barbers. Consequently, almost bald, his head appeared insignificant sitting on top of his chunky body. The lack of hair did nothing to improve his features. His small blue eyes had sunk away into fat. His nose had been broken at some point giving his face a lopsided appearance. To make things worse there was something reptilian about him. Perhaps it was the way he licked his lips repeatedly.

"It's definitely David Jones." DS James held up the driving licence card he had found in the dead man's wallet. "He has a set of car keys." He turned them over and over in his hand, examining the fob. "It's a Mazda. He probably drove here, so where's his car?"

"If he broke in, it's not going to be in plain sight." He looked round at Sam, "Go and have a scout outside, see if you can locate it. Harry, get those papers collected up off the floor and bagged." DS James sprang up off his knees. In contrast to his DI, he looked strong, fit and healthy. The sort of man who cared for himself; he would work out and be able to sprint after and catch escaping criminals. He knew full well that DI Benson was too fat and ungainly to carry out physical tasks, but he didn't mind. Harry was in awe of his brain power. The way he could identify evidence and shape it into a working theory never failed to impress him.

Sam came back in. "I've found it. It's a green Mazda sports car parked round the back and the engine's still warm. I checked all the doors. The kitchen door's locked but there are some French windows leading into the dining room that opened. I reckon that's the way he must have got in. What do you think he was doing here Sir?" The DI threw the question back at Sam. "What do you think happened?"

"Well," Sam said in a tentative manner, "it looks as though Miss Rose came in, saw the body and in a panic slipped on the glass. She hurt herself quite badly. She rang 999 at eleven thirty a.m. Then for some reason she went upstairs and found her friend. That's when I first saw her. I shouted and she appeared on the stairs asking where the ambulance was."

"Yes, but the question is, why did she go upstairs?" DI Benson mused, "Her friend, by all accounts was unconscious. She couldn't have heard anything. I have a different theory. I think she was already up there. She pushed David Jones and caused the mirror to fall on top of him. Then she went down, phoned 999 and indeed may have slipped or perhaps she deliberately injured herself. Where's the forensics team, they should have been here by now. It would be useful if we could find out the approximate time of death. Bob Saunders said it was after eleven a.m. when he met Caitlin Rose outside the local shop. Even if it was just after eleven a.m. it gives her plenty of time to get back here. Then she discovers he has broken in…"

"But Sir," Sam unwisely interrupted the DI's chain of thought, "if she was already upstairs, why didn't she get attacked? Why would she bother to make up a story that she came in and found him? She wasn't cool and calculated or anything like that. The paramedics said she was in shock. She had glass embedded in her leg. She didn't even seem to feel it. It doesn't make sense."

"Well laddie, it will become clear when we have examined all the evidence. Now I suggest you have a look round the house. You thought there might be someone else here. They could still be hiding." DS James smirked at his boss. "Be careful young Sam, the ghost might jump out at you. Whoooooo!"

"Cut it out Harry, have some respect for the dead."

"Scout round outside Sam, see if anything's been disturbed. Now, let's have a look at those papers. It appears they were important enough for a retired solicitor to risk his reputation by breaking into a house. What have they got to tell us?" DI Benson opened the evidence bag and sorted the papers out. He whistled. "I think we have our motive."

They heard a vehicle approaching, pull up, and doors slamming. "The cavalry has arrived." DS James walked over to the front door and called out a greeting. The pathologist, Dr Finch, looked up and raised his arm. He and the two technicians began dressing themselves in protective clothing, masks, gloves, boots; pulling up their hoods before entering. Dr Finch greeted the two detectives and walked over to study the body.

"Looks like he's broken his neck." He kneeled down and looked more closely. "His muscles are still relaxed. He has pallor but there's no discolouration of the skin. You can see there is only slight seepage of blood from the glass cutting into his neck."

"I know you don't like guessing Doc, but can you put

a time on it?" DI Benson gave what he thought was an ingratiating smile. "Well, in this case I think I can say death was pretty recent, within the last hour. Looks as though he was an intruder. Do you know what happened here?"

"No, we don't know yet. We think he came in through an open door, no sign of a break in. We also know there may have been two women in the property at the time, one of them was attacked. Harry, go and locate Constable Huxley. From his account a young woman was knocked unconscious in a room upstairs. We need to know who attacked her."

Dr Finch looked around the hall. "Was the mirror knocked off the wall in the fall, or beforehand?" He very gently lifted the man's protruding leg, carefully replacing it in the same position. "Yes, there's glass under his body. The mirror went first. The glass in his neck, by the way, didn't kill him. It's lodged in pretty well but there's little blood flow. There is, however, quite a lot of blood on the floor." He walked over towards the front door. "Ah here, about three paces from the front door, someone has been injured. There's a piece of glass with blood on its tip." He leaned over, picked it up, examined it then put it into an evidence bag. "I can just see a trail of blood on the tiles. I would guess someone has slipped and fallen on the glass whilst walking over to view the body. Then walked back over to the phone to call for help."

Dr Finch stood back whilst the technicians finished taking photographs of the body and its surrounds. "Thanks, you can take the body out now then and we'll have a look upstairs, see what that can tell us."

David Jones was placed in a body bag and zipped up. Dr Finch walked over and picked up several pieces of the mirror's frame. "This is pretty old." He looked up at the wall. "Dark marks where it has hung and the paint is lighter behind it. Look, the wire holding it up was corroded. Not surprising it broke." He started to walk up the stairs and pointed out an indentation in the wooden banister. "This looks fresh. Probably the mirror fell at this angle, struck the banister, broke and the whole thing went down smashing on the floor with some force."

He walked up the last few steps and bent over. "The carpet grip here is a bit loose. Although he's got trainers on, it's possible he caught his foot. This grip is looser than the one on the other side. The picture hook has come away from the wall." He reached out and wiggled his finger in the hole. "Don't think it's even been plugged. Probably been there for donkey's years. An accident waiting to happen." He stood on the top step, measuring the angles. "Strange place for a mirror. He may have been looking in it. Over balanced, caught his foot. Reached out to steady himself knocking the mirror off the wall. The noise of it falling and smashing down onto the tiles below would have unnerved him. He was holding a folder. Might not have wanted to let it go so hesitated too long to rebalance himself, and over he went."

The three police officers stood at the bottom of the stairs looking up at Dr Finch as he concluded, "That's what I think happened." DI Benson breathing hard, climbed up the stairs to join him. "How do we know he wasn't pushed."

"We don't, but it has all the hallmarks of an accident. He was an intruder. He may have been hurrying. You said a woman was injured up here." Sam called, "Shall I come up Sir?" The DI nodded his head. "Show Dr Finch where you found the injured woman, Constable." They followed Sam up the corridor. He pointed to the door. "This is the one. Last one on the right."

"There are a lot of boxes in here. Must be some sort of storeroom now. Where was the injured woman lying, Constable?" Sam walked over by one of the open boxes and showed Dr Finch where Sally had fallen. He described the scene, how her friend had sat beside her, her leg bleeding. He pointed out the blood stains on the floor. "I think she was sorting that box out. There's packing paper on the floor. The paramedic thought she had been hit with that lamp over there. Looks heavy enough."

"Thanks, Constable. We'll check for fingerprints in here." He walked over to the cupboard by the window. The top drawer had been left open. "He was looking for that folder." He shut his eyes for a moment. "Did he know where it was? Have you noticed anything else that's been disturbed Constable?"

"No Sir, but when I found his car, the engine was still warm. He wasn't here for long. As you say, he must have known what he was looking for and where it was."

DI Benson licked his lips and spoke for the first time. "We don't know that the intruder hit the woman. It could have been someone else. It all looks a bit too contrived to me. We need to get a statement off those two women. Where did the ambulance take them Constable?"

"I didn't ask Sir, sorry. I expect it's the County Hospital."

"Nothing more we can do here, Sergeant. We'll find out where they are and get over there tout suite."

"Thank you, Doc. Not sure I agree with all your theories, we'll see what the women come up with before they get a chance to fabricate their stories. Stay here

Constable, secure the property and get the tape up at the front entrance, then get back down to the station. You can take the statement from the chap who identified the body."

CHAPTER THIRTY THREE

Returning home, Bob immediately began to search the Yellow Pages. He remembered that was how Caitlin had found Charlie Bond; indeed there it was, "Charlie Bond Investigations". He rang. "Charlie, this is Bob, Caitlin's friend. I'm afraid there's been an accident in Rock House. Caitlin and Sally have been taken to the County Hospital. Cat was asking for you."

He heard a short intake of breath, "What's happened?"

"It seems David Jones broke into the house. He attacked Sally and ended up at the bottom of the stairs with a broken neck."

"Is Caitlin OK?"

"The mirror at the top of the stairs had come down and smashed on the tiles. I think she may have hurt herself on the glass. Luckily, the first person on the scene was one of our local bobbies. He told me what had happened. Can you get over to the hospital? The detectives who arrived at the scene are bloody awful. They're convinced Caitlin pushed David Jones down the stairs. She's going to need help."

Next he rang his Aunt Ann. Her reaction surprised him. "Oh, the foolish, foolish girl. She wanted to stir things up. What a mess. And Sal's injured through it. Cat's going to blame herself. Which hospital are they in?"

"They're at the County. Hold on for a bit Ann. I'd like to come with you but I have to go and give a statement first. It shouldn't take too long, then we can go together."

The police station was only a short walk away, but Bob took his van. He had promised to pick Ann up as soon as he was finished with the police. In the meantime, she would ring the hospital.

He parked close to the station, walking the last few yards towards the building. It was on the corner of the road. Solid and square, built of local stone, two chimney stacks on the roof and a concrete plaque over the door - Dorset County Police 1899. A hundred and three years of community policing, and now Sam had joined their ranks, keeping local traditions alive.

He went in and rang the bell on the front desk. A door opened and Sam strode through. Bob was surprised to see how nervous he still looked. "Follow me Bob." Then he murmured, "Top brass are here." He opened the door to Interview Room Two. A plain clothed officer was seated at the desk leaning over an open folder. He got up and smiled at Bob. "Bob, this is Superintendent Fletcher. He's going to sit in. He has an interest in the case."

"Oh, I've just come to give a statement. I identified the dead man, and I'm Caitlin and Sally's friend, that's all. I can't tell you much. I thought this wouldn't take long."

"I understand Mr Saunders. I won't hold you up for too long. I've been tracking Mr Jones and his associates. If you can give me the heads up on what you think he was doing in that house, I'd be grateful. Constable Huxley will take you through your statement and then we'll have a brief chat. Can I get you a drink? I expect we could all do with one." He smiled again and left, leaving Bob and Sam looking at one another.

"A superintendent getting the tea, that must be a first. What's going on Sam? Who is he?"

"He's a big cheese in the Fraud Squad. DI Benson called him in. He got here in double quick time. It must be something important. He'll be back in a minute. Can we begin the statement." Bob started his account, where he had been and why he had arrived on the scene. The Superintendent came back in with a tray of tea and biscuits. Offered sugar, Sam stirred two spoonfuls into his mug.

The Superintendent sat listening to Bob until he had finished his statement. "Mr Saunders, I understand you know Miss Rose well. Are you able to tell me what relationship Miss Rose had with Mr Jones?" Bob was unsure how much to divulge. He would stick to facts.

"Caitlin's mother was killed about thirty years ago. David Jones was the retired solicitor who administered the Trust Fund for Caitlin. She knew nothing about the fund until her stepfather's death about eighteen months ago. She hadn't expected an inheritance and accepted what she was told. She went to see Mr Jones a short while ago to ask him what he remembered about her mother. It must have set alarm bells ringing for him. He was clearly looking for something he thought she had. If you want to know any other details, you had better ask Caitlin yourself. She will want to tell you."

"You seem to be close to her. Have you been helping her?"

"She's a customer of mine and a friend and yes, I have been helping her. I'll be more than willing to tell you my part in it but I think you should hear Caitlin's story first. It shouldn't come from me." Bob sat back in his chair expecting a barrage of questions, but the Superintendent merely nodded. Bob blurted out, "Those two officers at the scene are going to try to stitch Caitlin up for murder. It's ridiculous. They were appalling."

"I'm sorry to hear that." The Superintendent spoke in a gentle voice. "The detectives will want to talk to her at some point and I will be taking a statement from Miss Rose as soon as she's fit to give one. We have to wait for the Pathologist's report, but as I understand it, all the evidence points towards an accident. Now, I'm grateful for your time, but I can see you are anxious to go to your young friends. I hope they both make a speedy recovery." Bob stood up; the Superintendent came around the desk and shook his hand. His composed manner was meant to reassure Bob. Both men were of similar height, able to stand face to face; each man stood appraising the other. The Superintendent's thin face shone with intelligence. Bob's face shone with uneasiness. "Good to meet you, Mr Saunders. Here's my card. Please don't hesitate to phone me if you need me."

When he had left the room, Sam let out a sigh of relief. "I don't know what to make of him, but he seems OK. Better than those other two." Realising what he had said he frowned. "You didn't hear that Bob, I'm not supposed to talk about my superior officers."

"No, you'll get into trouble. Look after yourself Sam and keep your head down. I've got to get to the hospital."

CHAPTER THIRTY FOUR

Sally regained consciousness in the ambulance. Joan, the paramedic, continued to monitor her whilst Caitlin held her hand to reassure her. She was confused and disorientated and had no idea what had happened. Joan explained that she might need a scan to ascertain the extent of the trauma to her brain.

The blue lighted ambulance made record time, pulling into the hospital within fifty minutes. On arrival Gary jumped out of the driver's seat, came round and opened the back doors. He asked Caitlin to wait in the ambulance whilst they stretchered Sally into A&E. Joan came back out minutes later to escort Caitlin in. By now Caitlin was limping badly. Her whole leg throbbed and the cuts on her arms and hands stung. Joan took her into a cubicle in A&E and drew the curtain. "You'll be assessed shortly Caitlin. I'll be giving the charge nurse a brief history. Sally has been taken for a scan, then she'll be admitted so they can keep an eye on her. When she's back you'll be able to go up and sit with her."

"Thanks, Joan. You've been wonderful. But is Sally going to be OK? She seemed so confused."

"It's likely to wear off. The doctor will talk to you both when Sally's back on the ward. You were doing the right thing, just keep talking to her. She'll remember what happened when she's ready. I must go. You're in safe hands now. Take care of yourself and good luck." Now she was alone, unsettled by Joan's kindness, she slumped over. Then she sat up, her whole body convulsed. She clutched her chest as though she was in pain. The tears she had kept back so she could support Sally erupted. When she heard the curtain being pulled back she tried to hide her emotional state, dropping her head to her chest.

She heard a gentle voice say "It's OK," and felt a hand on her shoulder. She looked up at a nurse in a pale blue uniform. "It's good for you to let it out. You've had quite a time of it." Sobs finally turned into gulps. The nurse handed Caitlin a box of tissues. "I'm sorry, I'm not normally a cry-baby."

"I'd be worried about you if you just sat there in silence." The nurse smiled, "My name's Cathy and I'm going to be looking after you whilst you are in here with us." She reached over and poured Caitlin a plastic beaker of water. Caitlin took a sip and tried to smile but it turned into a frown. "I'm a mess. I slipped on glass, but didn't take much notice of it at the time. I found a dead body, an intruder, in my house. I knew him. I still can't believe it. My mind keeps returning to an image of him lying there at the bottom of the stairs. He looked all broken. His glasses were bent and his glassy eyes stared up at me."

She shivered. The nurse sat down beside her and took her hand. "You've had an awful shock my love. It's bad enough that your home was broken into, but to find a body - terrible. What you are feeling is a natural reaction to what you witnessed. It seems awful now, but with the right help, you'll be OK. Now, let me have a look at that leg. The paramedic thought you may still have slivers of glass embedded in it. Are you in pain?"

"Yes, it is painful, but it's not half as bad as what happened to Sally. I shouldn't be so stupid."

"You're not being stupid. Comparing yourself to your friend won't help your pain. I'm going to take the dressings off your leg. See if I can see any more glass, then I'll redress the leg, clean up your other wounds and you'll be able to go up to the ward."

As the dressings came off, Caitlin felt herself regressing to a time when she refused to feel pain. It was happening again. A flash of memory erupted of a distressed child, pretending, always pretending. She moaned. "Try to relax Caitlin. I'm nearly finished."

Caitlin blinked, the nurse's voice brought her back to the present. She told herself she was in a safe place, but how could anywhere be safe? Her mind had been invaded by hate. Trying to appear natural she murmured, "You've done a real tidy job Cathy. It feels much better."

"I'll give you some dressings and painkillers to take with you, but I'd advise you to go and see a nurse in your local surgery within the next couple of days. Just to get it checked out. Now, I'm going to make you a cup of tea. I'll get you some painkillers too, they should help. As soon as we know where your friend is, we'll take you up to her. Just try and relax for a bit."

It felt like an eternity before Caitlin was wheeled up to Ward 7. She had remonstrated with the porter, but he insisted she sit in the wheelchair. She complied, feeling powerless. They went up in the lift. The porter was cheerful and very chatty, a man who enjoyed his job.

He wheeled Caitlin into a private room. It was light and airy, with a view of the busy dual carriageway below. The glazing let muffled traffic noise through. Sally was lying in bed, her eyes closed. Caitlin sat down on the chair beside her. Her hair was spread out over the pillow, tendrils of red curl escaping across her forehead and left cheek. She was very pale. Caitlin noticed she still had vestiges of mascara on her eyelashes. A few hours ago

Caitlin had feared David Jones had killed her. She shivered as she pictured Sally lying unconscious and unresponsive. How could she have let this happen to her friend?

Her thoughts were interrupted by a grey haired nurse, wearing a dark blue uniform bustling into the room. She had the sort of no nonsense look about her that would strike fear into the heart of an inexperienced nurse. She picked up the chart on the end of Sally's bed and scanned it. She was evidently satisfied with what she read. When she greeted Caitlin her voice was warm.

"I'm Sister Lloyd, I'm in charge of the ward. I understand Sally was struck by an intruder in your home. It looks as though you've both been attacked. What happened to you?" She squatted down beside Caitlin to examine her leg.

"I found a dead body at the bottom of the stairs." Caitlin looked down at her bandaged leg. "I fell on glass from a shattered mirror. Then I found poor Sally unconscious." Sister Lloyd looked surprised. "Oh my dear, what a dreadful experience. That explains why we've had the police on the phone. I've told them, under no circumstances would I have them on my ward. They will have to wait. Sally isn't fit enough to be interviewed." Caitlin looked over at Sally. "Is it normal for her to be sleeping. She regained consciousness in the ambulance. She was wide awake then." Sister Lloyd smiled. "Yes, don't worry, she's making good progress. Her vital signs are normal now. The doctor will be on his rounds shortly. He'll talk to you and Sally about her head injury. We have you down as her next of kin, is that right?"

"Yes I am. We look after each other."

They both looked round as an immaculately dressed man in a grey suit and a white shirt loosened at the collar strolled into the room. Tall and darkly handsome, he was calm and self-assured. He smiled and shook Caitlin's hand. She tried not to wince. "Hello, I'm Rohan Kumar, Senior Registrar, looking after Miss Thomas. I hear you two ladies have been in the wars." He looked over at Sally, "Ah good, Miss Thomas is waking up." Sally looked around, unsure of where she was. She smiled when she saw Caitlin and struggled to sit up. Dr Kumar sat on the bed beside her.

"You are one lucky lady, Miss Thomas." He pulled an object out of his pocket. It looked like a mesh ring. Caitlin knew what it was. He held it up as though he had just conjured it. "Your hair is wonderfully thick. You had it all tucked up on top of your head in this little gadget. Not only that, you covered it all up in a cap. Without it, the blow you received to your head might have caused major trauma. Because you were knocked unconscious, we scanned to make sure, but I'm pleased to say there's no sign of intracranial bleeding." He reached out and handed Sally her hair ring. "I remember," she murmured, "it was the wind. I wanted my hair out of the way. It gets so tangled in the wind." Dr Kumar's dark eyes twinkled. "That's good, you're beginning to remember already."

Sister Lloyd handed him Sally's chart. He skimmed it. "So, you've been dizzy and nauseous and your vision has been a little distorted. All normal symptoms after a blow to the head. They should subside quite quickly. We'll keep you in under observation tonight, and see how you are tomorrow." Sally's voice sounded weak. "I've got a horrible headache; I can't remember what happened."

"Sister will be round with the medication after supper. She can give you something to relieve your headache. Memory loss is typical after head trauma. It usually returns quite quickly, and I'm sure your friend here will help you all she can." He stood up and smiled down at her. "Time is a good healer. I'll drop in to see you tomorrow morning Miss Thomas." He turned to Caitlin. "You are welcome to stay with your friend for a while. No more visitors tonight though. Miss Thomas needs her rest."

CHAPTER THIRTY FIVE

The journey to the hospital passed without incident until Bob and Ann reached the outskirts of the town. It was early evening and rush hour. They queued all the way into the centre, turned off for the hospital and drove round several car parks trying to find a space. In the end, Bob drove up a residential road and managed to manoeuvre into a tight parking space. Ann and he walked the half a mile back to the hospital. By the time they arrived they were both tired and stressed.

The big double doors into the hospital's main concourse slid open and they hurried in looking around for an enquiry desk. The receptionist confirmed Sally had been admitted and signposted them to the lift and Ward 7. They were disappointed when they were informed Sally was not allowed visitors. They asked to see the nurse in charge.

Sister Lloyd welcomed them both into her office. They introduced themselves as family friends. "Sally is progressing well, we're going to keep her in overnight. Her friend, Caitlin, is sitting in with her at the moment, but it would be better if you were able to take her home. We did offer her some food, but she refused. I'm afraid they've both had a terrible shock."

"Does Sally remember what happened to her?" Ann asked, "We're assuming that she was attacked. Are you able to tell us anything?"

"I'm sorry, no. Caitlin says she found her, that's all we know. I really would advise you take Caitlin home or at least to a place where she feels safe. She can come back tomorrow. Just ring the ward first. There's a chapel area on the second floor with a comfortable sitting room for visitors. I'll explain to Sally and Caitlin that you are here and we will bring Caitlin down to you when she's ready." Dismissed, Ann and Bob went in search of the chapel and visitors' room. Arrows sent them up several corridors, down a flight of stairs; then the arrows disappeared altogether. When they eventually found the room, they both sank down into easy chairs and looked at one another. Bob scratched his head. "I hate hospitals. I never know what to do."

"It's stressful." Ann agreed, "I suppose we will just have to sit here and wait. Caitlin can't go home for goodness sake. It's a crime scene, and from what you say, it's going to need clearing before Caitlin and Sally can go back. That's if they want to go back there, after what's happened. What a calamity!"

"Look at it another way Ann. We could call it justice. We all know he was implicated in your friend Cessie's death. He only got what he deserved."

Sally had been given medication and had fallen asleep again. When Sister Lloyd told Caitlin her friends were waiting for her, she reluctantly agreed to leave Sally. This time, when the porter arrived, she refused the wheelchair point blank. He accompanied her as far as the quiet room, chatting all the way. She barely registered his voice and was relieved when he turned and walked back down the corridor.

She stood by the door, reached out and hesitated, her hand resting on the door handle. She observed two hazy figures through the glass panel. Ann and Bob. What on earth must they think of her. At that moment she understood how completely abandoned she had felt facing death alone. She wanted to cry out for help. A sense of dread was threatening to overwhelm her.

Ann pushed herself up out of her chair and put her arms round her. Caitlin's body was rigid. Holding her at arm's length, Ann gazed at her. As she feared, she saw guilt. "You poor love. How are you feeling?"

"I'm OK, a few cuts and bruises. Sal has a head injury, but the doctor said she was saved by her hair and the cap she was wearing." She looked at them, her eyes over bright, "Isn't that amazing?"

Bob put his arm around her and led her to a chair. "Stop trying to be brave, come and sit down love. I don't think you just have cuts and bruises. You look in pain."

In a faltering voice Caitlin began to tell them how she had found David Jones. She broke down when she told them how she had gone upstairs and found Sally. "He could have killed her. She was lying there so pale and still. She shouldn't have been there. She'd gone for a walk." Bob tried to reassure her but his words sounded wooden even to him. He didn't know how to comfort her. Caitlin stared, her face showed no emotion, her voice was cold. "I don't think anything will be the same again. What gave David Jones the right to come into our home? The man was a monster."

"He won't be able to hurt you or anyone else again." Bob shook his head, "I identified his body, I knew then I was looking at evil." When Caitlin registered what Bob had said, her face changed. It was no longer masklike. Her eyes filled with tears. "Oh Bob, you identified him? I'm so sorry. His dead eyes have stayed in my head ever since I saw him there. Horrible, horrible. If only Sal hadn't been there. He could have killed her."

Ann interrupted, "But he didn't. We can only thank our lucky stars that you and Sal are OK. I'm afraid I'm the reason she was there. I was driving over to the castle to meet some friends, saw Sally and stopped the car. I'd left the back window wide open for Coco to get some air. She saw Sally and jumped out of the window, ran round her and poor Sally tripped over, wrenching her ankle. I'm so sorry. It was all my fault. She tried to make me feel better by saying she had already hurt her ankle last night. I gave her a lift back and she said she might as well clear another box whilst she waited for you."

Caitlin's voice was very quiet, almost a whisper. "As simple as that. Fate has played a trick on us."

The three of them looked up as the door swung open, "Can I come in?"

CHAPTER THIRTY SIX

CHARLIE

So David Jones was dead. The first and last time I had seen him was when I photographed him as he left his house for the tennis club. His white hair slicked back; his beard neatly trimmed. His jumper slung casually around his shoulders. He looked smart, fit and ready for fun. A man who wanted to make a particular impression.

When he returned home unexpectedly I had just managed to get out of the bungalow. No time to check everything was in order. I had sensed him when I hid in the garden. He stood outside smoking a cigarette, even though he had an overflowing ash tray on the kitchen table. Had he known all along that I was there? Was he teasing me? But breaking into Rock House, that made no sense. He may have discovered I had taken some of the papers, but why think they were in Rock House? I could kick myself. I should never have agreed to leave the emails with Caitlin. I had noticed a change in her when she realised the part David Jones played in her mother's story. I feared she had been flirting with danger. Her mother's death had undoubtedly festered within her. However, the unravelling of it had only just begun. The pieces of the jigsaw barely revealed, let alone neatly sorted. Caitlin wasn't ready. I wasn't ready. It was all too soon. When Bob phoned to tell me what had happened, he said it was finished. Justice had been done. I wasn't sure I agreed. In addition, both young women in my protection had been harmed. I certainly wasn't finished.

It didn't take me long to get to the hospital. Whilst I

located Sally's ward I was transported back to the last time I had been there. My father was waiting for heart surgery. He was cheerful; looking forward to the future. I was glad I retained that memory of him. The planned surgery was too late, he had a heart attack that night and never recovered. It's hard when someone close dies suddenly. Grief hits, and when you are barely able to function, you are thrown into the bureaucracy of death. So much organising. All of it in a haze. My father had wanted a humanist funeral, a celebration, so we had a big party. I was able to say goodbye to him then, but I'm still not convinced he's really gone.

When I reached the ward I wasn't surprised to be told Sally couldn't have visitors. I asked to see the Sister in charge. She was startled when I told her my role in Sally and Caitlin's story. She reassured me she would not have the police on the ward until Sally was strong enough. She suggested I ring the following midday when the doctor would have completed his rounds. Sally might be ready to be discharged in the afternoon. If so, I could make arrangements to collect her. She then signposted me to the visitors' room. Off I went again.

Hospitals feel like an alien world to me. Long corridors closed doors opening onto wards, restricted areas. The bustle of a medical environment where each member of staff carries out their role enabling the whole to function. A world I normally like to appreciate from afar, preferably on the TV.

I glanced at my watch. I was hungry. The canteen was one floor down at ground level. I would suggest we all have something to eat and drink before travelling back. I saw the sign for the chapel and headed for the visitors' room.

I hadn't met Caitlin's friends, Bob the gardener and Aunty Ann. They were all sitting close together on low vinyl chairs with wooden arms. The sort of chair that makes you sweat but is easily wiped. They are never comfortable.

Bob got up effortlessly. I could see he was the fit, wiry gardener type. We shook hands. Aunty Ann rose with a little more effort. An older woman but agile. She was the tennis player. Poor Caitlin looked despondent and stayed put. Finding the body of a man at the bottom of your stairs, a man who may have been a murderer as well as a swindler, would have that effect. However, I figured it was more likely to be his attack on Sally that weighed on Caitlin's mind.

I greeted them all and got straight to the point. No point in beating about the bush. "I'd like to hear what happened Caitlin, but not right now. I've been up on the ward. It looks as though Sally will just be in overnight. We can't do anything here. I would suggest we all go down to the canteen for something to eat before we go. Cat, you can come home with me. I've made the spare room up for you."

Caitlin stood up with difficulty. She was wearing a dress. She usually favoured jeans. Her left leg was heavily bandaged. As I drew closer I could see blood stains on her dress and cream pumps. She had cuts on her bare arms. Her right hand had been bandaged. There was blood seeping through the dressing. She had dark shadows under her eyes. Her head drooped. I put my arm around her shoulder and started to help her towards the door. She picked up a package from the floor. Turning round I saw the other two following.

"The lift is just over there." I pointed, "It's only one

floor, not far. We'll all benefit from eating something. It's been a shocking day." Strange how people react when someone takes charge. They were relieved; happy to leave decisions to someone else.

It was quiet in the canteen. A few staff in white coats were snatching a few minutes away from their duties. I guided Caitlin towards a table in the corner. Bob went over to the counter and came back with cartons of juice and a selection of sandwiches. A practical man.

Caitlin seemed to be in a daze. I encouraged her. "Come on Cat. Have a drink and something to eat. It will help." She shook her head. "I can't believe what's happened. It's cruel. Sally in the wrong place at the wrong time, all because of a sweet little dog. It's incredible." Ann told me what happened with her dog and after that we sat in silence, eating and sipping juice.

Ann toyed with her sandwich then pushed it to one side. "Bob, you and I should go home. As you say Charlie, there's nothing we can do here. Sal can stay with me when she's discharged." She looked over at Caitlin, "I guess it's likely to be a day or two before you can both go home. I've some friends who do cleaning. When the police say it's OK, I can ask them to go in and do a deep clean if you like."

Caitlin nodded, "Thanks Ann and thank you both for being here for me. I was feeling so alone. I hope you don't feel you had a wasted journey. I'll go with Charlie. I suppose the police are going to want to see me tomorrow." I interrupted, "I'll sort that out Cat. Come on, if everyone's finished, let's go."

Caitlin limped out holding onto Ann's arm. Bob hung back with me. "Charlie, when I gave my statement there was a superintendent from the Fraud Squad there. He was very interested in David Jones, said he was already investigating him and his associates. He said he would want a statement from Caitlin."

"What was his name?" I had a sneaking suspicion I knew the answer.

"Superintendent Fletcher. He was a good man. I liked him." I have never believed in coincidences. Despite his subterfuge, I knew the John Fletcher I met in Cornwall was in the force. I'm glad Bob liked him. So did I.

CHAPTER THIRTY SEVEN

CHARLIE

Caitlin was uncommunicative on the journey back. Eventually, she closed her eyes. I left her to her own thoughts.

I spent some of the journey recalling John Fletcher. He had been in Cornwall for a similar reason as me - investigating Alice Brown. Being in the same B&B was serendipity, but being in that particular pub, and asking me questions about her, was not. Why on earth was Alice Brown of interest to the Fraud Squad? Apart from pretending to be Caitlin's cousin, what else was she up to?

I tossed around ideas, all improbable. That led me to think about how much I missed my father's wise counsel. He had a way of seeing the world, conjuring up new angles and perspectives. He would have liked this case. A real live mystery for us to solve. After he died, I sold our home. I couldn't bear to rattle round in that big old house without him. Even worse, I didn't have the time or skill to look after his beloved garden. I think he would have understood. I needed a new start. I used the money to finance my business and to buy a flat. I love the flat. It has a fabulous view of the sea. There is a small balcony with enough room for a few plants and a sitting area to watch the sun go down. Perfect for me. He would have liked it. I think he would have liked John as well.

I pulled in to my parking space at the back of the flats; Caitlin opened her eyes. "We're here Cat. You'll have stiffened up. Wait there and I'll help you out." I walked round to the passenger side and opened the door.

She was strangely compliant, allowing me to guide her towards the lift. She stopped and looked back. "I've left the bag of stuff the hospital gave me. Could you get it for me Charlie?" I left her at the door of the lift and came back with the package. She stared at me, her face glazed over, as though she didn't know who I was. I took her arm again and we rode up to the seventh floor. Inside the flat I sat her down on the sofa. Her eyes glistened then her head jerked up as she stared out over the water. "We're always surrounded by sea." She murmured, "It haunts me. We've been buffeted by those waves for millennia. Giving life and taking life away. Perhaps it will take me away too."

I sat down beside her. "We're drawn to the sea aren't we, that's why we live here. We're never far away from it. My father asked for his ashes to be scattered on the sea. He wanted to be taken by the wind at the end. You're thinking of your mother, and maybe when your time comes Cat, you will want to be taken by the wind too. But not until you have lived a full life. You're thinking about death because you've just been confronted by a violent death. He didn't deserve a good death." She winced, "It was his eyes, Charlie. I keep thinking of his eyes. Those horrible wire framed glasses of his twisted to one side. I hope they've taken him away."

"As soon as the pathologist examined him and confirmed life was extinct, he would have been taken to the mortuary. He's not in your home anymore Cat, and he can't hurt you anymore, because he did hurt you didn't he?" She didn't answer me. She turned away. When she looked back a grim smile drifted across her face. She nodded and bit her lip. "Do you think you might have any clothes that would fit me Charlie. I feel horrible. If I could just wash and change into something clean I'd feel human again." I smiled at her. "I'll find you something. You know me, the perfect sleuth – I've got clothes for everything. They might be a bit short but who cares." Caitlin looked down at her blood stained dress and shoes. "I think the shoes will come clean with a wipe, but this dress can go in the bin. I don't think I ever want to see it again."

The mood lightened after that. Baggy shorts and one of my extra-large tee shirts did the trick. Cat let me redress her hand. She had a deep cut on her palm. I flinched when I saw it. The bandage on her leg was intact. They had given her a large pack of paracetamol, but she didn't want to take any. I thought maybe she wanted to make herself suffer. Then she asked me if I had any whisky. Good plan.

She wanted to talk about Sally. She recalled the panic she felt when she saw her lying on the floor, thinking David Jones had killed her. Sally had been so excited to be part of the investigation, to act as look out as I searched David Jones's bungalow. Maybe they had both thought it was a game, although I had a strong feeling that Caitlin always knew what she was doing.

We both sat looking out at sea, sipping whisky. I could see she was beginning to droop. She looked grateful when I suggested bed. The whisky was doing its work. When I was sure she was settled I rang the station, informed them of Cat's whereabouts and offered to bring her in for an interview in the morning. Then I looked through my notes until I found John Fletcher's private number. Oh yes, he had some explaining to do.

We had spent a pleasant evening together in Cornwall. Almost like old friends; we laughed a lot. I had a suspicion that he was in the force from the moment I first saw him. It was how he looked, how he held himself. He wasn't your run of the mill blokey copper showing off, trying to get me into bed. He was thoughtful and kind and interesting to talk to. In fact, I wouldn't have minded getting into his bed but he didn't ask me.

Bob said he had an interest in David Jones and his associates. What was a superintendent from the Fraud Squad doing investigating Alice Brown and David Jones? What were they up to? Were there any others? I had the impression that Jones was a small fry, country solicitor with his hand in the till. He may have been involved in Caitlin's mother's death, but according to Bert who had been with George and Cecilia Rose that night, the police barely investigated, convinced it was an accident. Only one way to find out. I picked up the phone.

"Hello, is that Superintendent Fletcher? It's Charlie Bond. I'm a private investigator working for Miss Caitlin Rose." There was silence for a moment. "Hello Charlotte. I was hoping you'd call, but not under these circumstances." I choked, "What, you knew who I was all along? Why didn't you say?" He had the temerity to laugh. "No, I only found out when I asked someone at the office. I had a feeling you'd been in the force. Same as you probably did me. In fact, I thought you'd rumbled me." My turn to smile now. "Not until earlier this evening. I went to the hospital to help Caitlin and met Bob the gardener. He mentioned how much he liked you."

I knew better than to ask John what interest he had in the case. I told him I would be bringing Caitlin in to make a statement. "I'd like to see you as well Charlie. May I call you Charlie?" He carried on, "It's a criminal investigation now. We will do this formally. I'm willing to share information with you, but I want you to tell me exactly what has been happening to Miss Rose, and why she employed you. If you want to talk to her first, that's all well and good. She'll be interviewed by DI Benson, but I do want to speak to her."

"Alright John, I'll be in the station with Caitlin tomorrow morning, so I'll say goodnight."

CHAPTER THIRTY EIGHT

THURSDAY 1ST AUGUST

Caitlin and Charlie left the flat the next morning. Spotting a parking space close to the promenade, Charlie pulled in. She turned to Caitlin, "How are you feeling now?" In the early hours of the morning, Charlie had heard Caitlin cry out. One piercing scream then silence. She had lain in the dark listening; wondering if she should go to her, but no other sounds were forthcoming. In the morning Caitlin acted as though nothing had disturbed her.

Charlie had a special car technique. The comfortable old Rover seemed to have a calming influence on her passengers. The old leather seats and leather trims and wind down windows maybe brought back memories from another time. Clients often unburdened themselves in her dad's old car in a way they never would in the office. "You heard me cry out." Caitlin groaned, "I haven't left my body like that for years."

"What do you mean?"

"I tell this story of me having a great life after I'd been fostered out. I've told it so many times, I believe it myself. I gloss over the bad bits. The nights Sylvia spent holding me in her arms. I never believed I was having nightmares, although the doctor said I was. When I lay down and closed my eyes, I would transport into another reality. It wasn't only nighttime, sometimes it happened in the day. I did settle down on the farm and I think I stopped escaping into other lives by the time I went to senior school."

Charlie frowned, "So, what happened last night?"

Caitlin leaned forward, placing her elbow on the dashboard and scratched the back of her head. She ran her hand through her hair so it stuck up for a moment before it lay down neatly. "I was sitting in the front seat of an auditorium. David Jones was there as a ring master. I could see his dead fishy eyes staring at me behind his wire rimmed glasses. He wore a black top hat and tails and short black shorts and bright white trainers. He posed. His left hand on his hip, one brown muscular leg in front of the other. He held a whip in his right hand. When he cracked the whip, two clowns ran in. A tall one and a little one. They pirouetted in front of me. Their painted faces were shiny with greasepaint. Red painted upturned lips. Black paint round their eyes. They came closer. I saw who they were, and I tried to stop the vision, but I couldn't. They got closer and closer. I could smell their breath. Stale cigarette. I looked away from them, to try and banish them from my mind. David Jones pointed his whip at me, smiled and started walking towards me. That's when I cried out, and it broke the spell."

Charlie turned towards Caitlin. "Forgive me if I appear unfeeling, but you have to put this behind you. You have a job to do today. You have to convince the police that you had no opportunity or motive to harm David Jones. You've witnessed the violent death of a man who harmed you and you've experienced a night terror. That could be a normal reaction. Now you have to put emotion to one side. Get the statement over and done with. I'm not wanting to coach you, but repeat to me how you found the body. Can you do that?"

Caitlin nodded. She sat in silence for some moments. A distance opening up between them; then she shook her head, as though emptying herself. She began to speak in a monotone. Recounting what had happened step by step. She winced as she remembered how she had slipped on the glass. Holding up her injured hand as though she couldn't believe what had occurred. She described how she had initially thought there was a bundle of clothes at the bottom of the stairs. Then when she saw what it really was, how she had stumbled over to the phone.

"Hold on a moment Caitlin. You are in the hall over by the phone. Why didn't you go outside to wait for the emergency services? Why did you walk across the hall again, step over David Jones's body and walk up the stairs? Sally was lying unconscious in a back room, so you couldn't have heard her." Caitlin froze. Her eyes seemed to cloud over. She lifted her left hand and covered her mouth then she squeezed her bottom lip with her thumb and forefinger, clearly agitated by the question. Eventually she spoke, stumbling over her words. "I don't really know. It sounds as though I'm making this up but I thought my mother's ghost was upstairs. I've seen her up there before. I heard something and I just knew I had to go up. Something was drawing me on. Oh God, that sounds pathetic. They're not going to believe me are they? Do you believe me?"

Charlie reached over and touched her shoulder. "Of course I believe you, but the police may not. Now listen Cat, you have to tell it exactly as it was. Don't try to embellish your story, stick to what happened. Remember, there will be forensic evidence." Caitlin lifted her left hand to her mouth again. This time she gnawed at her thumb. Charlie thought how young she looked. A few days ago, when they had read the emails written by her stepfather to David Jones, Caitlin had recounted how, throughout her life, she had had to reinvent herself. She must have been a very damaged child. She was going to need expert help when this was over.

The two women sat quietly together, both deep in their own thoughts. It was Caitlin who broke the silence. "I'm worried about Sally. We should ring the ward. See how she is." Charlie, trying to recall what little psychology she had learned, was feeling inadequate. She was out of her comfort zone, unsure of herself, or how to proceed. She was concerned how Caitlin was going to react. Caitlin's question took her back into the present. "The ward has my number. If Sally's condition had deteriorated they would have rung. Sister Lloyd suggested we ring after midday. I expect she'll be ready for discharge this afternoon."

Caitlin crossed two fingers of her left hand. "I hope so. Anne had offered her a bed, so we could ask her to fetch Sally. Once the business in the police station is over, can you take me over to see them. I need some clothes and stuff from Rock House, then I can drive myself back to yours if that's OK." Grateful that Caitlin appeared calmer and was thinking about the future, Charlie nodded her head in agreement.

"You know, I could kill for a cup of coffee." Caitlin's eyes widened as she realised what she had said. "Oh dear, my big mouth. Seriously, can we go and get some coffee before we go to the police station. I've got a feeling I'm going to need it." Charlie smiled, "Good plan."

The café was a short drive away, close to the promenade. Caitlin struggled out of the car and stood looking down at herself, a wry smile on her face. No wonder she had dreamed of the circus. The baggy shorts and tee shirt Charlie had lent her looked ridiculous. The cuts on her arms were scabbing over. She held her injured right hand on her left shoulder and limped towards the door. She smiled as Charlie took her left arm. They walked through the café together and settled at a table on a paved area in the garden. The sun warmed them. A gentle breeze rustled the leaves of an olive tree planted in a huge earthenware pot close by them. It was early; they were alone. After they had ordered their drinks, Charlie sat back in her chair.

"I've got something else to tell you Cat." She began to tell Caitlin about her encounter with John Fletcher. "So, we now know something alerted the Fraud Squad to your antagonists. Whether that included Dennis, I don't know, but John was certainly interested in Alice, and he was aware of David Jones. They have got to have been up to some sort of major fiddle." She looked over at Caitlin and put her hands up, "I'm not dismissing what you have been through as unimportant, but there's something even bigger going on. I rang John last night when you were in bed. He wants to see you today if he can. He may sit in on your interview."

Caitlin looked nervous. "But he's a good guy right? I can tell him about my mother's death and everything? But doesn't this give me a perfect motive for being involved in David Jones's death?" She shook her head as though she was clearing thoughts away. "I promise you, I wasn't." She got up from the table, wincing with pain. "I keep forgetting about my leg. It hurts. I've just thought, what about you breaking into Jones's bungalow? Are you going to tell them what you found and where it is?"

Charlie got up. She stood beside Caitlin and put her

arm around her shoulder. "Leave that with me and it's going to be OK. We'll work things out. Let's get this over and done with, and while you're giving your statement I'll ring the hospital. In a few days you and Sally will both be home restarting your lives."

PART TWO

CHAPTER THIRTY NINE

CHARLIE

I found myself back at the station where I'd spent six weary years trying to hold my own against discrimination and misogyny. It all felt very familiar. Caitlin had been led away by a young female police officer. Poor woman. She looked timid. Probably experiencing the same sort of bullshit I had had to deal with day after day. My perfectly valid opinions being routinely dismissed. My ideas taken as their own. How many times had I sat in a briefing room being ignored whilst the men sat there puffed up with their own importance? Oh, I fought my corner every step of the way, it was exhausting. The last straw had come when a particularly stupid male colleague was promoted to DS instead of me. Well, my poor father's early death had freed me. I could hold my head high now. I was my own boss answerable to my clients and the business was proving a success.

Despite me jumping ship, the desk sergeant remembered me and welcomed me warmly. I recalled him being a genial sort of man. The sort who had no wish for glory. His dreams were probably of a comfortable life living on his pension and tending his garden. Patronising, but kind, particular to attractive young women. I inwardly chided myself for stereotyping. Wasn't that what happened to me? Anyway, we passed the time of day, then I asked to speak to Superintendent Fletcher.

"Could you just try to locate him Roy. Tell him I'm

here. All I want is two minutes of his time." Roy nodded and picked up the phone. I looked over to see Paul Benson and Harry James walking in the direction of the interview rooms. The very Harry James who had pipped me to the post. I shivered at the thought that it could have been me working with DI Benson. Although a good copper, once Paul gets an idea in his head he won't let it go. He's like a terrier worrying a rat until he gets the answer he wants. Truth or not. Caitlin was in for a hard time; she wasn't in good shape to withstand his style of questioning. I was glad he hadn't seen me. He knew how I felt about him and he was very good at bearing a grudge. When he knew I was involved it would make matters worse.

I was startled out of my reverie when I realised John was standing beside me. "Superintendent Fletcher, it's good of you to see me. Is there somewhere private we can talk?" I felt as nervous as a rooky. John's habitually kind expression helped calm my nerves. "I can only give you a couple of minutes Miss Taylor. Come on through." I followed him into a small interview room. "I'm going to observe your friend's interview, Charlie. The question is, did he fall or was he pushed? Benson and James will be tough on her."

"I fear you're right." He nodded, so I took that as an affirmative and continued, "She feels guilty about her friend Sally being injured. Benson will play on that. He could very easily tip her over the edge. Has anyone interviewed Sally yet?" John nodded, "Harry went over this morning. She confirmed she saw Jones before he hit her." It was Charlie's turn to nod. "What a mess. I wish I'd known what you were doing when we met in Cornwall. But look, I'm going to be an hour sorting things out, then I'll be back. She wants to go home to pick up some of her stuff, then she's coming back to me whilst we get the house cleaned. It would be better for her if you talk to her at my place. Could you come round later?"

"OK, leave your address with Roy. I must go now, they'll have started."

CHAPTER FORTY

"You're looking worried Miss Rose. Are you sure you've told us everything?"

Caitlin looked at the two detectives sitting opposite. She grimaced, Mutt and Jeff. DI Benson had questioned her again and again. He was clearly trying to lead her and becoming frustrated at his lack of progress. Caitlin was thankful that Charlie had already asked her to recount exactly how she had found the scene. She was able to recall the scene precisely; careful not to leave anything out or put anything in. She spotted DS James trying to hide a smirk several times. What was the matter with the man? DI Benson sat very still, never taking his eyes off her. He had a horrible habit of licking his lips. She was beginning to feel nauseous.

She shook her head. "I'm not worried, and I've told you everything."

DI Benson looked at the file in front of him. "Where do you normally park your car Miss Rose?"

"As I've already said, I usually park at the front. I wasn't concealing the car. I parked round by the garage because Sally and I were about to set off for the Cambridge Music Festival. I had camping chairs and picnic stuff to load up. The tickets are in Rock House if you want proof." DS James smirked at her again, speaking for the first time. "It all sounds a bit contrived Miss Rose. I think you concealed your car so David Jones would think there was no one in, but you were already upstairs waiting for him." He stared at her. "You look like a strong girl. A little push would have sufficed."

Caitlin stifled a nervous laugh. "How many more times do I have to say it? I only went upstairs after I'd discovered David Jones and phoned the emergency services. I came in through the front door, saw there was glass all over the floor. When I realised someone was lying at the bottom of the stairs, I forgot about the glass. Take a look at me." She held her right hand up. "I slipped on the glass in my panic to call for help."

DI Benson leaned forward, "I'm afraid that doesn't prove anything Miss Rose. You see, it just doesn't add up. Why would a fit man fall down the stairs? I think you pushed him. Otherwise, why would he have overbalanced and clutched at the mirror to save himself? After he had fallen to his death, you must have cold bloodedly stepped over his body. Satisfied yourself he was dead, then you went over to the phone to ring for help. For all we know you deliberately fell over to make it look as though you panicked."

Caitlin put her head in her hands and groaned. She looked up, glaring at them. "Why on earth would I do that? That wasn't what happened. How many more times do I have to tell you? **I did not push that man.** If you have any evidence, then arrest me. I came in here voluntarily this morning to give a statement. I've got nothing to hide. I went upstairs because I heard a noise. I did step over the body then. I thought I heard something up there." Her voice broke. "David Jones was a thief and for God's sake, he tried to kill my friend."

DI Benson narrowed his eyes as he contemplated her. "We found the French window to the dining room invitingly open Miss Rose. No, he shouldn't have been there, but I think you tempted him. He seemed to know what to look for and where to find it. How do you account for that?"

"I've already told you. I went to see him to ask him

about my mother's death. I let it slip that I'd found some old papers. Dennis Gough knew where I was storing the stuff from the attic. He must have told him." DI Benson smiled at her.

"How do you know Dennis Gough and David Jones knew each other Miss Rose? You haven't been able to explain that." DI Benson's dogged determination was beginning to rile Caitlin. Her calm demeanour had switched to anger. She snapped, "Instead of bullying me, why don't you look into David Jones's activities. How he cheated for years. Investigate my mother's death properly. You lot were quick to call that an accident, all those years ago. Did you know he was there when she went into the water?"

There was a knock at the door. DI Benson glanced up at the plain clothed officer who entered. He barely hid his irritation. The officer leaned over and spoke quietly to DI Benson. The DI shook his head in disbelief, then said, "Superintendent Fletcher has entered the room. Interview suspended at eleven forty-three a.m." He got up and lumbered out after the Superintendent, leaving Caitlin in the room with DS James.

She flashed at him. "When this is over, I'm going to put in a complaint. I've been stuck in this airless room for an hour and a half. You've asked me the same questions over and over again. I've answered you honestly. Unless you have grounds to keep me, I'm out of here. So what's it to be?" As if by magic DI Benson burst in through the door, his face contorted with anger. "You are free to go for the moment Miss Rose. We may need to question you again. Your friend is outside waiting for you."

Caitlin struggled up. Having sat in one place for so long her leg had seized up. "You think I did this deliberately, don't you?" She stood holding onto the chair, her face crumpled in pain. "I'm going to need help. I'd be grateful if you'd ask my friend to come in and help me, otherwise I'm going to fall over." DS James, a worried expression on his face, looked at his boss, who nodded. "Go and fetch her friend. You are good my dear Miss Rose, I'll give you that."

"I am NOT your dear."

CHARLIE

When I walked in I saw Caitlin standing up holding onto her chair for dear life. The knuckles of her left hand were clamped and white. Her face pale, drained of emotion. I hurried over to her, gently released her hand from the chair and rubbed it with mine. "You can let go of it all now Cat. We're going home." She didn't speak, simply nodded then rubbed her eyes with her bandaged hand. I held onto her left arm and we walked slowly outside to my car. She opened the passenger door and slid in, sighing with relief. I could almost feel my old car wrapping its arms around her. Fanciful I know, but true.

I walked round, opened the driver's door and sat down beside her. "Do you want to talk about it?" She bit her lower lip, then looked at me. She spoke softly at first. "Best to leave it here isn't it? Not take it with us. I just want to say, those detectives are bastards. It would have been so easy to have given in to them and confessed something I didn't do. God help all the vulnerable people they get their claws into. Bastards."

"Better?"

She shook her head. "To be honest, not sure if I'll ever feel the same again. Life will be different knowing those two detectives think I'm a murderer. Can we go? But I didn't see your friend John, I thought he wanted to see me."

"You did see him. He was the officer who terminated the interview. I don't know why for sure. I suspect the pathologist's report has come back. He does want to see you. I've asked him to come to my flat this afternoon." I glanced over and caught the look of horror on Caitlin's face. "It's OK Cat. He's not like the others. He's gentle, intelligent and thoughtful. I have high hopes we're going to learn how and why he's involved with your conspirators. So, shall we get out of here? Have something to eat back at the flat, talk to John and then go over and see Sally. Ann should be collecting her as we speak."

Caitlin put her head in her hands. "Oh my lord, with all this, I'd forgotten about poor Sally. I'm sorry I got her into all this. It was my fault, I should have figured the David Jones character out. I told him I'd found stuff out about my mother. He was surprised there was anything to find." Caitlin sat bolt upright. "I'd forgotten - when I got the key to the house, it was weird. I opened the door to nothing. The whole place had been cleared. A few pictures on the wall, that's all, and of course that mirror on top of the stairs. That's why he was so surprised I'd found something. He'd made sure there was nothing to find. Except they forgot the attic."

I felt a weight being lifted from me. I had been feeling uneasy. Caitlin could have deliberately enticed David Jones with the emails I'd left with her. But it wasn't that at all. She had given me the originals, but she had retained the copies of her mother's letters. That was what he was worried about. The death of Cecilia Rose all those years ago had come back to haunt him. I was beginning to think Cecilia had been murdered. I couldn't help giving a little whoop. Caitlin looked surprised. Particularly surprised when I punched the air.

"Oh, yes! I love it when a loose end gets tied up."

CHAPTER FORTY ONE

CAITLIN

I watched Charlie buttering bread to make sandwiches. The comfort of normal activity but I couldn't stop my mind from roaming. Charlie had said I could let go. It was over. If only. I transposed the picture of David Jones lying dead at the bottom of the stairs with another memory of Rock House. Closing my eyes, I was there again. I had just come from the solicitors and had the key to the house in my bag. It wasn't easy to find. The entrance was very overgrown, the sign obscured by undergrowth. I drove down to the front of the house. A jumble of childhood memories came flooding back.

I didn't know what to expect, yet I dreaded the idea of dirt and clouds of cobwebs resting on dusty furniture. I feared my father's essence would be in the house, that I would be able to smell him, even though I couldn't even remember what he looked like. I thought there might be a photograph of him in a silver frame. That I'd find his coat hanging on a peg by the back door. Maybe a pair of wellington boots or shoes left lying around.

What I found was nothing. I opened the door; a musty smell enveloped me. The hall was empty. I went through each room. Nothing. No carpets, no rugs, no furniture and no photos in silver frames. Even the kitchen was bare. No plates, no cups, no kettle, no toaster. The carpet had been left upstairs, that was about all. There were a couple of framed photographs screwed onto one of the bedroom walls. Old fashioned studio photographs. A young man, his dark hair greased back close to his skull, stood beside a seated woman. His hand rested on her shoulder. She wore a high-necked blouse and long skirt. Her hair pinned up and back from her face. They both looked solemn, concentrating on keeping their pose whilst the photographer did his magic work.

I went outside and sat down on a wall. It was drizzling but I just sat there staring at the house, wondering what on earth to do. Somehow, I switched my thoughts away from the father who had discarded me to an image I had buried deep in my consciousness – my mother standing at the top of the stairs. She was tall. She had beautiful, dark, curly hair. She wore a long grey dressing gown and she smiled as she called out to me. A three year old's memory.

I knew then, no matter what it took, I would make Rock House my home. It was meant to be. She wanted me back where I belonged. I went back down to the solicitors and asked why and how the house had been cleared. Mr Jones looked puzzled. He rifled through a folder but could find no mention of a house clearance. I ended up saying no matter. I had a clean slate to work with. After that I went in a search of a B&B and thought no more of it. I was startled out of my daydream by Charlie's voice. "You were far away Cat. Where have you been?" I told her the story of my homecoming. How I'd bought a bed and some camping gear and lived in one room until the house became habitable.

"It must have been David Jones who organised the house clearance, that's why young Mr Jones looked surprised. Charlie, do you remember what the emails from George to David Jones said? Sounds corny, but it was something like, 'you'll not get away with it this time', wasn't it?" Charlie nodded. I carried on, "He must have searched for any incriminating evidence when

George died. Maybe he didn't find it, so had the whole house cleared to be on the safe side. That's why he was surprised when I told him I'd found something of my mother's." I felt myself shiver. "What if David Jones found a way of doing away with George, so it looked like natural causes? He had the substitute next of kin in place. It was bad luck that I was found alive and kicking so they had to find some other way of getting their hands on the money."

Charlie nodded again. "That makes sense. But let's not get carried away. John should be here soon to help us unravel this. Your job is to give him the background. You could throw that into the mix, but he's going to need evidence. You made a good point in the car about the attic being forgotten. Maybe, just maybe, George Rose hid material up there. Surely he had his own computer to send emails. He may have copied material. When we can, we should go through what's left in the attic with a fine toothcomb."

Both of us were silent as we ate our lunch, trying to make sense of the last twenty four hours. I felt better for the food. I'd feel even better if we were free to go over and see Sally now. Patience is a virtue they say, but if I have to go through the whole finding of David Jones again, I'll go mad.

I wasn't much help clearing up one-handed and my leg was painful. Charlie insisted that I take some painkillers and put my feet up. It was very comfortable sitting on her sofa, my legs on a stool, looking out over the sea far below. I dozed off for a time; woke up with a start when the doorbell rang. I heard Charlie greeting someone, the door opened and Superintendent John Fletcher walked in, squatted down beside me and held out his hand. "Miss

Rose, I'm sorry you find yourself in this state. Are you in much pain?"

Charlie had described John as gentle and intelligent. I looked straight into a pair of hazel eyes. His gaze remained steady. His face was thin; he could have looked austere, but sympathetic eyes smiled at me, crow's feet accentuated. He held my left hand in his. It felt warm. There was something about his manner that is difficult to describe. I had dreaded another interview after this morning's performance but somehow I was OK. He held onto my hand for a little longer than I expected. He was summing me up. Suddenly I thought that I must look awful. Battered and bruised and dressed like a clown, which is exactly what I found myself saying out loud. He smiled, withdrew his hand and stood. "Would you mind if I sat down?"

I noticed he didn't disabuse me of looking like a clown, instead he picked up a chair, came and sat close by me. I noticed his well-manicured hands resting loosely on the arms of the chair. He was motionless, so self-contained. Time stood still. What was he waiting for? I found the silence unnerving; I cried out. "No matter what you've been told, I did not push that man down the stairs."

"I don't believe you did, Miss Rose. The pathology report backs up your story. I would surmise that he had just assaulted your friend and was in a panic to get away. His foot caught in a loose stair grip. He put his arm out to steady himself and caught the mirror. The mirror toppled first. He must have overbalanced and over he went."

At that moment I knew how much I had feared my own nature. The two detectives who bullied me had confused me so much that I had been on the brink of slipping into their reality. I was guilty. A man died in my house. I must have pushed him. It was my fault. If they had carried on with their interrogation, I would have cracked.

The Superintendent sat quietly watching my reaction; my struggle to understand myself. "I thought you'd be happy to hear that, Miss Rose."

"I am. I really am, but I'm devastated too. A man died in my home, and those detectives were convinced I'd murdered him. I always thought people were innocent until proven guilty. Those two thought I was guilty from the beginning. It was horrible. I was frightened they would bully me to a point where I just gave in and confessed. That's happened hasn't it – innocent people locked up?"

He didn't answer my question but simply said, "David Jones was killed through his own nefarious dealings. I'm sorry it happened in your home. I would be very interested to hear how it all came about. Are you happy to include Miss Taylor in our discussion?"

"Sorry Superintendent, I don't know who Miss Taylor is. Have you brought another officer with you?"

"Ah, let me explain. Charlotte Taylor is your investigator. Charlie Bond is her professional name." Well, that was a surprise, but using another name made perfect sense. Charlie Bond, Private Investigator. It stood out, brilliant name. Good to be able to switch it on and off. I'd only known her switched on, of course. I'd like a friendship with someone called Charlotte Taylor. I smiled, "Of course she can. Charlie's been incredible. She's kept a history - a timeline. I'm happy for you to examine it. You can see when the conspiracy began, who it involved and how it's progressed. We weren't so sure of why until a couple of days ago. It's been a rollercoaster and I'll have forgotten some of the detail."

"Thanks Miss Rose. I'll ask her to come in."

Did I feel relief? Yes, I wasn't going to have to tell the whole story again. I sat back on the sofa and shut my eyes. Maybe it was going to be alright after all.

CHAPTER FORTY TWO

Charlie opened the door to the lounge; looked in and turned round holding her finger to her lips. "Caitlin's asleep. She had a disturbed night. Let's leave her. Come on back into the kitchen."

They sat at the table facing one another. Charlie opened her folder. "I'll go through this with you, in return will you please tell me why you're involved with this case?" He nodded and sat quietly whilst Charlie talked. She went through what she knew about Caitlin's history and what led to her being called in to investigate Alice Brown. John asked, "At that time, what was your impression of Miss Rose?"

"She struck me as being naïve, a bit scatty. It was a game to her then. She changed as we learned more. She became more determined. Her aim has always been to find the truth about her mother's death. That's very important to her."

"And what was your impression of her friend Miss Thomas?"

"She was supportive and protective of her friend. I think she may have said that Caitlin was playing a dangerous game, so she was worried too."

"And as things unfolded? Tell me what happened." Charlie continued, "She was invited to meet David Jones. His son, Trevor, is Caitlin's present solicitor. She had asked Trevor about her mother's death. He had taken over the management of Caitlin's Trust Fund from his father, so he suggested she meet with him. She was confused and upset after that meeting, feeling she had given too much away. He expressed interest in the papers she had found in the attic. He wanted to know if she had been to the police with them."

"That's what led you to break into David Jones's bungalow? I presume that's where you found the emails?" For a moment, Charlie feigned surprise. "It's a fair cop. You're quite right John. There was a key hidden outside, it wasn't difficult to get in. But that skips over an important part of the story. Her friend Bob and his cousin Justin had unearthed a man who had been in the pub the night Caitlin's mother, Cecilia Rose, died. Caitlin and Sally went to meet him. His name's Bert Savage. He's terminally ill, has asbestosis, so communication with him was difficult. Bert said they deliberately bought Cecilia strong drinks that night because she was usually serious and 'po-faced'. He stayed inside the pub so didn't witness Cecilia going into the water. His friend Harry had been with them outside but remained sitting apart on the harbour wall. He heard a cry but thought no more of it. Some months later he committed suicide. Bert Savage blames George Rose for his death."

"So, at this point, Caitlin Rose is conflating her mother's death with Harry's suicide and blaming her stepfather, George Rose?" Charlie continued, "Yes, it was leading that way until I prompted her to repeat what Bert had said. It became clear that there was a third person there. Caitlin recounted how, as she was about to leave, Bert whispered something to her, which sounded like 'find the locker man'. We put two and two together and came up with Davey Jones's Locker. That was when we decided that I should have a look in David Jones's bungalow."

"I'm glad you've told me Charlie. We found fingerprints. You really shouldn't go breaking into people's houses." He wagged his finger at her. Charlie grinned hoping his was a playful gesture. "I know I shouldn't have and he may have realised someone had been in the house. He came back and I just made it out in time, so hadn't checked round. I ran and hid behind the shed in the garden. He stood on the kitchen doorstep smoking. My hay fever had been bad and I was worried I may have dropped a paper tissue."

"So, you found what you were looking for and took some of the incriminating material with you. I'm assuming you went through the material with Miss Rose. How did she seem after that?" Charlie frowned, "Deeply shocked, not so much because we now knew David Jones was up to his neck in what had happened, but that George Rose was protecting her. She hated him for abandoning her and was convinced he had murdered her mother. The blame switched to David Jones. It looked as though David Jones was defrauding her Trust Fund and possibly a murderer." John, his elbows resting on the table, his hands in prayer position, fingertips on his lips, mused, "So, she had the opportunity and the motive to want to harm David Jones."

"Maybe, but I would suggest she wanted him brought to justice, not dead at the bottom of her stairs. Apart from that, I'm not sure she did have the opportunity. The timings aren't right are they?" John sat back in his chair. "Paul Benson is convinced she's guilty. I'm not convinced, but there is something that doesn't quite add up. Not sure what it is yet. The pathologist backs Caitlin's story. I am minded to go with his report."

"So tell me why you are involved in this John. What were you doing down in Cornwall? You tried to pump me for information about Alice Brown aka Arabella

Rose. What's that about?" He got up and walked over to the window. When he turned to Charlie he had a preoccupied look in his eyes, his face serious and resolute. "I've been chasing a clever holiday and property scam. A lot of innocent people have been duped. That's what led me to Alice Brown. She was careless on one occasion. She left a fingerprint on some material she posted to a victim. She'd been involved in a minor fracas some years previously so we had her on record. One of my colleagues had been keeping tabs on her for some time. We knew she wasn't the ringleader, there had to be others. She was acting as an administrator. She didn't have the skills to prepare the documentation they used. Particularly for the bogus house sales."

"How long have you been watching her?"

"Several weeks, and yes, before you ask, we were puzzled by Miss Rose's behaviour. Following a man, unknown to us at the time, visiting Miss Brown." Charlie let out one of her little hoots. "Oh funny – you watched Caitlin hiding behind the hedge!"

"Yes, we did." He sighed, "It threw us off the scent for a day or two. Why don't you tell me why she was following Miss Brown's visitor. I've got a horrible feeling it's another long story." They both looked up as the door opened. Caitlin stood at the doorway.

"I seem to have come in at an opportune time. May I join you?"

John walked over to the door and offered Caitlin his arm. She smiled and refused. Limping over to the sink, she asked Charlie for a glass, ran the cold water tap for a moment, then filled it. She sipped the water, refilled the glass, went over to the table, settling down beside Charlie. Resting one side of her cheek on her left hand,

Caitlin looked over at the Superintendent. "So, you saw me doing my Miss Marple impersonation?"

"Not exactly Miss Rose. My colleague did and he was rather intrigued. Why don't you tell me about it."

"Charlie's doubtless spoken about the bogus cousin. My solicitor had her name and phone number on file. First I ever heard of having a cousin, I thought I was alone in the world. Anyway, I'd been down to visit her. Oh, I'd better tell you about Dennis. He was sort of living with me. I wasn't happy and eventually plucked up the courage to chuck him out. So, I was down in Cornwall visiting and I spotted him in the town. It did cross my mind that he was stalking me, but he was walking away with great purpose, nothing to do with me. I followed him and saw him go to my cousin's house. That's when I realised they were in cahoots." John sighed, "It's a bit of a tangled web Miss Rose."

"Oh please call me Caitlin, or Cat. I don't like being called Miss Rose."

He smiled. "Thank you, Caitlin. Did you hear me tell Miss Taylor why I'm investigating Alice Brown?" Caitlin shook her head, so the Superintendent repeated what he had told Charlie.

"Ah ha! Eureka! Hence the lawyer. I've led you to David Jones. That's why you're here. I'd bet my bottom dollar Dennis Gough is up to the hilt in any wrongdoing as well. Well, now you're here and involved, how about this? David Jones instigated my mother's death and I believe when George Rose threated him, he probably did away with him as well. I'd look for his wife, Babs, if I was you. She was no longer living in the marital home, but George Rose was referring to her just a year or so ago. He's probably a serial murderer!"

Charlie interrupted, "Cat, you're getting carried away. Stop, stop now. There's going to be a lot of work to do, but neither you nor I are actually a Miss Marple. Let the Superintendent and his team do the investigating. Unless the Superintendent wants us anymore." She looked over at him, he shook his head. "We should go over to Rock House, pick up what you need and then see how Sally is." She looked over at John again. "We are free to go into Rock House now, aren't we?"

"Yes, we've finished in there. Let me give you some advice Caitlin, give yourself time to heal. Leave the detective work to the detectives. We will talk again. We've got a lot to discuss, but right now, you need to look after yourself and your friend. Is that clear?"

"I'm sorry, I get carried away. I've been in a sort of whirlwind. It's gone round and round, faster and faster, culminating in finding David Jones dead at the bottom of the stairs. I wish I hadn't seen him. I think he was an evil man, but he didn't deserve an end like that." She turned to Charlie. "I'll go and get ready. Can I borrow a bag?"

"Of course, go and get ready. I'll see John out."

CHAPTER FORTY THREE

CHARLIE

Oh, my car! I'm going to keep you running somehow. Maintain and repair you, just like the old cars I've seen in Cuba. Still on the road. Ancient old American rattletraps, polished and loved.

Caitlin looked comfortable sitting back in the leather seat; almost happy. Happy to be going over to see Sally I guess. Then she began to talk, musing out loud. My car is so much better than a psychiatrist's chair. "I can't stop thinking about that first day back at Rock House when I realised my mother was calling me. You know, all I've ever wanted is to belong. It's lonely standing on the outside, never really being part of anything. An intruder, an interloper in other peoples' lives. They don't really want you, although they're generally polite. They sense you're not like them. It was different with Sally. We're similar and we cling to one another, as if we'd been in a shipwreck and had to hold onto the same raft for dear life.

Then, like a miracle, I was home. I'd found my place in the world. Local people began to know who I was. I started to feel part of the place. Maybe that was how I let my guard down. I allowed Dennis to get his claws into me. I'd wanted to be like other couples.

I tried to please him and couldn't understand why our relationship foundered so quickly. Maybe it never began. I had no experience of being in love or loved." She stopped talking. I glanced at her, sitting there, her expression no longer happy. She began to speak again. "I hate myself for what I did. Once I picked up with Dennis I virtually abandoned Sally. I was caught up in my own fantasy. That's all it was. Stupid."

I spotted a shady picnic area at the side of the road and pulled in. Tall oak trees towered above us. There were a few wooden benches on the grass, but we were alone. I opened my window wide to let more cool air in. "Cat, these things happen. Even if you hadn't been a target and Dennis had been genuine, relationships go wrong. Relationships also bring about change. Sally would have understood that."

Caitlin shook her head, "Yes, but you see, I think I sabotaged myself. I'd begun to feel a sense of belonging. Maybe I couldn't cope with that, not with all the crap I had inside me. I didn't deserve happiness. I'd done something to make my stepfather banish me to another life."

"Oh Cat, no. You were never to blame. You were just a child who should have been protected. Maybe in his own way, that was what happened. How do you feel now?"

Caitlin folded her arms and made a face at me. "I began by saying I wanted to belong didn't I? To get to know my real self." She grinned, "I was beginning to like who I might be. I like being able to make more friends and feel I can settle into a community. If he was protecting me, then some of those old feelings might just dissipate of their own accord."

I reached over and touched her arm. "You're very special Caitlin. You've got a great future. Promise me, from this day on, you'll stop blaming yourself; remember you had no control. Your dream of David Jones as a ringmaster was pretty true to life. I think we'll find that he had the whip hand on all those around him, including George Rose. John Fletcher has told us he believes

David Jones was a criminal. You were caught up in his machinations when all you wanted was to find out who you were. To find out who your mother was."

We both sat in silence, thinking about what had been said. No wonder I had found Caitlin such an enigma. She didn't really know herself, so how could anyone else? I had thought her a feisty young woman. I was right there. She would make something of her life. But there was still something niggling at me.

"Come on, we'd better go. Ann and Sally are expecting us." I turned the key and the engine started first time. It purred. I really would have to give the car a name, or maybe I should just call her "the old jalopy". Didn't quite do her justice.

Caitlin sat up. "I've just remembered something. There were two old framed photographs hanging in a bedroom, missed in the house clearance. At the beginning I thought they must be my grandparents. I showed them to Ann but she didn't think they were. What if they were George Roses's parents? We might never know, but he might have hidden something behind them don't you think?" I filed what she said in my mind somewhere, then forgot until much later.

We arrived at Ann's house. Caitlin walked to the front door. Her limp was improving. Good sign. She rang the bell. I heard scratching and snuffling then a delighted bark as the door opened. Sally stood there, beaming at Caitlin. They embraced, as a little brown dog ran rings around them. The dog spotted me; luckily Ann appeared and scooped the dog up in her arms.

"Coco, you naughty girl, stop it. Calm down." The little dog struggled in her arms, trying to get at us all. "Come on in you two, so I can shut the door. I don't want Coco running out into the road and causing more mayhem." She put Coco down, holding her hand up near the dog's face. In a stern voice she said, "Go on your bed Coco." The little dog panted enthusiastically and I thought she was set to run round us again, but she turned tail and hopped onto one of the sofas and into her bed. Ann raised her eyebrows. "Good grief, what a good dog." She laughed, "I didn't expect that! I'll just go and get her a treat. What would you two girls like? Are you hungry? Sal and I have just had some sandwiches. Can I get you something?"

Sally appeared remarkably well despite David Jones's attack. She was pale but otherwise I wouldn't have known anything had happened to her. I asked her how she was feeling. "They were very kind to me in hospital but I'm so happy to be back. My head's tender and I'm a bit achy. It was like a dream. Then this morning I remembered what happened. David Jones's face loomed over me. The hate in his eyes. I was in the wrong place at the wrong time. Typical of me. Ann told me what happened to him." She turned to Caitlin, "It must have been awful finding him."

Caitlin screwed her face up, then gave a rueful smile. "It was a shock, but strangely, it's already fading. We're going back to Rock House to pick up some of my things; you might want some too Sal. I'm going to face it down, confront it. He ruined part of my life, he's not going to taint our home for us."

Sitting there, watching the pair of them, I thought, yes, Caitlin's brave. She may also be adept at shrugging off trauma. Hiding it inside herself. I had noticed how, although she limped, she didn't complain about pain. I wondered if she had learned to contain pain as a child, so now she hardly felt it in the normal way.

Ann got us on to a more even keel. She brought a pot of tea and a plate of dark chocolate digestives – my favourite. We sat and chatted and planned. I was in bossy mode. Caitlin wanted to drive her car back to mine, but I wasn't having any of that. We had an appointment in the hospital to check her over in the morning, driving could wait until after that.

Danger still lurked. It was in the air. I wouldn't be happy until Dennis and Alice had been apprehended. Now, I needed to say what was on my mind. "Superintendent Fletcher was very generous with the information he gave us. We learned a lot more about David Jones and how Dennis and Alice might fit into the picture." I looked over at Caitlin, "Cat, you and I need to keep what he said absolutely confidential. What he made clear was that the police are now in control. No more investigating, and that includes me. So right now, although I haven't told Sally, I'm here as a friend and confidante, not as Charlie Bond."

Ann looked at me, a quizzical expression on her face. "What do you mean?"

"I'll help the police with their enquiries. They're running the investigation. We now take a backseat."

Caitlin clapped her hands. "So is Charlotte Taylor our friend and confidante?"

"I'm no longer working professionally for you Cat and I've grown rather fond of you all. But, when I've got the time, I will be sending you an invoice for the work I've done."

"If I didn't have this gammy leg, I'd dance round the room now. Thank you Charlie. You've no idea what this means to me." I winked at her and assured her I probably did. Caitlin and I nibbled biscuits, chatted and worked out a plan for the following day. Then we left with a list of things Sally wanted. First, we had to go to the local police station to pick up Caitlin's bag and keys, then I drove us up to Rock House. We sat outside thinking about what had happened inside.

"You've already had one accident on the glass. It's still going to be there until Ann's friend can do her deep clean. Just be doubly careful. I'll come in with you. Get what you and Sally need, then we'll go."

Arm in arm, we walked over to the front door. I took the key from Caitlin and opened it. She bent down and picked up something shiny just below the step. "I remember seeing this little bit of glass, picking it up and laying it down there. Then I looked in and saw there was glass everywhere, and I thought I should have moved that mirror. Maybe David Jones wouldn't have fallen if I had."

"Cat, you can do 'what ifs' until you're blue in the face. No, what is to be, is to be. This must have been his time. Let's go in and get this over and done with." We stood there staring. OK, glass all over the tiles, but nothing else to see. David Jones was long gone. We picked our way through the mess and went upstairs. Caitlin changed into a pair of her own long shorts and a shirt and slipped on a pair of blue trainers. She put the rest of the clothes and toiletries she wanted in one bag, and did the same for Sally.

Tomorrow the place would be cleaned and look as I had first seen it, when Caitlin had run down the stairs fresh from showering after her swim. It seemed so long ago. I hoped the image of David Jones lying dead at the bottom of the stairs would fade and eventually disappear from Caitlin's immediate memory. It was all you could hope for.

CHAPTER FORTY FOUR

FRIDAY 2ND AUGUST

Charlie assessed Caitlin across the kitchen table. She had eaten a good breakfast and seemed rested. The dark shadows under her eyes had lifted and her smile was back. She had removed the bandage from her right hand, exposing the cut on her palm. She was going to be left with a scar. It was a miracle she had only put her hand down to save herself. If the glass had penetrated her wrist, she would have been in trouble.

Charlie had to go to her office to pick up any messages and left Caitlin clearing up. When she returned, Caitlin was raring to go. "You must bill me for this last day Charlie. I appreciate your care of me, but I'm preventing you working. I'm going to pay you for today, whether you agree or not. After we've been to the hospital I'll be able to drive my own car back." She beamed at Charlie. A future without the dread she had been experiencing of late was opening up in front of her. They left the flat and drove back to Caitlin's local hospital for her eleven thirty a.m. appointment. When she emerged from outpatients, the bandage on her right leg had been removed. A dressing had been reapplied to the deep cut on her knee, but the minor wounds had been left open. The cut on her right hand had been redressed. She carried a paper bag; she opened it to show Charlie the contents.

"I can do my own dressings. I don't have to come back unless I'm worried. No swimming though. Not until it's fully healed, and I'm OK to drive."

By now it was midday. Charlie drove them over to

Ann's house. They checked up on Sally then went over to Rock House. Cleaning was in process. The front door wide open. They could hear the sound of voices and rock music. A tall man emerged carrying a yellow plastic bag in each hand. He was wearing a white tee shirt under blue dungarees, the front of which bore a large logo, Shipshape Services. His light brown hair was tied back in a ponytail, slipped through the hole at the back of a white baseball cap. He looked as though he hadn't shaved for a few days. Caitlin smiled at him, "I recognise you from somewhere."

"You've probably seen me in the White Swan. Our band plays there. I think I recognise you too." She studied his face. Deep set brown eyes and a broad natural grin. His nose looked as though it might have been broken sometime in the past; he had a scar on his left cheek.

He slung the bags into the back of a large white van bearing the same logo. They heard the unmistakeable sound of crunching glass as the bags hit the metal interior of the van. Caitlin flinched. He rubbed his hands together. "That gets rid of that lot. My brother's mopping inside the hall at the moment. We've had instructions to clean the whole house until it's sparkling, from top to bottom." Caitlin looked pleased. "Thank you. That'll be Ann's instructions, and she's right. Do the whole lot. I'm Caitlin by the way, and this is Charlie."

"Pleased to meet you. I'm Jed."

"I've only come to collect my car. This is my house. You know what happened here? I hope it's not worrying you. Last time I saw it…. Well, I think I'd rather not dwell on it." His grin was replaced by a scowl. "Yes, Ann told us what happened. If you don't mind me saying,

248

he'd got it coming. He wasn't trusted or liked in this town. When you come back, your home will be yours again. Shipshape and Bristol fashion, that's us."

Caitlin sighed, "Thank you. Come on Charlie, we should let them get on with it. I hope to be back tomorrow, and when this is all over, we'll have a big party and you and your band can come and play for us. How does that sound?"

Waving goodbye they walked round to the garage. Caitlin's BMW was still parked outside. She found the key in her bag and opened the doors and boot to let the hot air out. The bag of shopping for the festival was still sitting on the back seat. She leaned on the bonnet of the car, feeling the warmth of the metal on her skin. "I'm going to drive round the town. Have a walk on the beach if it's not too crowded. I might get as far as the North beach. It's where my mother washed up, and this is what all of this has been about. Her death and justice for her. I'm not going to mourn that man's death. Instead, I'm going to celebrate my mother's life, and my new life."

Caitlin and Charlie embraced. Charlie spoke for the first time. "You're going to be alright. The memory of what happened to David Jones will fade."

"Thank you Charlie. Thank you for all you've done. I'll see you later. One last night together in your flat. We can go out. I'll buy you a slap up meal." She grinned. "I'll hold you to that young lady."

Caitlin waited for Charlie to leave, then sat in her car, letting the familiarity of it wash over her. She had come home, but could she face it? She knew she had to come to terms with David Jones's death. Guilt overwhelmed her. She put her arms over the steering wheel, bowed her head and howled. She cried out when she heard a tap on the window, looked over and saw Jed's face. "Are you OK? No, you're not." He opened her car door, "Come with me. Let's go into the house, lay that ghost. It's the only way."

She looked up at him, tears running down her cheeks. What did this stranger think he was doing? She thought of shouting 'no, leave me alone', but somehow the oddness of his behaviour intrigued her. His voice was far from sympathetic. She complied, got out of the car with some difficulty and followed him back to the house. They walked through the front door together. It smelled fresh. The tiles were still damp. She walked over to the stairs and sat down on the second step. Looking down at her feet she said, "This is where I found him. He lay there. A look of horror on his face. The strange thing was he had blue latex gloves on. One arm outstretched, reaching."

Jed stood contemplating her. Hands on hips. Feet planted squarely. "He's gone now. He shouldn't have broken into your house. He hurt your friend. You have no need to be crying over him, so just stop it, right?" Caitlin couldn't help giggling. She thought of her social work training. There were no theories to cover his approach to grief. It was working though. Her giggles turned to laughter. Jed joined in.

"What's going on in here?" A man wearing the same uniform stood at the doorway.

Caitlin stared at a replica of Jed. Same height and build. Same brown eyes. But this man's hair was short, his nose straight and he was clean shaven. "Caitlin, meet my brother Adam, Adam meet Caitlin. I was just explaining to Caitlin that she has no need to be crying over David Jones." Adam smirked, "What, you mean our respected, upright and trustworthy solicitor? He's had his fingers in more pies than you and I could eat bruv, and we can shift a lot! No, don't waste your tears on him. Good riddance to bad rubbish I'd say." Caitlin got up. "Thank you. I don't know how you've managed it, but I feel better." Adam grinned, "My brother seems to have that effect on people. If we could bottle it we'd make a fortune. By the way, I love your house. I've just been looking upstairs to scope what needs doing." Jed looked surprised. "How did you do that then, fly?"

"No, I went up through the servants' entrance and up the stairs. This must have been quite a house in its time. I thought I was opening a cupboard but instead of shelves there was a staircase. Same door on the corridor upstairs. You have to admire the old builders, the thought they put into keeping the servants out of sight of their betters. I'm saying that tongue in cheek by the way."

Caitlin looked over at him. "We don't use that staircase. I normally keep it locked. Too steep and rickety. I suppose there must have been servants in the past." Adam surprised her by saying, "We can help you find out. We volunteer in the local museum."

"I have to thank you both again in that case. Thank you for helping me feel better. Thank you for cleaning the house, and thank you for your kind thoughts. I should be going now, leave you to it." She shook both their hands. Her right hand didn't appreciate their grip. She had forgotten the cut.

CHAPTER FORTY FIVE

Caitlin quickened her pace as she walked towards her car, propelled by an overwhelming urge to get away. She drove down into the town, parked her car. She walked over towards North beach, awkwardly clambering over the groynes until she reached a quiet spot. She found a large rock and sat down. She breathed in deeply, several times, blowing the air out of her mouth. She got up and stretched her arms over her head, then reached down to her toes, grimacing as she bent her knees. She sat again, stretching her legs out in front of her. The sea was calm. The tide was going out. She got up, carried on walking to the end of the bay and sat on the pebbles, thinking about her mother. Eventually she got up, limping a little, and walked back towards the town beach. She went into a local shop, bought some sandwiches and a bottle of water, and set off back to the car. She felt as though she was being watched. Maybe people already knew what had happened in her house. She decided to go back over to Charlie's flat. She would stop off somewhere quiet on the way and eat her sandwich.

She drove out of the town. The traffic was heavy so she turned off down a back lane. She was aware of an old blue Land Rover following her. She watched it in her mirror, tried to read the mirror image of the number plate. A game she and Sally often played. She drove up a long hill. The Land Rover was following her closely now. Just as she rounded the brow of the hill, she felt something hit her. The noise of it resounded in her ears. It was all in slow motion. She struggled to hold the wheel. She was off the road through a hedge and down a steep hillside; careering towards a clump of trees. She panicked, she couldn't turn the wheel. She braked hard but the car skidded. She felt the impact as she hit. She jerked forward, the seatbelt prevented her from hitting the windscreen. She felt a searing pain. The airbag activated. She blacked out.

A tall, blonde haired man got out of the Land Rover. He smiled as he stood looking down at the wreck of Caitlin's car. He slid down towards it. Pity the car hadn't burst into flames. He reached the car and tried to open the driver's door. It wouldn't give. He reached through the open window and tried the handle, no luck. He couldn't release it. He was wasting time. He strode round to the passenger door, pulled it open, leaned across Caitlin, unclipped her seat belt and began to pull her out.

He grinned to himself. He was enjoying this. He mouthed, "Time to say goodnight sweetheart."

His endeavours were interrupted by a loud shout. "What the hell do you think you are playing at. Leave the driver where they are. You'll cause more damage. I'm going to phone for an ambulance."

He swore. He let go of Caitlin, got out of the car and saw a man in blue overalls staring down at him. He tried to appear nonchalant but once the man had turned, he sprinted back up the hill to the Land Rover; he threw himself in, turned the key, and drove away. The man sitting in the van behind him talking on his phone looked on in astonishment. He tried to memorise the numberplate. Unbelievable. What a total bastard, leaving the scene of an accident. Probably didn't want the inconvenience. Well, he had got it instead. He would wait.

He got out of his van. Pushed himself through the gap in the hedge, and down to the car. He saw a grey BMW, its front bonnet resting on a tree. It didn't look too bad. The long grass must have slowed the car down. But how on earth could it have happened. He scratched his head. It didn't make sense. Was the driver speeding and lost control? If so, the car would have hit the tree head on and hard. He stood back to view the car. The right back bumper had been damaged.

He knelt close by the passenger door at the woman slumped sideways towards him. Her head was floppy. "Can you hear me? You've been injured. I've phoned for an ambulance. Try not to move anymore." He could see the woman was struggling to breathe. Her eyelids fluttered. She groaned. "Try to stay awake my love. Help's coming." He squatted down beside her, held her hand and continued to talk to her.

Fifteen minutes later he heard the siren. He clambered back up to his vehicle and waved at the ambulance. Two paramedics emerged. They ran over. He called out, "She's down there." The two paramedics clambered down to the car and surveyed the scene. One of them slid into the passenger seat beside Caitlin. The other paramedic managed to wrench the driver's door open.

The paramedic sitting beside Caitlin looked closely at her and frowned. He could see she was having difficulty breathing. What had happened here? The seatbelt could have fractured her ribs causing internal organ damage but she wasn't wearing a seatbelt. The airbag had activated, he could see bruising already forming on her face. "Let's get her out of here."

They extricated her carefully, stretchered her back to the ambulance. Within the ambulance the paramedics assessed her injuries. They gave her oxygen. The second paramedic got out and started the engine. The van driver moved his vehicle forward into a gateway.   The ambulance pulled away, blue lights flashing.

"We're taking you to hospital.   What's your name love?" A pair of blues eyes blinked at him. "Caitlin," she mumbled. He looked more closely at her. "Caitlin Rose? We've met before. I'm Gary. Remember me?" She looked up at him. Her blue eyes huge. She tried to sigh, but it hurt her. He gave her more oxygen. The ambulance started to roll. "We'll have you in hospital in no time. Just hang on in there."

It was Constable Sam Huxley who took the call. He was standing by his vehicle when he heard it come in over the radio. He was trying to calm Dorothy Beddoes down. He knew her of old. When he turned up she had been going hammer and tongs at her long suffering neighbour, Stanley Mason.

"Things from the shed have gone missing. Don't deny it, and you've taken all my pea sticks. Sold them down the car boot I daresay. Well, the police are here now, they'll get to the truth."

Stanley, a countryman through and through, was the same height as Dorothy. They were both small people; both in their eighties. She was wearing an old tweed skirt, a blue twin set, pearls and green wellington boots. Her hair was neatly coiffured. His hair was sparse. He wore a cream shirt tucked into a pair of baggy brown corduroy trousers. A pair of heavy looking brown leather sandals housed his gnarled, grimy feet. Three foot apart, they squared up to each other, neither of them giving way. Sam could see Stanley's fists were clenched.

"For goodness sake woman, why would I steal your things. I come here every week to help you in the garden. I do your odd jobs. I don't steal. As for taking pea sticks, they were rotten. You asked me to dump them last year."

"Did I?"

Sam intervened, "Dorothy, remember, we've spoken about this before. You gave most of your garden tools to your daughter, Deirdre. You can buy some new pea sticks, but it's too late for runner beans this year. Why don't you two go in and have a cup of tea? You heard my radio just then. I'm needed. I'll see you inside, then I've got to go." Dorothy looked up. "Oh, it's you Sam. You've grown."

"Yes, I'm grown up now." He smiled, "Come on both of you. No need for all this." He laid his hand on Stanley's shoulder and began to steer him towards the kitchen. Dorothy followed.

Sam hurried back to his vehicle and radioed in. He was eight miles away from the scene of the accident. He started the engine and sped away smiling. He liked old people. He could only hope they were the best of friends again. That is, until the next time. Maybe he would be like that when he was old and forgetful.

He arrived at the scene of the accident just in time to see an ambulance pulling away. He saw a man hurrying up the lane towards him. He got out and stood looking through the gap in the hedge at a car resting against an oak tree at the bottom of an incline.

He heard footsteps, and a voice speaking rapidly. "Officer, I was on the scene after the accident. I think I know what happened." Sam reached in his pocket for his notebook. "Could you tell me your name, Sir?"

"It's Pete, Peter Johnson. I was on my way to the next farm, when I saw a blue Land Rover blocking the road. I stopped; got out of my van, saw the car. A man was leaning through the passenger door, trying to pull the driver out. I shouted at him to stop. Bloody stupid fellow, he could have caused further injury. He got out and stood looking up at me. I went back to my van and phoned for an ambulance. Then I saw the Land Rover pulling away fast.

I went down to the vehicle. It was a woman at the wheel. The man in the Land Rover had dragged her so that she was slumped over the passenger seat. I spoke to her. I could see she was having trouble breathing, but I didn't want to move her any further.

I got back out and had a look at the car. There's damage on the back right-hand side, maybe the Land Rover collided with the BMW." Sam looked up from his notebook. "Can you give me a description of this man?"

"He was a big bloke. Over six foot I'd say. Powerfully built. He had blondish hair. He stood looking up at me and sort of flicked his hair back, like a girl. He legged it pretty fast." Sam intervened, "What sort of age would you say?"

"The way he handled himself, he could be late twenties, early thirties. A sporty sort of chap." Sam looked up from his notebook. "Do you think you would be able to identify him again?"

"Absolutely. I could see alright." Sam nodded, "Thanks. One last thing, did you notice the Land Rover's number plate?" He nodded. "Yes, I've got it written down. I only glanced as he was speeding away, it might not be accurate. Let me go and get it." Sam turned and peered through the gap in the hedge at the grey BMW resting on a sturdy looking oak tree. He considered the number plate; frowned, had he seen it before? The van driver returned and gave Sam a torn off sheet of paper. Sam glanced down at it, CFE 288D. He wrote the number down. "You say it was blue. Did you notice anything else?"

"Not really. I suppose it was quite clean. Probably not a farm vehicle." Sam nodded and smiled. "Is there anything else you can remember that might help?" The van driver shook his head, delved into his pocket and handed Sam a card. "Is that all?"

"You've been extremely helpful. We might need to have a formal statement from you. Can I call you on this number?" Sam glanced at the card. It told him Mr Peter Johnson was an agricultural engineer. He nodded and started to walk down the lane towards his van. He stopped, turned round and called out. "I might have seen that man before. I'll think on it."

Sam stepped through the gap in the hedge and scrambled down to the car. The doors were still open. If she had a bag, the paramedics had taken it with them. A sandwich covered in cling film and a plastic bottle of water lay on the floor. He looked in the glove box. He pulled out a black wallet holding the car's handbook. He saw a loose piece of paper within it. He pulled it out and stood back, nodding his head. That's where he'd seen the car. Two days before he had been at Rock House looking for a Mazda. He'd seen this car parked outside the garage. It belonged to Caitlin Rose.

He walked back up the slope, opened his car door and sat down thinking. Then he picked up his radio and called in.

CHAPTER FORTY SIX

Superintendent John Fletcher was being given a hard time. He held the phone away from his ear as the voice on the other end rose further. "For God's sake, I told you Caitlin was being stalked. Why hadn't you arrested him?" He sighed, "Calm down Charlie. We don't know if it was Dennis Gough. We've traced the Land Rover. We're trying to contact the owner. He's away on holiday. He may have lent the vehicle to a friend, or it might have been stolen."

"That's not good enough John. It must have been Dennis. Who else would have the opportunity and motive?" John Fletcher looked grim. Charlie was right. They had been concentrating on gathering evidence from David Jones's bungalow. Alice Brown was under arrest. Once she knew David Jones was dead, she had confessed to helping him with the scam.

"So far there has been no evidence against Dennis Gough. Nothing that we have found in David Jones's paperwork to involve him."

"Come on John, pull the other one. He was clearly involved with Alice Brown and David Jones. Have you forgotten what they were trying to pull? You know, David Jones had fabricated paperwork to make Alice Brown Caitlin's next of kin. It was obvious they were trying to hurt her. Well, it was obvious to me, but then I'm not a superintendent in the Fraud Squad am I? I was just trying to protect my client." He sighed again. "I hadn't forgotten Caitlin. With Jones dead I had assumed their plan had died with him."

"Well you assumed wrong." Charlie's laugh mocked him. He felt hurt by her attitude, then pulled himself up.

She had become far too involved with her client. But she was right, the damage to Caitlin's car and the testimony from the van driver pointed towards a deliberate attempt on Caitlin's life. For that he was sorry. He found it difficult to comprehend. Unless it had been an act of revenge, it didn't make sense. Even on a quiet road, there would always be a chance that another vehicle would arrive on the scene. It must have been carried out on the spur of the moment. If it was Dennis, why would he have taken the risk?

Charlie broke their silence. "I'm sorry, John. You're right, it couldn't have been foreseen. But she's sitting in hospital with broken ribs and a broken nose. Whoever tried to drag her out meant to hurt her. She's in a hell of a state. Have your officers interviewed her yet?" Before he could reply she fired another question, "Are you going to protect her? What's to stop him, whoever he is, trying again?" She couldn't hide the contempt in her voice.

John Fletcher remained calm. His voice was level and controlled. "A colleague has been to see Caitlin. She remembers the collision and the car careering out of control. When she came to, she thinks she heard a man talking, that's all. Rest assured, we're looking for Dennis Gough. We have a good description from the van driver. We have a constable outside Caitlin's room. If anyone shows up they'll be apprehended."

"Has the Land Rover been dumped? Surely Dennis has a car of his own. Why was he driving a Land Rover? Might be worth checking local garages, see if his car is being serviced or something. Caitlin said he works for a local Estate Agent. Have you made enquiries about him yet? He has a flat in town. He's that stupid he might just be lying low there."

"Thank you Charlie." He heard her snort. "No, I mean it. We are moving as quickly as we can on this. We will apprehend him and if he is identified by the van driver, then he will be arrested."

"Have you done background checks on Dennis Gough? Who is he, where did he come from? I'm not just angry about the attack John, I'm frustrated. I promised you I would stop my involvement, but I don't like loose ends. Dennis appeared like a bad penny after Caitlin moved into Rock House. It's clear he was part of David Jones's set up. What relationship did he have with him? Look, can we meet? I can be another pair of hands. I'm sure Caitlin would agree to continue employing me. Even if she didn't, it's what I need to do."

"I'm not going to be able to stop you am I?" John sighed, "Look, I have two good officers working on this with me. My sergeant, Simon Auger, and Constable Sam Huxley. Sam was the first on the scene at Rock House and first on the scene after Caitlin's accident. He's as keen as mustard and has local knowledge."

Charlie sounded impatient, "So, can we meet?"

"Tonight. I'll come to you. I've got my own loose ends to tie up here. I'll bring a takeaway."

True to his word, John Fletcher knocked on Charlie's door at seven thirty that evening. He stood holding a plastic bag containing a Chinese takeaway and a bottle of chilled white wine. Charlie opened the door and stood looking at him. Her expression was far from welcoming. She beckoned him into the kitchen. In silence, she took plates out of the cupboard and laid the table. John sat down. He nodded his head. "OK, say whatever you want to say, get it over and done with."

She sat opposite him, her arms folded. "You must

know how many women get murdered by their ex-partners. You should have treated Dennis Gough more seriously."

"Alright, point taken. In our defence, I thought you had her back. She was staying with you wasn't she?"

Charlie glared at him. "Don't John. Don't blame me for this."

"Charlie, think about it. Don't get so emotional. Once David Jones's death was out, we had to move quickly. We had all the evidence we needed to arrest Alice Brown. We're going through the correspondence from Jones's bungalow. There's nothing about Dennis Gough in the papers. We don't know yet what relationship there may have been between the three of them. Or whether there are more people involved. Remember, I'm investigating fraud."

Charlie uncrossed her arms, put her elbows on the table and held her head in her hands. They were both silent. He watched her closely. He was pretty sure she knew she was being unreasonable. He sighed, "Look Charlie, I'd like to work with you not against you. We have a forensic search going on to find out exactly how Jones operated. Files from Barrett and Jones have been requisitioned. We are going to be questioning Trevor Jones tomorrow. Sam Huxley broke the news of his father's death to him. Apparently, he showed little emotion. If anything, Sam said he seemed satisfied."

Charlie looked up at him. "You say you'd like to work with me. Include me then. I've been as closely associated with the conspiracy against Caitlin as you have with the fraud. Listen to what I've got to say. I'm not in the force anymore, but my gut instincts and analyses remain just as sharp, maybe sharper."

"Point taken again Charlie. I could bring you in. I've got Benson and James working on the Dennis Gough angle. They'll find him. Let me think about this. Come into the station on Monday. We'll go from there."

Charlie wasn't sure what to make of John's offer but agreed. "My instincts told me all along that Caitlin was in danger. I should have ensured she wasn't alone. I hoped she would drive straight back to my place, but she didn't. Dennis must have spotted her in the town and followed her."

"Well, you can soul search all you want, but you know as well as I do, human beings don't do what you expect. If they did, our job would be easy. Now let's eat."

CHAPTER FORTY SEVEN

SATURDAY 3RD AUGUST

"I feel as though I've been dragged through a hedge backwards not pushed through one!" Caitlin tried to laugh. She winced with pain from her broken ribs. She was in a private room in the County Hospital. She had woken up feeling the warmth of someone's hand in hers. Squinting upwards she saw Bob. When he saw she was awake, a fleeting look of guilt passed over his face. He tried to extricate his hand, but she squeezed it and smiled.

"My ribs are so sore, and I must look a sight." She reached up to stroke her nose. "The doctor tells me this will heal in a couple of weeks. I don't know which part of me hurts the most, they're all in competition. Just don't make me laugh."

"I'll try not to! You've got a great shiner developing there." He reached over and touched her cheek. They gazed at one another. "Stick with me Bob. I've got a lot of stuff to work through." She sighed and winced again. "They're saying all of me will heal without their intervention, and they're bound to need the bed. Maybe they'll let me go later. I'd like to wake up in my own bed tomorrow."

He squeezed her hand, "Ann and Sally plan to visit you this afternoon. The house is ready and waiting for you. When you're home we're going to look after you. You won't be safe until Dennis Gough is behind bars. The man's a lunatic. The police are taking it seriously now. There's a constable on watch outside." Her brow furrowed, "Are they sure it was him? Why would he have run me off the road?"

"He did it because he could Cat." He looked down at her hand in his. "Men like him see women as their possession. You felt you were being watched. The answer is, you were, he was stalking you. It was bad luck the traffic was busy yesterday and you took the back lane. He'd been waiting for a chance to get you on your own. It was a vicious attack. He could have killed you." Caitlin shivered, causing another wave of pain. "Maybe he didn't realise David Jones was dead and their plan exposed."

"You may well be right. The police are still looking for him. I've had a chat with Charlie. She was furious with her friendly superintendent. From her choice language, I don't think she rates the police too highly." Caitlin grinned, she could imagine Charlie swearing at John Fletcher. He would be calm and that would rile her even more. She looked up at Bob. "I'd feel better if I knew what the police were doing. Is that dreadful DI on the case again." Bob laughed, "I have a feeling they'll be rushing around like a load of farts in a colander. That's one of my dad's old sayings. Perfect description of the pair of them. A pair of farts!"

"No Bob, don't make me laugh." Caitlin held onto her ribs. "Oh, bloody hell." Realising what she had said, she apologised.

"I saw a different sergeant yesterday evening but I couldn't tell him anything useful. I saw a blue Land Rover behind me, and I felt it collide with the back of my car. I remember trying to slow the car down." She frowned, "I guess my old Beamer's a write off. Whoever did this to me is a total bastard." Bob looked at his watch. "Cat, I'm sorry, I'm going to have to go. The Ward Sister gave me an hour before the ward round. I think I hear them coming. I'll hang around outside. Hopefully you can come home later. I'll find out before I go and let Ann know. She and Sally can fetch you."

Caitlin closed her eyes for a moment. "I wish you didn't have to go. I know what I want to say, but I'm scared." She blinked through her two bleary, bruised eyes.

"Please never be scared of me. I want to hug you, but I don't want to hurt you." Her eyes filled with tears. "I don't care if it hurts. Hold me for a moment."

CHAPTER FORTY EIGHT

CHARLIE

I walked into the station. Roy, the same avuncular Desk Sergeant greeted me. This time he handed me a visitor's badge and called straight through to John Fletcher. He let me through. A young male officer asked me to follow him. He took me up the stairs and into John's office. John came out from behind his desk and shook my hand. "Let me introduce you to Constable Huxley, Sam this is Charlotte Taylor, known as Charlie."

I looked more closely at him as I shook his hand. Fresh faced, freckles on his nose, smiling brown eyes and tall, much taller than me. He was in plain clothes, blue trousers and a light grey sweat shirt hanging loosely on him. His dark hair was cut in a style I recognised from my teens. I wondered if he was a Beatles fan. He grinned and winked at me. "Morning Miss Taylor. I've heard a lot about you."

"All good I hope." John interrupted, "Thank you Sam. I hope Charlie will join us as a civilian investigator. I need to brief her, then I'll bring her in to meet the rest of the team." He looked at his watch. "Team briefing at ten thirty a.m. Tell the others please."

"Take a seat Charlie." John sat opposite me summing me up. There was a part of me that looked forward to being in a team again, but I was unsure of my role and the team's expectation of me. I had dressed carefully in a plain white shirt and dark trousers. I carried a brown leather document case over my shoulder. It contained Caitlin's notes and photographs. As a civilian investigator, I would be professional and maintain distance from John Fletcher and the rest of his team. I hadn't started off too well with young Sam. Cheeky blighter.

I wasn't sure why John wanted me on his team. I had already given him most of the information I had. I couldn't remember whether Caitlin had told him she believed her mother was murdered. I did remember her saying the police should investigate George Rose's death. Budgets were always tight. John must have pulled something out of the bag to want me there with them.

"Thanks for coming in Charlie. It's good to have you back."

"Why do you want me on your team John?" He turned away, got up, walked over to the door and shut it. He sat opposite me, his brow furrowed. "I observed you in action in Cornwall. Your creativity and tenacity impressed me. I think you will be able to unearth evidence others might not reach. I trust your instincts and your sense of justice."

"There are things I won't be able to do without a badge."

"Sam will work with you. He's a good officer and known in the locality." I thought for a moment he might allude to the David Jones break in. Clever man, his omission spoke louder. I was expected to work by the book. He carried on, "Sam has been busy going through the archives. He found Cecilia Rose's file. We went through them together, the notes were inconclusive. There was no mention of witnesses being interviewed at the time. It may be that we get nowhere, but I think Caitlin deserves closure. Alice Brown has hinted there may have been foul play involved in Cecilia and George Rose's death. His death is recorded as liver failure.

That's where you come in. I want both investigated. Paul Benson and Harry James are trying to locate Dennis Gough. I hope they will have news today. Other names are mentioned in David Jones's papers. I believe there may be separate paper trails. Our search at Barrett and Jones was futile. I understood from you that Cecilia Rose's house was cleared, it's a long shot, but there may still be something there." I shivered. It looked as though David Jones, a small town solicitor, a so called respected member of the community, had got away with murder.

"How are you going to sell this? Paul and Harry will hardly be happy having me poking around."

"Leave them to me. I want you to start with David Jones. Who was he? What was his involvement with George Rose? Talk to the old chap who hinted at David Jones's involvement the night of Cecilia Rose's death. Was he really there? Are there any other witnesses? It's a small town. People will remember her death."

"I'm not comfortable John, this is police work."

"I'm asking you because I believe you are the best person. Cold cases need the sort of investigative skills and sensitivity you possess. You've worked with Caitlin and have a good relationship with her. She's going to need support whether we are able to prove foul play or not."

"Who will I be accountable to?" John smiled at me. "You will be accountable to me. Sam will report back to the team."

"You're right, I want to see justice done. OK, I'll give it my best shot. How much of this are we going to share with Caitlin?"

"While Paul and Harry remain convinced Caitlin had a hand in David Jones falling down those stairs, you are not there to investigate her. All she needs to know is you will be exploring the events that led to her mother's and step-father's deaths. If you pick up any other evidence then I am relying on you to share it with me."

I nodded and looked at my watch. "About time for the briefing? Take me to the lion's den. You do know that Harry James got the DS job when I applied for it?" That got a smile out of John. He knew all about it alright. My mind flashed back to our first meeting in Cornwall. I'd liked him then even though I suspected he was a copper. Pity he hadn't been my boss back in the day. I'd probably still be on the force. But what was I thinking. No, I was in a better place. If Paul and Harry didn't like it, tough, they had no choice.

I followed John out of his office into the main area. I could see Paul and Harry sitting by the window. Paul looked as ungainly as ever. His shaven head, pink and sore. The top of his nose red and peeling. Harry, in contrast, looked tanned and healthy, a fine specimen, pity he had so little going on inside his head.

There was a third man sitting beside them. When I glanced at him I had to blink twice. He looked like a curly headed, blonde cherub with a button nose, and twinkling blue eyes. A grown up version of the child in the Bubbles picture. I walked towards him, holding my hand out. He sprang up from his chair and gave me a beaming smile. He was a little taller than me, maybe five seven, neat but chunky. He looked as though he could handle himself. A small Lord Fauntleroy, he probably had to learn bare knuckle fighting early on. We shook hands. Good grip – but I could match his. He beckoned me to a chair beside him.

"DS Simon Auger. You must be Charlie. I've heard a

lot about you." That's twice I'd heard the same phrase this morning. What on earth had they been cooking up about me? I sat down, crossed my legs and folded my arms. They weren't going to have the satisfaction of getting a rise out of me. I looked round the office. It felt so familiar. John had an all-male team. Now he had bought me in, the dynamics would change. Paul would see me as a disruptor.

Sam was standing near a table with a kettle just about coming to the boil. He asked us what we wanted, added teabags or a spoonful of coffee to mugs; he reached down and pulled a carton of milk out of a small refrigerator. He turned round, a resolute look on his face. "Come and get it then." Surprisingly, they did what they were asked. I could hear Paul muttering under his breath as he lumbered out of his chair. Some things don't change.

I settled down with my coffee. Took a notebook and pen out of my case and looked over at the board. I could see a picture of David Jones and Alice Brown. I recognised a picture of George Rose looking a lot younger than in the picture Caitlin had shown me. Caitlin's photo was missing and I couldn't spot Dennis Gough either. John stood in front of the board. "First of all, welcome to the team Charlie. Charlie is joining us as a civilian investigator. She's going to be working with Sam investigating the cold cases. Now, what's the news on Dennis Gough? Have you managed to locate him yet?"

Paul took a sip of his tea, licked his lips and spoke. "He's a mystery. Basically he doesn't exist. Given the date of birth he gave the estate agent, the only Dennis Gough on record died in 1972 at the age of three."

John shook his head in disgust, "Why doesn't that

surprise me? Have you managed to find where he worked?"

"He wasn't working Gov." Harry sneered. "He was a probationer at Gordons Estate Agents in November last year. They dismissed him when they checked his references. They were bogus. We've asked around. Nothing. We've hit a dead end."

I reached for a memory. "Hold on a moment, let me have a look in my notes." I scanned several pages, "Ah, here we are. Alice Brown once worked in the Spar at the top of the High Street. She'd been seen in the town and a shop assistant thought she sometimes stayed in a flat with a man. You could try asking up in the shop."

Paul stared at me, flicked his tongue over his lips and sniggered. "Thank you Charlie. We'll do that. Where did you get this information from?"

"The assistant's name is Edna Savage. She gave the information to Caitlin Rose." He grunted, "I see, well we'll follow it up, although I wouldn't trust Caitlin Rose further than I could throw her." John interrupted, "OK Paul, leave Caitlin to Charlie." He turned, "Harry, did Gordon's have any photo ID of Dennis Gough?"

"Sorry Guv, nothing doing there."

"Caitlin's back in Rock House, she'll surely have some photos of her ex-boyfriend, whoever he is."

"As you know her so well Charlie, can you get up there and see her today please. It's important we find this man. Sam, you go with Charlie." Sam looked over at me and smiled with satisfaction.

"Simon, you're with me. Trevor Jones has agreed to come in for questioning. We'll see him together this morning. We'll have another go at Alice Brown. She's got to know who Dennis Gough is and whether he was part of the holiday scam."

Paul got up, walked over to John. "Can I see you in your office John?" John looked at him and frowned. "Very well, but I'm warning you, I will not withhold information from any member of my team." I watched as Paul struggled to contain his temper. He turned to me. "Since when do we employ private investigators? Is she going to be subject to our rules and regs, I don't think so." Simon raised his eyebrows. "And you are Paul?"

"That's enough. Paul, come into my office now." Simon watched John shut the office door. "Don't worry Charlie. Paul's bark is worse than his bite. John's a good man, he'll sort him. I'm glad you're on board. Hope we can work together."

"Thanks Simon. Sam, you're with me. Let's go. I think you've been to Rock House before. You can tell me all about it in the car."

CHAPTER FORTY NINE

The entrance to Rock House was obstructed by a large white van. Two workmen were in the process of installing gates. They slowed; Charlie rolled down her window. One of the workmen stopped what he was doing and walked to the car. "Hello, what can we do for you?" He peered into the car and broke into a smile. "Hello Sam." Sam got out of the car and greeted the workman. "Hello Justin. You installing gates for Miss Rose?" He said, stating the obvious. "Yeah, trying to keep Caitlin safe. What are you doing here? No uniform?" He laughed, "They haven't got you doing detective work already?"

"What's so funny? I'm with Miss Taylor. She's an investigator working with us." He bent down to Charlie's window. "This is Justin, Bob's cousin." Charlie got out. "Hello Justin, I've heard a lot about you." She stopped and thought, I'm doing it now, it's catching. "Glad you're making the property more secure." She pointed, "Is that an intercom?"

"Yes, but it's not connected yet. I've heard a lot about you too, Charlie." Charlie stifled a giggle.

"We can park and walk down, save you moving the van." She got back in the car and reversed onto the grass verge. Justin and Sam were joined by the other workman. The three men moved the heavy metal gates across so Charlie could squeeze through. Sam followed her and they walked down the shady drive to the house. They stood regarding it in the sunshine. Charlie spoke first, "Terrible things can happen in houses. Sometimes I think it's possible to sense it, but this one just looks warm and welcoming to me."

Sam shivered, "Maybe, but I won't forget what happened here in a hurry. I'd never seen a violent death before. I was mesmerized by his staring eyes, then I looked up and saw Miss Rose standing there all bloodied. I radioed in for help. Paul and Harry turned up."

"It's time for you to meet Caitlin properly then. Let's go in." They walked up the steps to the front door and rang the bell followed by the sound of excited barking. They heard a chain being attached. Seeing Charlie, Ann took the chain off and opened the door wide. A brown bundle of fluff bounded out and ran round them in circles. Ann spoke firmly, "Coco, come." The little dog pricked her ears up and stopped for a moment, then she resumed, only this time, she made a running jump at Sam. He bent down and picked her up. "Calm down Coco, be a good girl." She licked his face. Her enthusiastic welcome made him chuckle. "It's you Sam. How are you?"

"I'm good, Mrs Saunders. I'm working with Miss Taylor. We've come to see Miss Rose." She frowned, "Should I be calling you, Constable Huxley then?" He shook his head,

"No, that's alright. Can we see Miss Rose?"

They followed Ann across the hall into a brightly lit lounge, sun streaming through the long front windows. Caitlin was lying on the sofa. When she saw them her bruised face broke into a smile; she struggled to sit up. Charlie walked over and knelt down beside her. "You're looking a lot better than when I last saw you. How are your ribs? I broke one once. Blooming painful."

"I'm alright as long as I don't laugh or move too suddenly." Caitlin smiled and turned to Sam. "Who's this handsome young man?"

"Constable Sam Huxley, Miss. I was here last week."

Caitlin's face fell. "Yes, I remember you now. I'd rather not remember that day." Deflated by Caitlin's remark, Sam apologised. "No, sorry, I didn't mean to remind you of it. How's your friend? Sally, wasn't it?"

"She's almost made a full recovery. She's in the garden. Ann, could you go and fetch her. She'll want to see Charlie." Charlie studied the composed young woman in front of her. Dark glasses hid her bruised eyes. A simple dressing covering the wound on her knee. Her right hand looked healed. However, studying her more closely, Charlie realised that there was a deep melancholy about her. She had mistaken immobility, the fear of sudden movement, for composure. Her physical injuries would heal. Charlie was less sure about her mental state.

"As of this morning, I'm a civilian working with the police. That's why Sam and I are here. I'm afraid, it's not just a friendly call."

Caitlin's face fell. "I don't understand. Why would you do that?"

"It's good news Cat. Superintendent Fletcher has taken what you said very seriously. He wants to reopen your mother's case as well as investigating what might have happened to George Rose. That's what Sam and I will be doing."

"Oh my God. Is that true?" She sat up straight. A spasm of pain crossed her face; she hugged her chest.

"Don't get your hopes up too much Cat, we might not find anything, but we'll do our best for you." Sally appeared in the doorway. Sam stared at her. He had last seen what he thought was a dying woman lying on the floor upstairs. Here she was as large as life. She looked young and vibrant, dressed casually, her face bare of makeup and hair tied back in a ponytail. She walked over and embraced Charlie. A wide smile on her face.

"Tell Sal what you just told me Charlie." Charlie stepped back and explained as briefly as she could.

Sam wanting to mark his authority, turned to the three women. "The reason we're here now is to ask if you have any photographs of Dennis. It seems he's vanished into thin air."

Caitlin bit her lip. "He never wanted to be in photos. He'd make a face or look the other way." She turned to Sally, "Could you nip upstairs to my bedroom. There's a photo album in the bookcase. There might be something." When Sally came back with the album, she and Caitlin sat on the sofa leafing through the pages. There were a lot of empty spaces. They got to the last page. "There's nothing here Sam. I'm sorry. Dennis must have removed them." Caitlin shook her head, "Why would he do that? He was vain, but that's ridiculous." She looked up from the album. "Hang on. I should have a photo of him. Early on in our relationship, I took quite a good one. He wasn't looking straight at me, so it's not quite face on. I kept it in my bag. It might still be there. The bag's upstairs."

"I'll go." Ann got up and made for the door.

Caitlin turned and shook her head. "He didn't want to leave a trace. What a scheming rat he was."

She came back carrying Caitlin's bag. "This is heavy Cat. You got the kitchen sink in it?' Caitlin smiled, "Let's hope the photo's still there. Turn it upside down on the carpet Ann." Ann and Sally got down on their knees. "Eureka – I think this might be it." Ann held up a creased photograph. She passed it to Sam. He looked closely. A blonde haired man, wine glass in hand, sitting on a garden chair. He knelt beside Caitlin, "Is this the one you mean?" She removed her sunglasses to look at the photo, revealing remarkable blue eyes. The skin around the eyes was beginning to heal, shades of yellow mixed with dark red bruising. "Yes, this is the one. I took it when we were first together. That's why I kept it close by me. To swoon over." She sighed, "I was an idiot."

"Can we take it? You can have it back." She nodded, "Keep it, I don't want it back."

Sam passed the photo over to Charlie. She looked over at Caitlin and smiled. "Thanks Cat. This will be helpful." She sat back in her chair, notebook in hand. "Remind me Cat, you said Dennis was secretive, that you knew little about him?"

"That's right. He told me his parents were dead. He had an uncle, but he never got round to introducing us. He didn't even tell me where his uncle lived. In a way I was glad. I wanted to keep him to myself. Then, later I began to realise how little he shared. Not just about his life, but generally. He didn't understand give and take. I began to feel like his servant."

Charlie and Sam looked at one another. Sam, following Charlie's lead, didn't disclose that Dennis Gough had falsified his identity. The Super had been clear. They were only there to ask for photographs. Annoyingly, they had to hand everything over to Paul and Harry. Sally sat down next to her friend. "Darling, I know you've struggled to understand what happened. I know what you're like, always trying to second guess; always taking the blame. We've said this before. Dennis was playing a part and he wasn't capable of playing it very well."

Caitlin sighed, "Then he ran me off the road. See, I don't understand that either. Didn't he know David Jones had been rumbled? Was he still thinking Alice Brown would inherit? Bloody stupid; he would have killed me for nothing."

Ann got up. "Well it's over now. We are going to keep you safe until that maniac is behind bars. You have to move forward Cat." She glared at Sam and Charlie. "You should get on with your jobs. Catch him. Don't come back here until you do. We all need to move forward. It's not fair to expect Cat to keep dredging up the past." She looked over at Sally and Caitlin; her expression softened. "Who'd like a drink? I expect we could all do with one."

"Let me help." Charlie got up and followed her to the kitchen. "I'm sorry, sometimes we have to ask tough questions. I know Cat's not safe until we find Dennis."

Ann frowned as she studied Charlie. "I'm staying here until you do." She switched the kettle on. "Are you investigating David Jones? What he was doing in this house?" She was no longer the friendly woman Charlie had first met. "I can't discuss that Ann, not my job. Sam and I are only reinvestigating the deaths of Cecilia and George Rose. It means digging into David Jones's past, the other detectives are investigating what happened here. Can I ask, do you remember David Jones as a younger man?"

"He was older than me. I didn't move in the same circles until later when I joined the tennis club. I remember his sister. She used to come to the club socials. I'm pretty sure she was a sister, not a girlfriend."

"That's helpful. Thanks Ann. When there's news, one of the detectives will keep Caitlin informed."

Ann spooned tea leaves into a teapot. She walked over to one of the kitchen cupboards; she pulled out a cake tin, found a large tray, placed mugs, plates, a teapot, a jug of milk and a bowl of sugar onto it. She regarded Charlie for a moment, her arms crossed over her chest, her face grim. "Now you're working with the police, it's quite different. You have to understand, we all want to protect Caitlin. The poor girl has been through hell. I don't know what those two detectives did to her, but she's terrified. They won't be welcome here. Maybe you would like to convey that to your new bosses."

Charlie swallowed. She felt an animosity that she hadn't experienced for years. As far as Ann was concerned, she had crossed over to the dark side. "I understand what you're saying but when I was offered an opportunity to do this, I was only thinking of Cat. She wants to find out how her mother died. I hope I can do that for her. Once my job with the police is finished, I'll be back to being Charlie Bond, PI again."

Ann shook her head. "I hope you're right." She pointed, "Are you good at carrying trays, there you are, make yourself useful."

On the journey back to the station Sam and Charlie were silent. Charlie remembered she had given John Fletcher the idea of being called in as some sort of investigator. Hubris. She thought she was important. When she'd asked John Fletcher why he had wanted her on the team, he flattered her. What he'd done was manipulate her and she'd fallen for it. Ann was no fool, she'd figured it out. The police still thought Caitlin was involved in the death of David Jones. What had John said, no secrets? She would have a duty to report any suspicions. She could kick herself for trusting him. She thought she was special. She hadn't considered how Caitlin and her friends would feel about her. How it would change the dynamics. She had engineered this, she would have to make it right. She sighed.

"Are you OK?" She saw concern written all over Sam's face.

"I mustn't do harm Sam. Whatever happens I mustn't do harm. We must concentrate on finding out about David Jones and the past."

Sam looked puzzled. "Yes, that's what we're doing."

CHAPTER FIFTY

The office was empty. Sam pinned Dennis Gough's photo on the board and scribbled a note for Paul Benson. The van driver said he had had a good look at the driver of the Land Rover. They should be able to ascertain whether that person was the man who called himself Dennis or not. Then all they had to do was find him.

Sam showed Charlie the desk that had been assigned to her. He settled down at his own desk, switched on his computer and began the search for David Jones and his family.

"Sam, wasn't Trevor Jones coming in today? We could ask him about an aunt."

"We don't know how he's involved Charlie. Maybe not a good idea. I should be able to find something online. Give me an hour. I think the Super left Cecilia and George Rose's file on the desk for you."

Charlie was startled, "There's a file on George Rose? So they didn't think he died of natural causes?"

"He was involved in a drink drive accident. His licence was revoked. Not much else in it."

Charlie sat at her new desk and tried to concentrate on Cecilia's file. She looked around her. What was she doing here? She wanted to run back to her own office, where clients chose her, briefed her and worked with her. She could have refused John. She had no one to blame but herself. Now she must concentrate on the job in hand. She must be utterly professional. Stick to the task she had been set. She was startled out of her reverie by an excited voice. "I've got her – the sister. She was born Janet Jones. She married a George Rose in 1959. Divorced in 1962."

Charlie got up and went over to Sam. She looked at his screen in disbelief. "What!"

He started to repeat what he had just said. "I heard you Sam. They were brothers in law? How come nobody knew that?"

"I suppose divorce was frowned upon back then. Families kept things quiet. We'd better find her." Charlie wondered if Sam had been a boy scout. He did indeed sound as keen as mustard. "Let's start at the local museum. They can point us in the right direction. We might just strike lucky. Janet was born in 1932. She'd be seventy now. She may still be alive."

"Hold on Sam. She's not that old, why did you think of the local museum?"

Hearing footsteps they both looked up. John Fletcher stood at the door. Eyebrows raised. "There's a lot of excitement in here. What's going on?"

"We've found the link between David Jones and George Rose, Sir. David had an older sister called Janet. She married George Rose in 1959. Divorced two years later."

"Good work Sam. Trevor Jones has just left for his office. He should know where his aunt is. Give him a call." Sam looked uncomfortable. "Should we alert him Sir?" The Superintendent smiled. "Trevor Jones does not appear to be a party to his father's plans. There's no evidence. He made his feelings very clear. Quite simply, he loathed his father. He was ashamed when he heard the circumstances of his death. Worried it would get into the newspapers. Not sorry he was dead."

Charlie spoke up. "I don't think Trevor Jones ever told Caitlin that George Rose was his uncle. We do need to tread carefully."

"Point taken Charlie, but families keep secrets. It's possible he didn't know." He lowered his gaze momentarily. "Maybe not probable. I might be wrong about him. See what you can dig up first. Anything else happening? Did you manage to find a photograph?"

"Sorry Sir, yes, I've pinned it up on the board. It was the only one Miss Rose had. Not full face." Charlie interjected, "He knew what he was doing. He hid his identity. Lots of empty spaces in the photo album. Luckily he missed one. Caitlin kept it hidden from him."

"Good, Paul and Harry will deal with Dennis. You two find that aunt, and I want you to talk to the old chap who was with David Jones the night of Cecilia's death. See if you can jog his memory a bit more. The man's dying, don't leave it too long." He walked over to the board, stared at the new image then strode back into his office. He shut the door.

Charlie watched John go back into his office. She grumbled to herself. It was inconvenient being on the other side of the office to Sam. She called over, "Let's start with Bert Savage, the chap who says he was there with Cecilia on the night in question. His wife's called Edna. They should be in the phone book. Make an appointment for this afternoon."

Charlie sat staring unseeingly at Cecilia's file. If David's sister had come to the tennis club socials and had been there often enough for Ann to remember her, the probability was that she didn't live too far away. The chances were Bert Savage might know her. He was friendly with George at the time, friendly enough to be out drinking with him. George and David Jones remained friends, or at least, it seemed they needed one another. Her thoughts were interrupted by Sam calling over.

"I've spoken to Edna Savage. Bert's in hospital. I've rung the hospital. We can go in this afternoon during visiting. He's not been well, but they've stabilised him. Visiting's at three."

"Thanks Sam. We've got some time to kill. Maybe your idea about the museum wasn't a bad one. Why don't we pay them a visit. Get some fish and chips first. I'm starving."

They sat on the harbour wall, guarding their meal from marauding gulls. They watched one gull swooping down to snatch a piece of battered fish from an unsuspecting tourist. "The reason the gulls are thieving from here, not out at sea catching fish, is because tourists feed them. Look at that man over there, throwing chips up for them. I think I'll have a word." Sam went to get up. Charlie held his arm. "You'll probably get a load of abuse. Get some signs made up asking people not to feed the gulls. That might work." He remained where he was sighing loudly. By now a flock of herring gulls was circling the square. Some were strutting around. Charlie shivered. There was a sense of menace about them with their long beaks. They could start attacking humans. A classic Hitchcockian scenario. Hardly likely.

A family with two small children and a white terrier dog saved them from further gull harassment. The parents had no control over the children or the dog. The children chased the gulls and the dog chased the children. In no time the square was clear of gulls. The children settled down to eat their chips. The dog settled down to watch the children eat their chips. His gaze unwavering. Every time a gull landed, the children chased them away, the parents took no notice of the drama going on at all.

Sam, who had finished his meal, shook his head in

disbelief. "Chaos. Doesn't do to want a quiet meal down here." Charlie offered Sam her remaining chips, he shook his head, got up and took their package to the bins. He came back, a determined expression on his face. "I expect those open bins get raided. The council should put in covered ones. I'm going to do something about it." He looked so serious, Charlie chuckled. "Sorry Constable Huxley. You were awfully solemn just then. It's great you care. You're going to be a fantastic community copper! Right, how long have we got? Time to have a quick mosey in the museum. I'd like to have a look at some of the old photographs. Get a feeling of how it was thirty years ago. Then we'd better go visiting."

CHAPTER FIFTY ONE

Bert Savage was tucked away in a side room beside the nurses' station. Dressed in blue checked pyjamas and a brown woollen dressing gown, he sat on a chair, an oxygen cannister beside him. He held the oxygen mask in his hand. He looked up expecting to see his wife. Instead, he saw the tall figure of Sam Huxley, followed by a woman. Police. He should have guessed.

Seeing the lack of chairs, Charlie went out and found two. When she came back in, Sam was on his knees beside Bert. Charlie put the chairs down and went over to shake Bert's hand. He wheezed and swallowed. "I trusted her, she said she didn't want revenge." Sam sat down beside him. "You know about David Jones. It was an accident Bert. Miss Rose wasn't involved." He held his mask to his nose and took several breaths. "She's bright. She figured out who I meant by 'the locker man'." Charlie intervened, "Bert, may I call you that?" He nodded, "It truly was an accident. He had broken into her house and he fell down the stairs." Bert sat weighing them both up. "So, what do you want from me?"

Charlie began, "You were friends with David Jones. We're interested in his past."

His eyes narrowed. "Why?"

"We have reason to believe that Cecilia Rose's death may not have been an accident. The case has been reopened. That's why we're interested in David Jones and George Rose. Their relationship could be the key."

Sam reached over and touched Bert's arm. "We want to see justice done Bert. Justice for your friend Harry too. Do you know anything about either of the men's past?" He shook his head. If he knew anything, he wasn't going to tell them. Sam tried again. "Did you know David Jones had a sister?" He nodded. "Janet wasn't it. She was his older sister. They lived in an old farmhouse up the other side of the hill."

"Can you remember the name of the farmhouse?" Bert seemed to be weighing up whether to tell them or not. Eventually he said, "It would have been Manor Farm. That's where they all lived." He shut his eyes, and breathed into his mask again. He sat back, exhausted.

Charlie got up. "I'm sorry, we've tired you out. You've been really helpful."

He looked at them both, tears in his eyes and whispered. "Just tell me it wasn't her revenge. She seemed such a nice young woman. I don't want to go to my maker with his death on my conscience." Sam crouched down, shaking his head. "I was there Bert. I answered the call. It was an accident, I promise you." He stared at them both; he nodded, leaned back in his chair and shut his eyes. They left quietly.

They sat in the car both thinking of death. Whatever had happened to Cecilia Rose that night was linked to the present. Death was stalking Bert. Neither of them wanted to press him too far. They might have to. He knew more than he was saying. At least he had given them a lead. "Did you notice, Sam. Bert said, they *all* lived in the farmhouse. Let's try and find it. There's an ordnance survey map in the glove compartment. We need to find that farmhouse." Ten minutes later, Charlie pulled out of the hospital car park. They were going fishing into the past. See what they could catch.

CHAPTER FIFTY TWO

They drove out of the town. Sam, following the map, directed Charlie to a network of country roads that all looked the same. High hedges on both sides. Narrow lanes with what seemed to be indiscriminate passing places. Meeting a tractor would be tricky. Eight miles out, they spotted a sign for Manor Farm Kennels on a crossroads. They followed the sign which led them up an even narrower lane. Charlie was beginning to worry they had taken a wrong turning. She was relieved when they saw an entrance with a small sign to the Kennels. She slowed down to a crawl and began to turn into the entrance.

"Look." Sam pointed, "I can't quite make out the small print. I'll get out and have a look." When he got back in he smiled in satisfaction. "It says, 'Proprietor, Mrs J. Morris' – fingers crossed, that's our Janet."

As they drove on, the drive widened. There were neatly trimmed hedges on both sides. The grass verge looked as though it had been recently cut. They heard the sound of dogs barking in the distance. They reached what might once have been a busy farmyard. The farmhouse was positioned further back, a solid looking stone built building, surrounded on three sides by a stone wall. There was a green wooden gate leading into the house. The entrance sign on the wall had a large arrow pointing to the right.

Charlie parked the car and they got out. She looked down at her feet. She had forgotten she had chosen open-toed black sandals that morning. A good choice for the office, not a farmyard. Luckily the surface of the yard was brushed clean. They followed the sign to a long rectangular building which looked as though it had once been a milking parlour. The sound of barking was getting louder.

Sam pointed to a door with an office sign. He opened it and went in. It was empty. They walked round the building to a field at the back. They saw two people on the other side of the field, with dogs on multiple leads. Sam waved, but they didn't acknowledge him. Too far away and too busy trying to keep the dogs in order.

"Come on Sam, let's go back and knock on the farmhouse door." They heard a voice. "Can I help you?" A woman emerged from the office door, carrying a small black curly haired dog. "Sorry, I was busy with this little one. This is Bunny. Poor little thing, she's missing her owners." She put the dog down, and told the dog to sit. "What can I do for you?" Sam took out his badge. "I'm Constable Huxley and this a colleague of mine, Miss Taylor. We're looking for David Jones's sister Janet."

"You've come to the right place then. Yes, I'm Janet, but I do know that my brother's dead, if that's why you're here."

Janet Morris was about the same height as Charlie. Her face showed no sign of grieving. For someone aged seventy and living an outdoor life she was remarkably well preserved. Her skin looked soft and fresh. Candid brown eyes returned Charlie's gaze. When she smiled her teeth were white and even. Her white hair was cut fashionably short in a pixie cut, and she wore clean blue jeans and a green sweatshirt with the kennels logo. Even her trainers were clean. Charlie remembered how Caitlin had remarked on David Jones's white trainers when she found him at the bottom of her stairs, and shivered.

"Why don't you come into the house. The girls will

be back with the dogs in a moment and it'll get noisy in here. Come on Bunny." The little poodle trotted after her.

Sam and Charlie retraced their steps. She led them round the back of the house, opening the door into a spacious kitchen. A huge cream AGA stood solidly against one wall. A kettle whistling softly on the hotplate. They followed her through the kitchen to a dimly lit front parlour. She went over to the windows and pulled up the blinds. The room didn't look lived in. Charlie guessed that the farmhouse kitchen was the heart of the household, not this showpiece of a room.

"Won't you sit down. I could do with a cup of tea. Would you like one?"..They both nodded. She went out, the little dog following, walking to heel. Charlie looked round the room. The furniture was comfortable enough. Practical dark brown leather sofa and chairs. Glass topped coffee table in the centre. A couple of Dorset Life magazines laid out. There was a large brick fireplace with a modern, clean looking, wood burner; a wicker basket on the side filled with logs. The mantel piece held a few ornaments and framed photographs. A long wooden dresser displayed more photographs. She was about to get up and look at the photos when Janet walked back in. Of course, the whistling kettle, tea made in no time.

Janet settled herself down in a chair opposite Charlie and Sam and gestured for them to help themselves. The little dog jumped onto Janet's lap nestling down contentedly. "Tell me why you are here? Trevor, my nephew, did hint that David's death was somewhat suspicious." Charlie took the lead. "He tripped and fell down stairs." Janet, her head on one side, regarded Charlie with curiosity. "He lived in a bungalow. Where were these stairs exactly?" She carried on, "Look, there's nothing you could say about my brother that would shock me. Even when he was a youngster, he seemed to get away with murder. Didn't seem to stop his machinations when he got older either. I washed my hands of him years ago."

"I'm sorry to say, he was in a house that he'd broken into. It appears to be an accident. But his death has led to questions being asked." Janet contemplated Charlie "You're Miss Taylor, yes? Not Police?"

"Yes I am and no, I was a serving police officer, but I'm working as a civilian investigator right now."

"OK, so what is it you want? You might as well spill the beans."

Charlie's thought processes moved rapidly. "You were once married to a man called George Rose?"

Janet frowned, "Good lord. I haven't thought about him for years. That was a lifetime ago. What's he got to do with David's death?"

"Their association seems to have been the catalyst for a set of circumstances that led to David's death."

Janet, clearly distracted, stroked the top of the little dog's head. "That sounds a bit too far-fetched to me. I suppose they must have kept up their friendship."

"Would you mind telling us what you do know about George and David? It might help. There are questions about their past linked to the present." Charlie, who was normally good with words, good at providing openings, was struggling to find a way in. "I'm not explaining myself very well am I?"

"Well, that's not surprising. It was always a muddle. Let me tell you how it all started. This was our Granny's house. It was the war, and David and I lived in London. Like lots of children we were evacuated to safety. When we came down on the train, there was a boy called George in the same compartment. He came with us to live with Granny. That's how it all started.

George was older – he must have been twelve. I was ten and David eight when we came here. Strange really, but George and David hit it off. Both of George's parents were killed in the blitz, and he stayed. Granny was like that. My father was a soldier and was killed in Italy, so mum came down and we all lived here.

I'd like to say George took advantage of my innocence, but growing up on a farm I can't make that excuse. I was seventeen and pregnant, we did what young couples did then, we married. It didn't last long. George couldn't cope with a baby. We never really had a marriage, so we divorced. He moved out and I stayed here with little Jennifer. We rarely saw George after that.

Years later he married Cecilia Roberts. They invited us to the wedding, but I didn't go. It all ended tragically; George was left with another child he didn't want. He fostered her out with one of Granny's old friends. Very odd. My Jennifer grew up not wanting to have anything to do with her father."

Sam interrupted, "Where's Jennifer now?" Janet sighed, "She had cancer. Died two years ago. It was a dreadful time. I have a grandson, Ian. He comes to stay here off and on."

"I'm sorry to hear about your daughter's death Mrs Morris. Can we go back to David and George? What sort of relationship did they have when they were younger?"

"David has a strong personality." She stopped, "I mean had. George was easily led even though he was the older one. They got into scrapes; poor George took the blame and the punishment. David was thoroughly spoiled, Granny and mum gave him everything he wanted." She shook her head and sighed. "About eight years ago, it turned out David had defrauded an old lady's estate. It all came to light when she died. Jack and I, that's my husband, paid it all back, otherwise he would have been ruined. We sold the majority of our land to do it. You see, David wasn't interested in the farm. We had inherited it together and Jack and I worked it as best we could. David had half his inheritance when we sold up and Jack and I started up the kennels instead. Jack died three years ago, so now it's just me."

Sam asked, "So, it wouldn't surprise you if we told you your brother's death was linked with other fraudulent dealings?" Janet grimaced. "So all we did to try to protect him was for nothing. My brother was a bad lot. That's always been difficult for me to come to terms with. So yes, back to the beginning of our conversation, I'm not shocked. I'm just terribly sad. He's ruined lives."

"How has he ruined lives?" Charlie spoke very softly.

"I was thinking of Trevor's mother, Barbara. We don't know where she is. Then of course, there's Trevor. He was his mother's boy. Once all this gets out – well, I suppose, Trevor's business will be ruined."

Distressed, Janet got up, gently cradling the little dog. She walked over to the window. "It's so peaceful here. I've tried to forget the past." She turned round to face them. "I'm not sorry David's dead. That's terrible isn't it. I'll go and see Trevor. I don't know if there's anything I can do to protect him. I hope he didn't know what his father had been up to, but if there's anything at all, he needs to come clean."

Charlie got up and joined Janet at the window. "You've been very honest, thank you. It can't have been easy. Can we come back if we need to?" She looked at Charlie, her face which had been so open and welcoming, looked drawn. "I'm truly sorry if my brother was the cause of any pain. Yes, of course you can come back. I'll give you my card."

Charlie walked across to the mantel piece and picked up an old black and white photo of two smiling boys. "Is this David and George?" Janet took it from her and nodded her head. "Happier times, I think." Charlie picked up another photo, "Who's this?"

"That's my grandson, Ian, Ian Morris. Jennifer had him very young. I don't know whether she got pregnant deliberately. She and Linda were together and maybe they wanted to be parents. They adored him. So, history was repeated and another boy was spoiled rotten."

"Do you see much of him?"

"He's been living with me for the last couple of weeks. I was beginning to hope he'd found a girlfriend and would settle, but it went wrong before he got round to bringing her here to meet me. He hasn't been very happy but it's been nice having him around and he likes working with the dogs."

"Is he at home now?"

"He's out, but he'll be back later. I think he intends to return to London. Nothing much for him here. He misses his mother and Linda's lonely up there all alone."

"Thanks Mrs Morris. You've been very generous with your time. We'd better get back to the station. It's been a pleasure meeting you." Sam looked over at Charlie, surprised she was winding the interview up. He had enjoyed listening to the story. Couldn't quite see what they had achieved, except now they knew for sure David had been a bad lot.

Outside Charlie turned and waved. "Come on Sam. Put your skates on. We need to get out of here." Sam looked at her in surprise. "Just act naturally. Get in the car." She drove away back down the drive and into the lane.

"What's going on?"

"Hang on Sam. Let me find a place to park up and I'll tell you." She drove further on then tucked the car into the entrance to a field. "The photograph of Janet Morris's grandson. If it wasn't the person we know as Dennis Gough, then I'll eat my hat." Sam started to say something. "No, we can't just wait here and arrest him. Radio it in. We need instructions."

CHAPTER FIFTY THREE

"Good work you two. The van driver has been in this morning and positively identified Dennis Gough. Stay where you are until Paul and Harry get to you. If he turns up before they find you, stay back and observe. Hold on a moment Charlie, I'll find Harry – you can give him directions to the farm."

Superintendent Fletcher put the phone down and walked out into the main office. "Harry, you're needed - my phone." Harry followed and picked up the phone. He listened then broke into a wide smile. He reached in his pocket for his notebook. At the conclusion of the conversation he swung round to speak to his boss. "I don't know how they did it, but it looks like we've got our man."

"Is Paul in the office?" Harry shuffled his feet, a guilty expression on his face. "He's gone out to get some grub. He won't be long. We've been trawling through hours of CCTV to see if we could spot Dennis in the town."

"Well, you can stop now. Whilst Paul's out, see what you can pull up on Ian Morris. As soon as he's back go and find Sam and Charlie. I want them back here."

They had been waiting for over an hour. Charlie broke the silence. "I've been thinking. We need to find some solid evidence to link David Jones with Cecilia Rose's death. So far, we've only got the word of a dying man. He didn't see the incident. I think we should split up tomorrow. You concentrate on trying to find anyone else who might have been at the pub or near the beach that night.

I've been thinking about George Rose too. He died of

liver failure certified by his GP. He'd seen the GP a couple of days before, so there was no post mortem. I keep going back to the liver failure angle. We only have hearsay about his drinking habits. What if the liver failure was caused by something else?"

Sam scratched his head, "What made you think of that?"

"Other substances can cause liver failure. I need to go through David Jones's emails to George. George was threatening Jones. He died not long afterwards. I don't believe in coincidences."

"The Super doesn't either, unless he's just trying to keep us occupied." Charlie raised her eyebrows and shook her head. "I wish Paul and Harry would put their skates on. I'm starving. Have you got any snacks hidden in here?" Charlie shook her head again. "I don't do snacks Sam." He looked disappointed, sat in silence for a few minutes then asked, "What would you do to find evidence from thirty years ago Charlie? In my experience, people don't remember what they did three weeks ago."

"You could start with the local papers. Journalists will have interviewed locals. Find out who the publican was then. Who was working there that night. It was a dreadful tragedy. It would have shocked the town's folk. You'll be surprised how much some people will recall. It might not give us anything solid but we have to cover all bases.

Once I've been through the files in the office, I'll contact Sally. We have to get back into Rock House. Go through the attic contents with a fine toothcomb. Caitlin said when she inherited the house it had been cleared, but luckily the attic wasn't. David Jones must have been searching for something in that house, something incriminating. We didn't find anything in his papers, therefore I think there may still be something there. Something that's been overlooked. Something that George Rose had on David Jones that led to George Rose's death."

Sam interrupted her. "I hear a car. Could be Paul and Harrys". They could hear a car slowly progressing down the lane. Sam got out. Careful to remain hidden, he peered over the hedge, then stepped out into the lane and waved.

Paul slowed down and Harry wound down his window. Sam crouched down. "You took your time." Paul glared at him. "It wasn't easy to find. How far are the kennels from here?" Sam pointed, "Just round the corner. We've got to get back to the station, so we'll move. No one will see you tucked in here." Paul called out of the window, "I take it he hasn't come back yet."

"No. His Grandmother said she was expecting him. We'd better get on our way."

Paul reversed to let Charlie move out and manoeuvred the marked police car into her space. Charlie completed a three point turn ready to go back. Sam jumped back into the car and they drove slowly back down the lane. As an oncoming car approached, Charlie moved into a passing space. The driver raised his hand to thank them. A man with blonde hair.

Paul and Harry waited for the red mini to pass and as it rounded the bend, they quickly manoeuvred out and followed it. They kept their distance until they saw the mini turn right. They moved closer and followed it down the drive into the farmyard. A tall blonde haired man extricated himself from the mini and stood watching them as they came in closer and parked behind him. Paul and

Harry got out.   Paul held his badge up and identified himself.

"Detective Inspector Benson, and this is Detective Sergeant James.   Are you Ian Morris?" He nodded. "We have reason to believe you were involved in a road traffic accident with a grey BMW on 2nd August this year, and that you left the scene before emergency services arrived."

"Ian what's going on?"   Janet Morris walked across the yard and stood by her grandson. "What's happening here, officer?"   Harry repeated what Paul had just said and turning to Ian Morris he added, "A man answering your description, driving a blue Land Rover, registration CFE 288D, was seen running from the scene."

"What have you done Ian?   You said a deer hit you."

"It did!   Why are you believing them?   It wasn't me. Anyway, if someone was running away how could they have a description of me?   They're fishing Gran, don't fall for it."

Janet Morris, clearly sceptical, frowned. "Well you had better go and clear this up.   If it wasn't you, I apologise.   I'm sure these gentlemen will give you a lift. Can I have my car keys back now please."

He handed them over, and she walked away from him. Obviously disconsolate, he hung his head. Harry walked over, took his arm. When Ian looked up, his eyes were full of tears.

CHAPTER FIFTY FOUR

"Don't get your hopes up too much. Ian Morris is likely to say it was an accident and he was trying to help Miss Rose. We haven't got an awful lot to go on."

Charlie who sitting across the desk from John exclaimed, "But it happened on the brow of the hill on a narrow country road. No one in their right mind would try to overtake there. That's the only manoeuvre I can think of that could have caused Caitlin to be shunted off the road."

"Point taken. It was dangerous driving. He could also say, he waited for another driver to come along to phone emergency services before leaving the scene."

Charlie groaned. "Have we nothing else? He's David Jones's nephew. Surely we can pin him down to something."

"We'll see. Paul and Harry will interview him, not your job. Have you been to see the old boy?" Charlie placed her left elbow on John's desk, hand on her chin, unconsciously imitating "The Thinker". She studied his face. She was acutely aware of her professional boundaries. She didn't need reminding. Working with the police had been like reverting to an old pair of shoes, discarded because they were no longer comfortable. Part of her discomfort was her fear that Paul and Harry would mess things up and she could do nothing about it. She had her own code of conduct. Her own values. She questioned theirs.

"Yes, we visited Bert Savage. He wasn't forthcoming. When we asked about the sister he said they *all* lived in the farmhouse. That led us to Janet Morris. I've got Sam in the library trawling through the newspapers around about the time of Cecilia Rose's death. We're hoping it will lead us to new witnesses. Don't suppose there's anyone still on the force who would remember it?"

John answered, "DI Hackett was in charge. Long retired but maybe still around."

"From what I read John, they assumed it was an accident from the beginning. I can't think we're going to learn much, but I'll try and locate him. I'm going to contact Sally Thomas and Caitlin Rose tomorrow to fix up a time to search their attic. Caitlin won't be fit enough to be there, but Sally might be. David Jones must have arranged to clear that house in case any incriminating evidence was left. From what Caitlin said, he was shocked when she told him she had found letters from her mother. Don't forget that letter John. It might be ambiguous but his reaction speaks volumes. David Jones lost his life in the search for it."

John Fletcher contemplated Charlie. She looked animated, her eyes bright and engaging. Keen and full of life. She had started at nine this morning. Whilst Paul and Harry had been bumbling around getting nowhere, Charlie had got stuck right in. She had motivated young Sam. Between them their actions had led to the identification and arrest of Ian Morris. He felt nothing but admiration for her yet knew he must keep her on a tight reign. He thought how she could have risen a long way in the Force, if only she had learned to work with her male colleagues rather than against them. He had liked her in Cornwall. Very much. Maybe, just maybe, when this case was wrapped up, there would be a future for them. First, he had to maintain her respect and help her negotiate her way through with Paul Benson and Harry James. She clearly did not respect them.

"Time you went home Charlie. As a civilian, we're paying you nine to five. I'd offer to buy you a drink, but I'm going to wait for Paul and Harry to come in with Ian Morris. Time's running out for us to keep Alice Brown in without charging her. We'll play them off against each other. See which one sings first."

CHAPTER FIFTY FIVE

CHARLIE

I drove home satisfied with my day's work. If Ian Morris was identified by the van driver then Paul and Harry would be the ones to disclose Dennis's identity to Caitlin. I sensed she still had a vestige of affection for him. His grandmother's description of him being a spoiled child was no surprise. One of the problems Caitlin spoke about was his lack of self-awareness. He took it for granted she would do everything for him. It was what he was used to. It explained a lot. I wondered how she would react when she found out he was David Jones's nephew.

Had David Jones lived in a fantasy world? Encouraged by the death of Cecilia Rose and the successful plundering of Caitlin's Trust Fund, he had gone on to defraud an old lady's estate. Then there was the holiday and property scam. Alice had worked from a home he had purchased from the Trust Fund money. David had hardly hidden his enterprise. They were bound to get caught eventually. As if all that wasn't enough, he had set up an elaborate trap for Caitlin. Why on earth go to such lengths to hide his nephew's identity? Why change Alice Brown's identity? As a fantasist he would have made his own reality, but it seemed he carried the others along with him.

Then there was George Rose. Janet Morris said he was easily led. I imagined David as an intelligent, manipulative child. He was eight, George four years older, yet George was led into mischief by David. George took the blame. It seemed their relationship remained unchanged as they got older. Cat had blamed

George for her mother's death. From what I had learned so far, he had been weak and ineffectual, not a murderer. David must have been shocked when George eventually turned on him. The devil was in the detail here. I must go back and trawl the emails again.

By now I was driving into my own neighbourhood and parked by a deli that remained open until eight p.m. I hoped they would still have some healthy food on offer. I remembered how poor my diet had been when I was on the force. Always grabbing something easy, a sandwich or a burger, drinking gallons of coffee. I'd had to wean myself off all that. I wasn't about to start the pattern again. I'm a frequent customer, so got a smile from Polly, the owner. She still had salad and quiche on offer – perfect.

I got home and dropped my bag of food on the kitchen table. I had an itch and I had to satisfy it before eating. I turned my laptop on and started to search. George Rose's death was too convenient, could he have been poisoned? He'd seen his GP three days before he died. It appeared he was known as a heavy drinker. So it was a fair assumption that his GP assumed his symptoms were caused by alcohol. I knew there was a deadly mushroom that could cause liver failure and it could be found in Dorset woods.

I opened my laptop to search. Here it was - Amanita Phalloides - commonly known as the death cap mushroom. Easily mistaken for common field mushrooms but they are the deadliest mushroom known to humans. They grow near broadleaf trees, such as oak and birch, and should not be consumed under any circumstances. People who survive eating them by accident describe their taste as delicious.

Consuming the mushroom can be fatal, leading to liver and kidney failure. A single mushroom can contain many times over the amount of toxin to be fatal. Eating a small piece is enough to kill an adult. Early symptoms of death cap poisoning are similar to having contracted a stomach bug. Only prompt medical attention can prevent fatal organ damage.

I knew from being on fungi forays where death caps could be found and so would anyone else who knew what they were looking for. If George had been given a meal containing a small amount of the mushroom, as an already a sick man, it could have led to his sudden death. I sat and thought about it. If he had been buried then a sample of his hair could prove my theory. He had abundant hair in the photo on the office board.

Had he been cremated? If not, would exhuming his body be in the public interest? David Jones was already dead. Then I thought of Alice. Alice of the mean little mouth. Poison was a woman's tool wasn't it? My stomach rumbled. It was a long time since Sam and I had fish and chips, and half my chips went in the bin. Time to eat.

CHAPTER FIFTY SIX

TUESDAY 6TH AUGUST

CHARLIE

I arrived in the office promptly at eight a.m. Sam was already at his desk. No sign of the others. I walked over to his desk. "Morning Charlie. I struck lucky yesterday evening. I found an article in the local paper from 31st August 1972. Cecilia Rose had been found lying dead on the beach the day before by a dogwalker. The journalist talked to the publican, Margaret Rudd. She backed up the story of heavy drinking. There was also a man, John Anderson, who'd been walking his dog along the promenade that night. He saw a man and a woman going into the water. On 1st September they ran a story about Cecilia and got a few words out of George Rose saying he was heartbroken etc. etc. I've just traced Margaret Rudd. She's retired and lives in sheltered housing near the school. I haven't found out who John Anderson is yet."

"Well done Sam. Can you go and see Margaret Rudd later on? I've got a feeling you're good with old people."

Sam grinned, "Yeah, I think they're my stock in trade. To be honest, I just like people and enjoy listening to stories."

"Yes, but always remember, people tell you what they think you want to hear, or if they have something to hide, they don't tell you much. Sometimes what they omit to say speaks volumes. Like Bert Savage yesterday. It's a long shot, but see if she remembers anyone else who was in the pub that night. Could you also see if you can locate the DI in charge of the investigation at the time. He's probably retired on the fat of the land somewhere."

Sam nodded in agreement so Charlie continued. "I'm going up to Rock House later. I want to talk to them about searching the attic. It might be better if I went on my own. Whatever Paul and Harry said to Caitlin has left a lasting impression. Learn from that Sam. Once trust is lost in the eyes of an individual, they will be wary of any police officer. It's not helpful. We should be fair and where possible act on evidence."

I couldn't tell whether Sam wanted a lesson on policing from me, but he was going to get one anyway. One of my pet dislikes is the use of the 'sitting with Nellie' approach. Expecting officers barely out of training to learn from officers who have forgotten what competent practice and good values are leads to the culture that I found abhorrent. I asked, "Do you know what happened with Ian Morris? Have you seen Paul or Harry?"

"No, but we have a briefing scheduled for eleven o'clock this morning. You should have had an email."

I began to walk over to my desk, then remembered I hadn't shared my suspicion about George Rose's death with Sam. I turned round and walked back. "I want a word with the Super when he comes in. I've got a theory I want to run past him." I explained how liver failure could be caused by a toxin found in mushrooms. I could see Sam thought it was a far-fetched, but I still had that itch. There was something niggling me that was leading me towards it.

John arrived with DS Simon Auger at his side. They disappeared into John's office. I went over and knocked on the door. "Morning John. Morning Simon, could I have a few minutes of your time?" I ran my theory through again. By now I had convinced myself my hunch was right. "Have you retained the keys to David Jones's bungalow? What I want to do is search for dried or frozen mushrooms." John nodded, "Do it." I asked, "Have you still got Alice Brown in custody?" Simon replied, "We're releasing her on bail this morning, on condition that she catches the eleven p.m. train and goes straight to her home address. She'll report in to the local nick every morning. She's a home bird – she doesn't even have a passport."

"I want to look at all David Jones's correspondence again. Particularly the emails when George Rose became threatening. From memory, it was early March 2001 and by the end of the month he was dead. I think Alice Brown may be smack in the middle of this. I'd like to interview her, but I met her in Cornwall as a prospective council candidate. She'd recognise me – may not be helpful." Simon grinned, "You can brief us Charlie. Go and search for your mushrooms first. I like the way you're thinking. Start with the character, get in their head. Find the motive, means and opportunity and pray for good luck."

"One last thing, do we know whether George Rose was cremated or buried? Could we find out and can you hold Alice Brown until I get back?" John sat silently contemplating my proposal. I could see by Simon's face that he sensed my growing eagerness.

"I do believe you're onto something. We have until ten thirty a.m. Take Sam, if you find anything call it in. We'll go from there." John had the last word, "Leave your car here Charlie. Sam can take a police vehicle. No creeping around this time."

We went in through the front door. A musty, closed up smell greeted us. The kitchen smelled rank. I unlocked and opened the back door wide. We looked around at the detritus David Jones had left behind. Half empty mugs and an overflowing ashtray still littered the kitchen table. "OK Sam, we're looking for dried mushrooms. Let's get started."

We wore gloves. I could feel my latex fingers sticking to half empty jars of jam. A bag of sugar had spilled its contents on one of the shelves. There were dozens of tins of baked beans, sardines and corned beef. It seemed he lived on a diet of tinned food, pasta and ready-made jars of sauce. Neither Sam nor I found anything suspicious in the first two cupboards. Then we opened a cupboard, one shelf filled with glass jars containing herbs. Someone had carefully labelled them in long hand. That's when I had my epiphany.

"Got it! It was when I was in Cornwall and I met Alice Brown's aunt. She said Alice loved nature and plants. She made up old fashioned remedies. These herbs must be hers. They're out of character for David Jones and his nicotine stained fingers. Keep looking Sam." We examined each jar carefully. Nothing resembling a mushroom. We carried on looking through each cupboard. We had drawn a blank. I could have screamed. I'd been so sure.

The small refrigerator just had an ice compartment, nothing in it. He didn't have a freezer, unless it was in the garage. "Charlie, if I had poisonous mushrooms, I wouldn't store them in my kitchen. I'd be afraid I'd forget and use them, or my mum would come in and cook me a surprise mushroom casserole. I'd hide them in a garage or a shed or something. Not in a kitchen." I looked up at Sam and nodded. "You're right. Let's split up. You try the garage and I'll look in the shed. Fingers crossed." I handed Sam the keyring to unlock the garage.

I stood outside taking deep breaths. It was good to be out in the fresh air. I remembered hiding behind that shed waiting for David Jones to finish his cigarette. I shivered. I took out a set of plastic chairs, a small electric mower and push bike before I could get inside. There was an old veneer shelving unit on one wall. It held rusty paint tins, oil canisters and glass jars filled with different sized screws and nails. There was a box holding pieces of material and another box full of different size paint brushes. Once upon a time this shed had been put to good use. I carried each article out onto the lawn to scrutinize them. I was beginning to lose heart until I spotted an old black tin box. I tried to open it but it was locked. I needed my bag; I went back into the house for the tools of my trade. It took me a few minutes jiggling around the lock, then it opened. I shouted, "Sam, come and have a look at this." Inside the box was a clear plastic bag. Sam held it up to the light. "I think we've found what we're looking for." Sam went to open the bag. "Don't touch that stuff. If that's death cap mushroom, you don't want to be breathing it in. Put it in an exhibit bag and seal it up." Whilst he did so, I figured out what we had to do. I looked at my watch. It was just before ten a.m. I fished in my bag, found my phone and rang John's direct number.

"John – I think we've found what we've been looking for. Were you able to find out whether George Rose was buried?" He answered in the affirmative. "In that case could you and Simon interview Alice Brown again before you let her go? Ask her about her relationship with George Rose. Let slip that we're treating his death as suspicious. If this is what I think it is, and she knows about it, she might panic and try and retrieve it. Sam and I will put everything back." I could hear John calling Simon's name. "Hold on Charlie." When he came back on he gave me instructions to return ASAP.

We hurriedly returned everything to the shed and drove back to the office. "I might be wrong Sam, but I think Alice Brown's motivated by money. If George Rose was going to get in the way, she and David would have disposed of him."

"Most people are motivated by money, aren't they?"

"I met her aunt in Cornwall, she dropped a couple of hints. I should have listened more carefully. What's the bet that Alice found out that George didn't own Rock House, so dropped him for David?" Sam didn't answer. He was concentrating on driving, leaving me to my thoughts.

Paul Benson was waiting for us in the office. "Drop that box and the stuff in it for fingerprints and testing. Simon and the Super have interviewed Alice Brown. They've let her go. Harry's tailing her. You are both to go back to the bungalow, keep watch. I hope for your sake you've got this right and you're not wasting everybody's time. You always did like melodrama Charlie."

I smiled, "Strangely enough, I'm acting on evidence Paul. Come on Sam, let's get going."

CHAPTER FIFTY SEVEN

DS Simon Auger didn't have a very high opinion of DS Harry James. He hoped he wouldn't mess up. When the call came in that Alice had taken a taxi and that he'd lost her, Simon sighed. He hurried into John Fletcher's office. "Harry's lost Alice. She may be heading to David Jones's bungalow. I'm going to get out there. Sam should be in position but I'm not leaving it to chance."

Charlie had parked the police vehicle in the next road and was standing outside watching David Jones's bungalow from a distance. She played Paul Benson's veiled warning in her head – you'd better not be wasting police time. She and Sam had made no bones about giving him Ian Morris on a plate. He would take the kudos for that. If she and Sam could prove David Jones and Alice Brown had murdered George, she would make sure Sam got the accolade, not Paul.

Paul had bullied Caitlin to such a degree that she remained terrified. Poor Caitlin, her life had been blighted by David Jones's greed. In her opinion, Alice Brown, despite protestations that she was only following instructions, was just as guilty of scamming the unsuspecting public as her probable lover, David. But did she have it in her to murder? What drove someone to murder? George Rose had been David's friend since they were boys. Maybe friendship was too strong a word. They needed each other and when George threatened to break their bond of silence, his days were numbered.

Her thoughts were interrupted when she spotted a taxi pulling up outside David Jones's bungalow. A small blonde haired woman got out. Alice Brown. She strolled up the drive. Looking around she picked up her pace and walked to the side gate. She opened it and disappeared from sight.

Charlie ran across the road and down the drive to position herself outside the side gate. She strained to listen for any sounds. At last she heard Sam's voice. "What are you doing here Miss?" Charlie felt exasperated and whispered to herself, "No Sam, show her your badge." She heard a female voice declaiming, "I'm not doing anything. I've just come to pick up something that's mine."

"Alice Brown, you are breaking bail conditions. You are under arrest." Charlie felt the gate being pushed. She pushed back hard to prevent it opening. A shout, "Stop there, Miss Brown!" There was a pause. Charlie breathed a sigh of relief. She heard Sam identifying himself as a police officer. She jumped as she felt a tap on her shoulder. "Simon, I'm glad you're here. She tried to run. Sam's just apprehended her."

They opened the gate. Hearing it, Alice turned round and glared at them both. "Why am I being arrested? I haven't done anything."

Simon stood squarely in front of her. "We are arresting you for breaking your bail conditions and on suspicion of causing harm to George Rose. You do not have to say anything but it may harm your defence if you do not mention when questioned something which you later rely on in court. Anything you do say may be given in evidence."

Alice stared at him. "No. I don't know what you are talking about. I haven't harmed anybody." She shook her head. "I don't believe this is happening to me."

Simon took her arm. "Come on, we're going back to

the station." Alice complied. She had tried to run. That wouldn't look too good. She walked beside Simon. He opened the passenger seat of the car and she climbed in. Sam, who had followed, sat in the front.

Simon leaned on the roof of the car. He beamed, "Your hunch paid off Charlie. See you back at the office. Team briefing's at two thirty this afternoon now."

Charlie walked back to her car and sat down breathing a sigh of relief. Alice hadn't specified what she was looking for. They would have to hope that her fingerprints were on the box and the plastic bag; that the contents of the bag would turn out to be poisonous mushrooms. Paul had said she liked melodrama. (Why was she letting him get into her mind again?) Well, maybe she did, but the path to her deductions had been clear. Proving guilt might be more difficult.

She started the car and began the journey back. She stopped to pick up some Danish pastries for the meeting. The team deserved a bit of a treat. She qualified that with – some of us do.

CHAPTER FIFTY EIGHT

Instead of going straight back to the office Charlie made the decision to call in at Rock House. She pulled in at the gateway. High wrought iron gates barred her way. She got out and pressed a button on the intercom positioned on the gatepost. A disembodied voice answered her. Sally. The gates swung open. She drove down the driveway and parked in front of the house. Sally came out to greet her.

She walked towards the car, a broad smile on her face. There was something vibrant about her. She had had her hair cut in a short bob. Her face looked different. Her eyes wider and brighter. Cheek bones highlighted with blusher. The freckles over her nose were more visible and made her look younger. It seemed to Charlie that her way of handling her near-death experience was visible in her fluid movements. As she got out of the car Sally held her arms out to her, reaching for her to hug her. "I'm so pleased you've come. Bob's here with Caitlin, and we've made a decision. Come on in. We'll tell you."

"You've intrigued me Sal. Lead on!" Sally took her arm and they walked in together. Charlie knew she was overstepping boundaries. She was in an uncomfortable position of perceived friend and civilian investigator employed by the police; walking a tightrope. The team were moving forward with the investigation. The earlier she could resume her normal life the better because the trust Sally and Caitlin displayed in her was precious. Whatever happened, she must hold that thought close. They had given her their friendship and she would not let them down.

Sally led her into the kitchen. It was the heart of this

house too – just as Janet Morris's had been. They were both old houses where so much time would have been spent preparing daily food. Had life improved because it was possible to purchase so much ready-made food? Convenient, but Charlie didn't think so.

Caitlin, who was sitting at the table, got up when she saw Charlie. She was still pale and moved stiffly but she too had a broad smile on her face. She walked over and kissed Charlie on both cheeks. Bob, who had been at the sink, came over and shook her hand. "It's good to see you all smiling. What's this decision you've made?"

Bob spoke first, "We've had the dreadful Detective Inspector Benson here with us this morning. He told us he'd found Dennis."

Charlie's eyebrows shot up. "Oh, did he?"

"Yes, his name's really Ian Morris. But you must know this?" Caitlin looked at Charlie, a curious expression on her face. "Yes, I did know. I've been busy, so I don't know the outcome yet. What did he tell you?" Caitlin took Charlie's arm, "Bob will tell you. It was fortuitous he was here this morning. I can't cope with that awful man. I could see in his eyes that he still thinks I'm the guilty one. He was hostile. Probably thinks I drove Dennis to harm me." She looked at Charlie, "I've not processed that he's really Ian yet. Come on, let's sit down."

"OK, so what did the Inspector tell you?"

Bob took the lead. "In a nutshell, Ian Morris is his real name. The Inspector had no explanation to offer us on that one. Said he couldn't divulge confidential information. So it was Ian Morris who confessed to stalking Caitlin. He was following her the day of the collision in a Land Rover he'd borrowed from a friend.

He admitted he was too close to Caitlin's vehicle as they reached the brow of the hill. She swerved and he slammed his foot on what he thought was the brake, but it was in fact the accelerator. He collided with Caitlin. It was all a terrible accident. He ran down to help her and tried to get her out. Good story isn't it? Particularly the bit about the accelerator and the brake!"

Charlie sat in silence for what seemed a long time. She frowned and leaning towards Caitlin said, "Is that all he told you?"

"Well, he said there were no witnesses. I don't think I swerved, but it's his word against mine. They could prosecute him for driving without due care and attention." She put her thumb to her mouth, gnawing at the skin. "I couldn't bear looking at that man. He kept licking his lips, like a lizard." She grinned, "You don't think he's an alien do you? He looks awfully like one."

Despite how angry she felt inside Charlie burst out laughing. "He can't help how he looks, but you are right. It might help you if you think of him like that. You know, the old technique when facing people – imagine them without clothes on, they're less scary. Same principal." Bob frowned, "No, don't. He's a dangerous man. Don't forget he tried to stitch you up Cat." The four people round the table instantly sobered up. Caitlin sighed, sat back, her arms folded. "Yes, but it's over with Dennis," She quickly corrected herself, "Ian."

"What do you mean? Is this about the decision you've made?" Bob spoke again. "Yes, we all listened to what the Inspector said and Cat's decided she doesn't want to press charges." Charlie, a puzzled expression on her face, looked at them all sitting quietly looking at her. "Really?"

318

"I don't want the hassle Charlie. Even now, I don't think he was all bad. He's going to get a warning, and I'll apply for a restraining order. What good is prosecuting him for driving without due care?" Charlie bit her lip. She could have said a lot, but it wasn't her case. How dare Paul come up here and tell them this cock and bull story. She would tackle what was happening here when she got back to the office. Endeavouring to look sincere, she said, "I'm glad, if it's what you want Cat." Bob looked at Charlie, friendly but with an edge. "You didn't just come up here to see us Charlie. What do you want?"

"Nothing terrible." She turned to look at Caitlin. "You remember you told me about the house being cleared and we figured out David Jones must have been looking for something George Rose had. It's a long shot, but Sam and I would like to come here to go through the rest of the boxes you said were still in the attic. Could we do that?" Caitlin nodded, "Of course you can. When do you want to start?"

"I'd like it to be tomorrow, but I don't know yet. I can ring you this evening and let you know. We are moving forward on this, but I'm not at liberty to share anything with you at the moment. When I am, I'll do so." Bob considered what Charlie had said and nodded his head. "Cat knows you won't do her harm."

Charlie had been given the code to open the gates. She stopped close to them. Instead of winding down her window she decided to get out. She stood deep in thought looking back down the drive. You couldn't see Rock House from here. The road was a little bumpy with grass growing up the middle. Its tall graceful beech trees provided a shaded green canopy. It looked idyllic but

Charlie felt heartbreak still lurked in the shadows. The misfortune of David Jones's death would fade with time but it wasn't over yet. The three of them had convinced themselves that Ian Morris would disappear from Caitlin's life if she didn't press charges. Yes, he was a weak and spoiled man, but he was part of a conspiracy. He was George Rose's grandson, a step-relative to Caitlin, although she didn't know it yet. No, it wasn't over.

Charlie punched in the numbers, the gates swung open with a hardly a sound. She drove away with a heavy heart.

CHAPTER FIFTY NINE

CHARLIE

I ran up the stairs to the office carrying my bag of pastries. I was later than I'd meant to be. John was standing by the board. The others were sitting close by. Paul called out, "Ah, Charlie, you're deigning to give us your company." I ignored him and sat down. "Sorry John. I decided to call into Rock House, wanted to agree a time to search the attic. Took longer than I thought." John was not pleased. "You should have called in first Charlie. Paul was out there this morning."

"Sorry, it was a spur of the moment thing." I turned towards Paul, "Have you given your report yet?" He shook his head. Ignoring us, John carried on, "Let's recap where we are: the investigation into the scam David Jones and Alice Brown were running is nearly complete. Alice Brown had been released on bail, but immediately broke the conditions of her bail and has been rearrested.

The substance she may have been searching for is in for testing. We will know the result in a few days. Her fingerprints were found all over the box and the plastic bag containing the substance. The theory at the moment, and it's only a theory, is that George Rose was poisoned to prevent him from whistle blowing.

Ian Morris aka Dennis Gough, has been apprehended and interviewed. He admitted he had collided with Caitlin Rose's car. After the conversation Paul had with her this morning, she has decided she does not want to press charges." Charlie put her hand up. John noticed but ignored her. "Quite frankly, as it stands, we have nothing to go on. She has said she will apply for a restraining order. She may get one."

Paul interrupted, "I explained where we were with this, but the woman was hostile. Virtually accused me of covering up."

It was my turn to interrupt. "I doubt that very much. You're projecting your own hostility onto her. She's terrified of you. Have you any idea what you've done? I'll tell you. You've made our job far more difficult." John tried to stop me in my tracks. He could see I had a rant coming on. When I was in the force, I kept quiet and seethed. I had no intention of keeping quiet. "If you and your sidekick showed some empathy you might get somewhere. There'll never be justice when you make theory fit despite the evidence; create guilt out of thin air using bullying tactics."

Unusually John raised his voice. "OK Charlie, tirade over. When we've finished, I'll see you in my office." He frowned at me. "To resume. Have you interviewed the ex-publican?" He hesitated, glancing at the board. Sam replied. "It's the White Horse, Sir. I've left a message. I'll ring her again this afternoon. Her name's Margaret Rudd. I know the name, but I can't place her. The incident was thirty years ago, hope she's got a good memory."

"You and Charlie are doing great work. Keep going for the present anyway." He looked over at me. "Get the search underway for any evidence you can find at Rock House. From what you've collected so far, you may just strike lucky. As I've said before, Caitlin Rose deserves some closure." I could see a softening in his stance but I was going to get a rocket from speaking out in the duty room. Quite rightly so, but it felt very satisfying.

"OK, we're finished for now. Simon, carry on with

the forensic work. Let's try to put that to bed. Once we have the results back on the substance, we might be investigating a murder." Paul looked as though he was going to explode any minute. He glared at John. He had tried very hard to pin murder on Caitlin. He was still convinced she had pushed David Jones down the stairs. Well, let him find the evidence. I was pretty sure there was none.

John asked me to follow him. Paul stared after me with a triumphant expression on his doughy features. I wouldn't be staying on this team for a moment longer than I needed to. John walked over to his desk. "Sit down Charlie." I did as I was told, and immediately apologised for saying what I had in front of Paul's subordinates. John sighed. "I thought you were better than that Charlie." He shook his head. "Look, I'm here on secondment because it was an expedient move in the circumstances. I'll be moving back to my old job as soon as we've wrapped this up. I'm not here to nurture Paul Benson's pride, but I am here to hold the team together."

"I understand that John. But Caitlin's motive for not wishing to press charges is because she's worried about police tactics. You know, we've not long had the Stephen Lawrence Inquiry. The force is institutionally racist. That's not the only institutional discrimination is it? Misogyny is alive and kicking. It's one of the reasons I left the Force. How often does training come around? Who goes on it with an open mind?"

"I've just explained Charlie, I'm not going to be here for very long. When you leave our employ I suggest you write formally to the Chief Constable with your complaint. That's the best I can do." I felt deflated. I was just a minnow in a murky pond. The big fish were ready to eat me up. I suggested as much to John. Affable again he smiled, and I felt even more deflated. "Have you ever thought about becoming an educator? You'd make a great trainer."

He was a kind man but I doubted whether he could have much idea of the task involved in training officers like Paul and Harry. A trainer might possibly change their behaviour at work, but as for changing attitudes and values – was that even possible?

"Thanks John – I appreciate the compliment. Can you imagine it though? Challenging prejudice and strongly held values. Walking willingly into the Lion's Den? Maybe one day - but the pay would have to be bloody good." He laughed, "They would probably pay you a fortune." He looked at his watch, "Go home now Charlie. You've put in the hours. I'll have a word with Paul later on."

Paul and Harry stared at me as I walked over towards Sam's desk. I took no notice. Simon looked up from the file he was working on, grinned and mouthed "Good on you." Sam, clearly embarrassed, greeted me with, "You OK?" I nodded, "Yes, of course." I wanted to reassure him. Everything was as normal as it could be with a civilian investigator disrupting the team. "How did you get on with Margaret Rudd?"

"She's got an appointment tomorrow morning, but can see us in the afternoon."

"Right, in that case we'll go to work in the Rock House attic in the morning. I'll check it out with them before we go. See you first thing." As I went to walk out I remembered the pastries. I went over, picked the bag up and put it by the kettle. "I'd meant to give you these at the meeting. Sorry boys. Help yourselves." I'm afraid

I sounded sarcastic. Maybe Paul and Harry were too thick-skinned to notice.

When I got home, I changed and cooked myself a meal. Having spent the last two days with police officers, I told myself I was not going to fall for John Fletcher despite my body telling me otherwise.

CHAPTER SIXTY

WEDNESDAY 7TH AUGUST

Sam sat fidgeting in the front seat of Charlie's car. "Look, I'm sorry I said those things to Paul in front of you. I lost my rag and I was out of order. Promise me – you'll never get to be like them. If there's one thing police work has taught me, to get the best out of people, whether innocent or guilty, be empathic and always be respectful. Does that make sense?"

"Yes it does and I do try." She couldn't help smiling. He was such a considerate young man. Hadn't been tainted yet and she hoped he never would be. "The other thing, Sam, is never do what I did yesterday, criticise a superior in front of their subordinates. There are much better ways."

They reached the gates of Rock House and were let in. Sally came out; she took Sam round to the garage to fetch the stepladder. Charlie meanwhile had gone into the house to be greeted by Caitlin. She emphasised they were only interested in finding evidence George Rose could have left behind.

"I know and we're both grateful. Could you do what Sally did before? Bring the boxes down to the spare room at the end of the corridor on the right. Later on, Sally and I can resume clearing it all." Caitlin still looked very pale. Charlie felt protective. "Don't do too much too soon Cat. You're still looking a bit peaky. Are your ribs healing?"

"Definitely, but it's only been five days and can take up to six weeks for bones to knit. I promise to be good." Charlie looked down at her knee. Caitlin said in a reassuring voice "Don't worry, I really am alright. My physical wounds are healing." Sam came in carrying the stepladder, so Charlie lost the opening Caitlin had given her. She had specified physical wounds. Her mental wounds went deeper. Charlie suspected deep, deep wounds locked away since childhood. Over the last few weeks, new mental wounds were being added to the old ones. No wonder she wanted Ian Morris's wickedness swept under the carpet. She was coping as best she could.

"Right, off we go Sam. Caitlin has asked us to bring the boxes down to the spare room. We've got lots of humping and shifting to do." They climbed the stairs, looking down when Caitlin called, "Shout when you want some drinks. It'll be thirsty work."

Sam rested the stepladder on the top stair and looked down at the tiled floor. "Jones didn't have much of a chance once he'd fallen. Those tiles are unforgiving. There was such a mess down there. Broken glass everywhere. Looks strangely normal now." Charlie tried to be understanding without success. "It was quick. He would only have had a few moments of fear."

"Terror's the word Charlie. You should have seen his face. I keep thinking of it. No matter what he'd done, he didn't deserve to die like that." Charlie wasn't in the mood for sympathy. "Yes, well, try and forget that now. We have a job to do, and we might find evidence to implicate him in murder, don't forget that."

"I'm learning from you Charlie. Even a murderer has some human rights. His death wasn't very dignified. I can't forget it. It wouldn't be right." He grinned at her, "But I will get on with my job." He erected the stepladder underneath the loft entrance, climbed up first, found the light switch, and called Charlie up. They looked around. The floor was boarded, it was tidy and well lit. There were still half a dozen boxes at the back of the room. They set about dragging them through the loft space to the access point. They were awkward but not heavy. Half way through Sam suggested he go down so Charlie could push each box over the access point and he could guide it to the ladder.

They worked well together. Within thirty minutes they had shifted all the boxes into the spare room. Charlie sat down on a chair. "I'm going to have aches in muscles I didn't know I had." She looked up at Sam, "You've hardly broken into a sweat." He laughed. "That's because I'm young and fit! Now we've got to search."

They set to, sorting and searching through each item in a box before moving on to the next one. Time was running out. They had an appointment with Margaret Rudd in fifty minutes. "Let's do one more box." Sam pulled out a large paper package. "What have we here?" He unwrapped it carefully. Inside were two portraits in wooden frames, sandwiched together, both facing inwards. Sam held one up. It was a painting of a pretty dark haired girl. Her hair was tied back in pigtails. She looked about twelve. A cheeky grin on her face revealed a front tooth, slightly overlapping the tooth beside it. Her eyes were bright and a remarkable blue.

"I know where I've seen that grin before. Caitlin has exactly the same overlapping front tooth, the same blue eyes. What's the other one Sam?" He held it up. They both stared at the portrait of a beautiful young woman. Long dark wavy hair cascaded over her shoulders. She was sitting on a wooden bench in a rose garden. She wore a floral dress. Her legs were bare and planted four square on the ground. She held a bunch of red roses in her left hand. Her right arm was raised, her hand resting on a marble statue. She was smiling for the artist. She looked alive as though she was poised to jump up out of the portrait and dance with sheer delight.

Sam looked at it in wonder. "She was beautiful. This must be Cecilia. Caitlin has the look of her. Not quite the same. She hasn't got the same vivacity. This is so joyful. If Caitlin's hair was long, she could be her sad sister."

Charlie got up from the chair. They hadn't got time to examine them properly, it could wait until tomorrow. "Can you take these down Sam. I need a pee before we go."

Sam was still staring at the picture of Cecilia as a young woman. "I hope seeing these will help Caitlin look as happy as her mother someday." He picked both portraits up and disappeared.

Charlie went out onto the landing. She couldn't remember where the toilet was. After trying a couple of bedroom doors she encountered a locked door. Never wanting to pass up a challenge, she reached in her pocket for her pen knife; she pulled out a special tool from the handle and jiggled it round the locking mechanism. She heard it click and smiled to herself. Her time was improving.

She opened the door expecting to find a cupboard. What she saw made her stop and stare. She heard Sam calling her and his footsteps running back up the stairs. She didn't want him to see what she had just discovered, so shut the door quickly. No time to lock it. She would have to leave it and sneak back up before they left. The next door was open. At last, a toilet. She went in, locked it and sat down to relieve herself. She heard Sam knocking on the door.

"After you. They have coffee and cake waiting for us, get a move on. We just about have enough time." She opened the door to see Sam hopping up and down. To her dismay she also saw Sally walking towards them down the corridor. Circumstances were conspiring against her. "I've just come up for a cardigan for Cat, she's feeling the cold. You two deserve a prize. You've made her very happy." They went down together. The coffee and cake looked inviting. Charlie managed to drink her coffee quickly hoping to make an excuse to go back upstairs. It wasn't to be. It turned out Sam was a stickler for time. He insisted they get to their appointment on the dot. The door would have to remain unlocked until tomorrow.

Sam navigated so they found the sheltered bungalows where Margaret Rudd lived. They knocked on her door and heard a disembodied voice calling to them through an open front window. The door was unlocked. They walked into a small, cluttered front room. Margaret Rudd was sitting in a reclining chair, her legs up. She needed a large chair. She was large. Her body swollen. Her bare legs puffy. The skin tight and red. Her face, in contrast, was of a woman in her early sixties. Made up, she was still pale, her skin remarkably smooth. She had emphasised her cheek bones with blusher, lending shape to her round face. Dark red lipstick accentuated her full lips giving the impression of generosity. Her neat greying hair was cut in a pageboy style. As an ex-publican, she was a woman used to being in the public gaze.

She looked up at them. Smiled when she saw Sam. He showed her his badge. "You don't recognise me." Her small brown eyes sparkled. "It's Sam isn't it. I used to help out with your scout group." She pointed to a small dining table. "Grab a chair both of you. Sorry about the muddle." Sam drew a chair up and sat close by her. "Of course, the scouts, I had a feeling I had heard your name before. How are you?"

"Could be better. I've turned into my Gran. She had the Dropsy too. Not much I can do about it." She looked over at Charlie standing in the doorway. "Who's this lady with you. Please come and sit down." Charlie smiled, picked up a chair and sat down close to the window. "I'm Charlie Taylor. I'm a civilian investigator. We've come to talk to you about the drowning of a young mother thirty years ago."

"Yes, Sam reminded me when he phoned." Her voice retained a strong midlands accent. "I'm not sure how I can help you." Sam took the lead, "We're interested in the night Cecilia Rose drowned. She was in your pub beforehand with a group of men, including her husband George. We were hoping you might remember how they behaved together. How much they may have had to drink." He held Margaret Rudd's gaze. "It doesn't matter how ordinary it might appear. It could help us build a picture of what happened." She looked puzzled, "But the police investigated her death years ago. Why are you so interested now?" Sam smiled. "We've come by some new information Mrs Rudd."

"Oh, please, call me Margaret." She observed Sam, a quizzical expression on her face. "So it wasn't an accident? I spoke to a police officer the day they found her. They assumed it was a tragic accident." He shook his head. "We don't know yet. What do you think?" She bit her lip, surveying both of them. Charlie could see dark red lipstick had smeared her front teeth. "I always thought her death was suspicious. I've mulled it over a lot since you rang. I do remember the group of them. The men were in high spirits. Well, as the evening went on, they all had a lot to drink. I knew George quite well. He was a regular. I didn't know his wife. I was surprised he'd married such a stunner. But it was as though she was with the other one. The good looking blonde one. He kept buying her drinks." She went silent for a moment. Sam sat patiently waiting for her to resume.

"It was busy that night. Warm weather, people coming in and out. The group of them sat at the table by the window." She shut her eyes. "I can see them there. Laughing and chatting. The woman was quiet though. Awkward. She looked out of place. The blonde one sat close to her. I'm sorry, I can't really remember anything else." Charlie asked, "You knew George. Do you remember the names of any of the others in the group?"

"The blonde one wasn't a regular, but it turned out he was a local solicitor. I don't recall his name. The other two I knew. They came in sometimes with George. Pair of local builders – Bert Savage and Harry Wallace. Poor Harry committed suicide. I haven't seen Bert for a long time." Charlie continued, "Do you remember them going outside? Did any of them come back in?"

"I'm sorry, we were busy. I really don't remember. The police came the following day and told me George's wife had gone swimming out there from Monkey beach and drowned. Terrible, but it happens. People are having fun, too much to drink...."

Sam interrupted. "Do you think they were all having fun Margaret? Do you remember how George's wife was behaving?" She shook her head, "No, not really. She was quiet. Maybe subdued. I wish I could remember more, but it was a long time ago." Sam smiled, "You've been brilliant. Do you think you could identify the blonde man if we came back with a photo of him." She nodded. "I'll try. What am I thinking – I haven't even offered you a drink."

"Don't worry, we've not long had coffee. Maybe when we bring the photo." Sam leaned over and took her hand. "I'm sorry I didn't recognise you at first."

"It wasn't fair to put you on the spot. I've been laid up a few years now. Not a lot the doctors can do for me. Pop in and see me again. If I'm not here, I'm often down in the big lounge with the others."

Charlie and Sam stood. Sam picked up both chairs and moved them back. "I'll pop in tomorrow with that photo. Thank you for your time and for all your help."

"I don't think I've been much help." Sam smiled down at her, "You'd be surprised."

Charlie walked over, squatted down and touched her arm. "You have been a help. We're very grateful." She got up and joined Sam. They went back to the car in silence. Charlie switched the engine on. It purred as usual. "What do you think we got from that Sam?"

"Well, at the very least, David Jones was being over friendly. Sitting close, maybe too close, buying her drinks. She was subdued and awkward. George often came into the pub with his mates. Why did he bring her that night?"

"My guess is they were setting her up. Plying her with drinks to cold bloodedly get her into the water. I can't see George being capable of murder, but the more we hear about David Jones the more I think he was capable of anything." Charlie tapped her fingers on the dashboard. "Remember his sister Janet suggested David was the schemer and George, his accomplice, took the blame."

"Come on Charlie – that doesn't prove either of them harmed her. It's all smoke and mirrors. We need some real evidence." Charlie raised her eyebrows. She put the car into gear, looked in the rear mirror and released the handbrake. "I can't see how we will find the evidence after thirty years. We've got a few more boxes to sort through, that's all. Caitlin and Sally had cleared loads of them beforehand, they may have chucked relevant papers out already. Then what? Let's get back to the station. We need to write this up and plan our next move."

CHAPTER SIXTY ONE

Charlie had had a restless night. Unusually for her, she had difficulty getting to sleep, then towards the early hours she dreamed of Cecilia. She saw her standing on a beach. She heard laughter as Cecilia stumbled into the water. Charlie wanted to warn her - "someone's following you". A wave broke over Cecilia and she fell face down. She saw an arm holding Cecilia's head down in the water, hair floating out behind her. She woke with a start, and sat up trembling. "Which one was it? George or David? If only I could see."

"Are you alright Charlie? You look as though you've seen a ghost." Sam stood beside her desk. "Can I get you a coffee or something?" She folded her arms twisting round to look at him. "I had a bad night, that's all. Yeah, let's have a coffee then get on back to Rock House. Finish those boxes. After that we can chase up the old DI from the original investigation."

Sam walked over to the kettle and turned it on. "Come on Charlie, you're normally optimistic. Let's put ourselves in George's shoes. He was an accomplice, but he was also capable of thinking for himself. For example, he spirited Caitlin away. Unfortunately we don't know how he felt about his wife. Was she a means to money or was he fond of her? He must have cared about her child." Sam snapped his fingers. "Of course, the portrait. Cecilia as a child. If he's left something, that's where it will be."

An hour later they were standing in the hallway of Rock House. Ann was there with Coco who ran around their feet waiting to be petted. Sam obliged, bending his long body to pick her up. She licked him with such enthusiasm he chuckled. He continued to hold Coco under his arm whilst he asked Caitlin about the portraits. Had they hung them yet? Could he and Charlie please examine them?

"Oh gosh, after you left yesterday Sal and I decided to take them to the framers. They're at Johnson's in the High Street. Did we do wrong?" Sam reassured her, "No of course not. Maybe we'll go down there now and have a look. We should have done it yesterday, our fault." Caitlin gazed at him. Her eyes no longer so bruised; for the first time Sam saw her as she really was. Not the shocked, bloodied young woman he had first seen at the top of the stairs, or the bruised and battered woman who had been run off the road. She was lovely. Tall, not as tall as him, but she stood well with good posture. She was calm and in control of her emotions. Her eyes really were remarkable.

"It's Thursday isn't it? Sorry Sam, I think he's shut today. He'll be open at ten tomorrow." Sam could barely hide his disappointment. "Never mind. We've got a few more boxes to go through this morning. We'll get on with that. Are you ready Charlie?" He looked over and saw Charlie deep in conversation with Ann. She didn't hear him. He looked back at Caitlin and smiled. "If you don't mind me saying, you look a lot better today."

"I feel better, thanks. I'm glad you're here Sam; we appreciate what you and Charlie are doing. I did freak out at the thought of a police officer being in the house. I shouldn't have. I worked perfectly happily with police officers in my old job. I trusted them to do the right thing. It was that detective. Him and his sidekick, they're the ones who freaked me out."

Sam hid his embarrassment by bending and depositing Coco on the floor. She scampered over to Ann interrupting her conversation with Charlie. Caitlin smiled over at Charlie. It seemed to Sam that they were studying each other. It was Charlie who broke their gaze. "We'll go up and do some more boxes."

Charlie let Sam go first. She tried the door she had opened yesterday. It was locked again. Charlie had seen it in her eyes. Caitlin knew.

Their search was futile. They had unpacked old clothes, sheets and blankets, china, books, and toys. The sum of people's lives, abandoned for other family members to see when they had passed. Sam was sorry strangers had been tasked with the job. He felt like a voyeur, unravelling a family's life, and so far, all for nothing.

Charlie drove back via the High Street, stopping at Johnson's. Sam got out and knocked on the door on the off chance that the framer was there. All was silent. In contrast to the closed and darkened shop, when they walked into the office it was buzzing. There was an air of energy and excitement. DS Simon Auger sprang up from his seat. "Great, just in time. I'll let John know you're here."

Charlie called out, "What's going on Paul?"

"We've made a breakthrough. The Super will tell you." Charlie was puzzled, Paul looked almost animated. Harry smiled in a smug Harry sort of way. Not quite the full ticket.

Superintendent John Fletcher came out, followed by Simon. Both of them with wide smiles on their faces. "Congratulations you two. The results are back on the substance you found. It is indeed Amanita Phalloides, the death cap mushroom." Charlie grabbed Sam's hands and cheered. "We did it Sam. You and I together." She saw John and Simon smiling in appreciation. "There's even better news, if you can believe it. Alice Brown has sung like a canary." Charlie let go of Sam's hands, suddenly serious. "You're joking."

John shook his head. "She's told us, with a solicitor present mind you, that David Jones asked her to collect mushrooms and dry them for him. She didn't know he intended to poison anyone of course. He told her, it was his insurance policy." Simon continued, "She also said, David and George had fallen out. Then the solicitor suddenly woke up. He asked to see his client in confidence and after that it was no comment all the way."

"I'm glad I stuck my neck out to get you in on the act Charlie." John acknowledged, "You and Sam have worked remarkably well together. You can learn a lot from her, Sam. We will take it from here. Paul's talked to the pathologist, his old friend, Dr Finch. He wasn't certain whether the toxin would still be present in a hair sample, as it's been over eighteen months since George was buried. We'll need permission from the Ministry of Justice and from his next of kin if we decide to apply for an exhumation. We've got a long way to go yet before we put the evidence together to make a decision."

"Deep breath then." Charlie exhaled. "Straight back down to earth. We've not got as far with our investigation into Cecilia's death." Sam spoke up, "We'll get there Charlie. We'll crack it together." John nodded, "I like your enthusiasm Sam. Keep going, we'll celebrate later. The drinks will be on me."

Left to their own devices, Charlie failed to shake off

the impact of her dream. It had left her feeling stale and, unusually for her, pessimistic. Sam, who as it turned out, was indeed her boy scout, tried to cheer her. "Come on Charlie, let's go and get something to eat. We can go to the canteen, or better still let's go out."

Charlie realised Sam was directing her to the café she had taken Caitlin to after David Jones had been killed. They went through to the garden near the very olive tree where they had sat. It was between lunch and afternoon tea, so it was empty. They ordered then sat in silence enjoying the tranquillity. It was Sam who broke the silence. "What were you and Ann talking about this morning?"

Charlie looked up, "I was asking her opinion. You queried whether George could have been fond of Cecilia. So I asked Ann. She said they always seemed friendly when she saw them together. So then I asked her how George had been after Cecilia's death. I could see she was conflicted. She wanted to slag him off – after all, she believes he's killed her friend, but instead she thought having a child was an encumbrance. He probably tried to do his best for her. She remembered going to the house shortly after Cecilia died. Mid-morning and he was still in his dressing gown looking dishevelled. Then to be fair to her, she said he could have been grieving."

"So, we're building a picture of a man who may have been involved in the murder of his wife." Sam thought out loud, "But he could be a decent sort of chap. So it's easy to jump to the conclusion that David Jones is the villain of the piece. Too simple though isn't it?"

"Well, it's never clear cut Sam. There's good in most people, maybe even David Jones. I dreamed of Cecilia last night. I could see her dressed as she was in the portrait, but she was confused and immeasurably sad. Then she stumbled into the sea and there was someone following her. A wave knocked her over and I could see an arm holding her head down. I was calling out to warn her, then I woke. I've got another lesson Sam – never allow yourself to get too close. It's bad practice to befriend clients. It affects your judgement and your actions."

"That's why you looked so sad this morning." Concerned, Sam sought to reassure her, but he found it difficult to find the right words. Charlie ended up reassuring him. "Look at what we have achieved so far. If there is evidence to be found we will find it."

The waiter brought their food; they ate in companiable silence. Sam insisted on paying. Charlie dropped Sam back off at the office to follow up on the DI who had been in on the original investigation. Charlie went home with the file. She had a vague feeling she had missed something.

Back in her flat Charlie settled down to read. She scanned the email dated 7th January 2001 from David Jones to George Rose outlining their plan. Between that date and 3rd March 2001 something had occurred between the two men. George feared David meant to harm Caitlin and had threatened him. On 29th March 2001 George was found dead.

She searched through the file for a copy of the death certificate. Skimmed it then looked at it more closely. The address he had been found at was given as 3 Hannam Place. So he hadn't died in Rock House. Was he staying with someone? A friend they hadn't located?

She read through the scanty police investigation into the death of Cecilia Rose. Something was bugging her.

Sam had discussed a newspaper report. There was another witness not mentioned in the police report. She picked up the phone and rang the office hoping Sam was still there. "A couple of days ago, before I led us off on the mushroom hunt, do you remember discussing the newspaper article you found? The one that led us to Mrs Rudd. There was a witness, a dogwalker wasn't there?" She heard the rustling of papers, then Sam came back on. "John Anderson."

"Well, either the police couldn't find him and didn't bother to note it or it was never followed up. There's no mention of him in the original report." Sam was silent for a moment. "I can do a search. I've found DI Hackett by the way. He died last year."

"That's a dead end then. See if you can dig up anything on John Anderson then call it a day Sam. We'll start again tomorrow with the framer."

CHAPTER SIXTY TWO

FRIDAY 9TH AUGUST

Johnson's opened at ten a.m. Sam and Charlie were outside waiting. Sam held his badge up and identified them both. The framer, not surprisingly, looked rather bewildered. However, he remembered Sally and Caitlin coming in and disappeared behind a curtain to find the original portraits. He came back with them and laid them on the counter. "Is there something wrong with these? Are they stolen?"

"No, not at all." Sam replied. "We're looking for something. Could you take the back off each of the portraits please." He turned each picture over then opened a drawer and took out a scalpel carefully cutting around the back of each picture. He took the tape and card away. There was nothing on the back of the card or behind either picture. Sam could hardly disguise his disappointment.

"These are lovely." The framer turned the pictures back over stooping closer to study them. Pushing his glasses back up his nose he exclaimed, "I recognise the lady. It's Cecilia Roberts isn't it?" Sam who had been so focused on the paintings and the secrets he hoped they would reveal, observed the framer for the first time. He guessed he was in his seventies. He still had a good head of white wavy hair. His face looked jolly, red cheeks and full lips. He wore round wire framed glasses. By now he was looking over the top of them as he contemplated his visitors. "I knew Cess. It was tragic what happened to her. I hadn't placed the dark lady who came with the portrait. Is she the lost daughter?"

Instead of answering, Charlie asked him a question. "How did you know Cecilia?" He looked puzzled. "Why are you asking?"

"The police have opened up the original investigation into her death. Constable Huxley and I are working on it."

"Well I never. I was an old beau of Cessie's way back when. She was a lovely girl. I was away when it happened so I didn't know about her death for some months. Now can you answer me, is the dark lady the lost daughter?" Sam nodded. "That's wonderful."

Sam looked disappointed again. He had thought for a moment the framer had some information, but he'd not been in the town when Cecilia died. He sighed, "Thanks for dismantling the portraits. Pity we haven't found anything, but we'll keep searching."

They went outside. Charlie suggested they walk along the seafront. Walking helped her think. It was a dismal day. Dark clouds promised rain. The first for a couple of weeks. The wind was revving up for a good blow. The beach was empty apart from a few brave souls. They walked to the far end in silence. Sam leaned on the railing. Everything was shrouded in mist. The sea looked grey and rebellious and he looked miserable. After their recent successes he expected everything Charlie suggested would turn out right. Then he remembered it was he who had suggested the painting held the key, not Charlie.

"I'm getting cold Sam. Let's go and get a coffee, then we could call in to Rock House before we go back to the office. We should tell them we've ended the search for now."

Charlie stopped at the entrance to Rock House. She

knew the code, but she wanted to flag they were on their way. When they pulled up at the front door, Sally and Caitlin both came out to greet them. Despite the weather, they stood outside arm in arm looking at the two detectives. Big grins on their faces. Caitlin burst out, "We've found something. Come and see." Sam and Charlie followed them into the kitchen.

"Charlie, do you remember when I described how I first saw the house? How it had been cleared but there were a couple of old fashioned photographs screwed onto a bedroom wall. I left them on the wall because I thought they could be my grandparents, although Ann didn't think so. Anyway, after what you said about the portraits, I remembered the old photos. We took the frames apart this morning. Look what we've found." She held up a blue floppy disc in triumph. "Weird isn't it? Fancy those pictures being left when everything else was gone."

Sam took the disc from her, "Have you got anything to play this on?" Caitlin said, "It might go in my laptop, but we didn't want to damage it in any way. What do you want to do Charlie?" Charlie thought for a moment, then looked at Sam. "I don't think we'd damage this by just sliding it into a laptop would we?" He shook his head, "Let's try it." Caitlin fetched her laptop and laid it on the kitchen table. "Well, here goes," she said as she opened it up and switched it on. "This is what we've been waiting for. You're the police officer, you do it Sam." Sam sat down and obliged. It opened to reveal two folders: one titled 'Caitlin', the other 'Confession'. Caitlin took a deep breath as she stared at the screen. Sally put her arm around her. "Please open the Confession document." He clicked on the folder and a document appeared.

6TH March 2001

My name is George Alfred Rose. I confess to being a co-conspirator with David Jones, formerly of Jones and Barrett Solicitors, to the murder of my wife Cecilia Rose on 29th August 1972.

David hated her because she chose me. He never forgave either of us. We stood between him and a fortune. I was powerless to stop him. I watched him buying her double vodkas. I followed from a distance when they went out skinny dipping. I didn't intervene even then. God help me. He swore it was an accident. He said she must have got into difficulty.

Two days ago he told me what he had in mind for Caitlin. When she was a child I hid her from him. I wouldn't allow him to use her as his plaything. Now she's turned thirty her Trust Fund will have to be wound up. I threatened him but he laughed at me. Told me how much he had enjoyed holding her mother's head under the water.

The doctor says I have very little time left. My liver is failing. I've lived with the bottle these thirty years, now I'll die by it. If I meet Cecilia on the other side, I'll beg for forgiveness. Her death is on my hands and I pray that David Jones rots in hell. He murdered my wife and means to murder her daughter.

I want to put my house in order before I die. I know I should go to the police. This is my insurance policy in case my time runs out. I have deposited a signed copy of this document with Musgrove and Kelly Solicitors, Bridport, Dorset.

No one moved. No one spoke. Eventually, Caitlin got up and walked over to the window. "What a pair of monsters. My poor mother. No wonder she was so frightened. George was a snivelling wretch. He knew it wasn't an accident all along. Defrauding the Trust Fund was as much his doing as his friend David's. I hope they're both rotting in hell."

Sally joined her friend. "Sweetheart, you've been looking for your mother for a very long time. Now at least you know. She's always been here waiting for you. Come outside for a few minutes. Feel the wind and rain on your face. It'll clear your mind."

When they had gone, Sam looked at Charlie. "Strange behaviour. What are we going to do now? There's a folder for Caitlin. Should we let her look at it in private?"

Charlie shook her head. "No, don't leave them with it. It's evidence. Open it quickly. They surely won't be out there long in the rain." A few minutes later they heard the door slam. Sam quickly closed the laptop. Whatever Caitlin and Sally talked about when they were outside, they came back looking upbeat. Caitlin opened a drawer and took out a couple of towels. She handed one to Sally. They both mopped the rain off their faces and hair.

Sally looked over at the others, "My hair saved me from the blow David Jones gave me, then I wanted it off. It helped take the revulsion I felt away. We had a ceremony by the statue, Caitlin got the scissors and cut the whole lot off. We buried the hair out there." She rubbed her head briskly, then said in a weird matter of fact way, "Cat's been saying she doesn't want to see any more. You can take the disc now." Charlie looked at her with a serious expression on her face. "Are you sure Cat?

It's evidence so we can't give it back."

"That's what we were thinking." Caitlin said calmly. "When you've finished with it, I'd like a paper copy of the documents. I don't want to see them again. I'll burn them and bury the ash by Sally's hair. It might sound macabre, but it's closure for us. George Rose had the opportunity when he wrote his will to leave me a meaningful letter. I don't want to see any more. I can only process so much."

Sam, mature beyond his years in some aspects, was puzzled. He was trying to decipher what Caitlin was saying. He was eager to do and say the right thing but found himself tongue tied. What do you say to a woman who has just found out her mother was murdered? Charlie interrupted his thoughts. "You have to do things your own way Cat. I'm glad your quest is over. My job with the police will come to an end soon. There are loose ends to clear up but as soon as we're at liberty, we'll give you the back story. By the way, Alice Brown is on remand."

Caitlin smiled, "Good, glad to hear it. Hope you've got her bang to rights. Can we ask you a favour? Sally and I want to do something, at least I do. We want to talk to Ian Morris. Is that possible?"

"Why?" Sam was shocked.

"I'm not pressing charges and I guess it's curiosity. You want to tie up loose ends and so do we. We want to know what their plan was. I think he'll tell me." Caitlin looked very determined.

Sam glanced at Charlie. She shook her head. He had no idea what he should advise and feared he would sound stupid. "Maybe, or maybe when the investigations are over. I'm sorry, I'm not sure what our procedures are in the middle of a case. I'll talk to Superintendent Fletcher and get back to you."

"Thanks Sam. Now take that bloody disc out of our house and go back to your superiors. I reckon you'll both get a commendation, don't you?"

Charlie drove down the hill and took the road by the sea. She stopped the car in a layby. "Sam, I think they both knew exactly what was on that disc. The other folder was blank because they deleted it. I don't want to believe it – but was that all carefully staged?"

"Why would they do that?" Sam's brow furrowed, "No, I don't think so. They appeared genuine to me. Bit weird though. Cutting hair off and burning documents. Bit witchy."

Charlie smiled, "Well, maybe so. I probably have an overactive imagination. Let's go. Catch the ferry; get back to the reality of the office. My mind's playing tricks with me."

CHAPTER SIXTY THREE

That evening, Superintendent Fletcher was true to his word. The whole team went to the pub and drinks were on him. Despite the joviality going on all around her, Charlie was quiet, full of misgivings.

John and Simon had forensically accounted for the missing money and assets from Caitlin's Trust Fund. They still had to establish whether Trevor Jones had been in on the fraud. The property and holiday scam Alice and David had been running had been bust wide open. Alice Brown was on remand for breaking bail conditions and would be up before the magistrates for the scam. The case would inevitably be referred to the Crown Court. She was in for a long stretch.

Charlie and Sam had fulfilled the task John had set them. Once they had the signed confession from the solicitors their investigation into the death of Cecilia Rose was over. They had not found the mysterious dogwalker mentioned in the newspaper article, but as Sam had pointed out, it was late at night. A positive identification would have been well-nigh impossible. George Rose's confession tied in with what the ex-landlady, Mrs Rudd, had remembered. She had identified David Jones from his picture.

Paul and Harry were working on the death cap mushroom angle. They might never establish murder. George Rose's life had been hanging by a thread anyway. Charlie thought it would not be seen to be in the public interest to exhume George Rose's body. Alice Brown would swear she was innocent. From what they had read in George Rose's confession, David Jones was more than capable of murdering his best friend if he felt threatened.

John, observing how pensive Charlie looked, took her by the arm and led her over to a quiet corner. "You're a good detective Charlie. Great result in double quick time. I have a feeling that being out with us isn't where you want to be." She looked him in the eyes. What could she see there. "It's been a privilege working with you all but I no longer think like a police officer. I have to get back to my own world. I've got work piling up."

"Understood." He grinned at her. "Loose ends too I suspect. Sam told me about Caitlin's request to meet Ian Morris. There's nothing to stop her as a private citizen. Will you go with her, continue to protect her?" Charlie looked over at the rest of the team, "What do you think?" She put her hands on his shoulder and kissed his cheek quickly. "So, when can I be made redundant?"

"Come to the team briefing in the morning. Write your final report; we know where to find you. You may be required to give evidence if the CPS decides Alice Brown should be tried for murder."

"What about her part in the bogus cousin conspiracy?"

He shook his head. "Report back on Caitlin's interview with Ian Morris if you think there are grounds to investigate. You've got my direct line. If you need any help all you have to do is call. Now come on, cheer up. You'll be free of us soon and we've got some celebrating to do."

CHAPTER SIXTY FOUR

CHARLIE

I spent Saturday typing up my final report. John came in around midmorning and isolated himself in his office. I had more or less finished when he offered to buy me lunch. Despite misgivings I accepted. He was perfectly charming. I spent far too long with him and before I knew it the day was gone.

I wanted a lazy Sunday but I knew I'd regret it. I couldn't put off sorting out my own work. The old office building smelled musty and slightly damp. My room avoided being drab because of the old mullioned bow window, but it was cramped. Maybe I needed to think about finding something more modern and convenient.

I spent the morning answering letters and generally putting everything in order. Several people were asking to see me urgently so I called them and made arrangements. I put off ringing Caitlin and Sally until the last minute. I wrestled with my conscience. Painful though it might be, I knew what I had to do. Once spoken there was no going back.

My final offer of help to Caitlin would be to locate Ian Morris and inform her of the links between him, David Jones and George Rose. Possibly that would convince her not to complicate matters further.

On Monday morning I caught the ferry along with the car loads of happy holiday makers. I envied them. I was expected so this time I punched in the numbers to open the gates and drove in. The rain had perked up the garden. Everything looked fresh and green.

Caitlin had made a remarkable recovery. I could see

by the way she walked that she was free of pain. In addition, she looked different, brighter somehow. At first I couldn't make her out. Was she was simply being herself? We stood observing one another. The eyes said it all. It was time for both of us to come clean. I was glad Sally was nowhere to be seen.

A few days ago I had messed about unlocking a door and saw the staircase to the kitchen. The scales lifted from my eyes but I still wanted to believe in her mother's ghost. The dark haired woman in the floral dress, the catalyst. I followed Caitlin into the lounge. We sat down opposite each other. I had no idea how Caitlin was going to react to my theories.

She was about to say something. I held my hand up. "No, don't speak. Let me start. When I've finished you don't need to agree or disagree. This is between you and me. No-one else." Caitlin bit her lip. Then nodded in agreement. "I couldn't work you out at the beginning then I began to realise you live by the tales you tell to protect yourself. Tales, that I came to believe, conceal the truth.

I noticed a marked change in your manner when we figured out there was a third man. The locker man, David Jones. Maybe having a name unblocked your memory. Sally told me that you sought out photos of David Jones as a young man. I think you recognised him, and then experienced some difficulty in adjusting back to the way you wanted us all to see you.

You also softened your attitude to George Rose, when you realised removing you from Rock House was his way of saving you. I was sure you already knew a lot more about your mother's death than you revealed to anyone. Why wouldn't you? You knew the Trust Fund had been misappropriated. You played the innocent beautifully but I think you were after justice from the beginning.

Dennis was a puzzle. This man who had come to live with you. When you saw him in Cornwall with the woman you believed was your cousin, you twigged. He had been using you, now you saw a way you could use him.

You employed me to find out about Alice Brown and start unravelling what might have happened to your mother. We made progress. I'm not sure when the point came where you decided to lay a trap. It might have begun with Sally. She was very keen to keep watch on the tennis court. When David Jones started to pack up, she said that she couldn't get a signal and had to run back to the top of the road to call. I went back there. The signal was strong. I nearly got caught in his house. I think you may both have planned a delay, hoping to arouse David Jones's suspicions.

You let everyone around you know exactly when you were leaving for the music festival. Then you deliberately stalled. You left the house with Sally hoping you were being watched. It was a stroke of luck you saw Bob at the shop, told him you had to rush so he thought it was later than it actually was. You went back with your shopping, parked out of sight and waited for someone to appear.

I realised the timings were wrong. On the morning of David's death, there was at least twenty minutes missing from when you said you drove through the gate and when you rang 999. It didn't make sense. Luckily Paul and Harry didn't pick up on it. They don't know you as I do. I knew you would have been more incisive. The phone was by your side on the hall desk. You would have checked his pulse, then dialled 999.

I remembered you said you described the ghost to Dennis and David Jones. Right down to her hair being tied back with a blue velvet ribbon. When you began to formulate your own deception, you may not have been sure who you would confront, but you gambled it would be David rather than Dennis. Dennis doesn't have the bottle.

The day David Jones was killed, you were wearing a floral dress. It struck me as odd at the time. You were about to leave for a music festival. Cut-off jeans and a tee shirt would have been more your style. If I'd carried out a search then, I'm pretty sure I would have found a wig. I don't think you told Sally that you hoped David would break in. You expected her to be out. You didn't know she had hurt her ankle and would come back to the house and go upstairs to sort more boxes.

You said, when questioned, that Cessie had done it. The police put it down to you being in shock. Bob had told them you were haunted by the ghost of your mother. In a way Cessie did do it, didn't she? When you saw David arriving, you ran up the back stairs and hid. Wearing the wig and the floral dress, you'd look almost identical to your mother. You waited for Jones to locate the folder you'd planted in the spare room. You may have heard a cry and thought it was a cry of triumph.

However it happened, you waited for him to leave the room, then stood near the top of the stairs. Maybe he heard something or saw your reflection in the mirror. You meant to confront him, or possibly frighten him, to teach him a lesson. I don't believe you pushed him. He thought he was seeing the ghost of the woman he'd murdered, panicked; lost his footing and toppled down the stairs.

You were just very lucky the police didn't do a thorough search. There might have been a different outcome if they had discovered the staircase. Possibly, young Constable Huxley was out of his depth. Too concerned with the living to worry too much about the dead; the DI and his sergeant too full of their own importance to check. Last night I was thinking of you and the house. Driving down through the beech trees and seeing Rock House, a solid but elegant three storey house. If the police had taken the trouble to think, they would have realised there had to be another staircase.

I've broken my own rule. I began to count you and Sally as friends, but if I thought for one moment you were a murderer, I wouldn't be sitting here."

Caitlin, a faraway look in her eyes, spoke quietly. "Can I speak now?" Charlie nodded, "Please don't think too badly of me. I knew you'd guessed when you saw the back stairs. I waited for you to tell your police colleagues, but nothing happened. Thank you for believing in me.

It started with George Rose leaving a note for me with his will. An envelope containing one sheet of paper. It said, 'We should have let you sleep.' On the other side, 'It wasn't all my fault, forgive me.' I puzzled over that. Had I seen or heard something? Try as I might, I couldn't remember, then slowly, as I settled into Rock House. Memories did start flooding back.

I went to see David Jones to ask him about my mother's will. I didn't recognise him. I saw a stranger. An eccentric older man hiding behind a beard and glasses. It was when I saw the photo of him as a young man, I realised he was the one I called Uncle Davey. No wonder I'd found him so creepy. He must have been very sure of himself to agree to see me. With what we know now I think he was unhinged. I was living with ghosts, but he was living in a fantasy. No matter that he'd ruined lives. There was no remorse.

When I was little, after my mother died, George Rose used to have friends round at night. They'd wake me up and take me down to join in. They petted me like a little dog. Said I was their mascot. Then Uncle Davey began to take me out on my own. The day it happened, I remember trees and a stream; sitting on a wooden bench. He often fondled me, I was used to that, but this time he unzipped his trousers. It was awful. He forced my head down. Afterwards I ran. He caught me and threatened me.

I became afraid of my own shadow. George must have figured out what was happening. I was never left alone with any of the men again. But one day there was a beach picnic with George and some other friends and David Jones was there. I was in the sea and felt hands pulling at me, dragging me down. I nearly drowned. Afterwards I remember white walls and a hospital bed.

I don't think he ever meant to harm me but I was frightened of George by then. He started locking me in my bedroom at night. He wouldn't let me go out of the house to play. Looking back now, I suppose he knew what was going on and did his best to save me. Soon after that he took me on holiday and hid me away.

I'd never told anyone about the abuse, it was too disgusting. I felt dirty. I locked it away. It made me different to everyone else I knew. I didn't like anyone touching me. I still struggle, and on the whole, avoid relationships. Anyway, most men aren't persistent enough to get past my barriers. Dennis did. That is – Ian. We were deceiving one another.

Sally genuinely had difficulty getting a signal that day by the tennis court. She was never part of my deception. I didn't even tell her I recognised and wanted to confront David Jones. I knew she'd try to talk me out of it. I was so mixed up by that point. I despised him. I was too emotional, unable to think straight. The day he died, I don't really know what I was thinking. You are right, I'd planned it, but I didn't think about the consequences of my actions. I just intended to frighten him so he'd confess. He saw me and I started to move towards him. He called out my mother's name. He looked terrified. That was enough. I knew what he'd done. Then he overbalanced on the stairs and he was gone. I promise you, I didn't want it to happen. I wish I could take it back.

I stood at the top of the stairs after the fall. I could see he was dead. Somehow I kept my nerve. I retrieved my handbag, ran down the corridor to the back stairs and straight out through the French windows in the dining room. I had to be super careful. There was glass from the mirror everywhere. I walked round to the front and opened the front door as though I'd just arrived. To give me time to calm myself I picked up a small piece of glass and laid it down outside. You're right, I am a decent method actor. I went over and looked down at his face. Then I panicked for real. He really was dead. It was no longer a childish game. I'd frightened him and I was responsible. I slipped and fell. I didn't even feel it. After I'd rung 999, I realised I still had the wig on. I meant to change. I stepped over the body and went back upstairs, that's when I found Sally.

I know you can't live your life wishing if only this or that, but if only George had left a proper clue and we'd found the disc before, none of this would have happened. With George's confession, we would have gone to the police and David would have been tried for murder. Instead we've been round and round trying to make sense of what could never make sense. I found the courage to tell Sally the whole sorry tale last night. That's why she's out now, to give us space to talk. I was going to tell you straight away but you beat me to it. I should have known you'd work it all out."

She broke off. Tears forming in her eyes. "I've let everyone down. Last night, when I'd come clean to Sally, I felt as though a ten ton weight had been lifted from me. We agreed I should tell you everything. I'm not naïve enough to think it's over or that I can be free of the past."

I got up and sat down beside her; took her hand in mine. "David Jones did his best to destroy your life. Rest assured, I'm no longer working with the police. As far as I'm concerned, it was an accident. There's nothing to be gained by investigating his death any further. As to being free – you were an abused child. There are therapists who can help you but I have a feeling you are partly there already. Am I right?"

Caitlin turned to me and smiled the saddest of smiles. "Yes, when I told Sally about the abuse and my deception she showed nothing but compassion. She's always known I was different and still accepted me as I am. She's a wise woman. We agreed I'm going to write it all down. We'll bury it with her hair and George's confession. Then maybe I can find some peace." She smiled at me. "I honestly did see my mother's ghost. Maybe I projected her, but she seemed very real to me." She got up and stood looking out of the window. It crossed my mind that she was unconsciously mimicking the stance of the ghost she had described.

"I'd see her looking out waiting for something. Sometimes I'd see her at the top of the stairs in a grey dressing gown. Pictures from my mind."

I asked, "How do you feel about her now?"

"Calm. I'm quite sure she was warning me. It didn't start until Dennis moved in. Now I know he's Ian, it feels different. She feels different somehow." As Caitlin had mentioned Ian, I asked why she wanted to see him. It was time I told her about the connections between them all. The chance meeting on a train that led to heartbreak and death.

CHAPTER SIXTY FIVE

"Sally's back." Caitlin turned away from the window, "Good timing." Charlie had feared what she had to say would push Caitlin towards denial. Instead, the opposite had occurred. She had confessed. As a rational being it was difficult for Charlie to put herself in Caitlin's shoes. She tried to empathise with Caitlin's thought processes; to understand why she staged such a bizarre deceit. She said all along she didn't want revenge, yet in the end, revenge was exactly what she achieved. It's said revenge is a dish best served cold. Yet Caitlin appeared genuine when she said she wished she could take it all back.

Charlie knew that if she handled the next part of the discussion well, it would go some way to enable Caitlin's recovery. Sally opened the lounge door. "May I come in?"

"Hello Sal. Charlie and I have had our heart to heart." She stopped speaking for a moment, observing our reaction to her light hearted words. Her tone of voice changed, "I'm truly sorry for what I've put you through. It was selfish and absolutely irrational but I was hurting so." She began gnawing at the skin around her thumb nail. "I've always tried to manage my life by burying the pain inside me." She stopped again, tears forming in her eyes. "Do I have to confess my sins to everyone?"

Charlie thought how strange the use of the word "sins" was. Cecilia had been Catholic. A male dominated religion based on sin. So the sins of the fathers drive women to desperate decisions. Cecilia's mother had been forced to give her baby up. Cecilia in turn had worried about her Catholic parents and her pregnancy. Women were still viewed as sinful in a male dominated society.

Brainwashed by the Adam and Eve myth into inferiority and powerlessness.

Charlie was careful with her words. "Cat, you haven't harmed anyone deliberately. What you did was wrong headed, but I think we understand a little more now. You've been hiding a very hurt child within you for a long time. You've faced up to what you did and why you did it. That's enough. There may come a time when you feel you have to say more, but right now leave it as it is. It was an accident. An evil man died."

The three women sat together contemplating what had been said. Charlie was reminded of Sam's response to both women last time he had been with them. A "bit witchy" he said. She'd have to have a conversation with him some time about how women can be cast as witches. Part of male brainwashing. She giggled to herself. When Sally and Caitlin asked her why, she told them what she'd been thinking. The three of them continued the feminist theme until Caitlin suggested lunch. Morning had become afternoon.

After lunch Charlie made the decision to tell them about the evacuees. She started with, "Are you sitting comfortably? I'm going to tell you a story. Imagine London during the war. Three young children escaping the bombing find themselves in the same carriage on a train chugging down towards Dorset. Ten year old Janet, her brother eight year old David, and a twelve year old stranger called George. Janet and David were being met by their grandmother. She lived in a farmhouse not too far from here. George was on his own. The grandmother offered to take him too, so they all lived together on the farm for the duration of the war. War destroys lives. Only Janet and David's mother survived. She came to live with them, and a new family was formed.

The younger boy, David, was spoiled. He was the master of the house. Superior by blood to the other boy, who was after all, only a stranger. He manipulated the older boy, soon had him dancing to his tune. George, in his thrall, took the blame for any misdemeanours.

The family stayed together after the war was over. Janet and George were now in their teens and experimented with sex. The inevitable happened, George and Janet had to marry and she gave birth to a baby girl. The marriage didn't last long. George left the family home. David left to go to university. Janet and her daughter Jennifer remained on the farm.

David eventually became a solicitor, George an electrician. You know what happened in 1968. Cecilia and George married. A marriage of convenience. Unfortunately George and David were still close. David envied George his rich, attractive wife. When he learned about the Roberts' inheritance he hatched a plot to rid George of Cecilia. He got away with it too. It should all have been hunky dory. George as an accomplice to murder couldn't go to the police. Fortunately, or unfortunately, Cecilia had set up a trust fund for her child. George was not going to inherit the house or the money. David took over the Trust Fund from Cecilia's original solicitor and the rest is history." Charlie stopped speaking for a moment. The sadness of the story etched on her face. The other two women sat in silence watching her. Neither of them spoke, so she carried on.

"If George hadn't hidden Caitlin away, it might have ended in tragedy for her too. Another terrible accident. Scroll forward twenty eight years. Trevor Jones, David's son, is now a partner in the firm. He has taken over the

Trust Fund from his father, believing it is all in order. The Trust Fund must pay out in full by the time Caitlin is thirty. David and George are in danger of losing their cash cow. George has no idea where Caitlin is. As usual, he goes along with David's plans. They dream up a bogus next of kin. Let's give George the benefit of the doubt, maybe he didn't realise what David had in mind. When he eventually figures it out he threatens to report David. That seals George's fate. Within a few weeks he's dead and the search was on for Caitlin.

Meanwhile think back to David's sister Janet. She had a child, Jennifer, by George. Divorced, she eventually marries and becomes Janet Morris. Jennifer took her stepfather's name. Jennifer wants nothing to do with her birth father, George. When Jennifer grows up she follows her mother's example and has a baby in her teens. Only she didn't marry. She moves to London somewhere and brings the child up with a female friend. The name of the child is Ian Morris, George Rose's grandchild and great nephew to David Jones. So, when Caitlin was traced, Uncle Davey draws Ian into his conspiracy. He's not a natural. He's been brought up in a loving female household. They spoiled him rotten. He's used to women admiring him and doing everything for him. In addition, maybe he's inherited his grandfather's personality and is easily led. He carries out his uncle's wishes. He even, it appears, ends up with murderous intent. Although, if we could give him the benefit of the doubt, it's possible running Cat off the road was a moment of madness."

Caitlin groaned. Sally took hold of both of her hands to comfort her. "You didn't stand a chance my love. How could you? David Jones, even in death, had his tentacles everywhere."

"How on earth did you find all this out Charlie?"

"Police work. We were looking for connections. Once we established David had a sister living close by, Sam and I went searching. Janet Morris is a charming woman. She runs a kennels. She clearly had no time for her brother. She had to sell most of the family farm to bail him out when he embezzled an old lady's fund – surprise, surprise. When we visited, I saw a photo of the man we knew as Dennis. Janet told us he had been living with her on and off. Sam and I left pretty quickly without telling her we were looking for him. Paul and Harry moved in later that day and arrested him." Caitlin frowned, "So when I kicked him out, he went to his grandmother's."

"We don't know for sure Cat, but probably. He may have been there on and off for months. He was sacked from the Estate Agents." Sally stopped me, "What's his grandmother like?"

"Straight I think. DI Benson said she had little time for her grandson when they arrested him. Asked him for her car keys back and walked away."

Caitlin got up and paced around the kitchen. "I need time to think this through. Shall we go and get some air. It's time the story finished. We just have to find the right way of concluding it."

CHAPTER SIXTY SIX

Caitlin looked down at Charlie's trainers. "They'll do. Are you up for a walk? I want to take you somewhere."

"Where are we going?"

Sally grinned, "I bet I know where she's going to take us. How are you at climbing up hills?" She turned to Caitlin, "To be kind, I could run us up to the top and then we can walk out onto the cliff."

Charlie turned the offer down. "No, that's nice of you Sally, but you don't need to. I'm reasonably fit."

"Famous last words," Charlie thought, as she reached the top of the reserve. Caitlin had led the way. She and Sally were like a pair of mountain goats. Striding up grassy mounds hiding the old quarry workings. They stopped frequently to let Charlie catch her breath; pointing out the view of the bay as though they always stopped every hundred steps.

At the top they walked through a gate and down a narrow road towards the cliffs. Charlie expressed surprise at the amount of traffic going up and down the road. Caitlin chuckled, "We have the most scenic refuse dump in the world. It's just round the corner."

We rapidly came across the tip in all its glory, gulls circling overhead. There were huge labelled metal containers for different forms of recycling. A necessary service but incongruous and ugly in such a beautiful place. We walked past quickly and carried on down a long track onto the cliffs. Charlie picked up her pace now the terrain was relatively flat. She managed to keep up as they reached a stone built stile. Caitlin almost ran over it. Standing at the top to survey the cliff before her.

"We're in luck. The bench is free." She jumped down

and Sally followed. Charlie looked at the stile in trepidation. A trip hazard if ever she had seen one. She stood on the first step and felt herself wobble. Holding on tight, she tried the second step. Caitlin could see she was in trouble. "Turn and sit down on the top Charlie. Then you can swing your legs over and feel for the step the other side. Stay there and I'll give you a hand." Safely back on the track, Charlie apologised. "I'm not sure what happened there. I'm not very good at this am I?"

"Come on, it's not far." Sally took Charlie's arm. Caitlin moved round and took her other arm. They walked across the field then took a barely discernible track to a bench. The three of them sat down together, looking out over the vast expanse of sea.

Caitlin spoke in a soft voice as though she was thinking aloud. "I wanted to come here, because this is where it all began. I made two decisions here that day. The first was to liberate myself from Dennis; the other to find out what really happened to my mother." She turned to Charlie. "I was told she had died in an accident. That's all I knew. I suppose as a child all I understood was - she was gone, she'd left me. The mystery of her death became part of my life. Perhaps it made me a bit more interesting, or maybe I was just busy trying to live a decent life, there was no time."

The two women sat gazing out over the sea; saying nothing, waiting for Caitlin to continue. She remained deep in thought. She reached for their hands, clutched them tightly and started to speak again. "OK, this is what I think. First of all, I'm not responsible for saving Ian Morris. Asking to see him again was a crap idea of mine. You both know, I have enough difficulty trying to figure myself out – trying to understand what drove David Jones is something else. I guess once he got away with one murder he thought he could do it again and again. He tried to kill me once when I was small. He was going to try again but this time he would use his nephew.

I can imagine the three of them together, David, Alice and Ian. Maybe they had a drunken evening and wrote down their plan on the back of one of Ian's cigarette packets. They must have thought it was great fun changing their names. Maybe Alice had always wanted to be Arabella. Small woman, full of spite. What I can't figure out is why Ian changed his name. There was no point. What would have happened if he had bumped into his cousin Trevor?

It makes me cringe when I think how I looked up to Ian. That is until I saw through his bullshit. We had very different values. Even under normal circumstances it would never have worked out. His Uncle Davey made a mistake thinking Ian was up to the job. He was a wimp and a bully. Mind you, I thought he wouldn't harm me, but then he did. Stupid fellow. Not capable of seeing anything through properly. So, despite everything I'm not going to slag him or any of them off. I was to blame for David Jones's accident. I don't think many people will mourn his passing. Alice will hopefully spend a long time in prison. Maybe a good woman will help Ian get back on track."

She stopped speaking and scratched her head. "What do you think?"

Sally shook her head in disbelief and repeated Caitlin's words. "Just listen to yourself. Maybe a good woman will help Ian back on track! Don't be a mutt. The nephew is as monstrous as his uncle. Think about it woman. He tried to kill you. Don't go through the rest of your life making excuses for the inexcusable. You have to face up to things. It's not some sort of fairytale. There's no happily ever after that I can see."

Charlie and Caitlin remained silent. Seeing how her words had impacted on Caitlin, Sally continued, "I'll tell you what I think. Look at us sitting here. See no evil, hear no evil, speak no evil." She grinned, "Only, it doesn't fit does it? The unfortunate fact is, we have been tainted with evil. There will come a time when it fades away to distant memory and then we can walk back up here, sit on this bench having become those three wise monkeys."

Caitlin smiled, "You are so right, my wise friend. Evil invaded everything. I think I've been trying to show you both that it didn't get inside me. I didn't mean to hurt him. I was heartbroken, acting out a hurt child's fantasy to pay David Jones back for his actions."

Sally nodded, "It's alright Cat. I think I understand. But please, don't go through your life trying to make excuses for others. Concentrate on yourself. In fact, be yourself. The self we love. Sorry, that sounds soppy. Let's get back to business, there may yet be repercussions. Trevor and Ian are first cousins. You can't tell me that he didn't know what Ian was up to."

"Agreed." Caitlin mused, "At the beginning when I went to see Trevor about my mother, I also told him I was going to ask a partner to leave the house. The first thing he did was ask if I was OK to confront him alone. He knew. I think he must also have known how the Trust Fund was manipulated for all those years."

Sally looked sombre again. "Oh no. I thought we were going to jettison all this. Can we bear any more?"

"Please Sal, don't look so sad. We can't just leave it."
She turned to Charlie, "I've yet to see your invoice
Charlie. I want to pay you up to date. Then, if you'll take
it, we have another job for you. I want you to untangle
Trevor and Ian's web. Trevor's mother has disappeared.
I want you to find her. Until I know what's happened, I
don't think I can put it to bed."

Charlie got up and stood facing both of them. "I
understand, and yes, I can do it. I like the word jettison.
You can push it over to me. I'll do what I can. In the
meantime, you two have to get on with your lives. Now,
we had better get back hadn't we? I hope the way down
is easier than the way up!"

Charlie stayed the night in Rock House. She slept
through the night unbothered by creaks and the sound of
tiny mice feet high up in the attic. When she woke she
understood the old house had recovered it's equilibrium.
Caitlin had accomplished what she set out to achieve.
Awful though the story might be, she and Sally were two
vibrant young women with a future ahead of them.
Charlie hoped to be part of it.

She stretched out on the bed, luxuriating as she
thought of the days ahead. Last night Caitlin and Sally
had talked about their plans. She had a new investigation
in front of her. She sighed with satisfaction. A job well
done. So far.

About the Author

Gill Calvin Thomas has retired from academic life and lives with her husband in Swanage, Dorset. She finds inspiration while walking in the Isle of Purbeck. Here, she is able to escape into a world of her own making, getting to know her characters whilst she plans the next twist and turn of a plot.

As writing has become a major part of Gill's life, she has withdrawn from taking a leading role in many community volunteer activities, although she has retained her interest in local and national politics. A lifelong feminist, Gill likes nothing better than a spirited debate on the issues of the day with family and friends. As her writing career develops, she hopes to explore those issues in her stories. Vex Not Her Ghost is Gill's first novel and she is currently working on her second.

Acknowledgements

I would like to thank Frances Usher for encouraging me to write. Thanks to my husband, Phil Blenkarn, for his proofreading and unwavering support. Thanks to Iola Harper, Pam Howdle-Smith and Michael Jacobs for reading my first unedited script and offering feedback. Thanks to Deborah Reddick for taking photographs. Thanks to my special friend Ann Collison and her dog Coco, who lent me their names.

None of this would have happened without Blossom Spring Publishing and their amazing staff. Clare Voet for her clear communication, Laura Cosby for doing a brilliant job designing the cover and Ruth Elizabeth Hales for editing my script so meticulously.

www.blossomspringpublishing.com

Printed in Great Britain
by Amazon